BEYOND THE YEW

HAROLD BELL

ST. PETERSBURG PRESS

Published by St. Petersburg Press

St. Petersburg, FL

www.stpetersburgpress.com

Design and composition by St. Petersburg Press and Isa Crosta

Cover design by Amy J Cianci and Isa Crosta

Paperback ISBN: 978-1-964239-25-5

eBook ISBN: 978-1-964239-26-2

First Edition

❀ Created with Vellum

LETTER TO THE READER

Dear Reader:

I remember when it happened, almost to the day. An unspoken vow, one I held for decades, about to see the light.

People, places, events, and a sense of purpose; stuff I'd collected over the years. A novel's worth of stuff, if properly assembled by someone with a knack for it.

My resume consisted of essays, written for school. That was over fifty years ago. I opted for on the job training.

A box of black Bics, a few college-ruled, spiral bound notebooks, and six months later, *Under the Yew* became a thing.

Historical fiction, set in the late sixties and early seventies. Characters from various backgrounds, united for a common goal. An emphasis on culture and current events.

The reviews were mixed.

Positive feedback included my knowledge of foreign shores and character development. Missing was a lack of wow moments and a sense of immediacy.

In the meantime, I discovered that I enjoyed the process of writing, frustrating at times but ultimately rewarding. Supplementing my own experiences with the help of Wikipedia, Google Maps, and daily editions of the Liverpool Post and Echo proved to be educational as well.

So, when a close friend read *Under the Yew*, she summed up her review rather succinctly. "What happened next?"

I accepted the challenge, got some more notebooks and another package of pens, and came up with *Seeds of the Yew*.

Seeds looked in on the Greenbank Gang five years later. It was a more concise, more focused work, containing elements not previously introduced.

The critics were warming to my rather unique style of prose.

I'd like to think that you are about to be rewarded for your patience, and that you enjoyed *Under* and *Seeds* enough to look forward to this next chapter.

I need to take a moment to acknowledge Sir Philip David Carter. Sir Philip was not a fictional character. He and his family were identified correctly, and his personal history in reference to his background and time with Everton Football Club is accurate. His family's ties with the clan are, of course, a complete fabrication. May Sir Philip and his wife, Harriet, rest in peace, and their memory live on in Gillian, Phillippa, and Terrence.

A nod is also due to the various other non-fictitious characters who were a part of the tale. With the exception of Margaret Thatcher, I'd like to take responsibility and apologize for any liberties taken with the likes of Gerry Marsden, Cilla Black, Paul Pilnick, Geoff Higgins, Mike Pinder, John Quayle, Wilco Hellinga, Margaret Aspinall, Heinz Christen, Joyce Hughes, Bob Craft, Lea Doyle, Phish, B. Getz, Sandi Wong, Ian Hamilton-Doyle, Jodi, Danny and Johan Cruyff, and Tim, Margaret, and Jessica Black.

Cheers!

BEYOND THE YEW
CAST OF CHARACTERS

The Greenbank Gang

The Barcants – Cyril, Colleen

The McTimons – Kevin, Cheryl, Seamus

The Pines – Benjamin, Faith, Hope, Grace, and Amos

The Carters – Lucas, Daniela, Jacob, Poppy, and Otis

The Ardavans – Abbas, Robin, Gabriel, Darcy

The Calderstones Crew

The McTimons – Ian, Phillippa, Nathan

The McTimons – Cyrus, Rose, Elizabeth

The Stillwell House

The Ardavans – Bashir, Penelope, Caspar

St. Petersburg

Eugene and Louise Pine

Cye and Astrid Ardavan

Tucson

Ender and Anne Linares

Port Of Spain

Michael and Allison Barcant

Catherine Barcant and Millicent Hathaway

TABLE OF CONTENTS

Hear what the teller of this history said
By stringing speech's pearls on verse's thread.
Nazami Ganjavi

PROLOGUE

They had been dubbed the 'Merseyside Six.' The tag was not a reflection of any perceived notoriety, it was just a nickname, a given in Liverpool once you become a known entity. Three pairs of siblings ranging from 19 to 23 years of age, nudged and nurtured by their kin and clan in a five home rowhouse in the leafy hamlet of Mossley Hill.

They were the direct descendants of 'The Fab Five,' a collective established some three decades past. Young pilgrims from vastly different backgrounds, coming of age and seeking a shared future in a land whose history and traditions called to them, and stirred in them a sense of challenge and wonder. They were the 'boomers,' the world around them a maelstrom of socio-political change and cultural transformation.

But change never stops, it just switches gears. This new edition of the 'Greenbank Gang' was analog in theory, but digital in practice. Their mark would be made in the new millennium.

CHAPTER 1
THURSDAY, 3 JUNE

Daniela Carter's mind was abuzz, random thoughts competing for space. Nothing too worrying, just a mental checklist she was composing in order to carry on the day-to-day running of the clinic. She found herself more and more occupied with managerial tasks of late and less time with patients, something she intended to remedy.

The Edge Hill Animal Hospital belonged to her now, lock, stock, and kennel. Julius Pope retired nearly three years ago, hanging up his stethoscope and taking up residence at Torquay, down on the southern coast in Devon. She missed Jools, a proper English gentleman whose guidance and counsel had transformed her from an eager clinician into a gifted healer. No doubt he would advise her to do as he did, hire a competent staff and don't worry the details. She had a plan for that, a little bit of restructuring.

Leaning against a table in the post-op room her thoughts turned towards home, just down in Mossley Hill, another Liverpool suburb. She was gently stroking the coat of an Airedale, cooing softly as the dog was emerging from anesthesia, and musing on the row house on Greenbank Road.

Her husband, Luke, didn't believe in fate and claimed there was no such thing as destiny. Finding purpose in chaos was one's greatest hope for a life well spent. The only mysticism he would entertain was karma as an aid to achieving happiness and contentment. One thing Dani knew for certain, she could point to one day in particular when forces aligned to create the life she enjoyed now.

She and Luke, a neighbor in her native Venezuela, hooked up with two of his friends, Cyril and Benjamin, from Trinidad and the U.S. respectively, with the idea of spending the summer and possibly emigrating to England. That led to 'The Day.' That day was the third of June 1969, thirty years ago exactly.

They were downtown, known as the City Centre, having lunch at Cooper's Food Hall. Luke's globetrotting, the guy had been literally around the world, included a stop in Tehran, where he'd acquired a close friend in one Abbas Ardavan, now standing before them carrying a sack of sandwich buns. The five of them had been devoted to one another ever since.

Their little enclave had grown over time, its occupants like inter-changeable parts, striving for individualism but always returning to the fold.

She was brought back to the here and now, her patient licking her hand appreciatively. It was time to button the place up and head for the hacienda.

The house sat opposite Greenbank Park, 235 acres in size and boasting a picturesque little lake. There was also a yew tree, massive and very old, halfway between the house and lake, dominating the view. The tree was a constant in the lives of Dani's loved ones; much had tran-spired beneath its canopy.

She had wondered if her 'boys' would remember the significance of today's date, the answer coming as soon as she pulled to the curb. All four of them were under the yew, dressed for a run and stretching out.

"Come na me sistah," Cyril chided. "We must train before we celebrate!"

CHAPTER 2
FRIDAY, 4 JUNE

Abbas Ardavan thought long and hard before answering the question, wary of being misleading or misunderstood. "Well, yes, I suppose religion is at the heart of the matter. The end result, however, will be much different."

The question was being posed by James Doohan; the subject was the current ethnic conflict in the Balkans. James owned the Baltic Fleet pub and had been a close friend of Abbas and his bunch since day one. He was curious as to the similarities of the turmoil in Yugoslavia and the revolution in Abbas' native Iran two decades earlier. "Iran is overwhelmingly Islamic; the revolution ensured that the government and the nation would be run by the clerics, with no western influence. There are multiple ethno-religious factions in Yugoslavia, my guess is the country will be split apart."

"They'd better get it sorted; those people are slaughtering each other!" James warned.

"Enshallah." Abbas replied.

James tended to the rest of his customers as Abbas sat back and drank his ale. Wow, twenty years had passed since the Ayatollah became Iran's supreme leader. The Ardavans had been targeted by the new regime, forcing Hassan and Aleah to send their son Cye to join his brothers Bashir and Abbas in England. What followed was a bold and risky effort by the gang, pooling their resources and sending one of their own on a thankfully successful mission to bring Hassan and Aleah safely out of Tehran.

Abbas missed his father, passed several years ago, a victim of cancer not caught early enough. He'd been happy on Merseyside, loved and respected by all that knew him. Graceful in decline, and seemingly content near the end, the community was reminded of him with an array of fine homes he had designed as an architect.

Abbas' mood brightened as he stepped outside the pub and was met with a cloudless and nearly warm day. Summer was just around the corner. The change of seasons signaled a shift in his workload; he'd soon have more command of his own schedule. Music was central to his life. He couldn't imagine existing without it. And he was blessed to have multiple fronts on which to channel his passions.

First of all, it was his job. He sat first chair flute in the Royal Liverpool Philharmonic Orchestra, where he met his future wife, the former Robin Quinn, a superb violinist. Their two children were following in their footsteps, they had their own little chamber ensemble at home.

Also, there was the Eclectibles, his band. It was a collective, consisting of a half dozen members, augmented by the odd musician sitting in or enjoying an extended run in the group.

On occasion Abbas was hired to go on the road with a big-name outfit, on tour for a run of shows. It was exciting. Large venues in different cities, performing with really creative people.

Tonight was another opportunity to play; open mic night at Dovedale Towers, the neighborhood pub. The Dovey was a blast, and they'd been having the sessions for so long now, you never knew who might show up.

Abbas loved playing so much he even could be found, from time to time, busking in the City Centre, usually giving his tips to the local rough sleepers, or homeless.

He caught the bus at the station at Strand Street by Canning Place, headed southeast to Mossley Hill. Halfway down the aisle on the left sat

Cheryl McTimons, smiling at the coincidence. Cheryl and her husband Kevin were rowhouse neighbors and part of his clan. He bussed her on the cheek.

"Thanks for saving me a seat!"

CHAPTER 3
TUESDAY, 15 JUNE

Cyril Barcant stood at center circle in a completely empty stadium. He kneeled and snatched a blade of grass, chewing it absently as his life flashed before his eyes.

Twenty-five years ago to the day he had donned the captain's armband and led Trinidad and Tobago against Italy in Munich's Olympiastadion at the World Cup. The Calypso boys exceeded expectations and Cy established himself as one of the game's top midfielders.

He felt fortunate to have spent all of his eighteen pro seasons at Everton, relatively injury-free to boot. His gladiator styled approach to the game had earned the normal array of knocks, strains, sprains, and pulls, but he had managed to avoid any extended time on the sidelines.

Upon retiring he took a full year and a half off, restoring some balance to his life and preparing for a 'second career.'

Coaching football required obtaining a license, commonly known as getting your coaching badges. Cyril had completed all five levels of certification, allowing him to coach anywhere in the world at any level or type of competition.

He thought long and hard about taking this particular fork in the road, coaching was, of course, easier physically, but required more of a commitment in time. His wife, Colleen, had put up with his being on the road for a very long time now.

Cy and Colly absolutely adored each other, she knew he'd hang up his boots if he thought she wanted him to. She also knew that the most passionate and vibrant men still nurtured the little bit of boy within. Cyril loved being with the lads and chasing the game. She had a career of her own and could never be bored living in the warren at Greenbank. Let the guy channel his muse.

Starting in the winter of 1989, he spent nine years in Everton's system, learning more about the behind-the-scenes running of a football club, and moving up through the ranks. He spent time with the various junior age groups at the academy, and eventually was promoted to manager Joe Royle's backroom staff with the senior team.

Offers began to arrive from other clubs as Cy became more confident in his ability to run his own team. He left the Toffees in '98 and took the whole year off to sort things out personally and reset himself.

At the beginning of the month Cyril got a call from Lorraine Rogers, the newly elected chairman of Tranmere Rovers Football Club. She wanted to make a splash with her first major decision and hire Cy to manage Rovers. The former ponytailed Prince of Goodison Park was moving across the river Mersey.

So there he stood, in the middle of Prenton Park, staring at the main stand, lost in thought.

"Oy! What the fuck are you doing in the middle of my pitch!"

"Just having a walkabout."

"I don't give a shite, get the hell off!"

Obviously the head groundskeeper and a young assistant, protecting their turf, now striding towards Cyril with the intent of giving him a proper dressing down.

"Easy boss, I've got permission."

"Like hell you do!" Then the pair got close enough and the man's expression changed.

"Corr, you're Cyril Barcant!"

"At your service."

The pair were dumbfounded, embarrassed, and staring blankly.

"I'm the new manager; Ms. Rogers and I just sealed the deal."

"Aces!" the young one said, "The best number six on the planet, you was!"

"Much appreciated. What's your name, lad?"

"Simon."

"And I'm John Quayle sir, head groundsman. Sorry for havin' a go."

"It's fine, part of the job. You chaps do good work. The pitch is excellent!"

"Thank you, gaffer. I'm excited, this could be brilliant!"

"I hope so, I'll work hard for your club. See ya around."

As they went their separate ways Cy smiled to himself. It was the first time anyone had called him 'gaffer.'

CHAPTER 4
THURSDAY, 17 JUNE

Benjamin Pine strolled up Duke Street to the shopfront at number 62. He unlocked the centrally located door on the two-story structure, stepped inside and turned on the lights. It was the Ropewalks area of Liverpool, not far from the docks. The larger streets here ran in a generally northwest to southwest direction, and were abnormally straight, a rare sight in the city. In times past, pre 19th century, rope-makers stretched their lines along these streets during production.

The building housed two businesses; his and Luke's, both begun some years ago. Big Ben Photography arose after Ben decided to strike out on his own, leaving the Liverpool Post and Echo where he worked as a photojournalist. Big Ben had nothing to do with a famous clock tower in London and everything to do with Ben's stature. He tipped the scales at 17 stones and was just a shade under 2 meters in height.

He'd loved being a newspaper man, learning the trade, chasing down stories, and the comradery of his fellow 'journos.' The demands of the job were many, however, and he decided that working for himself would afford more control of his own time.

Luke's feelings were similar and ran concurrent with Ben's, so the two had enlisted both Neff and Hassan, clan elders, to choose and develop their joint place of business. Neff found the place and greased the bureaucratic wheels while Hassan reimagined the building's interior.

Central on the first floor was a shared reception area behind which was a hall with two toilets, a custodial closet, HVAC equipment, and the back door. Ben's east side contained an office, a showroom, and a studio. Luke's west side contained two offices and a meeting room.

The second floor was special. Also divided in half, the east side was a flat; two bedrooms, sitting room, kitchenette, bath, and storage. Abbas and Luke's sons lived there. The west side was an events room, complete with stage, bar, toilet, and balcony out back. This is where Abbas' band, the Eclectibles, practiced, and a good place for the gang to make merry.

Scruff came with the building. Scruff, the attack cat, a very large yellow tom that took months to 'domesticate,' or at least allow himself to be looked after.

Ben made tea, updated his calendar, and was making a list of supplies he needed when Jude came in, today's *Echo* under her arm as she stowed her bag and brolly. She was Luke and Ben's only employee, serving as receptionist, secretary, office manager, and whatever else was needed for both companies. And she was worth her weight in gold. Her real name was Judith Baker, although the nameplate on her desk said Miss Moneypenny, a nod to the nickname Ben had given her when she was the editor's secretary at the *Echo*. She'd taken on more responsibility with the move but loved her job. The guys depended heavily on her, but she was basically her own boss and enjoyed a lot of freedom with respect to her schedule.

"Good morning, Benjamin!"

"Hey Jude!"

Sorry, he just couldn't help himself.

CHAPTER 5
FRIDAY, 18 JUNE

Lucas Carter stood pensive, one hand on hip, the other absently rubbing his chin. He was under the yew, the site of many past ruminations, a place that seemed to calm and guide his thoughts. An ageless observer, lending wisdom to those seeking solace beneath its boughs.

It only took about ten minutes to achieve the initial goal, a plan to prep and paint the rowhouse, a must prior to autumn's soggy arrival. Then Luke succumbed to a train of thought that often occupied his mind on a regular basis, his clan.

There were five homes in the rowhouse on Greenbank Road between Streatham and Bromley Avenues. Abbas' oldest brother Bashir lived there when Abbas emigrated from Iran. Then Cyril came from Trinidad to pursue a football career. He was joined a week later by Luke, Dani, and Ben; the four copped a hotel suite until another unit in the row came up for sale. Shortly after the McTimons moved in next door, and, along with Neff Boler and the Odegaards, all five homes carried on for a number of years.

Abbas bought the Odegaard's house when they retired back to Norway, and he and Ben established the short lived 'bachelor pad' at the middle unit.

The revolution in '79 forced the rest of the Ardavans, Hassan, Aleah, and middle bother Cye, to leave Tehran for England. Cye lived with Bashir and Penny while Aleah and Hassan moved in with Neff. This was in the midst of a baby boom. What started with Bashir's vision of a 'Greenbank Coalition' went full blown communal, prompting one wry observer to label the collective 'The United Nations of Mossley Hill.' Luke, true to form, felt the need to look after them all.

Cyrus McTimons, Kevin and Cheryl's youngest, was 33 and taught English Lit and Composition. Recently he wrote that 'the fruit from the tree rests under its canopy.' True enough, until it starts to rot. Luke felt strongly about a person's need to travel, an education in itself. To be grounded, well-adjusted, and ultimately happy you've gotta spend time in an aquarium, not a fishbowl. He was fortunate to have grown up in a handful of cities worldwide and was now content in place. It was time for the sons and daughters of immigrants to get their wanderlust on. They were raised in a good environment, with lots of diverse influence, but they needed to get out on their own, to stub their toes and follow an alternate muse.

The rest of the clan were groovin'. The Tweeners, as Luke called them, the McTimons boys and Rose and Caspar Ardavan, were all grown and gone though still on Merseyside.

The elders were getting on well, some still at the grind, some retired, some aged, and a few were gone. Time marches on, getting old is not for sissies. Hell, the Fab Five were all nearly fifty.

Luke suspended his reverie, the reality of the moment requiring his attention. He needed to get up to the office for an afternoon appointment; a new client had flown in for a meeting to discuss representation. He was no longer an educator, teaching language to adolescents at a nearby secondary school. He was an agent with his own firm, Carter Assets Management, representing mostly footballers. It was, at present, a one-man enterprise, with plans to hire his son after the first of the year.

Luke had trained for this field of work, unknowingly, for most of his life. His upbringing had shown him the world and its peoples, and how to navigate its subtleties. He was streetwise and savvy, known to many as the Fixer, and his communication skills made him a formidable player in any boardroom or meeting hall.

The drive up to the City Centre was uneventful. Luke was planning a meet and greet with the young Welsh defender, Gareth Roberts. The kid couldn't catch on at Liverpool and had been playing in Greece the past year and was miserable. He was a sound lad, Luke was planning to place him at Tranmere Rovers, give his buddy Cyril a new toy to play with. Judith greeted him at the door.

"Good afternoon, Lucas!"

"Hey Jude!"

She groaned inwardly; these yanks think they're so clever.

CHAPTER 6
FRIDAY, 25 JUNE

Carry each his burden, we are young despite the years
We are concern, we are hope despite the times
Happy throngs, take this joy wherever you go

"Geez, what a motley crew!" Ben had the Six up against an ecru shaded wall in his studio, making last minute adjustments. "Before the star witness arrives, I'd like to make the prediction that you're all guilty of any alleged crimes." Equal parts giggles and groans issued forth; Ben relished his role as the corny father.

He'd asked them to come in today for a group portrait. It had been years since the last time the camera had found them all together. Soon they'd be split up, most of them headed out, away from England. They were told to dress as they liked, hopefully something representative of who they were and how they felt at this stage of their lives. Now he thought that might have been a mistake.

"I think I'll let you guys choose the order in which you stand. Be equidistant, though, with only about a foot apart." That was an eye opener as well. Growing up together, all of Greenbank was really one big family, and had apparently installed a fierce sense of individualism within each of them.

On the left stood Gabriel Revaz Ardavan, turned 23 last month. The handsome one. His father's almond skin and wavy dark hair, and his mother's blue-gray eyes. Five feet, ten inches tall, looking sharp in chinos and a linen shirt.

Next to Gabe was Poppy Anne Carter, 21, also nicely dressed in a short skirt and a white, three-quarter sleeve blouse and sandals. Poppy was five feet, eight inches, with straight, light brown hair cut short and feathered at the edges. She had mischievous green eyes and a hint of her dad's wry smile. She certainly wasn't posh, more like retro-mod.

Jacob Neff Carter anchored the other end of the line-up, a couple of weeks of beard growth, tousled sandy blonde hair, and the remains of a shiner shading his left eye. Jake, turning 24 next month, was six feet even, 180 pounds, not classically handsome, more Bogie than Hudson, with tremendous presence. He had on blue jeans, a pair of trainers, an R.E.M. t-shirt, and his usual ever present but something's going on behind the scenes expression.

Next to Jake stood the kid, Darcy Lyn Ardavan, little miss 'I will not be ignored.' A smaller version of her brother and at 18 every bit as pretty as he was handsome. All the lads took notice when Darcy was present, the reason why Jake sported a black eye. She was five and a half feet tall, and her mannerisms echoed her mum's. Today she wore a tunic over loose cotton pants, a barrette taming her shoulder length wavy hair.

In the middle were Ben's own, Hope and Grace, identical twins, proof that the supreme powers held wondrous visions, and a sense of humor. Physically they were quite something to behold. Tall, lithe, athletic, with pale blue eyes and straight black hair, which in bright natural light a hint of ginger could be seen. They were attractive, self-assured, and possessed a quiet confidence, rare for those not quite 20 years of age. Grace's hair was to her shoulder blades, today parted on the side. She wore light cords and a V-neck jumper with moccasins. Hope's hair was shoulder length in a tight ponytail, silver hoops dangling from her ears. She had on short cut-offs and a peasant blouse, and the girl was barefoot.

Ben took a number of shots in different poses, adjusting light, depth, and shutter speeds on the fly. There'd be some keepers in this bunch.

There was a bit of a weird vibe present, he thought it was down to the realization among the kids that this was one more last thing to do before they were separated and gone off to parts unknown. He could tell that their thoughts weren't as in sync as usually was the case. This, he felt, was a good thing. Let them feel a bit of unease and discomfort; they'll come back stronger, better prepared for the future. You gotta know yourself in order to be of value to those around you.

"That's a wrap! Thanks guys." Ben started locking down the set and stowing his gear. "What's on for tonight?"

"It's the Dovey for me," Darcy said.

"Ah, a bit of culture."

"Me too," added Jake.

"I need to bathe first."

"Good idea Hope," her sister teased.

"Wait," Ben looked confused, "I thought you were Hope."

"Oh Dad!"

"Poppy and I have been sitting in class all day," Gabe reported. "We're going to walk down to the Mersey and stroll the Promenade."

"I need to shower and change."

"Go ahead upstairs Jake, I'll finish here and you can ride down with me."

"Cool."

An hour later the Greenbank gang at home were all busy individually dismissing the slings and arrows of the week's grind. Jacob had a chat with his folks then volunteered to feed and walk the dogs.

Otis was the Carter's yellow lab, his littermate Amos belonged to the Pine's. Big dudes, over 80 pounds. During the day, one of them stayed home while the other hung out at Erins Pharmacy, owned by Faith and Colleen, Erin being both of their middle names. Both dogs were nothing if not loyal and watchful; the clan their only focus.

Most everyone that was going to the pub were milling about under the yew when the trio got back. Jake left both pups with Kevin and Cheryl and joined the entourage taking the familiar hike up Penny Lane to Dovedale Towers.

Poppy and Gabriel walked west to the river at Albert Dock and turned south. It was breezy, but fairly warm and sunny—Gabe offering his arm as he talked about nothing in particular. Poppy could tell something was on his mind.

"What's up Gabe? You seem on edge."

"Yeah, I'm a bit nervous, if I'm honest."

"About what, your trip?"

"No, not really. I'm looking forward to it, for the most part."

"So?"

"Well, you know how it's been, the two of us, how close we are, in an unspoken sort of way."

"Yes. Kind of like brother and sister, but better, cause we're so honest together."

"Uh-huh. Only now I don't want to be like your brother."

She stopped walking as he turned to face her. She'd gone pale and looked hurt. "Gabe?"

"Oh no, that's not it!" He hugged her tight. "I want to be more than a brother to you. Much more!"

She saw the expression on his face and knew instantly. She couldn't believe it! Quickly she kissed him, softly and sweetly.

"Is that your answer?"

"I don't know. Just what, exactly, are your intentions, kind sir?"

"For us to have a proper love affair, if we can get past the weirdness of it all."

She giggled. "The idea does take some getting used to."

"The rest will tease us mercilessly."

"But won't it be great fun!"

"This has been on my mind a lot lately, Pops. I'm afraid if you don't want me everything will change."

"Well it wouldn't, not a bit. You should know that." She held him and whispered, "I love you. Behave yourself when you're away."

Gabe was joyous. "I can't believe it! Me and Poppy Anne Carter! You'll have me, really?"

"Me and just about every other girl in Liverpool!"

"I've never understood that, and I've never been comfortable with that kind of attention."

"Yes, I'm sure it's quite the curse. Boys are so dense sometimes. It's the whole package, luv. Your father's shyness and your mum's passion. When you're up on stage, lost in the performance, it's heady stuff. All the girls get wet."

Now he was blushing but didn't care. "Now I'm hesitant to go, just thinking about being with you. Really being with you. Can't wait!"

"Why should you have to, we've got all weekend!"

CHAPTER 7
SATURDAY, 26 JUNE

The world is a wonderful puzzle, everyone a piece and every piece fits
Every piece is alive making energy, energy pulls the pieces together
Into a round ball

Luke was back under the yew, staring at the house again. He was smiling this time; the plan was coming together. Next to him stood Nathan Philip McTimons, Ian's boy, Kev's grandson. He was Luke's lieutenant on the painting project, so appointed after solving the choice of color debate that had raged on for a week. "Why don't we choose one base color and let each home choose their own shade." Brilliant! That done, a common trim color for the whole complex still had to be decided on, Luke leaned towards a common decision agreed upon by he and Nate.

"Okay, write this down, left to right, facing the house. The Barcants, forest green. The McTimons, sea green. The Pines, jade. The Carters, olive. The Ardavans, hunter green. And the trim?"

"Well, we've narrowed the choices, I think, to stone and ash."

"Whaddya say boss?"

"Ash."

"Well done, very decisive. Okay, let's get Dani and head for your house."

It was a short drive down to the Calderstones area and Tweener H.Q., the semi-detached, or duplex, that brothers Ian and Cyrus McTimons owned. The units were similar in size to the ones at Greenbank—there were living, dining, kitchen, and utility rooms downstairs plus a den and bath. Upstairs were three bedrooms, two baths and an attic with a dormer window. Including Rose, three of the five 'Tweeners' lived here. The other two, Seamus and Caspar, were another story all together.

"Hello all!" welcomed Filly, Ian's wife. "Nate, how about you jumping in the shower right away; supper's almost on."

"Yes, mum."

"It smells great!" said Dani. "Curry?"

"Yes indeed, lamb. Rosie's in charge of rice and salad."

"Splendid!" Luke said, "Nate and I pretty much skipped lunch."

"The boys are out back with a tub full of ale."

"Nuff said!" He gave Filly a kiss on the cheek and went out the back door.

"Where's your two, Dani?"

"Jake's off with the twins and Darcy, last weekend before the trip, you know. Poppy's with Gabe. That's the big news."

"What do you mean?"

"The two showed up at the Dovey last night, plainly a couple now."

"Oh, that is big!"

"I'm sure we'll see precious little of them the rest of the weekend. They're probably up on Duke Street."

"The bachelor pad turned love nest."

"Deja vu all over, again. By the way, your anniversary is coming up."

"Yeah, next week."

Filly, nee Phillippa Carter, youngest daughter of Sir Philip Carter, Everton Football Club's chairman, met Ian McTimons at a big Eclectibles concert in '79. Aleah Ardavan had recruited her and her sister Gillian to help decorate the stage. Ian was home on a visit from the states, where he'd been living for a few years with Ben's folks in St.

Petersburg, Florida. They were married in '83 and Nathan was born two years later.

Filly checked the stove then she and Dani went into the garden to join the rest.

The clan loved their youngsters. Now that the Six were just about grown, the only two left lived here at numbers 10 and 12 Glendyke Road. Besides Nate, at fourteen, there was Elizabeth Rose McTimons, just turned five.

Lizzy and her parents were with Ian and Luke, enjoying summer's increasing grip on England. There had been a stone wall separating the gardens, but Ben and the brothers tore it down and built a storage shed in the northeast corner. There was a good-sized oak in the other corner and a firepit in the middle. The two couples and Dani sat up near the house, watching Luke and Lizzy chase each other around.

"Where's Nate?" Rose asked.

"Bathing. He's volunteered to set up the table and chairs so we can eat out here."

"Good idea, it's lovely out."

They talked about everyone's summer plans, always a confusing but eagerly anticipated time. All three McTimons brothers had been influenced by Dani's guys. Abbas bought Ian his first flute, Lucas inspired Cyrus to channel his love of literature into a teaching career, and Seamus joined Cyril at Everton. All three jobs provided for a light summer schedule. Home projects, holidays, and more time with the clan were on tap.

Cy and Rose were brought up to speed about Gabriel and Poppy. They weren't surprised at the news but were curious about the timing.

"So they finally figured it out," was Cy's reply. "The prophecy has been fulfilled," Rose added.

Her mother, Penelope, Bashir's wife, had predicted the union not long after Poppy's birth. Déjà vu indeed. Her own story, her's and Cy's, followed a similar timeline.

Cyrus was thirteen. Walking home from school one day he saw Rosie and her brother Caspar being set upon by two bullies. He intervened but took quite a beating. At the house she helped tend to him and when they were alone she kissed him, right on the lips. She was ten years old. The boy never stood a chance.

Dinner was delicious, the lamb succulent and tender, the curry not too hot, balanced by a bit of fruit in the salad.

They sat around for a while afterwards, catching up and looking forward. Filly suggested a walk in the park, Calderstones Park, one of Liverpool's jewels, whose border lie at the end of the block. They strolled by the boating lake and ended up watching the sunset from the Japanese garden.

CHAPTER 8
TUESDAY, 29 JUNE

Sometimes a wind comes out of nowhere and knocks you off your feet

England is very regional in its attitudes, customs, and dialect. Urban and rural areas guard and celebrate their past with fierceness and pride. On the other hand, the country is united, through government and the monarchy obviously, but also from a shared history and traditions built upon for centuries.

Liverpool, in the northwest, lies on the banks of the river Mersey, just before it empties into the Irish Sea. It's an area of considerable image and reputation, not all of it positive. That's to be expected; it's a big city, predominately working class and liberal. Economic swings and misfortune, brought about by global events or simply the machinations of Whitehall and Downing Street, tended to hit hard in areas like Newcastle, Manchester, and Liverpool.

The postwar boom was at first diluted in the '70s and then was stopped dead in its tracks in the '80s. Maggie Thatcher's 'solution' to the wretched economy brought Liverpool to its knees.

A severe recession kicked off the '90s; that led to the Tory party's ouster and ushered in Tony Blair. Politics raged during the decade but things were looking up. The country was exploring new tech and an increased sense of personal freedom, and Great Britain was becoming more popular around Europe.

In Liverpool a good barometer for the state of life in general were the docks. They had come back to life. The city of immigrants was on the rebound.

Immigration gave rise to Merseyside. There were strong communities of Irish, Welsh, West Indian, Middle Eastern, and Asian people adding to Liverpool's sense of identity. Immigrants in general, depending on their backgrounds, have seen hard times, and can be resilient and resourceful. Bring on the 21st century.

The country's regional identities had assumed monikers, a designation that could be a slight or a compliment, depending on which side you're standing on. People from Newcastle were called Geordies, people from Stoke-on-Trent were the Potters, Brummies were from Birmingham, and Liverpudians were called Scousers. Scouse was a type of stew, thick and hearty, a dish thought to have derived from Scandinavian sailors coming through the port. No matter your heritage, if you are born and bred in Liverpool, you are a Scouser.

Take for example the four 'Scouse Girls,' at present seated on the steps of St. Luke's Church. Poppy's parents were American and Venezuelan-American. The twins had an American father and an Irish mother, and Darcy, her folks were English and Iranian.

St. Luke's was known as the bombed-out church, its interior a casualty of war. The shell was intact, a small but beautiful sandstone Gothic structure with perimeter gardens and a carpet of grass.

"Why is it you're going to university this summer, Pops?" Hope asked.

"I'm desperate to get my nurse's certification; mum's so busy at the clinic."

"I thought you were a nurse."

"No, I'm a veterinary care assistant, one step below. Once I'm a registered nurse I'm cleared for more duties and responsibility."

"And a raise from the boss," Darcy added.

"Cheers to that!"

"So Poppy," said Grace, brightly raising a new subject, "Tell us about your weekend."

"Every detail," Darcy added.

She was already blushing. "Now girls, you know it's not polite to kiss and tell." She hesitated, "So we'll only speak about the multiple orgasms."

Eventually the conversation settled on both Gabe and Jake. Hope was melancholy. "I miss our guys already."

"Me too," her sister agreed. "Hope and I won't see them til Crimbo. A month after you two."

"Yeah, but you guys have your own adventure to keep yourselves occupied," Darcy countered.

"True, that. But I am excited for both Christmas and New Year's," said Grace, "When we're back together."

"When do you leave?

"The end of next month. It's pretty much all sorted."

"We are excited, this will probably change our lives," Hope said. "Maybe it's this new millennium thingy, but I'm feeling anxious."

"Well, this new millennium 'thingy' just happens to coincide with adulthood for us," Poppy declared. "Not to worry, no one's breaking up the Scouse girls!"

"Or the Six!" Darcy said.

"We'll have to break up for now," said Grace. "It's after four, I've got a meeting on campus to straighten out some transcript paperwork and then some errands to run. I should be home soon after dark."

"I'm going to check in at the clinic and Erins on the way down," Poppy said.

"I'm done for the day," said Darcy. "Hope?"

"Me too. Let's catch the bus, I need to bathe and get supper started. Dad and mum are both working till six."

Hope ate alone that evening; Ben and Faith were delayed. She cleaned up the kitchen and left a note saying she was going to Sefton Park to hear some live music.

She got home around ten. Her folks were still not there but Cheryl and Kevin were. It wasn't unusual to see any of the clan in anyone else's house and she didn't think twice until she sat down her purse and saw the look on their faces. She went suddenly pale.

"What's happened to my sister?!"

Chapter 9
Wednesday, 30 June

Darkness creeps in like a thief and offers no relief
Why are you shaking like a leaf, come on, come talk to me

G race had been taken to hospital just after six. She'd been assaulted. Faith was rung up at the pharmacy. She asked Colleen to track down Ben on her way out the door and drove in a panic up to the City Centre.

She was huddled with some doctors when he arrived, his presence filling the room with something akin to extreme menace.

"She's alright Ben!"

He looked at the doctors, "Talk to me."

"Your daughter's been badly beaten sir. No broken bones, and no obvious internal injuries, we've more tests to run to confirm. Doctor Cooper can further update you." The kindly, middle-aged man ceded the floor to a young woman, who looked confident and assured.

"Would you like to sit down, Mr. Pine?"

"No."

"Grace was not sexually assaulted. Apparently her attackers couldn't completely subdue her."

"How many were there?"

"Three. Her hands are bruised, and we found someone else's skin under her nails. She's a tough one Mr. Pine; we suspect she'll heal rather quickly."

"I need to see her."

"Of course. She's been asking for you, but first I should tell you to be prepared. Her bruising in some places is severe, and she's been cut."

Ben went pale, and seemed to draw up inside himself.

"It's just a flesh wound, a slash."

"Where?"

"Mostly on the left side of her neck, but it carries up on to her cheek."

He closed his eyes. Inside he was raging, equal parts despair and fury. He had to calm himself before seeing his little girl.

They spent all night with her, Hope arriving around eleven, clutching her sister's old stuffed teddy.

Luke was there at dawn. Ben met him in the lobby and gave him everything he knew, first about her condition and then the police report, which was not satisfactory.

She'd been in Williamson Square where she bought a barm from a street vendor before walking down Tarleton towards Church to catch a bus home. Two men rushed her into an alley where a third man waited by an open door. This turned out to be just an unused shed where they tried to bind and gag her. Suddenly she launched her own attack, after feigning compliance, putting one guy down. The other two got so frustrated that the big one just decided to wail on her. He used the knife on her then left. She'd passed out.

"What about cameras?"

"There were none right there, just each end of the block."

"How much have you talked to her?"

"Not much, she's in and out of it, we're just trying to be with her, keep her calm. She's scheduled for more testing and treatment most of the morning; gives us a chance to clean up and eat something."

"Good idea brother. How's Faith?"

"Better. It was scary Luke, at first, not knowing."

"I can only imagine. Look Ben, and listen. You stay off the streets, hear me? I'm on it!"

"I want these guys Luke."

"You can't do it from prison. This will take some time. You just concentrate on your family."

Something wasn't right here, Luke thought as he walked through the University of Liverpool campus towards his office on Duke Street. The account of the incident itself sounded like a botched kidnapping, not attempted rape. That didn't make sense.

He updated Jude, grabbed a cup of tea, and called Philip.

Sir Philip Carter was a good friend of Luke's, a former business adversary turned extended family. Philip was Chairman of the Board at Everton Football Club and Filly McTimons' father. Grandson, Nathan, was the apple of his eye.

Sir Philip pretty much had the keys to the city. Lucas explained what happened to Grace and that she was well looked after but would need some plastic surgery. Philip said he would do the research and get the best damn physician in England to her bedside at once. He was appalled that such a thing could happen so close to home and promised to give the constabulary a good 'kick up the backside.' At noon Luke went to Williamson Square and bought a barm, questioning the vendor, the other vendors, the rough sleepers, the shop owners, and anyone else he thought might have been around the day before. Then he walked down Tarleton, all the way to Church, eyeing every square inch of the landscape.

Luke tossed the barm wrap and napkin in a bin out in the glare and bustle of Church Street and stood, lost in thought. He had no answers, but did harbor a suspicion. He needed to talk to Grace.

He was glad she was asleep. Tears came to his eyes the moment he saw her, tears that quickly turned to rage.

He closed the door and grabbed a chair to take to her bedside as her eyes opened.

"Hi Luke."

"Hi sweetie, you got some owies."

"Yes sir, but they have good drugs here."

"Can I get you anything?

"No. Can you help me sit up?"

"Is it okay?"

"Yeah, I'm just a little sore."

He helped her readjust herself as he raised the head of the bed and got her an extra pillow.

"What's the latest from the doctors?"

"They think I have a slight concussion, otherwise not too bad. Mostly bumps and bruises. Contusions, they call them. They've got me on antibiotics and pain meds."

"Have the police been back?"

"No, they're supposed to come later this afternoon to ask me some questions. I wasn't too helpful last night but I remember more now."

"Can you talk to me about it?"

"Yes. Do you know how it happened?"

"Basically, I do. What's got me stumped is why it happened. It wasn't a sexual thing?"

"No, not unless it was something planned for later. I think they wanted to take me somewhere. They tried to tie me up and gag me."

"We're not rich people, Grace."

"Or famous, so I've no clue." She hesitated for a bit, then continued. "Something I didn't tell the police, or anyone else so far, though. You know that guy that hangs around the City Centre, the one that's always working the tourists?"

"You mean Silky Sam, the grifter?"

"Yeah, him. He was there."

"In the alley?"

"No, in the square. He was talking to the two guys that followed me down Tarleton. They approached me, said they were tourists needing directions. I told them they could walk with me to the stop and I'd put them on the right bus for the docks. They said they'd come down later, that they weren't done with Sam. Then they rushed me from behind, into the place with that horrible man. One look at him and I nearly wet myself. I knew I had to fight. Then he said, 'fuck it, this bitch needs a lesson.' He was so cruel Luke. I turned my head as he slashed me, he was aiming for my face!"

Luke leaned over and kissed a tear on her cheek. "Shush girl, it's over now." He sat silent for a long while, mulling it all over.

Grace reset herself and spoke again. "He's a big guy Luke, with an accent, eastern European. And the other two, just lackeys, it seemed. And Silky Sam? He was scared shitless, clammed right up when they talked to me, then kinda disappeared."

Luke sat up, hesitated, and started to say something. Then he smiled. He actually smiled. Now he knew.

"Honey, I need you to do something, or rather not do something."

"What?"

"Don't repeat what you just told me to anyone. Not here at the ozzy, not the police, and not the clan. Especially not your father. I'll tell him enough to keep him from going mental. It's a lot to ask but it's important."

"Okay, I promise, if you think it best."

He laid a hand softly on her chest. "I need to go now. You take care and mind the doctors."

As he was leaving, she called to him.

"You're going to do that 'Lucas thingy,' aren't you?"

He simply turned, put his finger to his lips, and winked at her.

As the door shut Grace smiled. She actually smiled.

CHAPTER 10
SATURDAY, 3 JULY

"Ah Luke, I don't know. They won't listen to me."

"Sure they will, Nate. You're the man with the plan."

"My dad and uncles, plus Ben, Abbas, and Caspar. And I'm their boss?"

"Absolutely! A very wise man told me that fortune favors the brave. Don't worry lad, they'll give you a chance."

All the prep work necessary before actually painting the house would be completed today. Luke left Nathan to his musings and headed for the Lime Street train station.

It was mid-morning on a breezy but bright day on Merseyside, the City Centre already bustling. It was day three of Luke's search for the character known only as Silky Sam. The fact that he hadn't been seen the past few days could be taken two ways. He was probably spooked, but that meant that he also could be of help.

From Lime Street he cruised past St. John's Beacon, Williamson Square, and then the main shopping district. He was headed in the general direction of the waterfront and was nearing the Strand when lady luck smiled down on him. Sam was climbing the steps to Chavasse Park, an oasis in the shopping district and a popular meeting spot.

Silky Sam had a reputation as a scam artist, one of Liverpool's local colorful characters living on the fringe. He had no taste for the nine to five, preferring to live off his wits and wiles. A grifter is what he was, but affable and basically harmless. Today his normally smiling, carefree nature seemed absent, replaced by furtive glances and a nervous manner.

Lucas caught up with him on the other side of the park, calmed him down a bit, and sat him down on a bench.

"You do look familiar. A high roller, you are."

"Not exactly, Sam. I'm sometimes seen in the company of some of the local gentry, but I make my living like you, working with people."

"What can I do for you Guvner?

"My name is Luke," he offered his hand. "We need to have a chat about what happened on Tuesday."

Sam's reaction told him he knew exactly what Luke needed to know.

"I had nothing in it, didn't even know it til the next day."

"I know Sam, just relax. I need the two that targeted that girl. You were with them just before."

"What two?"

Luke took a much sterner tone, "Sam, now you're lying, you were with those two when she walked by. And when they started up with her you freaked out and left."

The guy was stunned. He looked around nervously, seemingly having difficulty catching his breath. "You know her?"

"Very well."

"Is she close to you?"

"I love her like my own."

He softened a bit, "How is she?"

"Still in the ozzy, severely beaten. She was also slashed across the neck and face."

Sam closed his eyes, his shoulders sagging as he seemed to shrink within himself.

"Bad business, that."

"Out with it mate, we can't have that kind of evil in our city."

When he got back to Greenbank Luke pulled to the curb and stared in wonder. It was quite the scene—ten or twelve of the clan all over the rowhouse, scraping, sanding, power washing, humming right along. Nate broke from his labors and came over, beaming.

"Looks like a proper job site. Well done, Boss!" The kid just smiled.

"C'mon, I'll pitch in, let's get er wrapped up."

"Your foreman is quite the taskmaster Lucas!" Cyril carped. "I might put him on my staff at Rovers."

"That's okay Luke," Kevin shouted from the dormer in Ben and Faith's attic. "If you can't get here on time just come when you can!"

"Sorry, Kev, first round's on me."

All four McTimons guys went with Ben, Cyril, Caspar, and Luke to the Dovey for pints and pies. There was a good band playing, the Coral, a country-tinged quintet from Hoylake, over on the other side of the river in the Wirral.

After eating they all were in the performance hall, tapping their toes and enjoying the scene—Caspar, Nate, and Seamus up dancing with some of the band's girlfriends. Needing a fresh pint, Luke gave Ben the high sign and together they went in and sat at the bar.

"Whatcha got, pardner?"

"One very scared witness, who I was able to instill a sense of moral indignation in. And luckily, one perpetrator that can't keep a secret."

He went on to say that the three were a team, recently moving their operation to Liverpool from Manchester. The team was part of a network, which was part of an organization.

"They're human traffickers Ben, out of Albania. That's why they've come to Liverpool, for access to the docks. Down the Atlantic, into the Med, around Italy and up the Adriatic. There's a port, Durres, not far west of Tirana, the capital."

Luke explained that the two in the square that followed Grace were

Mancs. Their job was to identify the marks, chat them up, and get them some place where they could be snatched.

"A place where the third guy waited—part of the network. A man by the name of Liridon Gashi."

Ben was incredulous. "You got his name?"

"Yeah, Sam said the younger of the two-point men was a real talker. This guy Gashi is Albanian, apparently a big deal back home. A guy with a temper, and a reputation for cruelty."

"Which Grace got a taste of. Where can I find this guy Lucas?"

"I don't know. And I'm not telling you when I find out. We've got to step lightly here. Don't want to blow it now that we're close."

"I almost lost her, didn't I?"

"Yeah. It's kinda strange. She saved herself by fighting back. She pissed him off enough that it wasn't worth it. They would never mark up the merchandise; most of these girls probably get sold to the highest bidder."

"I couldn't bear that."

"I know. She's safe now, and the strength and grit that saved her will help heal her, inside and out."

"I'll tell ya," he continued, "this guy Gashi found out that Sam knew about Grace. He roughed Sam up and threatened his life. It took me a while to loosen him up. He said he had a sister down in Chester. I gave him 200 quid to go spend a week with her. I hope to have it wrapped up by then."

"You'll keep me in mind?"

Luke just smiled.

CHAPTER 11
SUNDAY, 4 JULY

That it's the ocean flowing in our veins
Oh, that it's the salt that's in our tears
Oh, 'cause we could have come so very far
Oh, in at least as many years

Dani woke up with both her yellow dogs, Luke and Otis, lying on each side of her, Otis snoring lightly. She lay still, thankful for the peace and quiet, and the feel of her boys. She heard the teapot downstairs begin to whistle, causing the guys to stir. Oh well, nice while it lasted.

Downstairs Poppy poured herself a cup, grabbed a shortbread biscuit, and settled on the loveseat by the front window. She missed her boyfriend and brother.

Next door, at the end of the row, a similar scene was unfolding. Darcy was out back in the garden, listening to the birds come to life as the day brightened. Abbas and Robin were in the kitchen, pondering breakfast.

The Pine household in the middle of the row was also minus one of the Six, but not for long. Grace was coming home this afternoon. Ben, Faith, and Hope were at the table, talking excitedly over scrambled eggs and toast.

"When do we leave?" asked Hope.

"Noon," said Ben. "We gotta give the staff time for their morning rounds and admin time to cross the T's and dot the I's."

"The doctors are surprised at her recovery," Faith remarked. "They'll check her over good before releasing her."

"She's ready," Ben declared. "She's a Pine, tall and strong."

"Oh brother!" Hope moaned. "Don't you ever stop?" Faith giggled.

"Look dad, here come the Barcants."

Ben opened the door. "Mornin' kids, you're up early!"

"Hey baby, it's the Fourth of July!" Colleen sang, channeling her best Robert Earl Keen.

"We're volunteering to walk the mutts this morning," Cyril said. "We know you guys are a bit distracted today."

"Sure, thanks!"

"I'll go next door and get Otis. C'mon Amos!"

"What time do you guys want to eat this afternoon, Faith? I don't know when you're going to pick up Grace."

"We should be back by two, Colly. How bout four?"

"Sounds great."

Colleen, along with Luke and Ben, were the only all-American clan members. Dani was half, and four of the Six had American heritage. Colly always was in charge of side dishes, Ben the bar-b-que.

"I invited George and April over," Faith said. "I'll ring them up and tell them to come any time after two."

"Cool." George Pearson and April Walker had been a couple going on twenty years now. They lived up in Toxteth near James Doohan and his family. James was the first friend Cyril had made after coming to Liverpool back in '69. George was the Eclectibles percussionist, April worked at Erins Pharmacy. George was American, April English.

As for the McTimons household, Kevin and Cheryl had house-guests. Two of the Tweeners had spent the night. Middle son Seamus and his wingman, Caspar Ardavan, Bashir and Penny's son, had ended up at Greenbank after an evening of who knows what.

Shea and Caspar weren't what you would call the black sheep of the family, not by any means. They were, however, very independent. And they hung together all the time.

Caspar was soft spoken, normally on the periphery of whatever was going on, the observer. As a kid he was always overshadowed, or at least drowned out by his older sister Rosie, the precocious one. With Shea he would come out of his shell a little, going clubbing or to a concert, pub crawling and chasing the birds. He had that Celtic Persian look about him, a big hit with the ladies.

Seamus was the rough boy, with roguish good looks and a devil may care approach to life. A long career at Everton had made him semi-wealthy and very popular, but he always kept his ego in check, saving any cheekiness for the pitch.

Neither man owned hardly anything, and only the government knew what they considered their official place of residence. Caspar did spend most nights down near Sefton Park at the Stillwell house, the home that Penny and Bashir inherited from George and Rose Stillwell, Pen's parents. Shea was there from time to time, but also was known to crash out at his two brothers' semi-detached at Calderstones, or at Greenbank.

"What would you lads like for breakfast?" Kevin asked.

"Porridge and sticky buns!" It was their favorite, and Cheryl was glad to oblige, loving the chance to spoil the boys anytime she could tie them down long enough.

A leisurely pace was the plan for the rest of the morning. Chores, reading the paper, and prepping for a shared Independence Day get together later, in the country the States got their independence from. That was a touch of irony.

Grace got home a little after one, much to everyone's delight. After five days at the Royal Ozzy, she had caught a case of cabin fever. Various parts of her body were still discolored from bruising and a sizeable bandage was on her neck and side of her face. Her gait was steady and proud, however, a smile on her face and that familiar twinkle in her eye. Some of the clan were tearful, both with relief and the sense that this had been very nearly the worst thing ever.

She was all over Amos and Otis, who gave her a good sniffing up, making their own assessment of the damage done. Amos stuck close to her the rest of the day.

George and April arrived with three apple pies and a gallon of vanilla ice cream and caught up with Grace while the Pine's garden was being prepared. The guys were at the grill wrestling with four racks of pork ribs and a big beef tenderloin. The gals were in the Barcant kitchen, putting the finishing touches on the sides. Colleen had settled on baked beans, potato salad, coleslaw, and corn on the cob.

Everyone had a wonderful time, eating, drinking, laughing, content just being with each other. Sometimes you realize how lucky you actually are, and the simple pleasures are more than enough.

Earlier, while still in bed, Luke brought Dani up to speed on his little side project. She always worried about him at times like these, and always wondered why he had to be everyone's keeper. It was just the way he was wired. After growing up a nomad, living somewhere new every couple or so years, he'd become protective of his family and friends, now collected and nurtured ever since he came to England. She had to admit he was well suited for the job, having acquired so much in the way of practical skills and street smarts in his travels. He was a very capable operator.

He'd also matured, allowing others to share with the 'heavy lifting.' And he always promised not to take any unnecessary risks, the definition of which they still debated.

When the day's festivities were over he went to the yew with Ben and sat, having a beer and polishing off the end of a joint. Big Ben was in a better place now, much more at ease, but still not satisfied. Luke filled him in on his plans and told him he'd keep in touch. Then he packed a few changes of clothing and some toiletries and headed for the now vacant flat at Duke Street. He needed to be in the heart of the city, closer to his prey. Lucas Carter was going hunting.

CHAPTER 12
THURSDAY, 8 JULY

You plant a demon seed
You raise a flower of fire.

The last three days had been difficult; Luke's plan had necessitated a complete change in his daily routine. He'd morphed from early bird to night owl.

Monday morning was spent at the central library, where he began his crash course in Albanian. He checked out two books, an English-Albanian dictionary, and a tourist's guide with basic conversational phrases and instruction on pronunciation. From mid-afternoon til nearly midnight he walked the streets in a fruitless search for any of his three targets.

He slept in as late as he was able, anxious to go again. He rose, showered, ate a big breakfast, and sipped a cup of tea while resetting the day's plan.

As good as the information he'd gotten from Sam was, the photograph he was given was just as valuable. He had to admit, the way the photo was procured was quite clever.

Sam had spotted all three of them together, before they'd seen him. It was in the gardens outside of St. George's Hall. They were standing by the statue of William Gladstone, deep in conversation. Somehow, Sam talked a tourist couple into putting a fresh roll of film in their camera and take several pictures of him. In turn he paid for the film and put them on the right bus for their next destination. Luke got the best of the lot, Sam's smiling face, and in the background, the two Mancs in profile and Liridon Gashi full on.

He left Duke Street at two and started working his grid, hitting the transportation hubs, tourist hot-spots, cafes and pubs. Luke had kept an eye and ear on the news outlets. There was nothing as far as coverage on Grace's assault or any of the other recent missing persons reports, all involving young women.

Luke's suspicions that the trio might drop their guard and resume their operation proved true. At four thirty he spotted Gashi's lackeys at Williamson Square, scene of the crime.

They were chatting up a couple of girls, about 18 or 20, Indian or Pakistani probably, who weren't buying whatever they were selling. Wankers. Luke seethed.

He shadowed them for several hours. These guys were lazy, not very observant, much too smug for their chosen profession. It was a leisurely stroll.

The mood changed considerably when they crossed Hood Street by the Queen Square bus station and Liridon Gashi stepped out of the shadows of the Royal Court Theatre.

The Mancs stiffened, their posture now very deferential under the man's glare. Luke understood why. The guy was a presence, threatening and malevolent. Just under six feet, dark eyes, buzz cut and thick, dark stubble. Over two hundred pounds of menace.

A short conversation, one-way and terse, was followed by a walk— the three of them making their way over to Hotham Street. They entered the Lord Nelson Hotel, a small budget lodging, old and out of the way.

Twenty minutes later the pair came out and scurried off, men on a mission. Luke stayed put.

Gashi didn't leave the hotel until after dark. He had cleaned himself up and was dressed decently. As it turned out he had a dinner date.

They were at Caesar's Palace, the popular Italian eatery on Renshaw Street. Luke couldn't resist, taking a stool at the end of the bar. He could see the table—Gashi now the subservient one, carefully listening to the well-dressed older man, also Balkan if not Albanian. He could also see, at the other end of the bar, the old man's bodyguard. This guy he wanted no part of. Luke finished his beer and waited outside.

The three parted outside the restaurant; Gashi walked back to the Lord Nelson. Luke had to make sure, and now he knew, this was the devil's den. Gotcha!

The previous morning he was up and at em, outside the Lord Nelson by eight. He wanted to know when this guy started his day. Two hours later he emerged and headed up by the train station for coffee and a copy of the Echo. Then he walked straight back to the hotel, pausing long enough to shove a woman who asked him for some pocket change to the cobbles. Luke waited three more hours outside the hotel before heading to Duke Street. He had all he needed.

In the afternoon he got with Judith to try to salvage the lack of client work he'd accomplished so far this week. He made a few calls, reorganized his schedule, and set some meetings for next week.

At the end of the day, he touched base with Dani and Poppy and had a brief chat with Ben before he checked out.

"I know it's late notice but I'm hoping you can stay down in the burbs tomorrow, well away from the City Centre."

"Uh, yeah, I guess. What's up?"

"Sorry, brother, you're still on a need-to-know basis. Just coordinate by phone with Jude if you need to, otherwise spend your day near the house and neighborhood. And make sure there's people around you, the more the better. All the time."

"Yes Bwana."

Luke walked down to the docks and strolled the promenade. He was leg sore but needed the fresh air and time to play out tomorrow in his head. He ended up at the Baltic Fleet.

"Lucas!"

"Hello James. Still here ay?"

"Just about to leave it for the night crew. You're looking knackered, mate. Everything okay?"

"Things are looking up, I'm about to wrap up a big project."

"Good for you. What can I get yer?"

"A pint of bitters and a plate of fish and chips, please."

"You got it!"

"Then go home, James. And give my best to Sarah and the girls."

Luke ended up eating every bite, along with three pints. Back at the flat he showered, copped a buzz, and listened to some music. Then he slept, sound and long.

This morning was cool and overcast, a spit of rain in the air. Good, this allowed Luke to wear a dark hoodie, cameras were everywhere.

Gashi emerged ten minutes later than the day before, and made the same morning run for coffee and a paper. Luke approached as he stepped away from the newsstand.

"Good morning, sir!" He was ignored.

"Excuse me please, I'd like a word."

"Fuck off!"

"But you're the guy, the one I'm supposed to see."

He hesitated. Met Luke's gaze. Scary. "You know, about the girl."

"What you talk about? I have no girl!"

"But I've got money, a lot." Luke flashed a big wad of folded bills.

"In five seconds, I beat you. Fuck off!"

"Çfarë nuk shkon, Liri. Nuk jupelqen të fitoni para?"

That did it. Gashi looked at him incredulously, his expression showing wonderment, suspicion, and anger. Suddenly everything had changed. Luke was locked onto the bastard now, but the guy now knew Luke wasn't who he pretended to be.

"You come to my office, maybe we make business." Luke hesitated. He needed to set the hook a little deeper.

"You have ladies there, at your office?"

"Pictures, only pictures. Business first." Again, Luke hesitated.

"Come, it's very close. Then we see the girls."

"Okay." He knew Gashi wouldn't separate from him until he found out exactly who he was and what his intentions were.

They entered the Lord Nelson and walked up to the second floor.

When Gashi unlocked the door, Luke had to make a decision. This was the point where there would be no debate with Dani on the subject of acceptable risk. He was walking straight into the lion's den.

"Nice place!" Gashi scowled at him. Luke decided not to waste time. "What I'm looking for is a white girl, English, or maybe American. A tall one. Athletic, with black hair and blue eyes. Not too soft, mind you. A tough girl, maybe with a scar on her cheek."

Gashi turned from the table where he had lain his coffee and paper, wielding an evil grin and a blade. Luke thought of Grace and met the son of a bitch halfway, blocking the thrust and locking on to the knife arm with both hands while kicking at the man's shins. He was getting clubbed in the side and shoulder by his opponent's weaker fist, so he suddenly punched him in the nose with his left. Gashi wrenched the knife hand free and slashed Luke across his left hip just above the thigh. Luke was able to grab his wrist on the follow through and smash it against the bedpost, sending the knife to the floor as they fell together against the side of the bed. They grappled, Luke managing to stay on top until the guy got his feet under him and thrust upward, sending Luke to the wall like a rag doll.

They both stood and stared, catching their breath, the knife halfway between them. Luke looked deep into his eyes. They were black, empty, devoid of anything seemingly human. This man had no soul.

"Now I butcher you."

"Fuck you will!"

Luke never made hard and fast rules in which to live his life, nor did he set too many goals to achieve during his time on the planet. He did carry some basic ideals, to guide his thoughts and decisions. One such tenet was the desire to live out his entire life without taking someone else's.

Oh well, can't have everything always go according to plan.

CHAPTER 13
SUNDAY, 11 JULY

That one day we may lay our hands on one another
And seek the healing for ourselves, this earth, and our young

33,830 — Sunday ECHO — 35P
11 July 1999

CITY CENTRE SLAYING ASKS QUESTIONS

The discovery late Saturday afternoon of a body in a Liverpool hotel room has raised suspicions of a human trafficking ring on Merseyside.

The victim, an undocumented Albanian national, was discovered by a chamber maid at the Lord Nelson Hotel on Hotham Street. A medical examiner estimated that the death occurred 48 to 60 hours prior to discovery. A do not disturb sign was posted outside the room.

Local authorities described the murder scene as an execution style killing, particularly grisly in its method. The deceased was in a sitting position against a wall, completely disemboweled. There was a handwritten note that read, 'Mothers against human traffickers' stapled to his forehead. Merseyside police have requested that anyone with knowledge of the incident come forward at once.

A spate of recent missing persons reports has fueled speculation of an organized cadre targeting young women in the area utilizing the docks as a means of egress. Lord Mayor Joseph Devaney has issued the call for law enforcement to form a task force to investigate the issue with the full cooperation of local civic leaders.

———

Ben read the article with growing alarm, although it did shed some light on Luke's morosity the last few days. Even this morning, when he dropped by to collect Amos for the morning walk, he seemed quiet and distracted. Man, just what the hell went down in that hotel room?

The girls were in the dining room, going over travel plans for the twins. He laid the front page on the table. "I read the news today. Oh boy." This wasn't a typical corny dad joke. Ben's tone conveyed real concern.

Faith read it and passed it on. "We've got to go over there."

"Yeah, let's grab a fresh cuppa."

"Hey girls, would you get the Ardavans? Take the paper with you."

"Okay mum," said Hope.

"Oh my God!" Grace looked pale after reading the story.

"You alright Gracie?" Ben asked.

"This is unbelievable! Is there stuff we don't know about Luke?"

"Probably. One thing for sure, he's the most loyal person I've ever met."

"Uncle Luke!"

"You got it."

"Come on, let's go help our guru get his mojo back."

Cyril and Colly were already there, having tea with Dani, who was reading the article for the first time. When she finished there were tears in her eyes.

"Mierda, I'm gonna have to clip that boy's wings. I'd give him hell if I wasn't so worried about him."

"He's been quiet."

"Now we know why."

"It's not something he can talk about," Ben said. "At least not openly."

"We have to hash it out with Lucas though," Cyril said. "But you're right, this stays in the clan."

"Hey everyone!" Robin chirped. "Where's Luke?"

"Still walking the dogs. Want some tea?"

"Please!"

"I'll get it mum," offered Darcy. "Dad?"

"Yes, thanks. Dani, you okay?"

"Morning Abbas, I'm fine," giving him a hug. "You know Luke, he just can't help himself."

"Everyone's protector, like a sheepdog," Hope said.

"Now he needs looking after," Faith declared. "We need our Lucas back."

The front door opened and in burst two big yellow blurs of fur, excited at all the humans about. Luke hesitated at the entry, trying to read the room. Uh-oh. He decided to try a bit of false bravado.

"What are all these people doing in my house? Otis, kill!"

"Here niño, sit down and read the paper. Then we'll have a chat. Kids, let's go scramble some eggs." Poppy, Darcy, and Hope followed Dani to the kitchen. Grace sat next to Luke on the couch.

He knew this day would come but was unsure how it would affect the situation. One thing for sure, he was in a funk and didn't know why.

He was clear headed and decisive at the scene, staging the room, erasing all evidence of his presence, and doing pretty well at disguising his limp as he left the area, sticking to the shadows.

He walked to Duke Street, then drove home. Dani freaked, then she and Poppy cleansed his wound, tended to his cuts and bruises, and wrapped his chest with ace bandages. At least one rib was cracked or broken. The knife wound was on his upper thigh, near his hip. He was lucky. There was no apparent ligament or tendon damage, but the slash was deep, close to the bone. Faith brought some antibiotics from the pharmacy. Poppy burnt his clothes in the Pine's firepit; there was a lot of blood, most of it not his. Dani stitched him up.

In the meantime, he'd gone quiet. 'It's over' was about all you could get out of him. Dani thought he might be in shock. He stared a lot, his voice metronomic when he did speak.

Now, reading the article seemed surreal, someone else's description of an all too real nightmare playing over and over in his head. Equally surprising was the sudden realization that reading the article was making him feel better. It was cleansing in a way. The ones who cared for him were getting the story without him having to tell it.

Luke finished the article and looked up; a room full of people were staring at him.

"Any comments on the reporting?" Ben asked.

"Journos, just a bunch of hacks."

Cyril grinned, "Is that you in there Lucas?"

"You don't have to talk about it, Luke," Robin offered. "We certainly understand."

"Thanks guys. I guess there's one thing I ought to come clean about. I didn't want to go into that hotel room, I could've let the police take over. But I couldn't see them sealing the deal. Somehow the guy would skate. I wasn't going to allow Grace to get involved. She'd have to testify against him and I'm sure that would really put her in harm's way. I was in the room looking for more to give the authorities, then he forced my hand."

"I was in a room alone with that man," Grace said in a dull monotone, "It still terrifies me." She edged up against Luke and put her head on his shoulder. "I'll show you my scar if you show me yours."

He smiled and kissed the top of her head. "You are precious."

"Thanks, godfather."

"I'm going to be fine, guys, really. Thank you all for the love."

"Lucas," Abbas said. "I've got to ask you one question though, then we'll all forget the whole thing."

"What's that, doost-am?"

"Mothers against human traffickers. What's up with that, and, stapled to his forehead?"

"Hey, you don't mess with Scouse mums!"

CHAPTER 14
MONDAY, 12 JULY

He's a rebel and a runner,
He's a signal turning green
He's a restless young romantic,
Wants to run the big machine

"I talked to my folks last night."

"Really, when?"

"Around eight-thirty. You were still out with Luca."

"And?"

"Dad wished me a happy birthday, then he put mum on, who blew my mind!"

"How so?"

"You wouldn't believe it Gabe. Grace was the intended target of a kidnapping ring. She kicked the shit out of one the three guys and was so much trouble they said fuck it and put her in the ozzy!"

"Damn, how is she?"

"Fine now, home and sassy as ever. You know the twins, forces of nature. We'll get the whole story when we get home in November. How was the meeting?"

"Good, I'm all hooked up. We've got a session on Friday."

"You're gonna wow em brother!"

"We'll see. They take their classical serious down here. We're next to Austria and Italy, the 'Holy Lands.'"

"You've got the creds and the chops, no problemo."

"How about you, did Laura enlighten you?"

"I'll say! We went into Zürich and walked the Bahnhofstrasse. That street has unbelievable wealth, probably bigger than the G.D.P. of most countries."

"And the language?"

"Any one you care to hear. What I liked is that all business is conducted in proper high German, not the Swiss German that's used colloquially, especially in rural areas."

"Cool, you ready?"

"Yeah, let's hit it."

They ran a lot, familiarizing themselves with the area, the heart of Switzerland. They'd landed at Flughafen Zürich two weeks ago; it seemed like only a few days.

Ben and Luke had met Luca Haller in Liverpool, Luca was in town trying to establish some points of sale for men's shaving products, produced at the factory inherited from his father. The three hit it off and spent time together, somehow resulting in the offer to host the boy's sojourn.

Luca married Laura about ten years ago. She had three children from a previous marriage—two girls and a boy. The boy was in the States presently learning English and checking out America for the first time.

The Hallers lived in a nearly 250-year-old farmhouse south of Lake Zürich, the Zürichsee, southeast of the city of Zürich. The house and the area were storybook gorgeous, on a slope overlooking the town of Wollerau and the lake beyond. Switzerland is divided into cantons, like states in the U.S. or counties in England. Schindellegi was in Schwyz, one of the three original cantons when the country declared itself so in 1291.

The trip was designed for several purposes—just to travel and learn about another part of the world chief among them. Also, to further their careers from a new perspective. Gabriel would play his cello with a new group of musicians, and study language, German and Italian. Lucas was nearly a licensed lawyer, or solicitor as they're called in Great Britain, not to be confused with a barrister, which is a trial lawyer. Luca was a Stanford educated lawyer and would serve as a mentor to Jake while here—sort of a new voice and different perspective. Jake wanted to get fluent in German as well. He was going to be an agent like his father, but with a law degree. He would travel, picking up talent wherever he could find it around the continent.

There was plenty to do around the property as well. The 'farm' was a hobby for Luca and Laura; there were no crops save hay, but there were animals. They had a chicken coop with a dozen hens and one cock; he was one happy dude. There were also four geese, some rabbits, a shepherd named Erlo and a cat named Pfüder. They had some sheep, the number of which varied. The sheep spent the summer in the mountains.

Erlo met them at the property line when they'd finished their run. They chased and bumped each other back to the house.

The lads had settled well here in the land of banks, chocolate, and alpine vistas. The Hallers were kind, inquisitive, and gracious folks. Time here would be well spent.

Tschüss!

CHAPTER 15
MONDAY, 19 JULY

This is where we walked, this is where we swam
Take a picture here, take a souvenir

Hope was entertaining a number of mixed emotions at the moment, all competing for time at the fore.

"A penny for your thoughts."

"Sorry, Darce. I've been distracted today."

"Duh!"

They were at the Otterspool Promenade, a long stretch of maintained greenspace south of the city. It bordered the Mersey and was a good halfway point for a run originating at Greenbank. The pair were having a rest and watching the river making its way to the Irish Sea.

"Are you worried, Hope, or sad?"

"No, a bit melancholy, it's fair to say, and anxious. But in a good way, mostly."

"Well, that answers all my questions." They both laughed.

"Sorry, I have to admit what happened to Grace shook me, but I've since realized that her recovery has been remarkable. And if she can bounce back so quickly, the rest of us can bloody move on as well."

"And?"

"That's the anxious part. I'm excited for the next two years, and confident. But the anticipation, it makes my brain go off in different directions."

"I think that's quite natural, with such big changes in the off. It just needs to happen, Hope. You'll be fine. Look out America!"

"You're right Darcy, thanks. Geez, I need to get over myself. How about you, when are you making your big move, so to speak?"

"I'm going to wait til next summer. That way I'll have all my basic courses over and done with. The Phil's pushing me to move to the Symphony now, but I'm not that great a student."

"So you're sticking with the Youth Orchestra. I thought you were getting good marks at school."

"They're alright, but I'm not taking any chances. By next summer I'll be taking mostly electives, then me and Viola will be kicking ass in the Royal Liverpool Symphony Orchestra!"

Hope giggled, "It's cool you named your viola Viola!"

"Hey, maybe we should head back. I'm starting to stiffen up."

"Yeah, I'm a little sore from painting the house."

"It looks great, ay?"

"It does. Greenbank's even greener now."

"Quite, Miss Jade."

"Indeed, Miss Hunter. You want to race back?"

"Hell no! Not with your long legs and super lungs!"

"Suck it up, Buttercup!"

Cyril was on his front stoop when they got back. With him was his long time protégé, Seamus McTimons. Shea also had a long career at Everton, the number eleven making mayhem on his opponent's left flank for nearly twenty years. He, too, loved the game enough to go into coaching, and nearly had all his badges. Shea was the only assistant Cyril brought to Tranmere, opting not to shake things up too much and keeping most of the staff already in place.

"Looking good girls!"

"Thank you, kind sir! Whatcha doing?"

"Whatcha think?"

"Talking football. Duh."

Both guys grinned. "Can either of you recommend a good center half, preferably a leftie?"

"Duh again!" Darcy scolded. "What do you think is standing right next to me?"

Hope struck a pose.

"We'll take her," Shea said. "She's better than what we've got."

"Too late, I'm already signed."

"When do you leave, Hope?" Cy asked.

"Ten days, on the 29th."

"Exciting times these are. Good luck!"

"Don't need it; we learned from you two!"

Kevin came out from his house next door. "What's all the yakking about out here? Darcy, I'm going to tell your dad you're hanging out with footballers again."

"You gotta go slumming sometimes, Kev."

"It builds character Da," Shea added.

"What's up Kevin?" Cyril inquired.

"Big news kids, I'm selling the business."

"What!"

"Come again? No more Kevin's Fish and Chips?"

"It's going to be a gradual thing, to get the new owners in, let them get sorted. By this time next year, I'll be a pensioner."

"That is big news, Da. Good on you!"

"Guess who's taking over the chippy?

"Colonel Sanders?"

"Ha, good one. No, how about George Pearson and April Walker?"

"Wow," Darcy exclaimed, "that sounds like a marvelous idea!"

"Yes mon!" agreed Cyril. "How 'bout dat. George going from the oven to the fryer!"

"Kitchen work is kitchen work. His experience as a baker will serve him well."

"I'm happy for them," Hope said. "They're due some good fortune, especially April."

"It was Cheryl's idea. And you're right Hope, such good people deserve a break. Now, instead of two jobs each with uncertain security they'll have something to build on. Not that it's easy-peasy now; a small business is hard work."

"They'll be okay," Shea said. "We sucked them into our little ecosystem, they'll be looked after."

"No doubt. Well, I'm off to meet them—an introductory tutelage, fish and chips 101."

"Give them our regards!"

"We're off as well," Cyril said. "A high-level meeting at the Baltic Fleet."

"Um-hmm," Darcy intoned. "A likely story."

"Care to join us?"

"Normally yes," answered Hope. "Particularly if this meeting involves other rich and handsome footballers."

"However," continued Darcy, "we've plans to meet Grace and Poppy at Pierhead to take the ferry to the Wirral."

"What's on?"

"A walk in the park and supper. Not sure where."

"Have fun, and stay together."

"Thanks Cyril, we'll be careful."

"Cheers!"

"Ta-ra!"

The girls went to bathe and change, check-in with the folks, and walk to the bus stop.

"All the men are protective of late. To be expected, I suppose."

"Yes, the only problem is that it's most dangerous when they're not about."

"You think your sister will be more timid now? In general, I mean."

Hope thought for a moment. "No, I think she will be more careful, but unafraid. I'm more worried she'll find the two Lucas didn't get."

CHAPTER 16
THURSDAY, 22 JULY

These are the days of miracles and wonder,
This is the long distance call

There was an abundance of savory smells, plainly evident as soon as the door opened.

"Good morning ladies, such a fresh and bright lot you are! How is everyone?"

"Hungry now, Gran. Whatever's in the kitchen smells wonderful!"

"Patience Darcy, it won't be ready for an hour and a half or so. I thought we might take a walk before we eat."

"It's a really nice day," Poppy remarked. "A cruise through the park would be perfect."

They were at what the gang referred to as the Stillwell House; their hostess was Aleah Ardavan. Aleah was the clan's elder, now in her upper seventies. She was a widow now, her beloved Hassan's passing several years ago now a memory that brought more smiles than tears. She lived here with her eldest, Bashir, and his wife Penelope, who inherited the house from her parents, George and Rose Stillwell. Grandson

Caspar was also a resident, when you could pin him down long enough.

"Hope, Grace, how does a walk sound?"

"We're with Pops, Aleah," answered Hope. "And Sefton's the perfect spot."

"Grace?"

"Lead the way, kind madam!"

The girls actually walked here to begin with. The southern border of Greenbank Park was Greenbank Lane, the western terminus of which was Sefton Park. The Stillwell house was two blocks past the other side of the park on the corner of Ivanhoe and Bertram.

Sefton Park is nearly big enough to get lost in. Aleah didn't want to take them the same way they'd come so she opted for a more southern route, skirting the bandstand, the north side of the lake, and walking around the Palm House—an immense events venue built of glass and housing numerous and varied plants from all over the world.

They found a couple of benches inside and sat, taking in all the strange flora and glasswork. Aleah sat next to Grace and took her hand.

"How are you dear, really and truly?"

"I'm fine, Aleah. Not afraid, or timid. It seemed a harsh and sudden manner in which to experience how cruel some people are, but I've come through it. I'm more careful now, more wary, but not scarred. At least not on the inside."

"She just got her bandage off yesterday," Hope reported.

"I noticed. May I look more closely?"

"Of course!"

Grace turned, fully exposing her left side. Aleah looked at the wound closely, with concern but no sign of shock, not even a flicker of a wince.

"This was done with a very sharp blade, which is good. It left a very narrow cut. And the doctor did a remarkable job." Then she kissed her cheek and turned her face back towards her own.

"There are those who will tell you it's hardly noticeable. They are lying, it's very noticeable. But it's mostly on your neck, and it will fade over time. She smiled. "I see it as a mark of character, and strength."

Grace hugged her. "You are sweet, and very wise."

"I've been around a long time. You pick up things along the way."

"Dad's still bandaged, for a few more days," Poppy said.

"That's what happens when you get sewn up by a vet," added Darcy. "Can't wait to see the scar!"

Aleah laughed, then paused, and for a moment was quiet. "I suppose you've all heard how Hassan and I came to Liverpool to live. You, Poppy, were just an infant then."

"We know you had to leave because of the revolution," Grace said. "And that Lucas went over to escort you back."

"And something about the U.S. Embassy," Hope added.

"I don't think we ever got the whole story," Poppy admitted.

"That's because Lucas doesn't like the attention, or he didn't want to alarm you. That man, well, he was in his twenties then. But that man flew to Tehran unannounced, made his way to the center of town, and bared himself in the middle of the road, halfway between a mob that wanted to rip him to shreds and some soldiers with their rifles aimed at his chest. All this just to get into the embassy, where he somehow convinced the ambassador and army intelligence to put himself and two Iranians on a military flight to Germany."

The girls were gobsmacked.

"To top it off, he got a private car driven by one of the Shah's secret police up to our house to take us to the embassy."

"That's secret agent stuff!" Hope exclaimed.

"That's a story for another time. Come girls, let's walk around the lake on the way home."

"What were Abbas and Luke like as teenagers?" Grace asked.

"Well, they were friends, not best friends, but close. Abbas was a dedicated musician, even then. He was also fascinated with western culture. I think he envied all the travel Lucas had done. Luke wanted to learn about Iran, and ancient Persia. I was in charge of the art department at school. He was a poor art student but always wanted to talk to me in Farsi. Oh, and girls, they both chased the girls."

"Typical," was Poppy's reply. "Mum says dad running into Abbas that day back in '69 was the start of Bashir's 'Greenbank Coalition' that everyone laughs about."

"Yes, Uncle Bashir still looks wistful when the subject's brought up," mused Darcy.

"It's fun to tease him about it. But you have to realize, it's what's led to all the weddings, and all you beautiful girls."

"Aww!" Poppy cooed.

"And some boys, it must be said," added Hope.

"The world can't be perfect, luv," her sister added.

Back at the house the smell of exotic spices assailed the senses, reminding the ladies of their appetites. They sat down to a platter of fesenjan, which was browned chicken and toasted walnuts, seasoned and simmered in pomegranate molasses. Some bread and a salad completed the meal. The twins ate heartily, Grace was able to start training again and the pair were doing a lot of roadwork and lifting weights.

"This is so delicious, Gran!"

"We can all agree to that!" echoed Poppy.

"Thank you. I only make it for guests so it's a treat for me as well."

They talked about the twins' trip to the states, now only a week away.

"You two must be excited."

"Definitely! Excited and a little nervous."

"That's natural. Embrace it, it's a whole new chapter in your lives."

"I'm a couple weeks behind where I want to be," Grace said. "Physically, that is. We've got to hit the ground running."

"That reminds me," Aleah said, trying to recall. "Ah yes, Alice Abrams, the poet. She wrote that, 'In life as in dance, grace glides on blistered feet.'"

CHAPTER 17
SUNDAY, 25 JULY

Hang up your chairs to better sweep
Clear the floor to dance
Shake the rug into the fireplace

In a scene repeated literally hundreds of times before, a sizeable entourage made its way up Penny Lane to Dovedale Towers. It was late afternoon, the mid-summer sun on its descent behind them. The gang had decided on a meal and some music, a bit of revelry and celebration to see the twins off.

"Ah, the minstrels are here!"

"Hello Emma." Ben greeted the Dovey's manager with a cuddle as the rest filed in.

"What's happenin' Ms. Cross?"

"You are, Sir Cyril. How's the new gig?"

"It's a challenge, my dear. But the lads are working hard."

The Ardavans stashed their cases in the performance hall while the rest put a couple of tables together. Colin came over to get the drink orders going.

"Hey all!"

"Hi Colin, how's Faye?"

"Splendid, Colleen. She may come by later to hear the band."

"Good, it's been a while."

"Where's the McTimons?"

"It's Cheryl's birthday. They're all over at Ian and Cyrus' house."

"So, what to drink?"

While Colin sorted the beer and wine list, the four young'uns were at the bar, already sipping on their pints.

"You know, in the states you can't drink unless you're twenty-one," Poppy informed the twins.

"You're kidding!" Grace was surprised.

"Nope."

"How am I gonna get my carbs?" asked Hope.

"More pasta, I guess."

"Why hasn't dad told us that?"

"Maybe he thinks you're going away to school to study, and earn your scholarship," cracked Darcy.

"Ha ha!"

Mae was behind the bar tonight, much amused at the conversation.

"So, they're breaking up the Merseyside Six?"

"They already have," answered Poppy. "Gabe and Jake are in Switzerland now, and the twins head west this Thursday."

"It'll just be meself and Pops," added Darcy.

"The times they are a changing," Mae sang in reply.

"Whoa now, quoting Dylan again are we?" came a voice from behind the girls.

"Geoff! Who let you in?"

"Come on Mae, you know my family used to own the place. I've still got a key!"

"Hi Geoff!" Grace said as she turned to face him. She knew everyone had to get used to and get over what happened to her, now awaiting his reaction.

"Hello luv," as he gave her a hug. "Un-huh, yeah, there it is. That's it? Blimey, I did worse than that shaving last week!"

"You're the best!"

"What do you think Grace? That's more important."

"Well, I've been playing it up quite a bit, sulking and looking pitiful. Getting some considerable attention and sympathy as well. But just between me and you? It's fucking boss!"

Geoff absolutely roared.

"There he is, chatting up the birds, dirty old man!" A collective 'Paul!' erupted from that end of the bar.

"Oh yeah, I brought the rest of the band, by the way."

Paul Pilnick, legendary Liverpool guitarist and session man, in the flesh. And trailing behind, George Pearson, the bongo buddha, and the ladies' favorite pony-tailed care bear.

"Evening all! Mae, may I have a pint of your best bitters please? I must go and set up my kit and it's such an arduous task."

"Of course, George. Geoff?"

"The same please."

Abbas wandered up to the bar, empty handed. "Where's all the serving wenches, I've a thirst that needs slaking!"

"Careful Abbas, it's hard to play the flute with a fat lip!"

"Yes ma'am. May I have a beer please?"

"That's better, nice boy."

Faith and Dani asked Emma what was on the menu tonight. The Greenbank gang had grown so much over the years and the Eclectibles so popular that when they came en masse like this they tried to take it easy on the kitchen staff.

"How about burgers? We've got a lot of beef."

"Burgers it is."

"Chips and coleslaw?"

"Please!"

Eventually everyone got fed, refilled their glasses and mulled about, catching up with friends and familiar faces from the neighborhood. A carefree, summer vibe was felt by all, fueled by comradery and the anticipation of live music.

On the green behind the pub the band was perusing Abbas' set list while adjusting the collective frame of mind. Lucas strolled up and joined the queue.

"Mister Manager, what's on?" Paul asked.

"You guys. I'm stoked. Anyone need anything?"

"We're all set. What's with the limp?"

"Just a little hitch in my git-along."

"Uh-huh, okay, we'll take the hint."

Luke's agency, Carter Assets Management, represented more than just footballers. He handled contract negotiations for musicians—the band and all five of the clan members employed by the Philharmonic, plus a few local actors and artists. So far Luke had grown the agency slowly but was preparing to ramp things up with the addition of Jacob next year.

The hall was filling up when they got back inside. Darcy was on stage, tuning her viola. The Eclectibles sound was ever evolving; thirty years of playing together will do that to any ensemble. The loss of their keyboard player coincided with the rise of Gabriel and Darcy's participation in the group. George's influence on the band had been tremendous. All the others had been expanding the collective toolbox with percussive accoutrements and the odd recorder or penny whistle. Ian McTimons, who sat in with the band often, had taken up the harmonica.

They took the stage to spirited applause; the spine of the group spread across the array of Persian carpets. George at center rear, anchoring his mates on each side. Geoff was left side, his electric bass and acoustic six-string at the ready. Paul was on the right, the big Rickenbacker strapped and humming, the Fender Strat waiting its turn. Two mic stands were placed between the guitarists, Faith and Dani's posts. A stand between them was loaded with noisemakers. The rest of the stage was open range, space for Abbas, Robin, and Darcy to rove about, making their magic.

Abbas had decided on an all-American set list, a nod to the twins' imminent western transmigration. They started with "First Recollection," by the Cowboy Junkies, and ran through Timbuk 3's "Waves of Grain," "Green Children" by 10,000 Maniacs, and Shawn Colvin's "Round of Blues" before ending with "The Book I'm Not Reading" by Patty Larkin.

The audience much appreciated the mini-set; Geoff had the sound mix spot on and the songs were well sequenced mid to up tempo selections of varying style. The girls traded vocals and sang together, showcasing Dani's sultry timbre and Faith's tenor, pure and strong.

Tunings were tweaked, gear readjusted, and some instruments were switched out for the next sojourn. Abbas stepped to the mic.

"Salaam alaikum, Scousers! I trust everyone is enjoying themselves thus far. Say, has anyone here ever been to Urbana, Illinois?" There were no takers. "Me either. It's not a big city, apparently, but a smaller college town. I don't know what its claim to fame is, but I can tell you it's produced one fine musical ensemble known as The Moon Seven Times. We'd like to showcase a few of their songs for you now. Paul, would you care to do the honors?"

"Why certainly! By the way folks, I've been to Urbana, on tour with Stealer's Wheel. Do yourself a favor and just buy the album."

Then he started picking his guitar, which in turn changed to strumming, arpeggio style, creating a repeating melody. Geoff and George picked it up on the second cycle, paving the way for Dani's story of an affected stranger in a dystopian landscape:

This is how the tale unfolds for everyone

Two verses and two choruses, drums, bass, and guitar steady on theme and meter, all the while the strings and flute were offering a counterpart sampling of accompaniment, building throughout. Dani delivered the last line of the second chorus amidst a full sonic tapestry:

But neither luminary gave off any real heat

Then it began again, Paul's ethereal chord progression. Luke had trouble figuring out just what effects he was using. The dude had an impressive set of pedals, stretching in an arc from his amp to his mic stand. When Geoff and George joined back in, it was in a staggered, stuttering manner, like they were trying to get the whole thing cranked up again. When the trio did fall back into sync, it was quite catchy. Dani delivered the last verse and sealed the stranger's fate.

"Neither Luminary" was followed by "Some of Them Burn," which started slowly. Paul again, a more traditional sound and melody. Faith stepped to the mic and started a tale of a woman at odds with those who would challenge her ability and focus:

The girl next door thinks I was born a little late

The account continued into a simple declaration:

Some of them burn for someone else,
Some of them complete themselves
Geoff and George set the pace for the second cycle, Abbas' flute popping up at the edges:
I'll hold my breath until it reaches
All the rooftops, where she still says
Some of them burn for someone else
Some of them complete themselves
Then Robin and Darcy started to play, the strings swelling, injecting into the song emotion and a sense of determination. Faith completed the thought:
One glowing wall at a time,
And some explode so bright.
The band fully cranked up now, the violin driving the sound home, allowing Faith to make her stand:
The girl next door, thinks I was born a little late
To slam her to the ground, and take her fire away
Everyone not already standing now rose, giving Faith her due.

The song called "Montgomery L" was a sort of love song, two star crossed lovers in a Shakespearian tragedy for modern times. Kind of folky at first, but on a slow burn. The rhythm section got to cut loose on this one, Geoff with impressive fret work and George working the timbales before picking up his sticks and locking into the groove. Dani told the story, night moves on the edge of town:
Steal a tire, roll it down the street,
To the burned-out hole where we once believed
We had them all fooled
Faith joined Dani when the rest came together on the chorus, sung twice as Romeo and Juliet bemoaned each other's demise:
The fools made you sleepy,
Sleep made you weak.
The weak ate your spirit
Naked in the street.
The crowd loved it! The lyrics were dark, and the music, constantly changing pace and morphing instrumentally, was not conducive to dancing, but it was compelling, and expertly performed.

That comprised the first set, nearly an hour's worth. The band broke, got fresh pints and mingled. Abbas sensed some pent-up energy in the room, and when they took the stage again he announced the need for 'everyone to boogie!'

They turned the place from an intimate listening room to a dance floor. The music was flowing from their instruments, calling out to everyone's rhythmic sense of movement. After a while Darcy abandoned her mates and got with cousin Caspar as Poppy danced with Colin and the twins just got up and danced. Ben stood by Emma, beaming as he watched the girls get their groove on.

"Just look at em Emma, youth and joy unfettered."

"Proof that the gods are wise and hopeful for us, Ben, and that they like to be entertained along the way."

CHAPTER 18
MONDAY, 2 AUGUST

Some days I can toe the line,
Some days I just straddle
One foot's talking Einstein,
The other's clearly babble

It felt like a Monday, a day when you wake up and go through the motions, hoping that sometime during the course of the day you'll raise your head and decide to make it more than just another Monday.

Rose McTimons met Faith and Amos at the front door of Erins Pharmacy. It was early, a half hour before opening time. Rose had dropped Elizabeth off at the Stillwell house; she stayed with Aleah most days.

"I need a cuppa, luv. Can't seem to get a start today."

"Go ahead and start a pot Rosie. We've got time."

Faith filled Amos' water bowl and gave him his morning treat. Putting on her lab coat she was thinking it was a bit of a slog today. Oh well, that's why they call it a job.

Faith and Colleen owned the pharmacy, bought from her father-in-law and his brother, Ray and Clive Mason. Ray was married to Faith's mother, Roisin, all three of them retired and living up in Kensington.

Casper was the third licensed pharmacist at the shop. Rosie kept the books and helped out on the register. They also had three other employees to help customers and keep the shelves stocked.

Colleen wandered in just before opening time. She put her bag and brolly in the back office and struggled into her lab coat. "Sorry kids, I'm stuck in first gear at the moment."

A general malaise seemed to pervade the air up in Edge Hill as well. Poppy was working at the clinic with Dani today, Mondays were typically busy.

Nathan would be in soon. He worked part-time but put in a lot of hours when school was out,

"I'm glad we've no surgeries scheduled today," Dani admitted. "I'm distracted for some reason."

"I'm in a bit of a funk myself. There has been a lot going on of late."

"You miss your buddies, Poppy?"

"Yeah, I do. It's just me and Darcy now. I've got plenty to occupy meself with, though. And it's hard to be lonely at Greenbank."

"True that. Something's always on."

"Like tomorrow, eh?" she said with a grin.

Dani hesitated, then remembered, and smiled. "Yes, tomorrow is special."

"What's the plan?"

"Nothing fancy, we're both busy. You know, Faith and Robin both have birthdays this month."

"Oh, that's right. The bunch of you are almost fifty now!"

"Hey, let's not get in a hurry, it's a ways off."

"Who's the eldest?"

"Abbas. He will turn fifty first, but not til the end of next year."

"Tick-tock. Tick-tock."

"Bratty kid!"

On the edge of the City Center, he who would turn fifty first was sitting first chair flute in the Royal Liverpool Symphony Orchestra, rehearsing a program to be performed in a fortnight down in Sefton

Park. Robin was close by, sitting with the other violinists. She was troubled, and Abbas was worried about her.

Her mum, Sylvie, was about to turn seventy. Her dad, John, was seventy-two. They owned Adam's Apple, a fruit and produce market on Allerton Road. Simply put, they needed to retire.

They had great help; their employees did all the physical work and the manager was a gem. But they both came in every day, and the grind had lost its ability to inspire them.

The Quinn's were having trouble with the idea of selling the business, the customers seemed like family and the market was the hub of their social life. Robin was considering taking over, then her folks could travel, or continue to hang out at the store. They'd be able to do as they liked, when it suited them.

Robin was a passionate musician, dedicated and skillful. Leaving the symphony would change her life dramatically. Could she fill that void by throwing herself into the family business? She certainly had lots of opportunities elsewhere than the orchestra to play violin. Would it be enough?

Abbas thought about Darcy, who would switch over to the symphony from the Merseyside Youth Orchestra after the first of the year. Maybe management would institute a three Ardavan limit on musicians in the symphony. Yeah, right.

Ben was thinking about his daughter as well. The twins left four days ago. Grace looked and acted non-plussed, but that was her nature. Physically she was fine, with no lingering effects from the assault aside from the scar. Ben wondered if she was carrying a scar inside.

He and Luke were in the office, sitting in the lobby. They were both planning the week ahead. Judith was printing out a list for each of them; the had-to-dos already committed to.

"There's no doubt it's on her mind from time to time, Ben, it's only natural. Time will fix it; it's the only thing that can."

"You're right, I guess I need time too, time to stop worrying about it."

"No such luck, pardner. We're parents, we always find reason to worry."

"What do you hear from Jake?"

"They're groovin'! Jacob is trying to separate proper German from all the local dialects and getting tutored on international law. Gabriel, besides trying to get along with four savage geese, has landed a guest chair in a local symphony."

"They've landed themselves in a good situation, me thinks."

"No doubt. Hey, what you got on tap today?"

"Nothing I have to do, just some organizing around here."

"You wanna go over to the Wirral later? I need to meet with one of Cy's players. He's on the ups and wants to discuss representation."

"Sure, why not. At the training ground?"

"No, at a pub afterwards."

"Even better!"

There was no mopey Monday for Cyril; he just didn't have the time. Pre-season was over, the first match of the 99-00 season was this coming Saturday.

The squad was looking pretty good; everyone working hard to impress the new manager. Cy was concerned about a couple of positions, but you never knew for sure until the games counted. There would be surprises.

A new manager was a daunting prospect for an established team— all the individual players wondering how it might affect their playing time. That's why everyone was bustin' a gut. Cyril knew they would work hard. He demanded it. It was team unity he was looking for; that's what brought good results. Man management was vital in building a strong football club.

He wasn't a big talker, given to flowery, rah-rah speeches about 'doing it for the Gipper.' His style was more easy going, and to lead by example.

They were all together now though, and looking at him expectantly. It was time for that first pep talk.

"Good work today lads. That was a quality session you put in. You've covered a lot of miles the past weeks, and it shows. Everyone's looking sharp. It's time now to set a routine, the way we act and the way we perform, match to match. All season long."

"You'll notice I've not been the taskmaster; no fire and brimstone."

He hesitated, then continued, "Dat's down ta me island roots, don't ya know!" That loosened em up.

"Seriously, I don't have a lot of rules. You're all men now, even if you're not all adults. "Just look after yourself, on and off the pitch. Be on time, work hard, and get on with your mates."

"We've a home match in five days, so let's start strong. When we're under it, everyone suffers. You pretty boys up front, get back and muck in. When we're finding joy, you lads in the back get in there and have your share. Cover for your mates, from pillar to post we work as a unit. Any questions? Good, now get yourselves cleaned up and over to the Seven Stars. The first pints on me."

CHAPTER 19
TUESDAY, 3 AUGUST

Poppy woke up early on Tuesday; the week was starting to gain momentum. She started a pot of water, cut up some fruit, and got a couple of boxes of cereal out of the cupboard.

Her mum came down and took over kitchen duties, so she put on a pair of jeans, a light jumper, and a pair of trainers to take Otis out for a jaunt.

It was a nice morning. Some ground fog lent a bit of mystery to the birds' chittering and the squirrels' early foraging, very aware of the canine presence. She let him choose the route, guided by scent and instinct and the need to reestablish his territory.

Today was her parents' 25th wedding anniversary. Her mum had to go to work, so her dad decided to go with her and spend the day together. And, they wanted her there also, which she was looking forward to.

Stories of the old days fascinated her. Every time mum or one of her 'boys' spoke of early times together, she'd get another bit of lore. The interrogation began on the ride up to Edge Hill.

"So, when did you guys first have sex?"

"After we were married."

"That's a load of hooey, Dad."

"That's a very personal question."

"Touche. Okay, how about the first kiss?"

"That's easy," Dani said. "Christmas Eve, '69, about ten minutes before we first had sex."

"Aha! Wow, you'd known each other for a year by then. Steamy stuff, that, I had to wait over an hour!"

Luke frowned. "Did I just find out that my daughter's been deflowered?"

Poppy stared blankly at him. "Duh!" Then she decided to change the subject.

"Do you miss Venezuela?"

"I miss the way Venezuela used to be, and have fond memories. It was a great place to grow up."

"The government, they're all Socialists now. Is that it?"

"The government is definitely the problem," Luke said. "They only claim to be Socialists. In reality it's authoritarian rule, ever tightening and growing more fascist by degree."

"So Gran and Papi are in Arizona for good?"

"Yep. Anne was raised in Tucson, and Ender's happy there."

"We should go visit."

"We're planning to, probably after the first of the year," Luke said.

"Okay, now let's talk about your other guys."

"What do you mean?"

"Did you know any of them before coming to Liverpool?"

"Just Ben, and only briefly. Luke and I flew up from Judibana and spent a long weekend at the Pine's just before flying over. Cyril met us at Lime Street Station and we just happened to run into Abbas."

"That story I've heard. Amazing!"

"And important. It's what led us to Bashir and Penny and Greenbank."

"And the Six! How did the guys find their girls? I know Abbas met Robin at the symphony."

"Yes, and Ben and Cyril met Faith and Colleen at the Dovey."

"And the rest is history."

Luke had a moment of déjà vu when they entered the clinic; his first job on Merseyside had been the office manager's kennel boy. That's when he decided to become a teacher. He was looking forward to today though, watching his girls heal critters.

The day passed quickly—Dani seeing the patients, Poppy assisting, or reading stool samples and administering meds. Luke chatted up the clientele, swabbed kennels, went out and got lunch for the staff, and generally made himself available. He briefly considered showing a nervous Mrs. Collins his hip scar, to show her that Dani would sew up her little poodle's belly properly, then decided against it. Dani had too many sharp objects at her disposal.

Poppy locked up at closing time and they drove home. Dani and Luke bathed, together, while Pops walked and fed Otis, then put out a plate of appetizers. Some of the gang were coming over for happy hour.

The Pines and Ardavans came, Darcy included. Colleen came, sans Cyril. He was still over at Rover's training ground.

"She's put up with you a long time, Lucas!"

"Yes, Abbas, I'm a lucky fellow."

"You guys dressed up real nice, Luke," Ben commented. "Where's supper?"

"Maranto's, on Lark Lane."

"Nice place."

"They've got some killer ribs!" added Colly.

"I could skip dinner and just have Dani's tequeños!" Faith said.

"Poppy made those. She's got the hang of it now."

"Oh, hey guys, I heard from Gabe today," Robin reported. "He and Jake send their best, and prost to the happy couple."

"I miss my boy," Dani lamented.

"I miss Robin's boy!" Poppy lamented. That prompted a few chuckles.

As they were leaving, Luke took an overnight bag for Dani that Poppy had secretly packed earlier. They had a wonderful dinner at

Maranto's, and a nice surprise when they left. When Luke went to pay the bill, the waiter said it had been taken care of. "Courtesy of the Greenbank Gang," the man said. Afterwards Luke drove to Duke Street.

"You need something from the office?"

"Yeah, but I want you to come inside and see it."

"Okay. I've not been here for some time."

When they went inside, he took her straight up to the events room. She grinned.

"You're a sneaky guy."

He'd decorated the space with old pictures of them and the gang, 25 years' worth. He put on some music, opened a bottle of wine, and lit a doob.

There was a small, gift-wrapped box on the bar. He handed it to her.

"Happy Anniversary." It was a bracelet, simple but elegant.

"Oh niño, it's gorgeous!"

"They tell me 25 years means silver."

"Verdad. Y plata es el camino a mi corazón."

"Where else might it take me?"

She just giggled.

They spent the night in Jake's bed.

Chapter 20
Wednesday, 11 August

There's a presence here
I feel could have been ancient
Could have been mystical

It was a modern scene, with all of the modern trappings, but Gabriel was feeling the heavy call of the past.

He was in the cantonal capital of Schwyz, having lunch with Jacob, Laura, and her daughters, Eva and Elisabeth. They were seated outdoors at a cafe on a roundabout in the center of town, across from a shopping center.

It was he and Jake's first trip to Schwyz, just a half hour south of the house. When they first arrived, Laura drove all the way through town, just a few miles, along the east side of a lake, the Vierwaldstattersee. She stopped on the side of the road and pointed to the other side of the lake. There was a clearing on the side of the hill rising from the lake.

"That is Rütli Meadow. It was here our country was born, in 1291. We celebrate our independence, as you know, on the first of August."

"Yes, it was right after we arrived," Gabe said.

"Independence Day," Jake mused. "I thought all the hubbub was to welcome us."

"We did not talk too much about you coming here," Eva offered. "The newspaper men would be quite bothersome."

"She's on to you, Jake," Gabe chided. "You can't take this guy too seriously."

Elisabeth giggled. The youngest at fourteen, she'd been taken with her houseguests, and very curious. Eva, nineteen, was more demur in her approach and despite the interest their boarders generated, she knew they were still basically just boys.

It was a beautiful setting. The town lay at a small valley's southern end where the terrain opened up, offering 360 degrees of forest, lake, and mountain. Just northeast of town two peaks, Grosser and Kleiner Mythen, stood sentinel.

They played tourist at the Victorinox Factory store, the complex literally right behind the café. Victorinox produced the iconic Swiss Army Knife; the guys bought some souvenirs for the gang back home.

They did make a brief side trip on the way down, to the town of Einsiedeln. Eva thought Gabe and Jake might want to check it out. As it turned out neither of them had heard of a Black Madonna.

The Benedictine Abbey of Einsiedeln housed one of the famous statues. This one was dated mid fifteenth century. It was a big abbey, with an elaborate monastic complex and library, a diocesan school, garden, and wine cellar. There were also stables, housing a breed of horse native to the region.

The abbey was established in the mid-800s by a Benedictine hermit and monk named Saint Meinrad. Eventually it became the largest baroque structure in Switzerland, and a sacred site for pilgrims.

A shrine dedicated to the Virgin Mary is the first thing they saw upon entering the church. At the rear was the chapel housing the Black Madonna, made of limewood and darkened over the ages by candle smoke and soot.

It was a humbling experience to stand in the place, in a land laid claim to by many since the time of Alexander the Great. A land so harsh, with its native peoples so strong and determined, that not even the Romans could fully conquer.

Lunch was great; schnitzel und spätzli mit grüner salat. There was some excited chatter on the way back. They needed to get home before the big event.

A total solar eclipse, and they were in a near perfect spot. Jake and Elisabeth were close to the house, picking fruit off the old Mirabelle tree. Mirabelle were a small plum, very tasty. Laura was planning to make jam. Luca came home in time, talking about all the people outside staring at the sky.

It was spectacular! Day turning into night, the critters wondering if the world was coming to an end. The pathway of total eclipse passed over southern Germany and into Austria, so very close. It was a time when mere mortals are forced to pause, and ponder the wonders of the natural world beyond their grasp.

The evening was a quiet one, spent at home. Laura talked to her son, Erik, on the phone. Erik was seventeen, in the states on a foreign exchange program, learning English and soaking up the culture. Laura was concerned. She said he was somewhat quiet and reserved, but seemed to be adjusting. Jake and Gabe were using his bedroom.

Jake found Eva a bit shy also. He thought she probably wasn't really confident speaking English. She came alive when they spoke German though, amused but impressed with the guy's efforts.

Elisabeth was anything but shy; precocious was her middle name. She was the guy's local tour guide, even arranging for Gabe to play his cello in a chilbi, a type of street fair, in Schindellegi.

Gabe was looking over some sheet music at the dining table. Jake and Luca were pouring over law briefs at the other end. Laura was working on a quilt while the girls watched television.

Quite the domestic scene, similar to what could be found on Merseyside, you might say. Gabe thought about the eclipse, how it must have bewildered early man. Even now, we ameliorate the mystery and mysticism of the unknown by gathering together, safe by the hearth.

Chapter 21
Friday, 13 August

When you greet a stranger, look at her shoes
Keep your memories in your shoes, put your travel behind
Keep your hat on your head, home is a long way away

Hope and Grace had also relocated to the mountains, over 5,000 miles away. They were in Colorado Springs, Colorado, nestled at 6,000 feet in the Rocky Mountains front range. At the moment they were wondering where all the oxygen went.

It was near the end of a football training session. Check that, soccer practice. The twins were Tigers now, members of the Colorado College varsity women's soccer team. Both were on a full scholarship. Classes hadn't begun yet, but the team had been on the pitch, check that, field, for the past ten days. The first match, er game, damn it, was a couple of weeks off.

They were adjusting to the altitude, feeling much more comfortable now than when they first arrived. It was worth it; the area was beautiful.

The trip over, including connections, took over 18 hours, the final flight landing in Denver late morning on the 28th of July. Their sponsors picked them up, loaded up their bags, and drove through the capital on the nearly hour and a half trip south to the Springs.

They were nervous about their host family, despite all the lengthy correspondence and phone conversations. It was a daunting prospect going off to another country and living with strangers. They could have lived in a dorm, or even pledged to a sorority, but their folks thought living in the community would be a much more immersive experience. Lucas agreed wholeheartedly; 'hang with the locals,' he said. It turned out to be a fabulously boss move.

Margaret and Jessica met them at the gate, and the four of them instantly fell into a group hug. Such was the level of excited anticipation. Like old friends, long separated and now joyous.

"Man, I thought we were gonna be late! Hi, I'm Margaret, and this is Jessica. Oh, you two are definitely twins!"

"It's easy to tell the difference after a while. I'm Hope."

"I'm Grace, here's something to help tell us apart in the meantime." She turned slightly, exposing her left side.

Margaret gasped and embraced Grace again. Jessica was silently stunned.

"Grace that looks fresh. This just happened recently!"

"Yes, about six weeks ago. I'm good now, we'll talk about it soon."

"As long as you're okay. Well, let's head downstairs. Tim dropped us at the curb. He'll meet us at baggage claim."

The four of them exited Denver International into bright sunlight and the thin, dry Colorado air. Tim Black stood with open arms, next to an old Volkswagen camper van, grinning like the Cheshire cat. He was nattily clad in cargo shorts, a native print shirt, and sandals.

"Hello lassies! Welcome to Colorado!"

Nearly as big as their father, and looking just as gentle, like a big ole teddy bear. Apparently full of corny dad jokes as well. It was starting to feel familiar already. The twins simultaneously kissed him on each cheek.

"He's a goner." Jessica declared.

The ride home flew by, there was so much to talk about. Life in

Liverpool, their family and friends. What they were going to study at college. The Blacks weren't much into soccer but were looking forward to going to some games and learning more about it.

They were avid mountain bikers, and why not, the terrain was as challenging as you like. They also liked to go camping and spend time with family, Tim had a little clan of his own that lived on the north side of the city.

The twins stared in awe as the V-dub came over Monument Hill on the I-25 interstate highway. Colorado Springs opened up before them, nestled against the front range. To the east, open plain, flat and brown. To the west the city was lorded over by Pikes Peak, all 14,000 feet. They passed by the Air Force Academy and Tim drove by Colorado College, just north of downtown.

The Blacks lived on a bluff in the foothills. It was a big house. Entering either through the front door or the garage you found yourself on the second level with kitchen, dining, and living areas along with two bedrooms, two baths, and a study. Hope and Grace each had a bedroom downstairs, which was partially underground. They shared a bathroom. The laundry room was down there, along with a storage area and a den.

Pepper completed the scene. She was a mini schnauzer, the cutest thing ever.

To top it off they lived on Friendship Lane, very apropos. The Blacks could not have been any more welcoming.

Speaking of the garage, besides having room for two vehicles, and tools, and a fridge, it contained eight or ten bicycles. Grace and Hope adopted a pair and rode everywhere, familiarizing themselves with the city and getting accustomed to the climate.

Today's practice had been a bitch, riding back up to the house would be too, Coach Ryan had run the team long and hard. Next week would be physically easier, with more focus on strategy, set plays, and dead ball assignments.

When they got home Jessie greeted them excitedly.

"Oh good, you're home. Guess what? We're going to the cabin for the weekend!"

"You have a cabin?" Grace asked.

"Yeah, we do. It's really cool. You guys get to sleep in the loft!"
"Where is it?" asked Hope.
"In the Sangres."
"What's a Sangre?"

CHAPTER 22
SUNDAY, 15 AUGUST

Oh, kiss the mountain air we breathe,
goodbye it's time to fly.
Sparrow climb, the air is thinner,
open wings cast this valley into shade.

Not to be outdone, Poppy and Darcy, like the rest of the Six, found themselves in the mountains. The Snowdonia range was not as impressive or extensive as the Rockies or the Alps, but it was only 80 miles from Liverpool.

It was a girls outing; their mums were with them. They'd prepared the evening before, and left at first light. The drive took less than two hours, leaving the city and driving across the Wirral, then crossing over the River Dee into northern Wales.

"I love these open country roads!" Robin commented.

Dani was driving the Victor, a Vauxhall Estate wagon. Light traffic and fair weather made for a good trip, circuitous through the area's hills and valleys. They passed through a series of small villages like Ruthin, Derwen, and Glasfryn—all humble and quaint.

They ate during the drive, fruit and pastry, with a couple of thermoses of tea. Each had a small pack, provisioned with an energy bar, some water, a windbreaker, and a change of socks. And, of course, since they weren't going to carry a purse, surely someone was packing a comb, a kerchief, and some lip balm.

"You've been up the mountain before, haven't you?" Poppy asked.

"A couple of times," Darcy said. "The whole family."

"This will be my fifth time," Robin added. "I think I was twelve the first time my dad drug me up Snowdon. I was knackered but it was brilliant!"

After passing through Pen-y-gwryd, Dani continued the ascent to Pen-y Pass, where there was a small complex catering to hikers. A hotel, café, bus stop, and car park occupied the crest of the pass, barren and wind-blown.

Two of the area's six or seven trails up the mountain originated here. The girls chose Pyg Track, the more direct of the two.

It was around six kilometers, or four miles, to the summit, none of it particularly steep. After an initial climb they traversed the lower slope of Crib Goch, one of the range's peaks. Sometime after they zigzagged their way up to where several trails combined for the final push to the top. This was Bwlch Glas, the pass between Snowdon and Garnedd Ugain, Snowdonia National Park's second highest peak.

A red kite was soaring high overhead as they reached the summit, just before noon. They were lucky; not many people had made the trek so far today. Snowdon was very popular. Literally hundreds of thousands of hikers chose this area every year.

The peak measured 1,085 meters, over 3,500 feet. Except for a few places in the Scottish highlands, it was the top of Great Britain. The Welsh called it Yr Wyddfa, dating back to the time of King Arthur. The area was rife with Arthurian legend and myth. Giants, fairies, and water monsters populated local lore, all linked to the mountain.

"The world looks a bit smaller from here," Darcy commented.

"So beautiful!" Poppy was amazed. "Makes you wonder why we haven't come more often."

"Oh look, the Isle of Man!" Robin exclaimed. "And Ireland! It is a clear day when you can see that far."

They spent nearly an hour at the top, taking pictures and chatting with other hikers, everyone boosted by their energy and endeavor.

They started back down the same way they came, descending past the uppermost craggy terrain and switchbacks. Then, above Glaslyn, llyn meaning lake, they took the other trail, the Miner's Track, back to Pen-Y Pass.

It was a little longer of a distance to cover but more scenic, passing by not only Glaslyn but also Llyn Llydaw and Llyn Teyrn. Here were wildflowers, including the aptly named Snowdon Lily. They even got to watch an osprey for quite a while, working the lakes.

The mood was light driving home. The muscles, a little sore.

"I know what we need!" Dani suddenly burst out. "A hot tub!"

CHAPTER 23
SATURDAY, 21 AUGUST

I'm a marquee veteran,
a multimedia bonafide celebrity
I've got an allergy to Perrier,
daylight, and responsibility

To many it would seem a fall from grace, or a major step backward at the least. But there he was, pacing the touchline, barking at his players, kicking every ball.

Cyril Barcant had spent nearly twenty years at the top. He'd walked on at Everton at nineteen and laid claim to the pivot in the league champion's vaunted midfield, a spot he occupied for his entire career.

In '74, Cy marshaled his national team's midfield to the World Cup in Germany. The Calypso Boys of Trinidad and Tobago were the surprise team of the tournament, making a deep run and narrowly missing out on the semis. Cyril captained that squad, announcing himself to the footballing world as the premier number six on the planet.

It was Trinidad and Tobago's only appearance at the World Cup, but the pony-tailed West Indian finished his career with more trophies during Everton's' brilliant mid '80s run. They won the F.A. Cup in '84, the European Cup Winner's Cup in '85, and league titles in '85 and '87.

He was a club legend, and could probably remain with the organization in some capacity. Wanting to stay in the game, he did progress as a coach in the Everton system, but something was lacking. So he decided to basically start over. He wanted to build a team like he had built a career, almost from scratch.

Tranmere were in the English First Division, the second tier. Cy's new career goal was getting Rovers promoted to the Premier League, making the Merseyside Derby a three-team affair.

In the meantime, he and the lads would do their work out of the limelight and under the radar, and that suited him just fine.

A sizeable contingent from south Liverpool had crossed the river to see the Superwhites host Huddersfield Town. Today, the fixture was scheduled for a three p.m. kickoff. They took the train over to the Rock Ferry station, just over a mile from Prenton Park. Cyril and Seamus had comp tickets for every game, even some access to the luxury boxes, but the clan had opted to buy tickets across from the main stand in the Borough Road Stand.

Poppy and Darcy had Rovers shirts on, leading the cheers. Colleen was there, along with Luke and Dani, Kevin and Cheryl, their other two sons, Cyrus and Ian, and Ian's son Nathan.

It was the second home match of the season, third overall, one draw and one loss on the books so far.

Seamus, Cy's assistant, and the rest of the coaching staff were in team training wear. Cyril was looking sharp in slacks, blazer, and light Rovers jumper.

Cyril was still not quite sure of his best eleven, although he felt the spine of the team was set. Defensively they were solid, both in the back and the midfield. They needed more offense, a challenge for most clubs, the more goals the better.

He started the kid, Jason Koumas, on a hunch. He scored in the sixth minute. Another youngster, Gareth Roberts, from nearby Wrexham, a northern Welsh hub, was not only solid at left back, but a terror on the wing with his overlapping play. Roberts was a client of Luke's, brought back home from a wasted spell in Greece.

Huddersfield, from west Yorkshire, put in a shift, you couldn't fault their effort. On paper they were the better side, expected to compete for the title after hiring Steve Bruce, the former Man U center back, as their manager.

Cy was proud of the boys when the full-time whistle sounded. Rovers had prevailed 1-0. Cyril got a hug from Shea before shaking hands with Bruce. Then he sought out the officiating crew.

"Well done Ray, I don't know how you manage it," Cyril complemented. Ray Olivier was the match referee; he and Cy knew each other well.

"I'm just happy you stayed off the pitch."

Colleen caught her hubby's eye as he and the players applauded the supporters. She was proud of her guy, he looked happy.

Darcy and Poppy each bought a copy of the matchday program, the Rovers Review, to save for Cy and Shea. One day they can look back and remember their first victory.

They all met up at the Baltic Fleet afterwards, pints and pies. James Doohan took the piss out of Cyril, as usual, for continuing to ignore the Reds of Liverpool as a career choice, then he staked Cy and Shea to their first pint.

"Well done, lads!"

Shea brought Gareth Roberts along. Gareth was a Scouser, so appreciative that Luke got him signed with Tranmere. And, at the moment, very much appreciative of the attention Darcy and Poppy were showing him.

James' wife Sarah was there. Dani, Colly and she got caught up on all the latest.

"Liverpool were beaten down at Middleborough, one-nil. Everton netted four at home," James reported. Some Toffee fans had come to the pub. They were excited to see Cy and Shea, asking about the game at Prenton Park and paying for their next round. Those two rarely bought their own ale.

They celebrated late, their song carrying out into the night:

Oh, a little bit of heaven fell down from the sky one day, and it nestled by the Mersey in a spot not far away. And where the angels found it, after looking all around, they said "Why don't we leave it there as Tranmere Rovers' ground.

CHAPTER 24
TUESDAY, 24 AUGUST

Like a mother's kiss on your first broken heart

No matter the species, the mothers of this world are nothing if not protective of their young. Mama bears, for example, are the epitome of vigilance and retribution where the safeguarding of their cubs is concerned. Number two on the list is probably Scouse mums.

The clan had their share. Cheryl, Penny, Rosie, and Robin were all proper English matriarchs, with an added sense of Liverpool grit and wit. That was key to the difference, that local determination of character.

Lineage was important; these traits were strengthened and confirmed through the generations. Rose Stillwell was an archetypical Scouse mum, instilling the tools of the trade within Penny, as she did with Rosie, who had already started young Lizzy on her path. Dani and Faith became mothers in Liverpool, influenced in no small way by the others.

Scouse mums imparted their wisdom through a variety of ways.

Youngsters could be cuddled and coddled, or smacked on the back of the head and led by the ear. Sometimes you might hear a colorful phrase, mum's way of informing, or just spurring one to think.

"Stop picking your nose or your head will cave in!"

Sometimes what you get is just good advice, on any number of subjects.

"If you pay cheap you pay twice."

And sometimes you get the appraisal, short and sweet.

"She's got a gob like the Mersey Tunnel, and her hair's like an explosion in a mattress factory!"

If things get serious, you'll not find a better ally or protector than a Scouse mum. There were nine days of violent rioting in Toxteth, a largely working-class community between Mossley Hill and the City Centre. Sarah Doohan's family were right in the middle of it. This was some years back, in '91. People protesting the government's managed decline of places like Liverpool had resulted in clashes with the police and a lot of destruction. Sarah and the other housewives on their block saw it out, facing down both sides to look after their own.

No better example of strength and drive to fight injustice and defend your loved ones could be found than in Margaret Aspinall.

One of the darkest days in Liverpool's history occurred on the 15th of April 1989. The Hillsborough tragedy, when 96 Liverpool Football Club supporters were killed, at Hillsborough Stadium in Sheffield. It was the scene of an F.A. Cup semi-final against Nottingham Forest, gone terribly wrong. The victims were crushed and suffocated.

Local authorities, realizing the threat of liability, immediately began blaming the fans. Late arriving, intoxicated, and thousands ticketless, local police and stadium management declared, all bullshit. The event was grossly mishandled. There were mothers on Merseyside whose entire family, husbands and sons, never came home.

Margaret Aspinall lost her 18-year-old, James. It was after midnight when she and her husband were told that they couldn't even see their boy, his body belonged to the coroner's office now.

The coverup began immediately, with certain media outlets in support. One in particular, *The Sun*, so enraged Liverpudians that every news stand refused to carry it. Even to this day, any printed mention of the paper refers to it as the S*n.

Telling her she couldn't embrace her son one last time turned something loose inside Margaret Aspinall. She railed, protested, and stuck her finger in peoples' faces. Then she organized. The Hillsborough Family Support Group was formed, giving voice to the victim's families.

It's a fight that continues even now. Scouse mums don't give up.

They deserve the best, these domestic stalwarts. If they've got a cob on, or seem a tad antwacky, be patient if they tell you to stop sagging off or geggin' in, and don't act like somebody knitted your face and dropped a stitch. It's your mum, and Scouse mums are the best!

Chaptar 25
Friday, 27 August

Collector of autographs, names upon photographs
Briefcase and spectacles, strange and respectable

They were crossing the Zürichsee, at its narrowest, not too far from the southeastern end. It was part bridge, part causeway, terminating in the town of Rapperswil.

"This is a pretty area," Gabe commented. He seemed to do that quite often of late.

Jake was along, sitting in the backseat of the family's Alfa Romeo sedan. Laura was driving. The destination was St. Gallen, Switzerland's northeast hub.

Laura's family was from St. Gallen; the city held a special place in her heart. It was beautifully situated between the Bodensee, an immense lake, and the highlands of the neighboring canton to the south, Appenzell.

It was less than 60 miles from Schindellegi to St. Gallen. After leaving Rapperswil the road opened up, a rural, ever-changing topography dotted with small towns. The conversation was lively, generally in

German, but switching occasionally to English for clarification. There'd been some fairly amusing conversations over the past weeks.

They entered the city, laid out southwest to northeast in an extended vale, and parked near the Altstadt, or Old Town, near the Abbey. Besides the Abbey, which pre-dated the city itself, St. Gallen was notable for its university, which housed one of the top business schools in Europe. It also had a football club currently occupying first place in the Swiss Nationalliga A.

"We have been in the auto along time. How about a walk?" Laura suggested. "We can take care of your business, Gabriel."

"That's a great idea. Lead the way."

"Do you not know where it is?"

"Um," he looked around. "That way," he said, pointing northeast.

"Ja gerne!"

They took the Museumstrasse to the Tonhalle, home of the symphony orchestra. It featured art nouveau architecture, constructed at the beginning of the century and refurbished just six years ago. Gabe picked up the program for the next performance, quickly scanning it to see if he had any questions.

"Hello, this is going to take some practice!"

Laura had introduced Gabriel to the powers that be at the symphony. She still had contacts in the city. After an audition he was offered a guest spot for his time in the country. The whole Haller family came to his first concert last month and were much impressed.

"Will it be difficult?" Laura asked.

"There's a cello concerto concluding the first half of the program, by Dvorak, in B minor. It puts the spotlight on our section. Check out the cover!"

"It is you Gabriel, your picture, on the front!"

"Let me see!" Jake implored. "Oh yeah, that's a Scouser!"

"This is really something!" Laura was excited, "We all should go to this concert!"

"It's typical to give a guest artist some attention," Gabe explained. "It should be a good listen though. The second half is Mozart's Jupiter Symphony, one of the all-timers."

"You'll blow that old longhair off the stage," Jake predicted. Laura chuckled.

"Still a bit early for lunch," she said. "Now I can show you what Sankt Gallen is most famous for."

They walked back, past the Abbey and the Gruningerplatz, stopping at the Globus department store to get Elisabeth a windbreaker. Exiting the west side, they crossed a pedestrian mall and accessed the Vadianstrasse.

There was a Credit Suisse office on the right-hand corner. Next to it was a cool looking building, with four stories on each side and three in the middle, ionic columns on the upper sections of all three. The façade, apart from window frames and trim, was a light rose in color. It looked like a palace of sorts.

"Textile Museum?"

"Yes, Jacob. This area has been the leading maker of these crafts since the 1600s."

"What all is included?"

"Really anything made from material, I think I have to say. Embroidery and lace are the best known. Early this century half of the embroidered goods in the whole world came from here."

"It's a beautiful building," Gabe remarked.

"Yes, they call it the 'Palazzo Rosso,' Red Palace. They have other forms of art also. Like jewelry, made from cloth."

"And quilts!" he exclaimed.

"Yes, Laura, you are a quilter!" Jake added. "Now we know why."

Laura smiled, "Come on boys, my treat. We should go inside."

Even the tickets were made of cloth. The place was fascinating. The history, the variety, and the craftmanship, beautifully displayed. Some were permanently housed here, but there was also space for exhibitions, allowing for works from other sources, some private collections, to be shown.

The guys were enthused to see a collection of quilts, and amazed at the different looks created by the artisans. You could stare at these for hours trying to figure out how they did it.

"Take a look at this!" Jake exclaimed, probably a little too loudly. "Gabe, check out the artist info."

"Laura Haller, oh my!"

Laura just smiled.

It was gorgeous. This was not your Aunt Bee's cut up pile of scrap cloth made into a patchwork quilt to warm your toes while watching the telly. This was art in one of its purest forms.

It was abstract in nature, not really depicting anything recognizable. But, somehow, it made sense. And it imparted a feeling, its tones and shapes almost bringing you inside, something untamed but strangely welcoming. Laura felt almost embarrassed at their silent stares.

Lunch was taken at the Zeughaus, in the shadow of the Abbey, or Furstabtei. Jake was thinking of upping his training routine. The rich Swiss cuisine, in cahoots with his lack of ability to resist temptation, was starting to take its toll.

Gabe saw a man looking their way from another table, maybe looking a little confused. After a bit he excused himself to his companions and approached, Gabe rising to meet him.

"Guten Tag!"

"Grüezi, mein Herr."

Jacob rose as Laura turned toward the man.

"Ah, Herr Stadtsprasident, guten Tag!"

"Nein, ich bien Heinz bitte."

"Okay, Heinz, hallo!" They laughed. "Ich mochte, dass sie sich treffen Jacob und Gabriel. Hey guys, this is Heinz Christen, St. Gallen's, how do you say, chief boss?"

"You mean the mayor?"

"Yes, the mayor."

"Stadtsprasident. Ist das richtig?" Jake added.

"Ausgezeichnet!" the mayor complimented. "You are both speaking German?"

"We are learning," Gabe replied. "I suspect your English is considerably better."

"You will learn quickly; it is all around you."

"You have a beautiful city, Herr Christen," Jake said.

"Vielen Dank! Where is it you are from?"

"We're both from England. Liverpool."

"Ah, yes. The Beatles and football. I was there once, even on the ferry across the Mersey."

"Excellent! If you come back you will have to look us up."

"Thank you! How is it you know of one of Sankt Gall's favorite daughters?"

They had a nice chat over a glass of Schützengarten, the local beer, along with the other two at Heinz' table, members of his staff.

Jake drove home afterwards. There was stuff to be done in the afternoon around the house and property. Topping the list was both Jake and Gabe writing a letter to Darcy and sending her a package. Her birthday was September the 3rd.

"She's your sister Big G. I won't be around every year to remind you!"

Chapter 26
Friday, 3 September

To rocky heights we climb
Under Pikes Peak light we shine
We are CC! We are CC!

"Pork and avocado burrito smothered in green chili. A month ago, I wouldn't have any idea what those words meant.""

"It seems you're a big fan now," Tim noticed.

"I could eat one every day!"

"How 'bout you, Grace?"

"Brglmff!"

"Careful, you'll choke!"

She finished chewing. "Excuse me everyone, I'm in a frenzy."

"You've got to be hungry. You two have burned a lot of calories lately," Margaret said.

"True, that," Hope said between bites. "The games have started now, though. Training will get easier."

"It's going to get boring if you don't let the other team score every once in a while," Jessica reported.

"Oh no Jessie, we love clean sheets."

"What?"

Tim was confused too. "We all like clean sheets, Hope. What's that got to do with soccer?"

Grace very nearly did choke this time. "It's a soccer term," she said, laughing. "It means you shut the other team out."

"Like a gaffer, that's a coach," Jessie proudly stated.

"Precisely correct, my dear. And what's a wobble?"

"That's when your team sucks!"

"Right on girlfriend!"

"What's that you got, Margaret? It looks good!"

"Cheese enchiladas, in a red sauce. Have a bite?"

"Sure, thanks! I really liked the staff at El Taco Rey, nice folks."

"Is Eddie the owner?" Grace asked.

"Not sure," Tim said. "It's definitely a family business, the Aguilars. I think Mama Rose is the official owner, but she's not there much anymore. Just Eddie and his sisters."

Margaret sat back and surveyed the scene, cozy and familial. This pair is becoming a nice positive influence on Jessica, now eight and continually curious. Hope and Grace were showing her things she'd not considered before, things she probably didn't know existed.

They were setting good examples, polite and respectful, industrious around the house, and thoughtful, very kind and thoughtful. This morning they asked if they could 'ring up' their friend Darcy in Liverpool to wish her a happy birthday.

And damn they were fun! Young, attractive, and full of life. Currently the only way to challenge them was on mountain bikes, and on the most technical trails. Now that the twins were altitude adjusted, however, it wouldn't be long until she and Tim would be left in the dust.

"I heard people talking about you at the game today," Jessica said.

"Really? Good things, pray tell."

"I think so. One man did call you both Amazons. I don't know what that means."

"That's a compliment, Jessie. Amazons were legendary. Big, fierce warrior women!" explained Tim.

"Whoa."

"You two have created a buzz," Margaret added. "I guess being identical twins is a big part of it. But the way you and the rest of the team are playing is remarkable. I don't think the Tigers have been good in a very long time now."

"A new coach usually boosts a club," Grace explained.

"I guess," Tim said. "But there's no doubt you two have been leading from the back, if that makes sense. Regardless, the talk on the sidelines is all about numbers four and five."

"Our mates tell us this early schedule is a bit soft. We've tougher competition ahead," Grace explained.

"We'd like a winning season." Hope continued, "Something to build on."

The squad had started strong under new coach Greg Ryan. He and his assistant, Stephanie Porter, had come in with a plan, one the players bought into. They trained hard, setting the bar for the entire season. A season where a system would be built, along with unity.

The start was good, three shutouts and seven goals scored. The test would come later, how would the team react to a losing streak.

The two center backs were not always so well in sync, at least not mentally. They'd always been the closest of friends, but also, at times, each other's bane.

Ben and Faith were never into keeping their daughters 'identical.' They never dressed them alike, or styled their hair to match, or had them pursue the same interests. They simply were not the same person.

Both Grace and Hope had always embraced this; the problem was they heaped pressure, not on themselves, but each other. It wasn't competition, quite the opposite actually. They wanted each other to be the best.

Somewhere along the line they figured it out, and accepted each other, warts and all. They were two different people who just happened to bear a strong resemblance to one another.

Even on a football pitch, where they very definitely looked a matched set, there were subtle differences. Hope was a lefty, Grace right footed, a coach's dream. Hope was probably the better pure defender, particularly in the air. Grace was more comfortable on the ball, and could dribble out of the back. They were both a danger on set plays; each had scored a goal so far.

Needless to say, dinner was great. Afterwards Jessica took a bath Margaret had drawn for her, changed into her jammies and watched some television. Despite autumn closing in the evening was warm, Margaret suggested sitting out on the back deck.

There was a glow silhouetting the mountains, deepening as the stars came alive. All four sat in a row facing west.

"I'm so glad we're living here with you," Hope said. "We've such a large extended family back home, I don't think we'd fare well in a dormitory."

"And definitely not a sorority house," Grace echoed.

"Yeah, you're not the type," added Tim. "Too much plastic."

"You sound like our dad. Same tribe at least," Grace remarked.

"We came of age in a magical time."

"I'd agree that the best ever music was made then," Hope said.

"Oh, by the way, I had a pretty long talk with Ben yesterday. He sends his best and says all's fine there," Tim said.

"And I talked to Faith!" Margaret said. "I just love her Irish brogue, it's grand!" she imitated.

"We're a confused lot," Grace admitted. "Mum sounds Irish, dad a yank, and Hope and I, pure Scouser!"

"You know what he told me?" Tim got up and went to the cooler he kept by the sliding door. "He said you might care for one of these."

Out came three bottles of Ivywild Pale Ale, from local brewer Bristol. A simultaneous "Yes please" sealed the deal.

"I'm going in to see Jessie to bed," Margaret said, "and get a glass of wine."

Tim continued, in a conspiratorial tone, "Ben also said you may occasionally, if we were okay with it, how shall I say, partake."

"What can I say," Hope replied, "we were raised by hippies."

CHAPTER 27
SATURDAY, 4 SEPTEMBER

In the locust wind comes a rattle and hum
Jacob wrestled the angel and the angel was overcome

"What do you think they're on about?"

"I've no idea, Pops."

"Gotta be big if they're calling a meeting."

"We'll know soon enough."

Darcy called Amos over. They were out of Sefton Park now, walking Greenbank Lane back towards home. The labs were lively this morning, sensing the coming change of season. They loved their early walks, especially when together. Today had been a long one, nearly an hour.

As soon as they passed the lake, they cut through the park, on an angle, past the yew and across the road into Darcy's house at the end of the row.

Amos and Otis lapped up a bowl of water and were fed while the girls shed their jackets and shoes. Abbas and Luke were at the table, perusing the *Echo* while Robin and Dani turned out some tea and pastry.

"It's beautiful out today mums and dads!"

"Seems so. Maybe I'll run to the river and back later."

"I'll join you, Luke. Perhaps we'll coax the ladies along."

"You have to promise to keep up," Robin teased, coming out of the kitchen.

Dani joined the rest, plopping down with a cup of Earl Gray. She looked pensive but resolved. "Lucas?"

"Okay, here's the scoop. The latest war in the Balkans has ended. NATO troops had to be called in. There's been a pact, the Kumanova Treaty, signed by all parties and so far things have been relatively quiet."

He continued, "The short of it is Abbas and I are planning to go there, to Kosovo, to help with the humanitarian aid efforts."

"Don't think the short version is going to be enough Da," Poppy said bluntly.

"It was my idea," Abbas interjected. "There's been some unspeakable things going down there. Some people are totally without hope."

"How dangerous is it?" asked Darcy. "So much hate, how can a peace treaty last?"

"Well, the bullies have been curbed," Luke explained. "None of the factions there can stand up to NATO."

"Kosovo, you say."

"Yes, the southernmost area of Serbia. See, back in '91, war first broke out in Yugoslavia. This was a couple of years after the death of longtime president Joseph Tito. He was pretty much a dictator, and kept the lid on all the ethnic tension by being a hard ass."

"It all boiled over then," Abbas continued, "and eventually the country broke up into six different ones. During the process the Serbs allied themselves within their own country, then they turned on their own minorities, primarily Muslims, some of them refugees from Albania."

"So what's the plan?" Poppy asked.

"There's a train, leaving England in twelve days, headed for Pristina, the capital. It'll be packed with supplies. You know, clothes, food, medicine, stuff people need right away," Luke explained. "We've volunteered to go and help."

"And how can you two help?" Poppy was not yet convinced.

"Mostly with language. Abbas found out he could communicate pretty well with Muslims speaking only Arabic when he made the Hajj. It's definitely not Farsi, but he can make do. And I've been playing around with Albanian for a couple of months now. Plus, we're two warm bodies, we'll do whatever is asked of us."

"Albanian. You mean like Liridon Gashi?"

"Come on Pops, you know there are good and bad people wherever you go."

"I repeat, how dangerous is it?" Darcy was proving to be a hard sell too.

"I don't foresee any problem during the trip. Once we arrive it depends how involved we become out in the city."

"Which is why both of them are going," Dani said. "Abbas can help Lucas with the definition of 'acceptable risk.'"

Luke looked a little sheepish.

"And you're both okay with it?" Darcy asked.

"We are," Robin said. "As Cyril would say, 'Satan lives there now.' There's been some real cruelty inflicted on these people."

"Over 20,000 Muslim women have been raped," Abbas said coldly. "The number of men and boys massacred won't be known until they find all of the mass graves."

Poppy gave it one last shot. "Dad, when are you going to stop fixing the world?"

"When it's fixed, luv."

It was the end of the debate.

CHAPTER 28
SUNDAY, 5 SEPTEMBER

Summer's going fast, nights growing colder
Children growing up, old friends growing older

Seamus and Caspar exited B. Shrigley and Son's Fish Market on Allerton Road. Shrig's was a south Liverpool institution; the guys couldn't remember a time when it did not exist. The Tweeners were having a fish fry over at Ian and Cyrus' house. The main course? Sea bass, baked, with grilled shrimp and steamed Guernsey oysters.

They drove over to Glendyke Road in Calderstones on a breezy, but bright afternoon. All of the McTimons were there. Cheryl was in Filly's kitchen helping get things organized; Kevin was in the garden with his two grandchildren having a frolic.

Rosie was in her kitchen as well. Cyrus and she were preparing rice and veggies and slicing up a couple of baguettes. Cyril and Colleen were looking on, anticipation growing towards the feast.

"Hallo, anyone home?"

"In here!"

"Aleah, welcome, I'm so glad you came!" Cyrus exclaimed, giving her a cuddle.

"How can I resist; nearly all my family is here."

"Hey all," Rosie said. "Dad, you brought flowers!" she exclaimed, hugging her mum and kissing her gran. "I'll get a vase."

"Where's my granddaughter?" Penny asked.

"Out back with Kev."

"Ooh, I need a word with that man," Bashir said, starting out the door. "I hear he's winding down the business."

"Don't get any ideas luv. Maybe after Lizzy gets her primary school over with," Penny cautioned.

"It's a wonderful day. Let's all go to the garden," Aleah suggested.

"You guys go on," Rosie suggested. "I've nearly got this sorted."

"Yes! I haven't seen Lizzy in ages," Colleen exclaimed.

Eventually they all made it out back and sat at two picnic tables pushed together, catching up and talking about the big day tomorrow.

A new school term was always a big deal with the clan, a little different every year as the years passed. Bashir and Cyrus were teachers. Bashir was the head teacher at Greenbank Primary and Cy taught English Lit and Comp at Calderstones Secondary, formerly Quarry Bank High School, where Luke used to teach, and John Lennon was an alum. Nathan was in his second year there and little Lizzy would ride to school with her granddad to Greenbank for her first ever school term.

Both youngsters were anxious and a little nervous, for different reasons. Lizzy, obviously, it was her first year. For Nate the reasons were a little more complex. He was still an underclassman; girls, bullies, and teachers could be a bit intimidating. And then there was that puberty thing, constantly rearing its ugly head, so to speak.

Cyrus remembered those days well. It was a time when he himself had struggled, thankful Seamus was still in school and Lucas one of his teachers. With this in mind he composed a list for Nate—short phrases to both challenge and guide the teen to maturity, or at least in the right general direction.

Aleah created a poster from the text, in a beautiful handwritten script with lots of artsy images around the border. She'd brought it with her, and shown it to Ian and Filly inside the house earlier.

"Aleah, we've a little time before supper, may we give Nate his gift now?" Filly suggested. "Things are likely to get messy out here soon."

"Good idea. Nathan, there's a cardboard tube in by my purse. Would you bring it out?"

"Yes, Gran." He hurried off, curious.

"I'm glad he doesn't call me Greatgran. It seems ancient!"

"Some beauty never fades, Aleah."

"Thank you Colleen, that's so sweet!"

"She only speaks the truth, Shahzadeh."

"Tasakkor, Cyril!"

"Khash mikonam."

Nate came out with the goods.

"Careful son. It's made of paper."

He opened the tube, slid the poster out, and unrolled it. "Wow!"

It was very well penned and illustrated. He read it once and turned it around for the rest to see.

'Pause and ponder. Stop to think. Consider the possibility. Wait for wisdom. Act on ingenuity. Weigh all options. Balance but teeter. Take while giving. Hope but defend.'

Again, "Wow!"

Leave it Cyril to break the silence.

"Wise words, me little brother, once we figure out what they mean. Dat uncle of yours is becoming quite the philosopher."

"What do they mean?"

"That's for you to decide," Cyrus answered.

"I'm guessing that every day you'll find something on the poster that applied to that day," Kevin surmised. "And hopefully, one day, you'll be a step ahead of that poster, you'll know its message before the question is asked."

"Huh?"

When the laughter died down Cheryl was able to allay the boy's confusion. "Not to worry Nate, as you can see it's confused the hell out of your granddad. It is good advice, though, heed its message, over time you'll cherish it."

Cyrus gave her a hug. "Scouse mums are the best!"

"I'll drink to that!" Ian toasted.

"I'll eat to that!" Filly said.

She and Rose brought the food out while Ian and Seamus set themselves up at one end of the table shucking oysters. Colleen grated some parmesan as Cyrus got everyone more drinks.

It was quite a spread. The food was great, the conversation lively. There was one small snag—Eizabeth wasn't having anything to do with an oyster.

"Come on Lizzie, try one. They're good cooked with the cheese sprinkled on!" her mum coaxed.

"You can have mine."

"See what you've missed all these years Cyril," Filly teased.

"Not completely, my sistah. I helped raise your husband, the rest of the Tweeners, and the Six. Besides, I've noticed something in the gene pool in this clan. Each generation is getting stronger, smarter, better looking. Mr. Darwin would probably freak out; it's like his theory of evolution in warp speed. I can't wait to see what kind of superheroes Nate and Lizzy turn out to be. And the Six, what happens when they start reproducing? No, I won't be a part of Bashir's clandestine plan for world domination."

As usual, Bashir sat smug, the grin on his face the only clue to his thoughts.

Colly smacked the back of Cyril's head.

CHAPTER 29
MONDAY, 6 SEPTEMBER

There's some debate about whether instincts
should be held in check
Well, I suppose that I'm a liberal
in this respect
I can't say I liked Robinson Crusoe,
but at least he didn't tie his dogs up at night

Otis was on the front stoop, cleaning up his paws after the early walk and feeding. He liked this season—crisp mornings and warm afternoons, the birds active in the yew with their chittering and busy movements.

Amos padded over from next door and sniffed him up, trying to discern where he'd been earlier. They'd done the business separately this morning, their people on different schedules. They were fascinating, these humans, and puzzling. They were in charge of things, everything really, the alphas of all living things, despite being so unaware, apparently, of the Mother's natural order.

They were lucky, he and brother Amos, their humans were kind. There sure were a lot of them.

The pack was aging, which was fine with Otis. He was too. He and Amos had lived all of their eight winters here, loved and loyal.

Besides the evening laying by the fire with a full belly, this was his favorite time of the day. On the stoop in the growing light, he and Amos, noses to the breeze. Their people would come from inside, one at a time or in small packs, off to all kinds of places, judging from the scents they brought home.

Dani was the best; she was a healer. He went with her sometimes, where other people brought their animals. He had duties there, to make sure it was safe. Amos went with Faith quite often, he had duties at the place where she helped humans, not critters. Their mates, Luke and Ben, had other duties. Amos had no idea what they were. He did know they both sometimes smelled like cat.

Oh boy, here comes Darcy. She gives good lovin'!

"Hey boys, aren't you the handsome ones! Can I sit between you for a minute? How 'bout an ear scratch? Oh man, I've been slimed! Okay, gotta go to school."

Otis wasn't sure about all the whelps getting older. It was nice not to have to be so alert all the time; he and Amos were becoming the clan elders. Some things they missed though. Extra food, little ones were messy. More play time too, chase and fetch and hide and seek.

Who knows ... maybe their time with a new litter wasn't over yet. The Mother works in her own way.

The Six were of age now, and had been rutting for some time. It wouldn't be long until they chose mates, and that meant whelps weren't far behind. Humans mated for sport as well as reproduction, and came into heat during every moon. He and brother Amos weren't too sure about spending their retirement getting their ears and tails yanked on.

There was no use in pondering matters you couldn't affect, something Otis and Amos excelled at. Their pack leaders were gentle and caring, and they responded with obedience and dedication. Trust was mutual.

They were taken out, all over the city, to see and be around others of different species. Socialization, it was called. Otis had seen and heard much, and sampled many scents. There was a lot of cruelty, and avarice, and in some cases just a lack of discipline. Humans could be reckless. Even he knew that to co-exist sometimes basic instincts had to be curbed. A lack of respect for the natural world would only serve to bring the species down.

CHAPTER 30
TUESDAY, 14 SEPTEMBER

Catch the mist, catch the myth,
Catch the mystery, catch the drift

It had taken time, two or three years, but the memories now brought smiles instead of tears. This day in particular, so bitter-sweet, had now begun to be celebrated.

Neff Boler was born ninety-five years ago on this date. He passed peacefully in his sleep during the spring of '94. You couldn't argue that he was taken too young. He'd led a long and accomplished life and was known and loved by many. Still, it was the saddest day ever on Greenbank.

Neff was the rowhouse's first resident, a divorcé whose ex took their daughter and moved away. He could easily have turned into the old curmudgeon, warning the neighbors off his lawn and becoming more isolated over time. A bit of melancholy did impose itself, but Neff had neighbors, and after all this was Liverpool, a city with a big heart.

The Odegaards lived next door, now the Pine's home. Peter and his wife Berit were from Norway. Peter worked for the Cunard Steamship company until they relocated down at Southampton. Berit's cooking and Peter's curiosity about the area drew Neff out. He worked as an historian for the city. Then Bashir and Penny moved in on the other side, at the south end, and started a family.

All thoughts of a hermitic life ceased once Dani and her boys came to town. Neff was drawn to these pilgrims, and became their sage. The more the clan grew, the more he reveled in taking part in their lives.

The Carter's lived in Neff's house now, his ashes in an urn on the fireplace mantel. He bucked the traditions of his generation by not being buried in a local cemetery. 'I've taken up enough space,' explaining his decision to be cremated.

Ben had taken a small vial full of Neff's ashes this morning. Pursuant to his wishes, they would be scattered at the last of five locations, places that he loved and identified with. This Ben had decided to once a year, on Neff's birthday.

The first year everyone gathered under the yew, a miserably sad affair, the memories painful. The next year those who were able rode the ferry and cast ashes into the Mersey on the outgoing tide.

The Kop at Anfield saw an emotional tribute to Neff the year after; Dani and Faith cueing an extra rendition of "You'll Never Walk Alone."

The noted ceramicist Julia Preston Carter joined Ben and some of the others at the Anglican Cathedral last year. Julia was a longtime friend of Neffs. Ben thought their age difference was the only thing keeping them from getting serious about a closer relationship. Julia found a nice spot in the cathedral gardens for Neff to have a rest.

The task would be completed today, a labor of love to be sure. Ben let the others know when and where, hoping some would be able to attend. He was at the office, preparing to lock up and head out. Luke and Jude were doing the same, both wanted to go with him.

They entered the gated grounds of the Bombed-Out Church just before six, greeted by Poppy and Darcy. Cheryl and Colly were there, their hubbies still at work.

Abbas said he and Robin would stop by Edge Hill and pick up Dani on the way.

It was no accident that Ben chose St. Lukes for last. The clan had come here often. Lots of memories were made in this idyllic little sandstone church.

They gathered on the steps outside the apse, sitting and reminiscing.

"It's warm today," remarked Abbas.

"My mom called a day like today Indian summer," Dani said.

"There won't be many more like it, I'm afraid," Cheryl warned.

"The old man's coming." Ben smiled. Neff used to say that.

"Coming to the wedding was my best memory of St. Lukes," Judith said. "And the wedding itself was the most amazing I'd ever attended!"

"It was special," echoed Robin. "We all got to take part and the guests had a fantastic time!"

"And Neff!" Abbas exclaimed. "What a class act! He performed the perfect ceremony. Without notes, I should say, with grace and dignity."

"And no small amount of panache," Luke added.

There was no doubt the gang had changed Neff. The man was raised a proper gentleman, buttoned up and squared away. A fellow who rarely colored outside the lines and went about his duties without deception or duress.

Over the years things changed. He was buttered up and softened into a lovable patriarch, the old and young seeking his company and counsel. And he could orate like a parliamentarian, but be just as happy having a frolic with the dogs and children.

Neff's memorial service was held here at St. Lukes. The place wasn't big enough. The cathedral itself probably wasn't either. People from all walks of life filled the church and the grounds, and were lined up against the gates and fencing surrounding the property. It was a gray and dismal day, and Liverpool wept for one of its most honorable sons.

CHAPTER 31
MONDAY, 20 SEPTEMBER

Mystic rhythms under city lights, or a canopy of stars
We feel the powers, and we wonder what they are
We feel the push and pull of restless rhythms from afar

It was called the Kosovo Train for Life, as its headboard boldly proclaimed. The movement that brought about this unprecedented humanitarian aid effort was initiated by retired British Rail personnel and supported by the government. Authorities from other nations 'got on board' as well, a necessary step considering the train would pass through a dozen different countries.

The mission was closely coordinated with the guidance of the United Nations Kosovo Force, who would hopefully see to security along the route, particularly down in the Balkans.

Abbas and Luke traveled down to the Midland Rail Station at Butterly, near Derby, early last Thursday morning. They met with Neil Howard and John Morris, the project's main organizers, to get themselves lined out. They were taken to a siding, where 700 tons of goods sat waiting to be loaded. Coordinating the effort with the help of local volunteers was their assignment.

They were lucky to be included in the first place. It was Abbas' idea, but it was Lucas who talked their way aboard, utilizing the irresistible Carter method of making friends and influencing others. They were sure to make themselves useful along the way, but this would be their chance to immediately ingratiate themselves with all the train nerds.

The assemblage departed the next day for the Kensington Olympia Rail Station in London, where there was an official wave-off in front of the media and the public. The train itself consisted of three British Rail Class 20 locos and six wagons, owned by Direct Rail Services.

The 2,800-mile route began by entering France via the channel tunnel and making for Lille. There were sixteen aboard, a mix of people, mostly male, from the rail industry. There was a journo, Andy Flowers, a very likeable chap, thrilled like they were at being included on the journey.

From Lille the train entered Belgium and stops were made at Namura and Liege before making for Germany.

Traveling by rail through Europe is the stuff of dreams for many vacationers. Luke and Abbas were quite enjoying the experience thus far. It wasn't first class accommodations by any means, but the guys learned that changes to the train's configuration was in the offing.

An extended stay in Aachen, Germany provided for the addition of nine more wagons, loaded with goods gathered by the families of the British military stationed locally. The train also gained three service cars, a sleeper, a restaurant car, and a supply car for the sixteen passengers. Luke and Abbas had a compartment to themselves, right next to Andy Flowers and Major Poyntz, no first name.

The weather had turned; the area was becoming socked in with low clouds and a light drizzle. No matter, they were all in a pub having beer and schnitzel.

A little over 400 miles to the southeast, Luke and Abbas' sons were soaked to the bone and muddier than they could ever remember.

Luca had gotten Gabe and Jake up early and driven to the Muotathal, an area made up of a number of valleys and surrounded by mountains and glaciers. It lies to the southeast of Schindellegi, past Schwyz down near the canton's border with Uri.

They were there to get the family's sheep and bring them home for the winter. It was typical for people who owned small flocks to have shepherds who lived at elevation tend their sheep during the late spring and summer months where they could graze the high pastures.

It was a group effort. All the sheep in the area were driven down into the valley where the small flock owners came to collect them. The spot was well chosen. A natural pen formed by a steep hillside and the fence bordering the road itself. Wide at one end, where another fence spanned the thirty or so yards from the road to the hillside, it narrowed to nothing at the other end where the road curved around the hill, a distance of about seventy yards.

They parked the Alfa and walked to the center of the pen's wide end, where a central gate stood. A small fleet of rag tag trucks and trailers sat waiting to be loaded, one of which Luca had hired for his sheep.

Gabe once again felt that pull, here in the Alps. Those ancient rhythms' call, in a country whose 700 years of history and tradition paled in the memory of all that came before. The men surrounding him now were of hardy stock, soft spoken for the most part but possessing a time-honored ethos and boisterous spirit.

The ceiling was low, a misty fog sealing the scene. The only thing more pervasive was the sheep's bleating, constant and insistent. Jake couldn't figure out if they were freaked out, apprehensive, or excited.

One guy pointed out to Jake and Gabe how to tell the sheep apart. His dialect was hard to parse out, but they understood that each animal had a good-sized splotch of paint on them, the color and location of which identified who the owner was. Then the fun started.

One of the trucks was backed up to the gate. Then everyone was informed of what the man's sheep looked like. Then everyone waded into the bleating mass of ovine flesh and wool and started culling the lucky winners.

The method was simple—grab a handful behind the neck and another on top of the rump, get them pointed the right direction, and make for the truck. Repeat steps one, two, and three until the man gets all his stock in his truck. Then do it for the next guy, until it's done.

Getting the sheep's cooperation was easy; staying upright the whole time was not. After a while it was easy to spot the two rookies in the group, and the lads took a lot of teasing in the process.

Finally it was done. They had to strip their clothes off and throw on a spare set as well as cover the car seats.

"I've got mud in all my nooks and crannies!" Jake exclaimed.

"We should bathe as soon as we get home," Luca warned. "It's not all just mud."

CHAPTER 32
WEDNESDAY, 22 SEPTEMBER

These are strange days, funky indeed
Still all we really need is the truth to fall,
shed light on the shadows

The twins had the afternoon off, no classes and no scheduled team activities. So instead of hanging around campus or going home they rode the bikes straight up Cascade past Fillmore and over to Tile Traders.

Tim and his older brother, Tom, owned Tile Traders, a distributorship for ceramic and stone products for home and business. The building was super cool—an old movie studio featuring a really unique design. Basically, it was a large round hub with several spoke-like extensions. The store sold not only tile, stone, and glass but all the associated materials needed to install and maintain the finished project.

Tim and Tom had paid their dues in the past—hourly wages laying tile for years on end. Going into the supply business was a struggle for some time, the payoff coming with an economic boost and a sustained building boom.

"Hi Bob!"

"Hello twin!"

"Come on now, you can do better."

"Grace! You're the one that would walk right in and challenge me."

"It should be easy by now, I'm the good looking one."

"I might agree if your sister wasn't standing right there. Hi Hope."

"Hey Bob, how's business?"

"We're busy today."

"Good, we're here to help."

"Yeah? Okay, but probably not in the back. Those young bucks are worthless with you two around."

"Too bad, I wanted to drive the forklift."

"That's a good one. You ever hear of OSHA?"

"Is that a him or a her?"

"Oh man! Tell you what, go see Heidi, we've got inventory coming up."

"Um, I don't know, Bob, we only know how to count using the British system."

"Huh?"

"Gotcha!"

"Scram!"

They found Heidi in the showroom, perusing a clipboard nearly overloaded with sheets of paper.

"Well, what a nice surprise!"

"Hi Heidi, what's on?"

"What's on what?"

"Sorry, what's going on?"

"Oh, I see. Man, I just love the things you come up with!"

"We do get misunderstood from time to time."

"Please don't become too Americanized."

"Don't worry, sometime we'll have a chat about Scousers."

"Sounds interesting, I think. By the way, Nicole was so thrilled to see you two play soccer. She really likes to play but I'm not sure about her team. I don't know that she's getting much in the way of learning the game."

"The younger the more difficult it is," Grace said. "Some of the kids, and some parents, consider it babysitting. It's fun, but just a temporary thing."

"Time sorts it Heidi. If she continues, and her love for the sport grows, she'll find her way." Hope explained. "We'll help out; one day she'll be ripping off her shirt like Brandi Chastain! In the meantime, Bob said we may be able to help you. We've the rest of the afternoon off."

"For sure! We've got to get ready to take inventory. And let me tell ya, it's a pain in the ass."

"That's one thing that's the same the world over!"

"We've done it before," Grace added. "Mum's the co-owner of a pharmacy and our next-door neighbor has a veterinary practice. Lead the way!"

Tim loaded the bikes in the Vdub at quitting time and drove up the hill towards home.

"I'm troubled, ladies."

"Oh, do tell, kind sir," Hope urged.

"It's the whole Y2K situation. Is it going to be a thing or not?"

"How do you mean?"

"Well, some people are calling for the end of the world. Not me, that's too extreme. But I do wonder how some might react, even if nothing happens."

"Like people who feed on this type of, em, uncertainty, I guess," Grace surmised. "They may see it as an opportunity."

"Uh huh. Then there's the theory that the grid and infrastructure will collapse, cause the machines won't know how to act."

"We've heard of that even before coming to Colorado," Hope said. "Our lot back home aren't what you would call techies, by any stretch of the imagination. But our youngest elder, Cyrus, says any problems arising from digital malfunction, as he puts it, should be minimal."

"Hmm, I guess I'll just fall back on what I learned from Kwai Chang Caine."

"Who's that Tim?"

"That cool guy on Kung Fu."

Both girls giggled. "And just what wisdom did he leave you with," asked Hope, warily.

"Will worry change the future, Grasshopper?"

"It's spooky how much you're like our dad."

When they got home the girls were in the kitchen figuring out dinner. Jessica was looking at a cookbook while Margaret pulled ingredients from the cupboard. Pepper was supervising.

"Honey we're home!" Grace announced.

Margaret had the cutest laugh ever. Just one of her many assets. Another was keeping reins on her hubby. 'The man's a boy,' she'd simply say.

"We figured out this millennium issue on the way home, dear."

"Yeah, what's the verdict?"

"We don't know what's going to happen so we're not gonna sweat it."

"Good, we've other fish to fry."

"Such as?"

"Well, we could start right here in our own city with the religious right. I mean, to each his own when it comes to religion but these people want to censor my personal choices. Focus on the Family, what a joke! Focus on your own damn family!"

"Uh oh, here she goes."

"Let's go up the road to Denver. A bunch of old white guys under the dome speak with forked tongue. What the hell? You're there for your constituents, not yourselves. Same in Washington, where Senator Fat Pockets gets legislation for corporate tax cuts on a whim but the minorities, the poor, women, gays, and vets are left to fight for every single thing that they usually don't get. Hell, let's get global! War, famine, genocide, all with an extra dose of hate. People killing their neighbors in the name of God. Me thinks the pinball table is on full tilt. So, how was your day?"

"Peachy! Hope and Grace spent the afternoon at Tile Traders. They put a pretty good shift in."

"You girls have endless energy! What's the secret?"

"We're still teenagers, for another couple of months, anyway," Hope said.

"You okay Margaret?" Grace asked.

"Oh yes, I'm fine. I just like to rail against the man from time to time."

"You go girl!"

"You need to meet Lucas," Hope said. "He's our man of the world, he fixes things.

"I've heard of Lucas. Remind me."

"He lives next door with Dani, the vet. Their kids, Jake and Poppy, part of the Six."

"He's somewhere in eastern Europe right now, on his way to Kosovo with a relief effort mission thingy," Grace explained.

"That's very admirable. Plenty of people care; to act on that belief of cause doesn't happen often enough."

"Tell ya what, all you ladies. You too Pepper. Go on back and get clean and comfy and get it all figured out. In the meantime, Samuel Adams and I will prepare this evening's cuisine."

The five of them gathered in the master bedroom as Margaret turned to the twins.

"Sometimes you have to be reminded of why you keep them around."

CHAPTER 33
SATURDAY, 25 SEPTEMBER

Sleep comes like a drug, in God's country
Sad eyes, crooked crosses, in God's country

The past four days could best be described as a lesson in reality. The next few days was anybody's guess.

The layover in Germany was beneficial, they'd taken on the added supplies for Kosovo and the comfort cars for those on board, and enjoyed a nice respite in town. Tweaks had to be made after leaving Aachen; the train was a half mile long now. They were primarily mechanical adjustments and power issues having to do with coupling hardware, the compressor, and brake system.

Luke was a godsend dealing with these problems. He was the only one that spoke good German. Andy helped as well, his German poor but he was more familiar with train and rail terms. Abbas was a big hit; he'd brought his flute along and played some in the evenings. The group had meshed well along the way, the guys were hearing lots of stories about the industry from those who'd lived it.

Crossing the border into the Czech Republic at Decin they picked up a local pilotman, Petr Psota, for the run to Breclav. He and Andy got on well, Andy spoke a bit of Czech. They learned that each other's favorite two things were drinking beer and speaking English.

They spent a day traversing the Czech, Slovak, and Hungarian countryside without any snags or delays. The big 20 Locos were an anomaly in this part of the world, as well as the train's length and configuration. They attracted a lot of curious attention at the sheds and stations passed along the way. The noise the engines produced alone brought people out of their shops and houses.

Breclav was the last stop before Hungary. Everyone got off for a stretch and some supplies; provisions were very inexpensive locally.

It was a quick trip to Budapest, the train able to maintain speeds of over sixty miles per hour nearly the whole way. Luke and Abbas had an interesting time talking with Joyce Hughes, the only woman aboard.

Joyce was executive in charge of European train movements for the British army. The lady was fascinating, and much interested in the both of them. After trading histories, she professed a curiosity as to why the guys lobbied so hard to come along. "The rest of us are hopelessly besotted with rail travel, why on earth would you go to so much bother?" she'd exclaimed. Abbas spoke to the past, and referenced he and Luke's feelings with respect to the immigrant experience and how that experience could turn for the better or come to a tragic end. Joyce seemed much taken with Abbas' concern and passion. It reminded her the trip would take on a new look and feel in the coming days.

At Budapest they disembarked for a tour of the terminus, Keleti station, and the marshalling yards. It was an overnight stay. Andy Pearce, the safety officer, had a list of provisions to be brought on because they were to lose the restaurant car further down the line. A walk around the old town and a meal out was a nice diversion.

The train roared back to life the next morning and the team rumbled through Romania, refueling at Bucharest. From there they were to pass through Bulgaria, the northern tip of Greece, and up through Macedonia into Kosovo.

Their route was much further east than the shortest way possible. They could've left Germany and headed south through Austria and right down the Balkan Peninsula, a much shorter overall distance. Ten years of war scuttled that plan, much of the infrastructure was still down and tensions, even hatred, still existed.

Despite a few snags along the way, the trip was a scenic smorgasbord. All three countries, Romania, Bulgaria, and Greece, were equally diverse in terms of geography. Valleys, hills, mountains, and lakes all were in abundance and ever changing, with villages and towns popping up at random.

Entering Macedonia things changed. Not so much the landscape, but man's influence on it. This was a land much affected by war. The citizenry here had a different look about them, hollow, disaffected. It wasn't lost on Luke how the conflicts in this region had progressed from north to south. War first broke out in Slovenia and Croatia and worked its way down to Bosnia, Serbia, Montenegro, and Kosovo. People here just might be bracing for the inevitable.

They had crossed into Macedonia yesterday, and in Macedonia they still sat.

It was a holdup, in more than one sense of the word. Local authorities, either sensing an opportunity to line their own pockets, or allying with ethnic Serbs, demanded a hefty wad of cash for continued passage.

They didn't get it, and weren't going to, the team was resolute. A thirty-six-hour standoff ensued, during which the other side apparently saw the error of their ways. Either that or they'd been threatened by NATO.

Regardless, the engines started up again and the train rolled down the track towards Kosovo.

What fun and games lay ahead?

CHAPTER 34
SUNDAY, 26 SEPTEMBER

*You can strip the trees, foul the streams, try to hide
in a progressive dream, ease into the comfort that kills.
Before I do that, I'll grab my pack, and disappear,
with Billy from the hills.*

Hope stepped out onto Friendship Lane as the sun was rising from the eastern plain. It was chilly, low 50s, the slight breeze bringing the subtle scents of evergreen and sage.

It was very quiet, the neighborhood still mostly in slumber. Pepper was working the vegetation on one side of the street, trying to parse out what went on during the night. It was her favorite time for a walk, everything so fresh, the dew serving as an appetizer before the morning meal when they got back to the house.

The lane was mostly an elongated circle following the contours of the bluff it straddled. The land in the foothills here was a series of rises and ravines at the base of the front range.

Hope was into checking out the local flora and fauna. This was such a dry environment compared to Britain. The Blacks and their neighbors were pretty creative landscaping their properties, a combination of grasses, trees, shrubs, rocks, and yard art. After two months in the area, she was finding out that high desert plains have a surprising amount of life if you knew where to look.

When it came to critters, you had to look no further than thirty yards down the lane where a coyote had just come out from a stand of blue spruce. A male, judging by his size, a thick winter coat building for the coming season. All three of them stood silent and mute, at first from surprise, then to gauge any possible danger. After a seemingly long ten or fifteen seconds the big guy moved on. Pepper spent quite a while sniffing up the scent he left.

Grace was sitting in the dining nook having a cup of tea with Margaret. Jessie was occupied with a glass of orange juice and the comics section of the Colorado Springs Gazette.

"Hey Jess, would you slide that skin cream over to me please?"

"Here you go."

"Thanks." Grace squeezed some onto her finger and massaged it into her skin along the scar line on her neck and cheek.

"Does it bother you Grace?" Margaret asked.

"Not really. It used to be itchy and a bit tender. Now it just feels a little tight, I guess is how to best describe it." She noticed the look of concern and decided it was time to address it. "Would you like to hear the story now?"

"Only if you are comfortable with it. But I'm afraid you're going to tell me this was no accident."

"It was most definitely not an accident."

Grace told her story, the approach in the square, attempted snatch, her defense, the assault, the hospital, and her release and recuperation.

Margaret took her hand, the first tear rolling down her cheek. "That's a hell of a story, Grace, a nightmare, really. And combined with what I've learned about, and plainly seen in you during these last couple of months? Well, you're a strong and beautiful young woman."

"Thank you Margaret." She sat back, looking not quite so confident now. "It comes back on me now and then, during quiet times, or when I'm in bed."

"I can imagine. These images will fade over time, I'm sure. It will get easier to bear."

"I know. Thanks for that. I do need some reassurance at times."

"So, did the police catch the guy? I hope they castrated the son of a bitch!"

"No, but he was found less than two weeks later. The matter was handled privately."

Margaret didn't immediately respond. She sensed going any further would take the conversation into dangerous territory. When she did speak, her words were measured.

"I don't suppose this man remains a threat, to you or anyone else."

The beginning of a smile tugged at the corners of Grace's mouth. "We Scousers look after our own."

Tim came up from the downstairs storage area toting as much stuff as he could manage.

"There's gold in them thar hills ladies!" was all he had time for as he disappeared into the garage.

Hope and Pepper came in the front door, Hope shedding her jacket and shoes while Pepper raced expectantly into the kitchen.

"We saw a coyote!"

"Yeah, where?"

"Straight down the street, just before the bend."

"So cool!" Grace was psyched.

The foothills were rife with wildlife trails, a natural funnel between the burbs and the mountains, The twins had already gotten used to seeing rabbits and deer on a regular basis, and hawks were nesting on the property. That was probably the reason they hadn't spotted many other types of birds.

"Okay," Margaret began, "I'm gonna whip up a pot of oatmeal and some toast. Girls, how about getting your personals packed and we'll get this show on the road."

Now they were all psyched. Prior arrangements were made with school and work for taking the next two days off. All five of them were going to the cabin.

The 'gold' that Tim was referring to was the changing color of the leaves of aspen trees, an annual autumnal affair. Driving into the highlands at this time of the year was a popular diversion.

Aspens are communal, you might say. Groves share root systems, shallow and ever spreading. Each stand is its own little community. The brightness and color each leaf takes on every year can be debated, depending on who you ask, but all agree it has to do with moisture and temperature. How much and when can lead to yellow and gold, even orange and red hues lighting up the mountainside in patchwork patterns.

It was roughly seventy miles from the house to the cabin, south by southwest. They left town via the foothills and passed both the NORAD facility at Cheyenne Mountain and Fort Carson's down range acreage before accessing Highway 50 at Penrose and heading west to Canon City. After stopping at a market, they got on a steep, winding dirt road and traversed the wooded and relatively low elevation Wet Mountain range. The cabin lay on the west facing slope of the range in a shallow valley. The view down the draw was magical—nothing man made in sight.

"Okay campers, let's get unpacked and organized. Then we'll take a hike!" Tim was psyched.

"What about lunch, Dad?"

"We'll take some snacks and feast later this evening."

Tim and Grace emptied the van, setting everything up on the front deck. Margaret, Hope, and Jessica carried it in and set it in place.

It took some time and village, getting the cabin built. Tim did all the tile work and helped with as much else as possible. Friends, family, customers, and a variety of hired craftsmen combined to produce a wonderfully rustic structure, modest in size but almost hobbit-like in charm and function.

The deck was huge, and elevated, with rough storage underneath. The first floor had a bedroom, living area, dining nook, kitchen, and bathroom. The front half with the nook and open area was floor to roof. The back half featured an open loft for sleeping and storage.

There was a small peak just off the east side of the cabin that they had named Black Mountain. The twins hiked up there last time by themselves. It was a quick climb, fifteen minutes max, and it offered some nice views, but today Tim promised a much 'heightened' experience.

Bob and Sandy Craft owned the property just west of the Blacks, the same Bob that worked at Tile Traders. All was quiet in this part of the dale as the group started up the ridge.

It was rocky, with brush and evergreens, and occasionally some aspen, along a winding route of game trails leading to the top. They settled in a saddle between two rock outcroppings, sheltered somewhat from the wind but open to the west.

The reward was a broadside view of the Sangre de Crisco range of the southern Rockies. Rising from the Wet Valley, the Sangres spanned a hundred miles from Poncha Mountain to Blanca Peak. The range was isolated, dramatically showcasing its peaks, ten of which were over 13,000 feet, another five topping 14,000.

The tree line in this part of the Rockies was set at 11,000 feet, and all the forest below was splashed with the brilliant tints and shades of aspen trees. It was wondrous, a scene you could just sit and gaze upon for hours.

Fruit, bread, and cheese was the fare, plus a biscuit, em, cookie rather. They all faced west when they spoke, the conversation not limited or in any way guarded.

"How long did it take us to get here?"

"You mean to this point in our lives, or just from the cabin to this place?"

"Grace, we changed continents, but we still have the same father."

"Looks it, luv."

"Huh?"

"Jessie, do you think your dad is funny?"

"Not terribly."

"It seems my talents are sporadic and unsustainable."

"Not so, noble sire, the peasants are cheeky in jest."

"Huh?"

"One hour and nine minutes."

"What's that mean?"

"That's how long the hike up here took."

"Such a beautiful view!"

"That mountain over on the right is Cottonwood Peak."

"Yeah, know any more?"

"Only a couple, Crestone Peak and Crestone Needle, over there to the left."

"And those bald streaks in the forest, that's the old Conquistador ski area."

"Where?"

"Right there, above and slightly to the north of Silvercliff and Westcliff."

"Speaking of Westcliff, there's a place there called the Feed Store. That's where we're feasting later."

"Oh, we get to go into town, Pa?"

"If yer chores are done, youngin'."

"Done em all, even slopped the hawgs!"

"Don't think the Scouser and the cowgirl is a good blend, sister."

Hope leaned into her granite backrest, a silent grin displaying the sense of peace she felt. These people have allowed us into not just their home but their lives, and their friendship is genuine and freely given. She was glad her parents had the foresight to acquire both British and U.S. passports for her and Grace.

"Me thinks America, with all its lands and peoples and bold ideas of manifest destiny, is worthy of a sustained and dedicated study into the American soul and psyche."

"Huh?"

CHAPTER 35
WEDNESDAY, 29 SEPTEMBER

I saw a war widow in a launderette
Washing the memories from her husband's clothes
She had medals pinned to a threadbare greatcoat
A lump in her throat, with cemetery eyes

The Kosovo Train for Life did finally make it to Kosovo. It arrived a couple of days late, its passengers harried and feeling somewhat uneasy, but the unlikely project had been completed. The assemblage of tangible aid, 8,000 tons, had traveled 2,800 miles through twelve countries over a ten-day period.

The team was nervous after the delay in Macedonia. They'd been threatened by Serbian workers from the local rail system. It was a tense standoff, the tacit threat of NATO's peacekeepers finally saving the day. This all played out in Skopje, just 50 miles from their destination.

The mood lightened as the train neared Fushe Kosove station on the outskirts of Pristina, Kosovo's capital city. Locals lined the tracks, shouting and waving, some of the women tossing wildflowers.

Post trip plans were varied. The train itself was staying in the region as part of the aid package, including the engines. Four members of the group were staying for training purposes. Most of the rest would return home by rail, they were, after all, train geeks. Abbas and Lucas were planning to ride the rails for only the first 180 miles, due east to Sofia, Bulgaria, where they would catch a plane to England.

Somehow the unloading and distribution of all the goods got sorted. Local authorities organized and saw to the logistics for getting the right stuff to the right people, loaded up and safely to its destination. Safety was an issue; violent flare ups were a common occurrence. Kosovo, a newly formed republic, was 4,000 square miles of raw emotion and recent tragedy. Much resentment still existed.

The uncertainty of the situation, plus a chance encounter, resulted in Luke and Abbas' decision to postpone the trip home for a day.

A row broke out during the unloading of school and medical supplies for some small communities outside Pristina. Lucas went to investigate and arrived on scene as a man rudely pushed a woman to the ground, soiling her pants and blouse. The lady was spunky, jumping up and rejoining the fray, vociferously arguing her case. The guy, tall and lanky with a malicious sneer and really suspect personal hygiene, grabbed the woman's arm and started to twist it. Luke rushed in and stiff armed the man in the chest with the heel of his hand, stunning the guy into a menacing grimace.

"Çfarë nuk shkon më ty?" Luke said, asking what was wrong with him. An indecipherable litany of invectives poured from the man, curse words mostly, Luke guessed. He didn't have a clue.

"He says I don't get any of these things," the woman replied in accented English.

"A keni dokumente?"

"Ja ketü," she answered, taking out her list from a satchel she carried.

"Eja më mua. Ti qendro ketü!" he instructed, telling her to come with him, and tall and smelly to stay put.

They went to Neil McNicholas, the operations manager, who parlayed with the government liaison, trying to get the matter resolved. As it turned out the woman was a part of something truly remarkable.

Her name was Ermina Murati, from the Village of Krusha e Madhe, southwest of Pristina. She drove a truck with an 18-foot van body to the station for supplies for her village by herself. Her paperwork was in order. The guy hassling her was a Serb loyalist. Luke grabbed Abbas and they loaded the truck while getting acquainted and learning more about her plight.

"You speak a little English."

"Very little. You speak some Albanian."

"Also very little."

"What is your country?"

"The United States, but I live in England. Abbas also, but he is from Iran."

Ermina perked up a bit, likely to be more trusting of an Islamic person, regardless of which ever sect they belonged.

"Where do you sleep?"

Luke shrugged his shoulders. "Maybe here, at the station. We need to take the train to Sofia."

"No more train today, only tomorrow. You can come to my village, help with truck. Tomorrow I bring you back. Tonight I feed you, and you sleep there."

"Are you sure it's okay?" Abbas asked.

"Yes, I am boss now, I have no help," she said, pointing at the truck.

Abbas looked at Luke and got the high sign. He hesitated, Dani's presence looming large, the concept of acceptable risk rearing its ugly head again.

"We have too much here to put on the truck. If we can come back early tomorrow we can help before we get on the train."

"Yes, very early."

Luke smiled.

"The ride to Krusha e Madhe took about an hour and a half, long enough for the guys to be struck speechless by Ermina's account of what war had done to her little corner of the world.

Back in March, when NATO started its air campaign to end the atrocities the war had fomented, the Serbs decided to go all in while they still were able. The Serbian Special Police came to Ermina's village and separated the women and children from the men and teenage boys, telling them to go to Albania or else. Then the males were stripped of any identifying documents and taken to an abandoned house on the edge of the forest. There they were slaughtered, between 90 and 105 of them, between the ages of 14 and 73, mercilessly gunned down.

Luke was badly shaken, Abbas visibly upset. Ermina remained stoic, somehow numbed to any further outward displays of grief. She'd lost her husband, Arben, but was thankful to have her little girl, Agnesa, just six years old.

There was little left of Krusha e Madhe when the women returned three months ago; most of their homes had been burnt to the ground. But somehow, right when all seemed lost and hope was nowhere to be found, these women steeled themselves, determined to reverse the misfortune brought upon them through man's ill will.

They banded together, pooled their resources, and started clawing their way back, their spirits boosted with each incremental bit of success. The shock the guys felt at first was being allayed with the more recent positive developments.

Their arrival at the village was met with much cheer and excited confusion, the unloading process slowed by the women's curiosity and goodwill. The tour Ermina took Abbas and Luke on around the area showed progress, but there was still a mountain to climb in order make Krusha e Madhe viable again.

The evening meal was simple but tasty, followed by watching the sunset from the front porch. Little Agnesa played with the family's two vizslas, fine animals that were good watchdogs. Luke had brought along a couple of bottles of wine and Ermina allowed herself to enjoy the evening's respite.

They spoke only of the future, the past now an unwelcome visitor that brought only sad memories.

"How did you learn to speak English, Ermina? It really is very good."

"Through other people like me, at medical training. I am a veter, um, animal doctor."

"Really, Luke's wife is a veterinarian!"

"I love animals. Mostly I look at farm animals, but pets also. Arben tended the farm, some crops and a few dairy cows."

Luke's mind was churning; these people needed help in so many ways. The beginnings of several ideas began to take root in his subconscious.

Sleep came easy that night. It had been a rare good day in the village, another step forward. They were up at dawn and headed back to the capital.

Abbas and Luke loaded the van back up, sneaking some extra medicine and food into the cache. Afterwards the guys treated Ermina to a late breakfast before they boarded the train.

Through tears she hugged and kissed them both, nearly unable to speak. They were at a loss for words as well, humbled and in awe at the strength and character of one who so much had been taken from.

The world needed a lot of fixing, probably always will. Luke and Abbas were heartened with the knowledge that there were people like Ermina Murati in it.

CHAPTER 36
SUNDAY, 3 OCTOBER

She's the wave, she turns the tide
She sees the man inside the child

C all it what you will, happy hour, meeting, chat, even hen-do. But make no mistake, it was members only. If you weren't already present, you'd best keep your distance.

They were under the yew. A casual observer would think it a normal gathering. Quaint, you might say. Colleen, Cheryl, Faith, Dani, and Robin, heads of household for all five homes in the rowhouse. Matriarchs, keepers of the apron strings, and, if necessary, the strings of the proverbial marionette.

References to an important cabal of the past were noticeable, a round table with an exact number of chairs. But here you wouldn't find the principals dressed in armor and chainmail, and quaffing flagons of mead. Here were capris, knit blouses and jumpers, with glasses of red wine.

It was an open forum as far as subjects for discussion was concerned, each of them encouraged to speak freely. As if.

"You got your guys back, ladies!"

"Yeah, Lucas was worn out."

"Abbas as well. He had a massive supper, chatted some with Darcy and I, then went to bed and slept for ten hours."

"So, mission accomplished, I gathered. How was it for them personally?"

"Luke said the train ride was fascinating, and the trip overall very sobering. He's always freaked at the cruelty people can inflict on one another."

"Yugoslavia, or what was Yugoslavia, has been in and out of war for ten years!"

"I hear they had a little side trip adventure."

"Of course, it's Lucas."

"Dani and I still haven't got the full story on that."

"I think Abbas is not one to color outside the lines much, but he seemed very affected by what he saw there. It's possible he got led on a bit."

"And Luke always protests being called a leader. People tend to follow him though."

"I've a theory. Pack mentality is a thing; everyone's aware of its power. Our guys are nearly the opposite. They tend to be bolder on their own, and more measured, more calculated, when together."

"Wow, I never considered that!"

"Ya know, they've been through so much together, and for so long."

"Yes! And they're more careful together, to look after each other. That make sense?"

"Love thy brother above thyself."

"I think that sentiment runs through the whole clan, sisters."

"Kumbaya!"

"Yeah, maybe we've smoked enough weed."

"You too much, girl. Uh-oh, now I'm sounding like Cyril. By the way, are we sorted for when he gets home?"

"All taken care of. Kevin and Ben are grilling, Luke and Abbas making the sides, and Poppy and Darcy are baking the cake."

"How many candles?"

"Forty-eight."

"Time marches on."

"The man's still a fine specimen."

"All our boys have stayed fit."

"Your four have been a good influence on Kev. He's in as good a shape now at sixty-six as he was at fifty-six."

"It's good you're selling the chippy. The both of you can travel and spend more time with your sons and their families."

"And help them along like you did with ours."

"I can never repay in kind the influence you had on my sons."

"You raised them, luv."

"But you inspired them, showed them how big the world really is."

"Kumbaya!"

"Hey, I've news, hot off the press!"

"Do tell!"

"Abbas has mercifully put an end to my dilemma over mum and dad. As of January one, we are taking over Adam's Apple."

"Oh Robin, this is huge!"

"Both of you!"

"Grocers, that'll take some getting used to."

"I can't picture you not at the Phil."

"Produce is my life."

"You should do well; everyone loves Adam's. And now the whole clan will go nowhere else for fruits and veggies.

"Your folks must be so happy!"

"They are, it should be a smooth transition."

"I'll bet Ian sits first chair flute now."

"And there'll still be two Ardavans in the symphony."

"True that. Darcy comes over from the youth orchestra, also on the first."

"That's a change in plans, I thought she was going to wait til summer."

"She was worried about her marks in school, but she's doing fine."

"What's the latest from your girls, Faith?"

"Aspen trees, mountain bikes, and Mexican food. I wonder if they're going to school and playing football."

"I wouldn't worry. They've always gone to school and played football, two things they're very good at. The new things are what gets them excited."

"Good point. They just want to share what's different in the day to day."

"I've noticed that with Jacob and Gabriel. Instead of language, lawyers, and musicianship, we get fondue and sheep."

"Mothers tend to worry when their sons get preoccupied with sheep."

"Oh stop it!"

"Hey, what time is it?"

"Nearly five."

"Cy's due soon, Rovers played at Crewe Alexandra."

"Crewe is in Cheshire, right?"

"Yes, he and Shea should be along anytime."

"Perhaps we should motivate, give birthday boy a proper welcome."

"Right, let's finish the joint."

CHAPTER 37
FRIDAY, 8 OCTOBER

And the only sign of life is the ticking of the pen
Introducing characters to memories like old friends

The combined offices of Big Ben Photography and Carter Assets Management were humming with activity. Lucas was just about caught up with some needed correspondence after his latest jaunt. Judith had several balls in the air—tracking down clients, setting appointments, and sorting the mail. Benjamin was applying a bandage to the back of his hand after Scruff went Cato on him upon entering the building.

"He likes you Ben, otherwise he'd ignore you."

"So it's true then. Love hurts."

"On so many levels."

Cup in hand, he went into his office, ninja cat on his heels, and sat at his desk. It was obvious that Jude had been in a funk of late, understandable for a number of reasons. She'd turned forty early this year, and she'd been without a love interest even longer. She had friends and was fairly independent, not lacking confidence and certainly not shy. Mick

Lyons leaving town without her had hurt deeply, but that was a long time ago. She'd be fine; the girl was a fox.

Ben was in a good mood. Today he was going to dust off his journo's hat and do some writing.

The Liverpool *Post* and *Echo*, Ben's employer for more than 25 years, was always interested if he had a freelance piece to offer, and sometimes contacted him with a request for something specific. Such was the case today.

A retrospective of pop culture in the '90s. He'd penned articles in the past on the subject, for the '60s, '70s, and '80s, so he would pull those for review before starting. Right now he was going to list some ideas in a notebook and categorize them for an outline.

Technological advances were the overlying theme of the decade. The internet, Google, beepers, CDs, voice mail and e-mail were now part of the norm.

News events captured the wonder and imagination of anyone who might pay attention, reduced to acronymic form for expediency. The rise of HIV, the fall of the USSR, and the pure spectacle of OJ in an SUV.

High tech brought new images to the big screen, sparking a rise in the popularity of animated films as well as special effects wizardry fueling the Star Wars and Harry Potter franchises.

Television got bigger and bolder as more and more households got wired for cable and satellite. Crime dramas were hot, and the sitcom audience tuned in to New York City to laugh at the frivolity and dysfunction of *Seinfeld* and *Friends*.

Familiar names continued to top the bestseller lists in literature. Those not glued to the boob-tube looked forward to the latest from Clancy, King, and Koontz.

The world of fashion was, as always, a no rules no holds barred polychromatic riot of shapes and textures. An early '90s trend towards minimalism sputtered under the weight of flannel and camo. At least we got the Wonderbra.

The common vernacular evolved, and in some cases devolved, into words and phrases tailored for the times. Good cop-bad cop, happy camper, and crack baby. Eco-safe and politically correct. Boom-box and rolodex. Going postal.

And then there was music. Ben tried not to be too cynical when it came to the subject. It was a great passion of his and he felt fortunate being a teenager in the '60s. For him the years between '64 and '72 was the golden age. Not that good music didn't exist before or after, and certainly not that some of the stuff from that period was less than stellar. Some of it was inane.

The British Invasion of the mid '60s brought more to America than Beatle boots and the Freddy. The music itself had a basis in the blues, skiffle, and the other roots traditions. Young people of the time, influenced by a series of world events and the temptation to 'tune in, turn on, and drop out,' immersed themselves in the counter-culture movement. The poets among them picked up a guitar and rock music went every which way imaginable. Soul, funk, jazz, psychedelia, and compositions that refused to be labeled all found committed acolytes. The alt-country, highly educated, Texas troubadour Rober Earl Keen was lying in a motel bed one evening, trying to decide what to call his music. He looked out the window and decided on 'Best Western.'

Songwriters and lyricists became the scene's philosophers, their ability to inspire and mobilize helping to further support for the popular movements of the times. The powers that be were wary of the younger generation's icons, names like Lennon and Dylan.

So what changed since then? There were plenty of talented musicians and good songwriters, and lots of new innovations in sound equipment and recording techniques. Ben's theory centered on two factors—the end listener and the industry's marketing and research practices.

No one listened to albums anymore. Vinyl and tape had been replaced with compact discs. The new generation's attention span had shortened a bit; they wanted video with their music, and dancing.

Girl and boy bands ruled; Destiny's Child, NSYNC, the Spice Girls, and the Backstreet Boys regularly topped the charts. Their concerts featured elaborate stage set-ups and lots of extras.

The revolving door of music genres continued. Punk and metal lost some of its attitude and luster while hip-hop and gangsta rap established themselves in the inner city and grunge in the suburbs.

There was a new four-letter word in music, Napster. Two kids in a college dorm figured it out—a way to store individual songs on computer and access them at will. Other file sharing sites followed, Audio Galaxy, Lime Wire, and Soul Seek, to name a few. This created a huge problem; the musicians themselves were having their work given away. What the hell? Ben was confident the situation would get resolved, but when? Greed was a powerful thing.

New technology was a boon to those getting started in music. Equipment was more versatile and less expensive, allowing for a better sound in smaller spaces through added portability and innovations such as wireless components and solid-state circuitry.

He'd been scribbling for nearly two hours, lumping ideas and info by subject into a collection of runes and hieroglyphics. With a postscript reminder to reference the coming of the latest end of days he decided to end the session.

On the way to the studio he made a mental note on a post-postscript. The article would include a welcome declaration—disco is dead!

CHAPTER 38
SATURDAY, 16 OCTOBER

Cogs and grunts and hirelings,
A meeting of a mean idea to hold

Jacob Carter was proving to be his father's son more and more all the time. The physical resemblance was strong, despite having his mother's green eyes, but it was his developing mien and manner that most reminded others of his resemblance to the 'Fixer.'

Even before coming to Switzerland, he'd come up with an idea, kind of a side project, to accomplish during his stay. He wanted to secure his first signing for Carter Assets Management.

Gabriel had to go to St. Gallen a lot for symphony rehearsals, so Jake tagged along and attached himself to the St. Gallen Football Club. The timing was fortunate. They were having a stellar season at the moment, comfortably in first place in the country's top division. He'd been to five of their matches, and attended any open to the public training sessions he could. He even got to know some of the club's internal staff, the result of a liberal dose of that intoxicating Carterian charm.

His best sources, the ones whose job it was to really take the pulse of the football club, were the reporters, specifically beat writers for the local paper, the *St. Galler Tagblatt*.

The list he'd compiled at first was lengthy—players of quality and maturity. From this list he struck the ones who already had agents; he wasn't ready yet for that part of the business. Also culled were the youngest players, particularly the home-grown academy products.

It was tough. The team was flying, the players buying in to new manager Marcel Koller's plan. The former Swiss international had brought a couple of studs with him; Ghanian striker Charles Amoah had become the leading scorer. Jake learned, however, no matter the current situation, there were always those looking for a move.

Wilco Hellinga was one of these players; Jacob intended to facilitate that move. He was a likeable chap. Jake had introduced himself at an autograph session. He had no representation because thus far in his career he hadn't needed it. He'd always found employment through contacts and reputation. He did see the value of having an agent, especially now. He and Jake's relationship became personable before any agreements were made. They naturally got on well and came to like each other.

On the field of play he was a different animal, known as the hardest man in Swiss football. Jake thought of him as the Dutch Cyril Barcant. Similar in stature at 5' 9" and 155 pounds with massive thighs, Wilco also played in the number six slot, defensive central midfield, marshalling the area in front of his defense. He was 29 years old and at the top of his game.

This evening the Espen, which is German for aspen, were hosting F.C. Aarau, from the north central part of the country. Jake and Eva were Wilco's guests, seated with the relatives and friends of the players. Eva played the game as a schoolgirl and was excited to be in such a prime spot. The stadium's name was Espenmoss, or aspen moss, the origin of which eluded Jake. It was a cozy setting, a little over 10,000 in attendance on the east side of the city.

The green and white machine rolled on; the score three-nil at half-time. St. Gallen put it in cruise control after the break, the supporters chanting "Whoa Sankt Galla, Sankt Galla Ole!" The match ended up 4-1, Wilco got a yellow card.

Jake and Eva were invited to go to the Einstein afterwards for a pint. It was a pretty classy place near the Aldstadt. The three of them took a quiet table away from the bar. Wilco wanted to talk about something specific.

"We heard a story about you tonight."

"Yes? Don't believe it."

"I remember reading about it," Eva said, backing Jake up.

"Uh oh."

"Back in February, at the Letzigrund. Something about a bull."

Wilco laughed out loud. "Not such a big thing. The poor guy was freaked out, more afraid than me!"

"He was Zürich's mascot, right?"

"Yes, his name was Maradona, really big. He was new to the team. Rescued from somewhere. He got loose and was running on the pitch."

"But we were told you were the only person not to take to the stands," Jake countered.

"He was chasing those people. I was frozen!"

Eva was cracking up.

"You got booked again tonight, I noticed."

"The referee does not like foreigners."

"Either that or he didn't like three fouls in five minutes."

"Eva, you are too smart for me."

"I was surprised to learn St. Gallen is the oldest club in continental Europe," Luke said.

"Since 1879."

"Wow, that's older than Liverpool, and almost as old as Everton."

"Only five years older than Tranmere," Wilco said, with a rather inquisitive glance Jake's way.

"Oh, you've been studying up on Rovers?"

He hesitated, not wanting to misspeak.

"I was, how you say, confused? No, I was in a conflict, not knowing what to do."

"Conflicted."

"Yes, that sounds better. I have good relationship here in St. Gallen; I talk the truth to the gaffer. The club will release me if I want it. They understand the business. Before I met you I was having my offer in

Germany, F.C. Nurnberg. The contract was good, but not so much the team."

"Do you think that you would like England?"

"I think I would like to play for Cyril Barcant, even in Timbuktu! I did not know he became a manager of his own team. Do you know him personally?"

"He's my godfather, we've lived in the same rowhouse all my life."

Wilco Hellinga was grinning from ear to ear. "Okay Jacob, I now have an agent. Take me to England, to the godfather."

They stood and shook hands, then Wilco hugged and kissed Eva, lifting her right off the floor.

Chapter 39
Friday, 22 October

Oh my peer, your veneer is wearing thin and cracking
The surface informs that underneath the underneath is lacking

The interpersonal dynamic among the students at Colorado College was understandably complex. Its reputation as one of the top liberal arts colleges in the country, along with its ideal setting, attracted ten times the number of applicants that could be admitted to the 2,000-member student body. It was a diverse lot, with a large percentage of both out of state and international attendees representing an array of ethnocultural backgrounds.

It's a private school. The tuition was steep and the twins were reliant on their scholarships to attend. They and others that shared the same circumstance, the so-called jocks, were an example of the way cliques, real or imaginary, are perceived. Fraternities and sororities were another good example, an easy excuse to lump people together, give them a label.

Who's to blame? The wealthy, the spoiled, the immature, the self-entitled? All of the above, Grace felt, and it pissed her off. She had no patience for putting on airs. Where do people get off judging others as nerds, or knuckle-draggers, or eggheads, ragheads, or even deadheads. What's wrong with deadheads, anyway?

Colorado Springs is a red city politically, for the most part. A number of conservative organizations are based there. Focus on the Family is one. A church, basically, but a huge one that very much combined religion and politics. 'Focus on your own damn family,' Margaret would say. You would think Colorado College, with all its diversity, would be immune to sentiments of censure and exclusion.

Hope didn't share as much concern over the issue, taking more of a pragmatic view overall. 'Screw em!' was her take. Give them a chance and if they're going to be boorish then don't waste your time.

The twins did find plenty of kindred spirits among the student body, and were impressed with the intelligence and passion of the faculty. The curriculum was taught in a most unusual way, referred to as the block plan. Each student would complete one course per month, only studying that single subject each morning in intense classroom instruction, followed by instructor led sessions in the lab, or afield, depending on the type of course. This left 3 or 4 days off at the end of the month when students were encouraged to explore the area, the region, even the state. The idea was to more fully enrich the overall experience. Living off campus with locals more than accomplished this goal.

The college itself was established in 1874, just northeast of downtown, straddling both Monument Creek and Cascade Avenue. All of its early buildings were now on the National Register of Historic Places, and the campus continued to grow right through the present day. It also was referred to as one of six western 'Ivy League' schools, a term the more gentrified class liked to use.

The range of studies offered was very ambitious. Languages, including Russian and Chinese, were available, as well as Anthropology, Environmental Studies, Political Science, and the Arts. Over 80 programs of varied study existed to both challenge and educate. Both Hope and Grace were taking Spanish, plus assorted courses in Human Biology and Kinesiology.

In their downtime they would hang around school some, mostly at the Worner Campus Center, which was akin to a Student Union Building. The school also operated KRCC, a National Public Radio outlet, which they enjoyed listening to. The programming was all over the map, making a program schedule a must.

All the school's athletic teams competed in NCAA Division III, except for men's hockey and women's soccer—both Division I. The hockey team had a strong program, often ranked in the nation's top ten. The soccer team had a real heyday in the entirety of the '80s and into the '90s, including two finals appearances. From '92 on, the program lost its mojo, thus the decision to hire Greg Ryan and refocus on recruiting.

The Pine sisters were earning their education on the road today, in Tucson, Arizona. The Lady Wildcats were hosting them at Murphey Field, east of the downtown area. The game was highlighted early on the schedule on Friendship Lane, the twins looking forward to seeing two very special people, Ender and Anne Linares.

Dani's parents, retired now, and living in Anne's hometown. Anne was the clan's hippie matriarch, a favorite of the Fab Five. Anne met Ender in his native Venezuela while on her own late teenage sojourn, eventually encouraging her daughters to do the same. The socio-political climate in Venezuela became untenable due to a string of autocratic heads of state bringing strict laws and a horrible economy, prompting the Linares' relocation to the States.

They were waiting at the athletic complex when the team bus rolled in, wanting to spend as much time together as possible.

"Oh my word, you're all grown up!"

"And beautiful!"

"Hi Anne! Hi Ender!"

"It's so good to see you guys, in your town, no less!"

"Hey, I can still tell you apart, after how long, two, two and a half years?"

"Has it been that long?"

"It's easier now, to tell us apart."

Grace turned to the side, exposing her scar completely.

"Not so bad, huh?

"Not bad at all, Grace."

"Siempre seras bonita."

"Gracias, amable señor."

"And what's your two's secret, so young and lively."

"And so very handsome!"

"I don't know, I thought this dry desert climate was baking the juices right out of me."

"We're digging on it. Colorado's getting chilly."

"Is that your coach looking this way?"

"The assistant, we better go."

"Good luck in the match, we'll be watching."

"We want to hear you as well."

"Go Tigers!"

The game itself was defensive, and physical to the point of confrontation. Neutral observers were treated to a high energy contest, full of commitment and endeavor.

The Wildcats were members of the Pac-10 conference, home of some of the heavyweights like UCLA and Stanford. They clearly had no respect for such a small program toiling away in the Mountain West. They got a rude awakening.

It was a battle waged mostly in midfield, where Erin Simons and Sydney Stoner locked down the middle of the park. The other team resorted to the long ball, which Hope and Grace just weren't having.

Ties weren't popular in the states. It was compared to 'kissing your sister,' a phrase Grace dismissed as lame if not misogynistic. So after a scoreless 90 minutes they played 30 minutes more.

Halfway through overtime, frustration got the better of the Arizona number 9. Hope leaped to clear a cross with a header. The forward came from the side with no chance at the ball; she wasn't even looking at it. Instead, she undercut Hope, who landed awkwardly on her shoulder and neck.

The whistle blew immediately, the ref on the way to administer justice. Grace, who didn't think justice would be properly served, got there first. She slammed into the player from behind, face planting her into the turf.

"We come in pairs, bitch!" They were both booked and thankfully not ejected.

The game ended in a draw. Hope went straight to the trainer's table.

The twins got permission to have dinner with the Linares before flying home. They talked long into the night.

"Now I know where to go for a bodyguard," Ender said wryly.

CHAPTER 40
SUNDAY, 24 OCTOBER

Much as you'd like to hear what the daisies have to say
They'll come to get you if you act that way

"Hey Pops, your Papi and Gran Anne saw the twins day before yesterday."

She was getting ready to take Otis out for his morning constitutional. Her dad's declaration stopped her at the bottom of the stairs.

"Huh?"

"Hope and Grace were in Tucson, playing football."

"Oh cool! What else?"

"I spoke to Anne, your mother was at the clinic. They're fine. Ender's into cooking and they both got new bikes. Anne's dealing with the city's zoning department, something to do with a new strip mall in the neighborhood. Fascists in bed with corporate carpet baggers are the words I believe she used."

"Gran's so boss!"

"That she is."

"I miss em. You think much about going to Arizona for a visit?"

"Every winter."

She chuckled, "Yeah, it's Baltic out today. There was frost on my bedroom window."

"Bundle up for the walk."

"You betcha!"

She got her coat, scarf, hat, and wellies from the mud room and Otis' collar and leash from the foyer then stopped, turned, and went to the table where her dad sat to give him a hug.

"Thank you! What's that for?"

"You were due a cuddle. Plus, I never said how proud I was of you and Abbas, what you did going to Kosovo. Especially after giving you a hard time about it."

"Understandable. And it's nice to be cared for."

She hesitated, "I'd like a chat sometime, to maybe discuss what happened in that hotel room back in July."

"Another time, luv."

"Okay." She kissed his cheek, joined Otis, and opened the front door.

"What's happening!"

"Geez Darcy, I nearly wet myself."

"Young ladies must be alert at all times."

"Yeah, yeah. You never know where danger may be lurking."

"Morning, luv!"

"You're on it this morning, what's on?"

"I've a date!"

"Groovy! Who's the lucky chap?"

"Sid Roberts."

"Your mate at the symphony?"

"Yup. He's a dear. We're going to see The Sixth Sense at the Woolton."

"So he's not one to garner any special favors?"

"No, just a friend. I think he feels the same."

"You're the prettiest girl I know, Darce. I doubt he'd pass on your affections should you offer."

"He plays the French horn Poppy."

"Oh, I didn't realize! How could I even think it."

"Come on, let's get the pups over to the park."

Porridge, fruit, and tea were on the menu when she got back at the house. Dani was up, reading the *Echo*. She always said it was the only way to see if her husband's been off making news somewhere."

"What are the plans today?"

"Your mum and I are seriously planning to do as little as possible."

"Amen! And you?"

"Well, I think I'll go to the clinic and see to the boarders right away. Probably get started on the supplies order to be placed this week as well."

"That reminds me, I need to add to it."

"Why is that?"

"Your dad wants to send some stuff to his girlfriend in Kosovo." Luke raised an eyebrow.

"Just kidding, it's a great idea. We'll send as much as possible."

"Hard to imagine what she's up against. You feel sorry for the animals when people themselves are struggling," Luke said.

"I've an idea, Mum. Ya think it'd be worthwhile to ask the vet school to send a shipment? We could even petition other vets in the city for donations, give it to the university, and ship it on to Ermina? They might even have some old but serviceable equipment they could spare."

"I'm sure they do, and could, help out that is," Dani replied. "Getting someone to cut through the red tape and make a decision would be the hard part. Who could possibly get that accomplished?"

A pregnant pause ensued, after which Luke announced, "I gotta go to the library."

Dani grinned. "He's hooked, but it may take a while to reel him in."

The Edge Hill Animal Hospital was quiet, until Poppy opened the door. A long, low, moaning howl issued forth.

"Poor baby, come on out of there." It was a mutt, about 60 pounds, some kind of hound mix, kept overnight as a precaution after a fairly routine neutering. "Whatcha sad about? Lonely, hungry, or because you're singing the high notes now?"

She checked him out thoroughly. Satisfied with his condition, she rang his owner up and said she could come collect him. While she waited, she looked after the only other guest, a calico named Splotch. She'd been spayed but no one was coming to pick her up. She'd been left at the front door last week during the night. Poppy named her, and wanted to find her a good home.

It was a little after 10 when she locked up and caught a bus to the City Centre. First stop was TJ Hughes, a department store on London Road north of the university. Nothing too exciting—socks and panties, plus a scarf she couldn't resist even though she had 4 or 5 at home.

Then it was Boodles on Lord Street, probably Liverpool's most trusted jeweler. She wanted to get Gabe a present; he'd be home in a few weeks. He didn't wear jewelry much, and wouldn't wear a ring or dangly type of bracelet because of his cello. She also didn't remember ever seeing him with anything around his neck. Finally she decided on a Swatch watch, something he'd wear when he chose. Even that took a while, there were so many to choose from.

She copped a bacon butty from a street vendor near the bus stop. Two actually—one she gave to a rough sleeper along the way. As she sat and ate, her thoughts turned to the coming months, and all that it entailed. Next month she would turn 21, the month after she would attain her Veterinary Nurse Certification. Big plans for the holidays were on tap, then came 'that millennium thingy' that the twins were wondering about.

All in all, more than enough to ponder in the next ten or so weeks. She'd worry over next year when it got here. Enshallah, the Ardavans would say.

Whoa, that gave her an idea! She got home, stowed her things, jumped in the Vauxhall, and drove back to Edgehill.

"Come on Splotch, there's a lady you should meet."

She knocked on the front door, carrier in hand. Aleah answered, and was silent. Uh-oh, this may have been a mistake.

"Naneh hello, have I come at a bad time?"

Aleah hesitated, then smiled, and made the cutest sound—a mixture of wonder and glee.

"Not if you've brought me my new little kitty cat!"

CHAPTER 41
SATURDAY, 30 OCTOBER

I know the barricades
And I know the mortar in the wall breaks
I recognize the weapons, I've used them well

Splotch was settling in quite nicely at the Stillwell house. After just six days she'd decided on and claimed her three primary places of repose for morning, afternoon, and night. It was a careful process; comfort, temperature, and logistics were some of the factors considered. She felt good about her choices. Now she could start training the staff.

Stillwell was Penelope's maiden name, George and Rose's only child. She inherited the house, a grand manor near Sefton Park in a very nicely appointed neighborhood, and now lived here with her husband, mother-in-law, and, most of the time, her son. Ardavan was the name on the post box now.

Bashir sat in his favorite chair, thankful that the cat hadn't chosen it, and read the *Echo* after breakfast. Penny and Aleah were still in the kitchen, Caspar was getting ready to go to work at Erins Pharmacy. He worked most weekends, filling scripts and running the show so Faith and Colleen could be with their families.

After a bit, Bashir realized he was staring at but not reading the paper. Concentration was a problem at the moment. He set it to the side, closed his eyes, and let his mind go where it may.

He'd been uneasy of late, something nagging at the corners, just out of reach. There was no obvious reason for it; life in general seemed to be on cruise control.

It hadn't always been smooth sailing. Bashir could easily point to the time when he and Penny's life, thought to be cozy and on track, was turned upside down. That was the summer of '69.

His youngest brother came to England, fresh out of high school, wondering if Liverpool could also be his place to settle. Some kind of karmic, cosmic strangely wonderful force aligned the stars and dropped Cyril Barcant, Lucas Carter, Daniela Linares, and Benjamin Pine into his life and the lot of them into Bashir's and Penny's lap.

It was a joyous chaos of sorts, going to school, finding work, establishing themselves in a foreign country. He and Penny were their guides, their big brother and sister, they in turn becoming little Rosie and Caspar's aunt and uncles.

Bashir endured many jokes and much frivolity over his concept of an allied approach to life, the famous Greenbank People's Coalition. The blueprint was a sound one, however, and still endured, even though the Fab Five made it more commune that coalition. Then came the baby boom.

The five had some practice at child rearing, with not only Rose and Caspar, but also Kevin and Cheryl McTimon's three sons Ian, Seamus, and Cyrus. Penny and Cheryl, classic Scouse mums, provided the early guidance and instruction. It was helpful, but still all hands to the pump with the arrival of the Merseyside Six, all within a five-year period.

The gang, along with the whole region and most of the country, saw hard times in the late '70s and all of the '80s. The coalition, in spirit and practice, saw them through it.

The clan even had an outpost on the other side of the pond. St. Petersburg, centrally located on Florida's gulf coast, was the home of both Bashir's other brother Cye and his wife Astrid, Dani's sister, and

Ben's parents, Eugene and Louise Pine. They lived just three blocks apart.

And now the whole unlikely experiment was undergoing a reboot. The Tweeners, as those at Greenbank had dubbed them, were raising their kids and navigating their careers as their parents did. And the Six? They were at the same point their folks were 30 years after that fateful summer of '69.

So, why the unease? Why not just finish out his career and become the happy pensioner, surrounded by Splotch and the grandkids. Maybe by that time he'd be ready, tired enough to step back and satisfied enough to enjoy it.

Perhaps, in the meantime, a change in routine, or a trip somewhere, possibly some new challenge to take on, an engaging side project. Various members of the clan were always taking off, gallivanting around the globe. At present most of the Six were in the Rockies and the Alps. Maybe he should find his suitcase and knock the dust off it.

"Bashir!"

Geez! What just happened!

"Are you asleep? The kids still have my Mixmaster!"

Hmm, maybe I'll take a journey over to Calderstones, he thought. Small steps first.

CHAPTER 42
SUNDAY, 7 NOVEMBER

Maybe he's caught in the legend
Maybe he's caught in the mood
Maybe these maps and legends
Have been misunderstood

Gabriel was conflicted. In three days' time he and Jake would be back in Liverpool, something he was really looking forward to. Leaving Switzerland was not something he was looking forward to. The elders always spoke of the educational value of travel. They never mentioned that the experience affected the heart as well as the head.

It was four months he would never forget, and the elders were right. A lot had been picked up, a new level of maturity attained. Now conversant in German and familiar with the customs and history of his host nation, Gabe had also furthered his craft, performing with a completely new set of peers. More and more, however, he felt that getting to know the Swiss themselves would be what he would value most.

The last fortnight had been great. He and Jake were able to stay close to the lane that the Hallers and their neighbors the Muellers and Tschopps lived off of. His stint with the symphony was finished and Jake had sealed the deal with Wilco, so time spent going back and forth to St. Gallen was over.

The last three days had been varied and interesting. The bulk of Friday had been spent shearing sheep. What a trip! Since bringing them back from the mountains they'd been grazing the rich green grass on the property. There was a dozen total, including three lambs, two of which belonged to Zanzibar, Laura's favorite. Balthazar, literally the black sheep of the family, was the only other one with a name. The Hallers didn't name too many of the animals on the farm; the freezer contained too many of their ancestors.

Jake took on the job of moving them around the area, a tricky task at best. They had a portable pen, a strand of wire with an armload of light stakes attached and hooked to a solar powered electric supply mounted on a stake of its own. It was pretty easy to move around; you needed to from time to time to allow the sheep a fresh patch to graze. The challenge was getting all the flock to get with the program. They were skittish by nature; slow, steady movements and soft words of encouragement were a must. Oh, and make sure the power pack is switched off before touching it with both hands. Jake learned the hard way.

The shearing took place at the Muellers', another challenge for the sheep whisperer. Their barn was near the top of the lane, and the little baaastards didn't want to go. It was just Gabe and Jake; they were at odds for a solution.

"Well, I don't know if this would be frowned upon, but I've an idea," Jake said. With that he picked up one of Zanzi's lambs and started towards the Mueller's place. A photograph would've won a Pulitzer— the young shepherd, babe in arms, leading the flock single file up a country lane. The little dude peed on him.

Mrs. Mueller spoke good English. She and her husband were middle-aged, just the two of them, living where the lane met the road, which led to the highway up to the town of Shindellegi. They'd arranged for someone to come and do the job—two guys, one was actually from Australia. What a character! A hairy, crusty, wild-eyed, storytelling, sheep shearing son of a something. But he was good, and fast! Gabe and Jake brought in the sheep, one at a time. The Aussie sheared them and his buddy collected the wool and directed traffic. Once underway the process moved right along, except for the ram.

The guys were told not to bother; he needed special handling. Jake took it as a challenge, and got knocked on his ass. The Muellers were much amused.

Yesterday morning was a quiet one, fogbound but not too cold. Jake helped Elisabeth with some homework while Gabe tended the oven slash heater slash fireplace, the proper name of which he was still unaware of. It was an amazing fixture, you might say—a simple but versatile and efficient sort of appliance.

It was like a huge cube with six-foot sides, forming the boundary between hallway, kitchen, dining, and living areas on the ground floor. Thick walls, like a massive kiln, off-white in color with decorative tiles. The hallway side had a large opening, mostly clear for stacking firewood, but also equipped with racks for cooking. Once lit, the cube gradually warmed, and emanated heat, warming not only the entire first floor, but the two floors above as well through passage holes in the ceilings at each corner. Another cool thing was the bean bag looking cloth bags Laura sewed together. Inside each she placed dried pits from a cherry tree in their garden. On really cold nights you could take one of the bags to bed to use as a footwarmer after heating it up on a rack in the oven.

The afternoon was spent with the children. Eva and Elisabeth wanted to take them down to Wollerau, nearby on the shore of the Zürichsee. The Tschopp kids tagged along. Theo and Natalie owned the farm adjacent to the Hallers. Theirs was a working farm, and they were raising four children, hopefully, in Gabe's mind, to help with chores. The eldest and youngest were boys, Hans and Levi. In between were Anna and Luisa, about the same age as Eva and Elisabeth.

It was a street fair, common throughout the country in the autumn. A parade, music, vendor stands, food and drink, lots of costumes, and people milling about, enjoying the sunshine now that the morning fog had lifted. Heisse Marroni was the big hit—roasted chestnuts, in small 100-gram bags, warm and so tasty. Levi, probably 10 or 11, was a heck of a cute kid, with a smile that let you know the wheels were turning. He was a chip off the old block, as they say. Natalie had a picture of him at 2 ½, sitting on his dad's tractor in a box welded next to the seat.

Supper was on the Scousers. The boys wanted to take their hosts out for a meal and a glass of wine. Luca suggested Attilo, an Italian eatery just a short drive to the east by Feusisberg on the Dorfstrasse. The food was very good. Jake and Gabe both had lasagna, but the highlight of the evening was the view! From their table you could see the hillside down to the lake, the lights twinkling in a random pattern. And beyond, the lake itself, sparkling in the moonlight.

"That is where we will be tomorrow," Luca said with a gleam in his eye.

As much as Laura loved and excelled at quilting, it was matched by Luca's passion for sailing. They all went this morning, waiting until about 10 to cast off, the sun high enough to warm things up some and the wind picking upas the day progressed.

The boat was impossibly beautiful, a national 45, single masted, a craftsman's delight. Beatrix was her name, all wooden and polished to a deep, reddish glow. The sails, lines, and fittings were in top order. You could tell she was loved and properly looked after. You could probably sail anywhere in a vessel like this. Luca said she wasn't real fast, but cruised at a pretty good clip and was steady in rough seas.

Luca was a natural. You could tell he'd logged a bunch of nautical miles, and he took on a wistful air when talking about some of the trips he'd been on.

It was near dark when they got home. The boys tended to the animals while the girls bathed and Laura put together some cheese, meat, bread, and fruit to munch on.

Now they were all cleaned up, fed, and snug cozy near the fire, the kids drinking hot cocoa while the adults sipped on spiced wine.

Just three more days. There was very little to do as far as travel prep, maybe a couple more souvenirs for the clan. Jacob was bringing home a footballer for his dad—that would cause a sensation. Gabriel wasn't to be outdone. His father was getting an Alphorn! He was delighted to find out they could be broken down into three pieces. He thought of Abbas as soon as he saw and heard one, but didn't know how to ship it.

Poppy was waiting, and the symphony, and his family and friends. He would go home willingly and happily, his head full of maps and legends. And faces.

CHAPTER 43
SATURDAY, 20 NOVEMBER

Do you remember
Chalk hearts melting on a playground wall
Do you remember
Dawn escapes from moonwashed college halls

The subject had been on the table since they were toddlers, so long ago now that no one could recall who first raised the issue. Possibly Faith or Colleen, with something like, 'oh, I can just picture it, Gabe and little Poppy, such an adorable couple.' Fun to talk about. Lots of people fancy themselves the matchmaker, but rarely does such a prediction become reality.

Yet here they were, very much a couple, a situation everyone in the clan would have to adjust to. It was comical in a way, from playmates to school chums to big brother little sister. How far would this progression go?

Everyone wanted a piece of the boys when they got home, Poppy waited her turn. The stories they told and the excitement they shared plainly exhibited how big the experience was for them.

Home ten days now, a routine was being reestablished. Poppy still lived at home. Her courtship with Gabe, which started the weekend before the trip, resumed in earnest. They were taking it slow even though they planned to spend tonight together at the flat.

Poppy had a roommate of her own the last eight days, Wilco Hellinga. On paper Lucas knew all there was to know about the Dutchman. Now he wanted to get to know the man himself. Luke had tested the waters around the region as to where to place the midfielder. Three clubs were interested. West Bromwich Albion was dismissed out of hand; they were in danger of relegation and were just trying to save their season. Luke presented Wilco with two choices—Leeds United and Tranmere Rovers.

Leeds were flying in the Premier League. They were playing in Europe as well, but manager David O'Leary admitted he was looking for backup at midfield and anybody signed would probably sit a lot. At Rovers, Wilco would earn almost as much, but even though Cyril made no promises, he would get every chance to prove himself. In the end Wilco showed maturity, and that he was still up for a challenge.

"I'm nearly thirty Lucas. I get too stiff to sit on the bench. And I want to still learn more the game. Cyril Barcant for me is the best. I will play for Rovers. Okay?"

Poppy was Wilco's cultural guide to Liverpool, showing him the sights in the afternoons after training. He and Otis bonded from the get-go and Dani thought he was a wonderful houseguest—polite, engaging, and helpful. The family was in no hurry for him to find his own place; let him get a better feel for the area first.

Lucas, Jacob, Gabriel, Poppy, and Darcy were guests in the VIP section at Prenton Park this afternoon for a four o'clock match hosting Nottingham Forest. The midpoint of the season was nearing. Rovers were hovering mid-table as Cyril continued to mold the team's style and composition. After a scoreless first half Cy decided to let his new player off the leash.

He didn't score, and he didn't assist, but the new number six keyed Tranmere's three-nil victory. His positioning, communication, and work rate were spot on, a solid shift. Defensively he was the 'you shall not pass' stone wall, the guy loved a tackle. He was a clean player, not reliant on the dark arts to control the middle of the park. His arrival frustrated Forest so much they saw four players booked and one ejected.

They all went to Duke Street after the match, the Eclectibles were up in the rumpus room for a session. Geoff, George, and Paul, the core of bass, drums, and guitar were set up, accessorized with voice and orchestration courtesy of Dani, Robin, and Abbas. Gabe and Darcy tuned up and joined in, Gabriel particularly anxious to get back to rockin'.

Poppy, often coaxed into some background vocals herself, lately had been singing more, taking some direction from Faith and her mum. Faith wasn't present tonight; she and Ben were hanging with the tweeners down at Calderstones. No doubt Poppy would get a chance to belt out a few numbers.

So, with the boys back in town and the family that stays together because they play together was back together again. The Eclectibles cut loose. Mistakes were made, high signs missed, lyrics forgotten, and a couple of times they had to stop altogether. No one cared because when they were lockstep they soared!

They had a small audience, a few Tranmere players, including Wilco and fellow Dutchman goalie John Achterberg, as well as both players from Wrexham in North Wales—Gareth Roberts and Jason Koumas.

There was a table stacked with pizza boxes and some other munchies, plus plenty of ale. The footballers were hungry; everyone was thirsty.

"Is pizza popular in the Netherlands, Wilco?"

"Pizza is everywhere, Darcy."

"That's a good thing. What's your favorite street food back home?"

"Patats mit mayonnaise, number one."

"Chips and mayo?"

"Yes ma'am."

"Okay, I'll have to give it a try."

"John makes his own, even the mayonnaise."

"Ooh, now I'm really excited."

"Small pleasures, big happiness."

"That's brilliant!"

"Like your music."

"Aw!"

All this while Geoff's bass was laying down a solid, driving groove augmented by Gabriel's half note interplay in the same octave but a higher key. Abbas and Robin took turns soloing while George kept them all in the same frame. Poppy danced with Gareth and Jason, the trio lost in the moment.

"Dance like nobody's watching."

"It's the only way I dare, Dani."

"C'mon Paul, I'm betting you can cut a rug."

"I prefer giving others the itch to boogie!"

"Let's do just that."

Paul strapped on his Stratocaster and quietly checked its tuning as Dani tapped her mic. Robin cued the rhythm section and ended her solo with typical flare as Paul's crybaby wah pedal transformed the opening chords to "Tales of Brave Ulysses" into a mystical preamble, setting the mood for Cream's classic Greek saga.

Dani's voice, low and cautionary, lured the listener in while George's cymbals and both guitars swirled, gathering force:

You thought the leaden winter would bring you down forever
But you rode upon a steamer to the violence of the sun

A sharp rap on the snare brought guitar, bass, and cello in all at once, a singular sound that threatened to come apart but held, raging to match Dani's now forceful snarl:

And the colors of the sea
Bind your eyes with trembling mermaids
And you touch the distant beaches
With tales of brave Ulysses

Through the first two verses, George, Paul, Gabe, and Geoff somehow produced a feral, predatory sound, bound only by the structure of the composition while Dani relayed the tale. Then the song slowed, and segued back into the introductory theme, recoiling into itself:

Tiny purple fishes, run laughing through your fingers
And you want to take her with you
To the hard land of the winter

Again, from the hush to the rush, poor Ulysses:

Her name is Aphrodite
And she rides a crimson shell
And you know you cannot leave her
For you've touched the distant sands

The last verse was followed by one last lull, after which Paul went off, his Strat wailing its tremeloed riffs like sirens to the sea. Everyone not on stage looked like they were melting into each other, a mass of kinetic groove.

Gabriel's cello had been an important addition to the band; the instrument itself was becoming more and more popular in rock music. For one, it had the widest range of sound in the band, allowing it to be utilized for both melody and harmony. Also adding to its versatility was that it could be played with or without a pick, as well as plucked, or, most commonly, bowed. Gabe was enthusiastic tonight. Except for some music played for the Hallers and their friends, he'd only performed classical music in a symphonic setting for the last four months.

"Hey, is this a private party?"

"Shannon, Cindy?"

"In the flesh!"

"Oh my word, welcome!"

Robin was first in for a cuddle, "We heard your parents were back on Merseyside from the Doohans. Have you come back as well?"

"No, no, we're just here for the weekend," explained Shannon.

"And your handsome escorts, welcome lads."

"Handsome husbands, luv. This is Simon."

"And this is Callum," Cynthia added. "The children are with mum and dad."

"Pleased. I'm Robin, and the man fondling your wives at the moment is my husband Abbas. Kids you said?"

"And how," Cindy explained. "My son Dennis is six, Shannon's girls are nine and eleven."

Abbas took Simon and Callum for a beer and to introduce them around. The band broke and the couple dozen people now in attendance grazed and chatted for a while, mostly divided by gender.

Simon Hargreaves and Callum Stone were partners, both from the Midlands. They had a carpentry business, employed occasionally by

Shannon and Cindy's father, Dennis 'Bones' Waters. Bones, and more importantly, his wife Donna, liked and approved of the two hard working young men and nature had taken its course. The Waters adored their grandchildren, and their daughters loved Liverpool still, so it was always a fun weekend for them all.

"We've heard about the 'Merseyside Six,' Dani. There were only three the last time I saw you," Cindy said.

"Well, later that same year Faith and Ben had twin girls. They're off in the States at school. Then Robin had Darcy the next year. Look, there's Gabe and Darcy with my pair sneaking off to the back balcony."

"Oh for heaven's sake, what a dummy I am. Of course they're adults now!"

"Most of the time."

Now it was a party, food, drink, music, and a willing set of participants. As it turned out the new guys were players, maybe not to be compared to the band, but they worked well together, Simon on guitar and Callum on harmonica. Geoff set Simon up with his acoustic. Callum's harp was always in his pocket, and they did their thing. Little by little others joined in, adding to their songs before encouraging them to stretch it a bit, and improvise into a jam. You could tell the two were thrilled with the collaboration.

Jake, Gabe, and Poppy were beat by the time everyone had gone home, but they still talked into the night. Four of the six were together again, and next month the twins would join up with them. A happening was planned, something the three of them discussed excitedly.

Gabriel and Poppy slept together for the first time since June. They just fell into bed, too tired to make love. They made up for it in the morning.

CHAPTER 44
WEDNESDAY, 1 DECEMBER

Pretty soon we'll all be tumblin' like a barrel thrown from the top of a
waterfall

The first day of the last month of the century. That was Abbas' first thought as he opened his eyes that morning. A big month for the clan, lots of moving parts. Like most mornings he laid still, assembling his thoughts. Robin was still asleep, breathing softly, her butt up against his hip.

He rose quietly, a bit of mischief in his head, and padded downstairs in his slippers. Above the sofa against the north wall, that's where it was mounted, his newest fascination. He lifted it from its brackets, all three and a half meters, and marveled once again at its heft, and its smooth lacquered curves.

Carefully, he climbed back up the stairs, by-passing the second floor and continuing up to the attic. There he opened both dormer windows and leaned out, sampling the chill morning air. Then he carefully positioned his instrument, business end to the heavens, and let 'er rip.

The Alphorn's notes broke the still morning's slumber, scattering the starlings busy amongst the yew's branches. Other reactions were varied.

Darcy sat bolt upright in her bed just coming awake. "What the hell?" Robin just shrugged; boys will be boys.

Next door Lucas was at the downstairs table drinking tea. He smiled to himself; his old buddy was following his muse. Daniela and Poppy were in the kitchen giggling.

Ben thought it might be some kind of air raid warning at first, then had a chuckle of his own. Faith was out with Amos and Otis in the park. They had the best seats in the house. She liked it. The notes were low and slow, very peaceful with an ethereal quality. The dogs' instinct and past traditions suggested the hunt was about to start.

After a few minutes it ceased, then began anew. Five notes, repeated, distinct, and somewhat familiar. Colleen was the first to parse it out, the same five notes that were featured in that movie, *Close Encounters of the Third Kind*. Colleen was superstitious. Just who or what was Abbas trying to call forth. It was only a month before the end of the world for Pete's sake!

Back downstairs Abbas ran the gauntlet of sideways comments and disapproving looks and hung 'Alpina' back up. With a smug and satisfied look, he joined his girls at the table.

Poppy came over with her cuppa and made it a foursome.

"I think Darcy and I should have a trip of our own."

"Wherever it is, don't bring back anything you can't keep to yourself," Robin advised.

"I'd be happy to stay with the Hallers. The boys plainly had the time of their lives," Darcy said.

"Their daughters would probably be thrilled!" Abbas added. "Luca and Laura seem quite interesting, talented as well."

"Jake said that Laura could take a pile of rags and create something to make the angels weep!"

"Jake is Lucas 2.0," Robin declared.

"Not a bad thing, Mum."

"Not at all. But, as Dani says, that dog needs a leash sometimes."

"Oh, did you hear? Luke ran into Sam last week in the City Centre."

"Silky Sam?"

"Yep, dad said he stayed with his sister in Chester for several months instead of a couple of weeks. She was a single mum and he was a big help. He and dad had a long talk about what happened. You know, to I guess agree on how to address the subject going forward."

"Which basically means don't," Abbas said bluntly.

"Exactly. Dad must've been moved by the guy, though. He offered him a job."

"Wow!" Which is all anyone could say, the very idea took some getting used to.

The Carter's were the next to show up, followed closely behind by the Pines, both to offer their review of the morning musicale.

"Come on Darcy," Robin said. "Let's scramble up some eggs. Might as well feed this lot."

The conversation got lively, the topics numerous. Somehow though, it always got back to the present, as in present month, December. The first day of winter, the holiday season, with all that entailed, and the coming new year. If that wasn't enough the clan had some goings on to add to the schedule, good things, things to look forward to. Sure, there were rumblings of gloom and doom in the new millennium, but so what? It had always been that way. Screw the agents of the apocalypse.

As was his nature, Ben kept one foot in the real world.

"This is Wednesday kids, check the time."

"Oh shit, we gotta get a move on!"

CHAPTER 45
SATURDAY, 11 DECEMBER

It's a drifting time,
people are fascinated by screens,
no idea what's on the other side

The twins were about to put a bow on the first term of their junior year. Grace and Hope were due a pat on the back. They'd taken on a tremendous challenge and responded well to the opportunity.

The Tiger's soccer season was deemed a success even though they played .500 ball, the first non-losing campaign since '91. The program had fallen far since the '80s heydays; a rededication in funds and focus had paid dividends. A bit more recruitment in certain areas would fuel a continued rise in their fortunes. The Pines had done their part, anchoring a much-improved defense.

Now their focus was solely on their studies. They very much liked the block plan system of taking subjects one at a time, accruing credits along the way. The simplistic approach seemed to ease the learning experience.

They'd settled well culturally too, both on campus and in the community, especially up on Friendship Lane.

Hope was at the table in the nook by the kitchen, helping Jessica navigate the family PC. She was careful not to get carried away. Her computer skills weren't a whole lot stronger than Jessie's. Neither she nor Grace were tech-savvy, and to be honest, didn't care to be. It was a necessary 'evil' nowadays, and they didn't resent it. Technology was a wonderful thing. Hope was just trying to limit her screen time; it seemed people more and more were solely occupied with the small space at arm's length.

"Hey Tim," she called, pausing his attempts to get ready to take Pepper out back to the park. "How much memory does this bad boy have?"

"Dunno dear, that's milady's department."

"Hmm, I thought you were that high-tech man of the times."

"Oh no. All this new-age stuff, I can't tell the difference between tai-chi and chai tea."

There were no bad dad jokes this time, that was pretty clever.

Margaret and Grace returned from their little adventure, a mountain bike ride in Ute Valley Park. Colorado Springs had an awesome array of public access to mother nature. Ute Valley was 420+ acres, huge for a city park, and left completely natural save one small, nearly unnoticeable parking lot next to the nearby middle school. Its best feature was its topographical diversity, oval in shape from its bottom, a sandy drainage, up to its rocky bluffs, with meadow and wood in between.

This morning it was sporting a winter coat, seven or so inches of snow, freshly fallen yesterday late. They went early, within an hour of sunrise. Grace was pumped.

"Just like home with the fog, only nearly silent! Our tire crunching the snow was the only sound."

"It was kinda surreal, we never saw anyone," Margaret echoed.

"But we saw a pair of owls, right off the trail, about fifteen yards. We spooked them, I suppose, but they just flew along the trail, from tree to tree. It was like they were escorting us!"

"Well, we're jealous. We've been lost in the wilds of the internet," Hope reported.

"You know what?" Margaret started. "If we had those cool go-pro cameras on our helmets we could be watching it on that computer right now!"

"Wow, that's an idea!"

"Wild!"

"And we could add a soundtrack!"

"Hey, where's Pepper? Margaret asked.

"What about dad, Mom?"

"Oh yeah, where's Tim?" The twins were much amused.

"They're both in the park."

"Okay, how about this. We've only snacked this morning. Let's get organized and have a late lunch out somewhere and pig out. Then we can snack healthy this evening?"

"Perfect Margaret, I'm on board."

"Second that."

They ended up in town, at Phantom Canyon Brewing Company. It was a prime location, right downtown at the corner of Pike's Peak and Cascade. Housed in a three-story building, the ground floor featured the main dining room and bar, fairly upscale. The top floor contained the restaurant's offices and such, off limits to the public. The gang opted for the second floor. It was unique.

Completely open around the perimeter, with floor length windows on three sides, the space was filled with pool tables. The center had a small bar and the room's MVP, a massive pizza oven.

They had a blast! It started to snow again; Hope and Faith had never seen anything like it. Big, wet flakes, softly floating to earth in the still air. All the downtown area was decorated for the holidays, glowing in the diffused light. It was peaceful, and beautiful!

"I shall miss you all while we're away," Grace moaned.

"Yes," Hope agreed. "Christmas with the Blacks would be fabulous!"

"Crimbo!"

"Right you are Jess!"

"Me thinks you'll be satisfactorily occupied during your time away," Tim offered.

"It will be good to see our mates again," Grace admitted. "We've all been so busy this fall, there'll be plenty to catch up with."

"Is it supposed to keep snowing?" Hope asked.

"Yes, we might get dumped on pretty good."

"Perhaps we should head back up the hill," suggested Tim.

"Hey, you guys didn't have any beer," Hope pointed out.

"We were gonna wait til we got home," Margaret said. "To celebrate with you ladies."

"That's a good idea!"

"You girls finish up. I'll go get a growler filled."

"What's a growler?"

"A jug. It holds a gallon of beer. I was going to get some pale ale."

"Hold on," Grace said, looking confused. "You mean you can buy ale to go?"

"Yeah. And you can bring it back for a refill."

"What a country!"

CHAPTER 46
SUNDAY, 19 DECEMBER

Sometimes we live
No particular way but our own
Sometimes we visit your country
And live in your home

The clan's first western outpost was established in 1974, in St. Petersburg, Florida. The whole thing started innocently enough. Ben's parents, Eugene and Louise Pine, offered up a bedroom to Dani's little sister Astrid so she could finish school locally. Ian McTimons followed—Kevin and Cheryl's eldest scratched his 'travel and see the world' itch living with the Pines, also getting his degree and furthering his craft with the local symphony before returning to England. Then it was Cye Ardavan, the middle brother, forced to flee his country and an established career, struggling on Merseyside before coming to Florida.

Astrid and Cye were still in St. Pete, married 15 years now, and living 3 ½ blocks away from the Pines. Both couples were happy, living quietly in Lake Pasadena Estates near the center of the peninsular southern part of Pinellas County.

Cye and Astrid were career driven professionals. When it was remarked upon that Astrid seemed to possess her sister's knack for science, that person had no idea. She'd risen quicky at the Mote Marine Laboratory in Sarasota before accepting a position heading up the research department at the Clearwater Marine Aquarium.

Cye's knowledge and skill in the field of architecture was well established before coming to the states. He loved it, and was dedicated to its theory and application right from the start. He'd worked for a local firm for the past twenty years, furthering its reputation as well as his own. It had enabled him to expand his portfolio to a wide variety of projects.

The Pines' careers were behind them, and they were deservedly enjoying the fruits of their labor. Eugene's storied past included field work for the CIA, an ambassadorship to the UK, and two stints as hometown mayor. Louise, who started out as an accountant for a travel agent, became Gene's partner. She was part secretary, advisor, hostess, and liaison—an entourage of one.

The Pines and Ardavans spent a lot of time together when Cye and Astrid weren't working. Dinners, outings, and local events, here in the 'Sunshine City,' with occasional trips around the bay area. They were also content to just hang out in the neighborhood together, where the conversation often turned to the clan itself. Today there was no need to postulate or presuppose goings-on in respect to their family and friends —the Merseyside Six was in town.

They all flew in yesterday; Cye and Astrid spent half the day at Tampa International. The rest of Saturday was spent settling in. Unpacking, dealing with jet lag, and spreading the love preceded a good night's sleep.

This morning the Pines and their guests, Jacob, Darcy, and, of course, their granddaughters, walked down to the Ardavans for a morning cuppa. Their house, on the northeast side of the diminutive Lake Disston, featured a modern look—a one-story stucco with sleek lines and terrazzo floors.

For breakfast the whole crew walked back west to Gene and Lou's, a more classically styled home, one and two story, with lap siding and oak floors throughout, except for the kitchen and bathrooms. It sat on Lake Pasadena's southwest side, a half mile from the Ardavan's.

There'd been non-stop chatter from minute one, so much to catch up on. And so much to discuss going forward. A two-week stay was on tap, with no time to waste.

The Six had brought a chaperone to the party, Robin's excuse to include herself, the line between her and her charges already beginning to blur. Gabriel, Poppy, and she stayed at Lake Disston.

They were all together now at a local eatery. It was early evening and the gang was tucking into a traditional Sunday roast.

"The Horse and Jockey, we've one in Liverpool," Robin said. "Up in Melling, near Kirkby Park."

"This one's been around for a while," Gene pointed out. "A dozen or so years."

"Looks like home," Darcy declared. "Phone booth, post box, English ales, football gear. It's boss!"

"And a football match," Jake said. "Chelsea hosting Leeds at Stamford Bridge."

"Up the Whites!" Poppy exclaimed, which drew a few echoed chants from the bar.

"Yes, quite like an English pub," Hope remarked.

"Except for the shorts, sandals, and t-shirts," Cye noted. "Best of both worlds, I say."

"I would like to propose a toast," Gene began. "To Darcy, the Royal Symphony's newest star. And to Poppy, Liverpool's newest veterinary wunderkind. Also to Gabriel and Jacob, our ambassadors to the Alps. And to Hope and Grace, purveyors of all things Scouse in the Rockies. The Six! Our path and purpose in the new millennium!

"Cheers!"

Robin was tearing up. "I've got my Neff back!"

"I appreciate the compliment, my dear. But I'd have to bow, I believe, to the lovely Aleah as the clan's elder statesperson."

"Gran is a class act," Gabe said. "I see her quiet wisdom in my Uncle Cye." This prompted a brief pause, Cye at a loss for words.

"Kumbaya!" Jake to the rescue.

The food was very good. Everyone had the Sunday roast, some with chicken, some with beef. Veggies, potatoes, Yorkshire pudding, and dark gravy. Scrumptious!

Gabe noticed a man walking over from the bar, pint in hand. He was of medium height, dark hair, fit looking with a mischievous grin and a slight twinkle in his eye. He rose to meet him.

"Hello."

"Hey all, I was just wondering how so many Scousers were allowed in the country?"

His accent gave him away.

"Ya can't fool us, soft lad!" Robin admonished, with a grin. "Most of us are from Mossley Hill."

"It's a pleasure. Lea Doyle's my name."

Gene introduced himself, then did the honors.

"I'll never remember all them names so I'll stick with the ladies."

"You are definitely from Merseyside," remarked Grace. "Or nearby."

"Chester, to be exact."

"Red or Blue, mate?"

"Red til the day I die. But if I'm honest, I played for Everton as a schoolboy. They dropped me."

"Oh, that's tough for one so young," Astrid sympathized. "There seems to be a lot of Brit expats in St. Pete."

"Loads of em, in and out of here at the pub all the time. Well, I'll leave you to it. Cheers!"

"Cheers Lea!"

Suddenly the bar erupted; a raucous cheer complete with flying suds. Stephan McPhail had scored for Leeds in the 66th minute, breaking the deadlock.

"Rovers seem to be holding their own," Astrid said. "We don't get to see them, of course."

"Cyril's given them a jump; they're hoping to end up mid-table, something to build on."

"That sounds familiar," Grace said.

"We'll be better next year," Hope vowed.

"Where's the team lacking?" Gene asked.

"We need a couple of box-to-box midfielders, and a nine."

"The universal quest, a dependable number nine," Jake said.

"Well then find them one, mister sports agent!" This from Louise, throwing down the gauntlet.

"I'm powerless when it comes to amateurs, Lou."

"I suppose. Well, how about after next year? There's going to be a women's pro league in the States; you can get my granddaughters in the big time!"

"Consider it done."

"Goal!" More suds flew.

"Two-nil, McPhail got his brace!"

They made their way home after the match, ending up in the Pine's lanai. Cye had the big news, his mood excited but cautious.

"I've decided to strike out on my own." He went on to explain how he'd come to love the city, and wanted to work locally to help to literally change the shape of its future. "I predict that soon St. Pete will undergo a boom of sorts, and that the population will see a rapid increase. The image of green benches in Allah's waiting room will be forgotten.

Jacob had a question, after he stopped laughing. "And what's your vision for a better St. Petersburg?"

"Homes reimagined after a prior existence as something different."

Robin perked up, déjà vu had stuck. "You mean like your father did in Liverpool?"

"Yes my sister. And I will honor him with the name, Ardavan Concepts and Design."

"That's wonderful Cye," Hope said. "I've seen examples of his work. It's brilliant!"

"Well done mate," Jake said. "Bashir will burst his buttons!"

"Ah yes, the coalition," Gene remarked.

"How's the New Year's Eve plans shaping up?" Darcy asked.

"All set," Gene reported. "We pick up the vans a week from Tuesday. I've got the tickets and all that information; you guys just need to get supplies when the date gets closer."

"We're going Phishing!"

"I'm so excited!"

"I've never been to a music festival really, just some one-day affairs back home."

"I can't believe it's in the middle of the swamp!"

"What about Y2K?"

"Screw it, I say WHY2K?"

CHAPTER 47
CHRISTMAS

And so this is Christmas, I hope you have fun.
The near and the dear ones, the old and the young.

Abbas could be forgiven if he decided to be mopey or put upon because his immediate family had abandoned him over the holiday. He would have a hard time trying to elicit any sympathy at the moment, however, he was half naked in a hot tub with three lovely ladies.

Dani's vow to purchase this bubbling wonder had come to fruition, and it was a beaut. Room for six with lots of comfy molded seating, and rotating jets aimed at all the right places. Honey brown teak surrounded the spa, the platform, roof, and removable sides all but immune to the changing weather's harsh effects.

Colleen sat next to Abbas, and across from them sat everyone's Christmas presents, Catherine Barcant and Millicent Hathaway. Cat was Cyril's younger sister, Millie her partner for over 20 years. They were both Trinidadian. Cat ran her own travel agency, Jaunts and Journeys. Millie, who recently retired from being a stewardess, was working at the agency until, in her words, her next occupation presented itself.

"Me thinks Christmas in Trinidad would be a better scenario," Colly suggested. "It's abnormally cold this year."

"But it feels like Christmas!" Catherine countered.

"True," agreed Abbas. "And it will still feel like Christmas in April."

"When we're toes in the sand at Maracas Bay," reasoned Millie. "I see your point."

"Did someone mention Maracas?"

"Kev!"

Kevin was on the move, sporting nothing but a pair of swim trunks and a glass of Bailey's on the rocks.

"Make way, I'm coming in hot!" He snuggled in between the Trinis, much to their delight. The McTimons held a special place in Cat and Millie's hearts, Port of Spain was Kev and Cheryl's favorite holiday destination. Time spent there with both the girls and Cat and Cy's parents, Michael and Allison, was the best. It was Cheryl that the two young lovers confided in when they first came out to the clan.

Inside the dress code was also casual, new jammies, a Liverpool tradition. The guys were in charge of brunch; Luke was slinging eggs while Ben fried bacon and Cy buttered toast. Otis and Amos supervised. Dani, Cheryl, and Faith were in the front room coordinating their contributions for a feast over at the Tweeners house at Calderstones later that afternoon.

"I'm looking forward to it!" Faith said. "Children at Christmas is a must."

"I'll bet Lizzy's in a frenzy right about now," Dani said.

"Nathan's getting a bike," Cheryl reported.

"Wow, Nathan got a bike, look!" Faith exclaimed.

Sure enough, there he was, peddling up the front walk, bright and shiny.

"At least I think it'sNate. All I see is fog breath coming out of a muffler!"

Dani opened the door. "Get in here boy, it's Baltic outside!"

Nate waddled in and shed a couple of layers. "Hello everyone, Happy Crimbo. I got a bike!"

"Yeah you did, it's boss!"

The boy just beamed.

"How about a cuppa cocoa?"

"Yes please."

"We're glad you rode over. How's everyone at your house?"

"Fine. Gran is there now, she kinda took over.

"Christmas is her thing Nate. What did she do for pajamas this year?"

The lad turned sheepish. Instead of speaking he just took off a couple more layers. Faith covered her mouth, Cheryl laughed out loud. The kid was head to toe South Park characters, and they'd killed Kenny.

"Mum said they plan to eat supper at four but everybody can come when they like," he said, putting his jeans and long tee back on. "Dad's cooking a whole pig!"

"That sounds great!" Dani replied. "I know you probably want to ride your bike back but how bout some breakfast first?"

"Yes please!"

Two hours later it was three hours earlier in St. Petersburg, strictly from a hands on the clock perspective. Lou and Gene, along with their guests, Jake, Darcy, and the twins, walked up 3rd Avenue and around the east side of Lake Disston to Astrid and Cye's house. Christmas glowed in the growing light, a reminder that holiday traditions were celebrated in all climates. After all, Jesus was born near the desert, his parents wore sandals.

"Merry Christmas!"

"Merry Christmas!" Astrid was excited.

"I just spoke with Ian; they send much love! Everyone's headed over there later for supper.

"Good, Greenbank is probably feeling a little underpopulated this year," Louise remarked.

"I wouldn't feel too sorry for them Lou," Cye said. "Catherine and Millie are visiting."

"Ian said he and Abbas took them busking in the City Centre last evening. Apparently they turned Church Street outside Marks and Spencer into a dance off."

"I wouldn't doubt it."

"I fear our sleepy little Burg's not measuring up when it comes to holiday frivolity," Gene wondered.

"Nonsense!" chirped Gabe. "Just being together's enough for me. Besides, I've got sun, sand, surf, and seafood!"

"And we're going Phishing!"

"I would venture to say," began Astrid "that just like the Fab Five, the Six need only to be in the presence of each other, and surely frivolity will follow."

A lazy morning ensued, conversation over coffee, tea, and pastry. The Christmas parade was on the television, and Hope and Grace talked to Margaret. There was snow on the ground in Colorado.

The Six were much taken with Iggy, Astrid's iguana. He was a marine iguana, well adapted to life in and around the water. The dude had his own kiddie pool. He was a rescue someone had brought into the aquarium and Astrid decided to adopt him. She took him to work some days, strutting along on his custom-made lead. Louise had stitched his name on the collar and Jurassic Park on the leash.

In ones and twos, they all eventually made their way over to the Pine's. Estrogen coursed through the kitchen, a traditional dinner was being assembled and prepared. The ladies were exacting in their preparations, dictated by handed down recipes and fueled by Champagne Chambord.

The enticing aroma proved to be too much for the guys, who fled on foot for a tour of nearby Admiral Farragut Academy. There they were visited by the ghosts of Christmas past, Carter and Pine, clad in full naval regalia.

Their bravery and sacrifice were rewarded upon their return.

"Wash up boys, it's on!"

Was it ever! A turkey and a ham. Sweet potatoes and green beans. Scalloped potatoes and corn pudding. Crescent rolls and pumpkin pie.

"This is delicious Louise!"

"Splendid!"

"I've never had corn pudding before!"

"Pass the rolls please."

"More beans please."
"How about you Grace?"
"Brglmff!"

CHAPTER 48
WEDNESDAY, 29 DECEMBER

Set the gearshift for the high gear of your soul
You've got to run like an antelope out of control

Now Jacob knew why his father routinely demurred when being called the Fixer. Luke knew his skills paled when compared to Gene's. The former diplomat had the ability to do things quietly, behind the scenes. It was remarkable the way everything had come together the past couple of days.

They ran errands on Monday, groceries, personals, propane, and a trip to Bill Jackson's. It was a sporting goods and outdoor gear supplier. There they bought a lantern and some freeze-dried meals. These were to be their only hot food during the trip, along with tea and oatmeal in the mornings. Bread, cheese, fruits, and nuts would sustain them in the interim. On the way home they bought ten five-gallon jugs of spring water, which Gene described as their most precious resource.

Yesterday morning Gene took his granddaughters a short distance to meet with a business contact offering a unique product. His name was Carl and he rented Volkswagen camper vans.

"They're both checked out, gassed up, and ready to go Gene. Good morning, ladies!"

"Good morning, sir!"

"Pleased to meet you Carl. These buses are the coolest ever!"

Were they ever! Carl handed Grace a set of keys to the green one. 'Magic Bus' was neatly stenciled on each side; 'I can see for miles' across the front. On the back it was 'Going mobile' on the top of the Who's iconic circle and arrow logo.

Hope's bus wasn't a bus at all. It was the 'Yellow Submarine,' complete with portals and periscopes, and a mod paint job. The artwork was excellent!

All but Astrid and Cye crossed the Howard Frankland bridge to Tampa in the afternoon, a dry run for the twins to get accustomed to driving the vans and a chance to play tourist. Ybor City was the destination, a long-standing Cuban settlement on Tampa's eastern outskirts. They had lunch at the Silver Ring, Cuban sandwiches and deviled crabs the fare. Next stop was Tampa Bay Brewing Company, just off the main drag on 15th Street. It was an historic building, built of brick like nearly all the other structures in the area. Teddy Roosevelt and his Rough Riders were staged there before heading for Cuba back in the 1890s during the Spanish-American War.

Tampa Bay Brewing Company's owners were John and Vicki Doble. One of their sons was the head brewer. Gene and John were old friends. They'd worked together for the government back in the day, during the time the clan never asked questions about. Vicki, a Brit, ran the place, John was head schmoozer.

The Dobles took the gang upstairs, normally closed during the weekdays, and they had a nice chat while sampling some beers. They left with six big growlers full of Old Elephant's Foot India Pale Ale.

The Merseyside Six, with Robin in tow and temporarily redubbed the Seminole Seven, left St. Pete at first light. They exited Pinellas County via the Sunshine Skyway bridge and accessed I-75, driving south past exits for Sarasota, Venice, Port Charlotte, Fort Myers, and Cape Coral. Just before Naples they made their only stop, a shopping center containing both a gas station and a Publix supermarket. Here they filled the tanks and bought sub sandwiches and as much ice as they could load into their coolers and the van's ice boxes.

The interstate took a hard left and became Alligator Alley, an arrow straight highway cleaving the Everglades between the coastal cities of Naples and Ft. Lauderdale. Their destination lay just over halfway across, the Big Cypress Seminole Indian Reservation.

Gene's three-and-a-half-hour travel estimate was spot on for the first three hours, the last half hour took over four hours to complete. A new tribe had taken over the swamp, all part of the phamily. It was stop and go now, mostly stop. Jake and Gabe got out and walked, easily staying in front of the rest. They ended up in a caravan of RVs and cars from the northeast, friends all banded together for the pilgrimage.

"Collectively we're from Jersedelphia!" the dude said, introducing himself as B. Getz. "How bout you guys?"

"Liverpool."

"England?"

"Yes sir."

"Far out man!"

"Far away too."

About a half mile back two V-dub camper vans full of the fairer sex was garnering a lot of attention. A trio of beaded, tie-dyed, plaited phans were quizzing Grace on her awesome magic bus. When they moved on to the yellow submarine and approached the driver's window, they came to an abrupt halt, stupefied.

"How'd you do that?" Sometimes it's fun being twins.

The pace picked up once they exited the interstate at Snake Road. The two lanes north into the reservation were slow, but steady all the way up to the check-in stations. From there they were directed to their camping spaces, next to one another up on a newly cleared lane named Barrymore.

Here they were lucky or, was this another of the Fixer's subtle touches? They were in the northwest corner of the nearly 500-acre camping area, between a drainage ditch and a stand of cypress trees. They were coincidently adjacent to B. Getz and company, who'd circled the wagons and already begun their bacchanal.

They set up a solid bank at one end of their combined space, vans on the corners, tent in the middle, folding tables and coolers filling in the rest. It all faced the woods. Gene's old shortwave radio was tuned to FM 91.7, Thin Air Radio, a temporary station broadcasting on site, staffed by phans. It kept them in the loop.

Phish's minions had descended on Big Cypress a month prior and erected a small settlement. There were first aid stations, a post office and general store, and a Ferris wheel. There were also art installations, including a rock garden, ice pyramid, and paper airplanes up in the trees. A boardwalk wound its way through the wet ground around some of the cypress stands. They were expecting 80 thousand people, making it Florida's 10th largest city. Tribal police were in charge of security. So far their only complaint was all the hippies wanted to pet their horses.

The rest of the afternoon was spent either hanging out or walking around, checking out the set up or making new phriends. The Six were electric, amongst their contemporaries in America. Somehow that carried a significance they couldn't explain, even if they were aware of its presence.

Robin was aware; she'd felt it building for the past ten days. It amused her that they were nervous, the lot of them, even though they hadn't the foggiest. They needn't be; she'd stand any of them next to anyone else's kid. Three days from now the Six would add another layer of maturity and awareness and move on.

Dusk brought the gang back together. They cleaned up and ate, then set up for some fun and games. The only thing Gene Pine hadn't hooked them up with was reefer. Astrid, to everyone's surprise, did the honors. A pipe was stuffed, and a growler popped open, followed by a recap of the day while sharing stories.

There was no music scheduled until tomorrow afternoon, so the Eclectibles' string section unpacked their instruments and began to thank the native forefathers for permission to inhabit their tribal lands. It took about a minute for their neighbors to start to wander over, the music the magnet.

They played Phish's music mostly, melodies and extended jams, punctuated here and there by Poppy's singing of the band's very unique lyrics. The onlookers, more by the minute, began to mingle and sing along. Soon there were no strangers, only new phriends, sharing all they had in common and celebrating all their individuality.

Some brought their own instruments, percussives mostly, and the Swampwater Orchestra was born.

The Beatles "Within You Without You" was the highlight, Poppy's dancing hippie gypsy, the image inhabiting most of the faithful's dreams in the wee hours. Robin was much amused.

CHAPTER 49
Thursday, 30 December

A thousand barefoot children outside,
Dancing on my lawn

Jake awoke, and his first thought was that he'd died and gone to heaven. Enveloped in a strange light's glow, Hope was against his right side, arm across his hip. Grace was on his left, her head against his chest. Suddenly he was sad. Did God have to take the twins as well?

Outside the tent Robin had started some water, and she and Darcy were talking to B. Getz.

"So neighbor, when's the next performance? You folks are crazy good!"

"Thanks B, I imagine we'll crank it back up this afternoon. We'll be the warm-up act."

"Cool!"

"How many shows have you been to?" Darcy asked.

"Oh, probably close to fifty by now. You?"

"This is our first."

"No kidding, wow! And Big Cypress, no less. It will probably change your life!"

"I think it may have already done so."

He laughed, "Wait'll you hear the band."

"We have most of their albums. They're a goofy lot, but their music is brilliant!"

Jacob and the twins crawled out of the tent, stretching limbs and peering through mussed hair.

"Dude!"

"Oh, hi B!"

"Jacob, did you say you brought some stamps with you down here?"

"Yes ma'am, they're in the glove box in the Sub."

"Splendid. I bought some handmade post cards yesterday."

"I heard about an area where people are selling all kinds of things," Grace said.

"It's over near the stage area, in a campground," B said. "Everything from grilled cheese to tie-dye."

"We'll have to check it out."

"I don't know if it's your bag or not, but I wouldn't cop any man-made psychedelics here. I'm hearing bad things."

"Thanks for that."

"Oh hey, I actually came by to ask you guys over for breakfast. We're cooking up a bunch of eggs and pancakes."

"You sure? There's seven of us," Robin cautioned.

"There's thirty-seven of us, a few I haven't met yet. Come on by!"

"Thank you. Pancakes sound great!"

"With blueberries!"

"Now you've got my attention," this from Gabe, who just emerged from the bus with his arm around Poppy.

"Dude!"

Breakfast with the Jersedelphians was both appetizing and entertaining. Collectively they'd been to hundreds of Phish shows and possessed much lore and a lifetime of memories. Their anticipation was off the charts, hoping for a career high from the Burlington natives.

The rest of the morning was spent wandering around and mingling with the crowd. Jake counted license plates, giving up after noting 37 different states and a handful from Canada. Darcy had a conversation with one of the tribal police about airboats and chickees. Poppy and Gabe met a couple from Louisiana, got stoned, and wandered around in a hardwood hammock. Robin and Grace went shopping in the most unusual market imaginable. And Hope? She crawled back into the tent and read for a bit before falling back asleep.

The gang got their groove back on around two, after a lengthy tuning session. This had been a problem ever since they landed in Florida. The humidity had affected subtle changes in not only the relationship between the strings and the tuning pegs but also the wood of the instruments themselves.

There were more than a dozen others present when they kicked off with a long, slow burner. Poppy's only lyrics, early on, initiated a fifteen-minute jam, building in intent all along the way.

In the evening I undo my belt,
Split open and melt.

By the time it was over their audience had nearly tripled, and their juices were flowing. The Ardavans had wowed them, taking turns driving the jam forward, raw, powerful, and very psychedelic. Now, to invite them in.

A lighter vibe, "Bouncing Round the Room," Poppy stirred the embers.

And I awoke, and faintly bouncing round the room,
The echo of whomever spoke.

They were ready for the singalong, and knew right when to join in.

That time in and once again I'm bouncing around the room.

Their new mates repeated the mantra, over and over until the whole campsite was bouncing around.

They played another 45 minutes or so, the mood light and engaging. Energy was building, Phish Nation was queuing up for something epic. Robin sensed the Eclectibles would have trouble sustaining the vibe.

"See you at the show!"

Phish had been a steadily growing entity since 1983, at the forefront of the jam band scene since its inception. The genre, widely accepted as the offspring of the counter culture's poet laureate, Jerry Garcia, had several features at its core. Musical improvisation, extended jams, and a dedicated fan base had created quite a body of work, quirky and wondrous.

Phish had amassed an impressive catalog of original music thus far, and they weren't afraid to experiment, either with the music itself or their business model. They toured extensively and kept the tickets affordable. They even set up a section at each show for tapers, whose recordings were shared and swapped nationwide. Also, it was typical at Halloween for the band to cover other's albums, the whole thing, in sequence. And Big Cypress wasn't their first festival. They'd treated phans in the past at gigs like the Clifford Ball, the Great Went, and Lemonwheel—upping the ante at each opportunity.

Late afternoon saw the faithful gravitate towards a 26-acre meadow on the other side of the Ferris wheel. The stage was massive! It was set up with the back and sides up against the woods, creating a natural setting.

Phish is a foursome. Trey Anastasio on guitar, Mike Gordon on bass, Jon Fishman on drums, and Page McConnell on keys. Separately they were top drawer musicians, highly skilled and versatile. Together they became far more than the sum of their parts. Phish was innovative and exploratory, an organic arsenal of aurality.

Grandiose description of their sound and music could not be extended to their appearance and demeanor. Four guys looking pretty much like the average dude in the audience, save Fishman's dress, strolled onstage to absolutely no fanfare or bombast. With kids in candy store grins, they took up their instruments and tossed out a surprisingly clean and clear "Water in the Sky," obviously chosen for its 'filter out the Everglades' lyric. A cover followed, Traffic's "Light up or Leave me Alone," which the crowd took as an invitation. The band brought out Chief Billie, their host and tribal chairman, early in the set for a couple songs. The chief was quite a character and a singer songwriter to boot. The band backed him on both a traditional welcoming song, "Che Tun Ha," and one of his originals, "Big Alligator."

The gang was planted in front of the crew on the sound board, out of the crush and enjoying the quality of the mix. This was a muti-sensory experience; they were swept up, reveling in both the music and the communal vibe. First set highlights included "Limb by Limb." Gabe dug how the song morphed from a jangly, call and response, almost disjointed practice exercise into a full-blown monster jam, each member feeding the beast. The twins got into "Ghost," with its uber cool slow groove and atmospherics. They were already in motion, lithe and sultry, feeling every note. The set ended with "Character Zero," a real rager.

The Everglades was settling into another gorgeous sunset as everyone refueled and recharged for the evening's phestivities. Chicken, pasta, bread, and beer were on the menu, along with a side of chatter. The band had more than delivered, there was no letdown after all the anticipation.

The whole scene was part of the pull; people here were kind. It was a relaxed and welcoming atmosphere.

A couple of puffs and a fresh mug of Old Elephant's Foot put the Eclectibles in a creative state of mind. That and the fact that people started coming round hoping for some tunes stirred the gang into another session. B Getz showed up with Sister Bear and Fluffhead and announced, with a bit of panache, "Maestro, if you please."

Poppy sat the first half hour out; the Ardavans were in the classroom. Robin started with a simple, repeated set of four notes, changing only one note at the end of each set. Gabe joined with his own four note sequence, in a distinctly lower key. Then Darcy, perched in the middle, her four notes a combination of the other two. This was repeated until it sounded 'whole,' for lack of a better term.

Robin then took her leave, a melody, staying in key, meandering within the structure laid down by the other two. Then it was Gabe, introducing his own melody, a counterpoint to Robin's, but still following Darcy's cadence. Darcy's escape was when it all came together, her melody complemented and completed the other's groove. From there they took turns soloing. They ended perfectly together, all at once. They'd completed Phish 101 in a half hour.

There must have been forty or fifty people present, their reaction almost embarrassing. Jake noticed someone familiar in the crowd. A guy, a little older than most of the rest, in a floppy hat, obviously digging the strings. He topped off Robin, Gabe, and Darcy's mugs while suggesting they play a song he'd heard them play back home a lot.

"You're up Pops."

Gabriel got em started, low and slow. Robin and Darcy joined up, tentative, all three of them coming together. Then swelling, Poppy's cue:

Tumbling greens, a pickup screams alone above the square
Whoa, sing softly
Above the trees where Billy breathes we float upon the air
Whoa, oh

Hope and Grace came to Pop's side, a little help from her friends:

Softly sing sweet songs, softly sing sweet songs

The strings breathed again, then swelled anew:

Silent scenes in motion means, I'll wake you when we're there
Whoa, sing softly
Time it seems, in broken dreams, to sleep beside the stair
Whoa, oh

Two more sets of 'softly sing sweet songs' by the three sirens preceded another deep breath as the song changed completely. An instrumental finish, composed to lure the listeners in, build the emotion to a precipice, then softly ease them back down to earth.

There was no audience participation on "Billy Breathes," only hushed, rapt silence. Sister Bear had tears in her eyes. Floppy Hat looked like he was melting in place. Much appreciation and compliments followed before the happy campers wandered off to prepare for Act II.

The familiar stranger came forward and doffed his hat, introducing himself with a smile.

"Hello Page," Jake began. "This is quite an honor, I'm Jacob."

"The pleasure's mine Jacob. I'm glad your friends stopped playing. I was thinking no one would show up later if they didn't!"

"Not a chance, you lads are amazing! Allow me the honors. This is Robin and her brood, Gabriel and Darcy. Poppy's my sister and Hope and Grace here are also part of our extended clan."

"I'm more than delighted folks! Your take on 'Billy' is the most beautiful piece of music I've heard in quite a while."

"Your music is inspirational, kind sir," Darcy gushed. "It's our first time hearing the band live."

"Oh, where is it you're from?"

"Liverpool. You don't tour a lot overseas, it seems."

"No, that' true. It's logistically challenging. We've got a lot of stuff to lug around."

"True that," Robin said. "We're excited for tonight. Our neighbors here were telling us about your light shows!"

"We're fortunate to have such great fans. By the way, you three are classically trained I'm betting."

"We are, members of the symphony back home. We also have a band, the Eclectibles."

"Cool name! Maybe Phish need a little Eclectization."

"That's a nice thing to say. We've not much original music to draw from, though."

"No no, I mean a collaboration, as in you guys play with us."

"Wait a minute," Gabe interjected. "You mean both bands, together, at the same time?"

Page chuckled, "Yes, here, tomorrow, the afternoon set. Come join us for a few tunes."

The Ardavans were gob smacked, and tongue tied.

"Allow me to re-introduce myself," Jake began. "Jacob Carter, I represent the Eclectibles through Carter Assets Management, Merseyside."

Now Page was laughing out loud.

"Here I have my staff, Hope and Grace Pine, in charge of security, and the occasional background vocal duty."

Now everyone was laughing.

"My clients would indeed be willing to share the stage in a gesture of international goodwill and the pursuit of the arts."

"Fine, I'll have my people contact your people and parse out both the setlist and terms of participation."

Even Jake succumbed to the merriment. "Meaning?"

"Let's jam!"

Poppy squealed. "Can we make it très psychedelic?"

"Trey's always up for the psychedelic, and he loves orchestration. Don't worry young lady, we'll make em all split open and melt!"

The Seminole Seven pretty much floated numbly through the rest of the night. There were highlights, the playful syncopation of "Taste," and the twins' hypnotic gyrations during "Gotta Jiboo." The night's first set ended with Led Zep's "Good Times, Bad Times," and Trey's soaring lead guitar. Intermission was a trip back to the campsite for a mug of ale and a respite from the throngs. There was a note under one of the Sub's wipers, a list of some songs from which to cull tomorrow's picks. The gang was touched. The list was chosen with an obvious consideration toward the band's guests.

The nightcap was lengthy and varied, the seven all in. Chris Kuroda, the Wizard of Light and the band's unofficial fifth member, was incredibly in sync with the music, giving the sound a visible presence. It was easy to let go, carried along by all the sights, scents, and subtle sounds, and 80 thousand new best phriends.

Sleep did not come easy, echoes and vibrations still coming in waves. When it faded they slept, long and deep, dreaming of the Wolfman's brother, antelopes, and the Weekapaug Groove.

CHAPTER 50
NEW YEAR'S EVE

Steal away before the dawn,
And bring us back good news.
But if you've tread in primal soup,
Please wipe it from your shoes.

Back when only native Americans lived in Florida, the peninsula was dominated by the Seminoles. Lesser tribes occupied some of the coastal areas. The Calusas and the Tocabagas were prevalent among the mangroves on the west coast, but it was the Seminoles whose influence white settlers had to contend with.

Three wars later nearly all these people were relocated to Oklahoma with only about 200 left to hide out in the swamps. This was the mid-1800s. It wasn't until after the turn of the century that the federal government allocated land in the Everglades for the Seminoles to live in peace and revive their customs and traditions.

Chief Billie and the elders assured everyone that this new 'tribe' would be welcomed on their ancestral lands, and that the spirit and goodwill they showed would bring good fortune to both them and their hosts.

Jacob lay still in the tent, soothed by the twin's synchronized and metronomic breathing. He was thinking about his hosts, and what they might be thinking of their guests. He felt his tribe had been respectful and treaded lightly here. It was a kind bunch; they cared for their peers. Not many groups of like-minded souls this large could pull something like this off.

The sun was well up, but it was quiet. Phish Nation was recharging for the main event. Darcy and Robin were up, but they were over by the main gathering area, called the Delta. They'd taken a box of shortbread biscuits to share with the tribal police having their morning coffee.

Gabriel exited the bus and started stretching. He was feeling that call again, just like in Switzerland. Rumblings from the past, faint, indiscernible, but there. He didn't care to have them explained; he liked the mystery, and the myth. Heady stuff for the modern mortal.

It was nearly noon by the time all of the seven were together at the campsite, and the combined energy level was palpable.

"We need to be over there in an hour or so," Jake alerted. "With all our stuff. We won't be able to come back here til nearly dark."

"They'll really be rolling out the red carpet, it seems," Poppy remarked.

"That's cause you guys are really good," Hope said. "They're excited."

"And because they're all pros, with an eye for detail," Jake explained. "This is a big deal. They want it all to happen just so."

"We'll kill it, I can feel it!" Gabe was psyched.

"I'm nervous," Darcy confessed. "So many people!"

Grace wasn't having it. "Nonsense, you're a bigger show off than your mum!"

"Just pretend you're at Duke Street. Concentrate on the stage, you're just jamming with a bunch of guys," Hope advised.

They turned up by the stage just before one-thirty and were led around to the band's encampment. These people definitely were not roughing it. The gang was properly looked after, as well. Hot showers before changing into the nicest clothes they'd brought. A buffet was laid out, and they grazed and got acquainted with some of the crew and band member's families. They didn't know who was who, introductions were without titles. It was 'Hi, I'm Jason,' or 'Hey guys, I'm Susan, this is Pat.' They were made to feel relaxed and comfortable.

Then they met the rest of the band. Page did the honors. As if! Robin walked right up to Jon.

"Hey Fishman, where's your muumuu?"

"Oh, I only wear it while performing, or campaigning for Bernie Sanders."

"Okay."

"Trey, what a pleasure! I was telling Page yesterday you guys should tour abroad more. I could break the band big in England."

"Ah, you must be Jacob."

The twins were chatting up Mike, and he was paying attention.

"Keep it up Mike," Grace said. "You'll supplant John Entwistle as our favorite bassist."

"That's big praise ladies. Ole Thunderfingers is the man! I hear you sing back-up and handle security."

"We do indeed," Hope answered. "Are you going to behave?"

He grinned. "Until you tell me not to."

"Thanks, I think."

Page took the floor. "Well folks, we were thinking we should all sit and have a little session. We can go over these arrangements and sift out the vocals and just see if we need to tweak anything."

"Good idea," Robin said. "It'll make us feel more comfortable."

"I've heard you guys, don't forget. You'll be more than fine. We actually would like some feedback; you tell us how to make this work better."

"Fine. Let's do it."

So they played, and talked, and tweaked, and altered, and enjoyed it all immensely. The guys went off to change for the set while the gang went up on stage so the sound engineers could mic up their instruments and test them. These sound guys were meticulous, their equipment the latest. All Robin, Darcy, and Gabe had to do was breathe on their instruments to be heard.

Showtime came. There was plenty of space to see the band from the side of the stage, some of it elevated. The seven joined some of the family and crew to take it all in. Nice work if you can get it. Looking out over the crowd was dizzying, and surreal. There was about to be a happening.

Phish took the stage as the roar of the phans enveloped the scene. They opened with "Runaway Jim" then genre jumped through a half dozen songs, including "Tube," "Punch you in the Eye," and even "Bouncing Around the Room," before settling into "Roggae," a nice little mellow meanderer. This was the Eclectibles' cue. Instruments at the ready they awaited their intro. Trey stepped to the microphone.

"Good evening! How we doin' so far?" The response was positive. "We'd like to introduce our new friends to everyone. I know some of you have already met them, or at least heard them. They've come all the way from Liverpool, in England! Wow, yeah, and what's more, they came over in a yellow submarine! So please welcome them to the stage everyone, the Eclectibles!"

A chair was brought out for Gabe, placed between Mike in the middle and Trey on the right, stage facing. Robin and Darcy were between Mike and Page, on the left. Poppy had her own mic, next to Trey's. They saluted the crowd with their bows. Heightened anticipation coursed through the audience.

Trey, with the slightest backing from Mike and Fish, played the intro to "If I Could." And with the chord change he sang:

Take me to another place, she said

And Poppy answered:

Take me to another time

Then again:

Run with me across the ocean

Float me on a silver cloud

This she extended, leading into the chorus, which they sang together:

If I could I would, but I don't know how

If I could I would, but I don't know how

If I could I would, and I'd take you now

The band's steady rhythm through the chorus died back down, even lighter than the beginning, to highlight the second verse duet. This time it was Poppy first:

Stay with me till time turns over
I want to feel my feet leave the ground
Take me where the whispering breezes
Can left me up and spin me around

A second chorus ensued. At its end the strings, in a supporting role thus far, came to the fore, strident and ever insistent. It also cued an addition to the chorus, which again they shared:

If I could I would, take you now
Hear you laughing as we go, take you now
Flipping backwards through doors and through the windows
Take you now, I'm melting into nothing

Two more simple half choruses while bass, drums, and keys built the momentum, leading to one last chorus, then the strings took over.

Phish sat on the groove while the Eclectibles delivered a stunning, forceful 12 note melody, changing pitch until high on the scale all four guys sang their plea, and Poppy's answer, always the same but varying in delivery:

If I could I would
But I don't know how
If I could I would
But I don't know how
If I could I would
But I don't know how

Then all seven musicians quickly, but gently, brought it all back down to earth.

You could hear a pin drop, for about a second.

"Oh man, we don't get to play that song often. Thanks guys." Trey was smile bound. "Okay folks, now it should come as no surprise, back home these people have a second gig, as members of the Royal Liverpool Philharmonic Orchestra. I can't even hardly say it!" The audience ate it up. "We hope to make them feel at home with these next couple of songs."

Page got things started. The man had so many keyboards it was hard to tell what he was playing. It was, however, almost instantly recogniz-able. Poppy was side stage for this one, Trey did the honors:

Let me take you down cause I'm going to
Strawberry Fields, nothing is real, and nothing to get hung about.
Strawberry Fields forever

This was iconic John Lennon. The chorus came first, followed by the verse. The strings came in on the second chorus. The album's orchestration featured cello, and Gabe stayed true to the original. His mum and sister got to have a bit of a frolic with Page; together they subbed for the album's horns.

Through two more cycles they played on, the music swirling and weaving its way through the psychedelic soup. The lyrics begged transla-tion, but was better off leaving that to the listener.

In the last chorus the last line, "Strawberry Fields forever," was repeated three times. Then the confused jumble of sounds that served as the album's fade out was changed to a five-minute improvisational jam. Phish 202. Inde-scribable, except to say that the stars of the show laid it down for their guests to play on. And play on they did, Gabe locking into Mike, feeding on his bass line and adding to its depth and texture while the girls raged with Page.

B. Getz and company were euphoric. They were close to the stage, their eyes disbelieving what their ears would swear to. Live music is a series of moments; this was one not soon forgotten. Some of their own, plucked from the crowd and connecting with their anointed gods.

Trey looked around at his bandmates as waves of adulation and appreciation washed over them. They were quietly amazed at what just happened. You could almost hear what they were thinking, 'fuck it, let's double down!'

Page's opening piano chords drew a gasp from even the crew, they were going for the holy grail. Poppy stepped to the mic and took a deep breath:

I read the news today, oh boy
About a lucky man who made the grade
And though the news was rather sad
Well I just had to laugh
I saw the photograph

She sang all four verses as Page led the others through the tale. The guy in the car blew his mind, was he really from the House of Lords? The film about the English army, did they really win the war? You just have to read the book!

The she addressed the crowd, telling them all:

I'd love to turn you on

Instead, Page led them down the garden path, then the rabbit hole as the band followed, creating a cacophonous din, the intensity building to the sudden release.

The whole structure changed during this middle part, pacier and steady. Trey took the mic and described the start to "Everyman's Day":

Woke up, fell out of bed, dragged a comb across my head
Found my way downstairs and drank a cup,
And looking up, I noticed I was late
Found my coat, and grabbed my hat,
Made the bus in seconds flat
Found my way upstairs and had a smoke
And somebody spoke and I went into a dream

A dream like segue followed, back to the original structure and societal confusion:

I read the news today, oh boy

This time the din built and became incessant; something was really going on here. After all, wasn't the end of the world just hours away?

The final chord, struck by everyone simultaneously and allowed to die on its own, was replaced by appreciative mayhem. They just wouldn't stop voicing their pleasure at the unexpected quality of what they'd witnessed. The Eclectibles took their bows and exited backstage to a bunch of hugs and high-fives.

They finished the set side stage, sipping water and groovin' on the band. "Split Open and Melt" was performed, along with "Horn" and "Guyute." "After Midnight" closed the session, a preview cautioning the listeners to be ready for the coming marathon.

In the interim they stayed at the campsite, mostly out of sight. They were determined to see out the last set; if the band could play all night then they could damn sure stay up to cheer them through it. A toast was proposed at seven; it was midnight on Merseyside. Grace had a question;

it stumped the rest. "What time is this millennium thingy happening, which time zone?" Wow, no one had thought of that. Or was it already happening, hour by hour, the planet brought to its knees little by little, east to west.

Ben had thought of it. He'd been down at the *Echo* when midnight first struck, somewhere out in the Pacific. So far so good. New Zealand and Australia were still above water. He didn't believe it all anyway.

At the other end of the scale was Colly. Cyril was careful not to tease her, she was the superstitious one. It made no sense to tell her they were powerless to affect the situation, and that Ben was almost sure to be right—it was a non-issue. She believed all of mankind was careening towards the apocalypse!

CHAPTER 51
SATURDAY, 1 JANUARY

After midnight, we're gonna let it all hang down

Aw hell, the computers didn't even take a dump. At least Colleen had settled down, somewhat. She wouldn't totally relax until tomorrow, when the whole world would have a chance to take stock and declare itself fit for the 21st century. From where Cyril stood at the moment, it was hard to maintain any sense of alarm or concern.

He was in Greenbank Park with Amos and Otis, and it was obvious that Mother Nature wasn't having any of this doomsday chatter. It was a beautiful morning, fairly cold, but dry and clear. The pups were sniffing up the brush around the lake, Cy trailing behind, the landscape becoming clearer with the rising sun.

They ended up under the yew. Cy took a seat. He was in no hurry to get back inside, times like this were rare. His job required him to be elsewhere nearly every day, often out of town. No complaints; he felt lucky to still be in the game, but he also loved his clan, and cherished time spent in their company. Just over thirty years had passed since he and

Luke, Dani, Ben, and Abbas decided to make a home in their 'new world.' Looking around now it seemed a masterstroke. Together they'd accomplished so much more than they could have individually.

Cyril saw change coming. He and Colleen had talked about it recently. Bashir's talks about coalition had turned to thoughts of legacy. The Tweeners had apparently satisfied their wanderlust and were content in place. And the elders, well, they were getting elderly. He and the rest of the Fab Five were still fulfilling their unspoken vows to make it on Merseyside. They may all decide to retire to warmer climes one day, but for now they were going to continue, together, to give back to the city that fostered their idealistic dreams all those years ago. So, where was this change Cy was predicting coming from?

The Six of course, Cy's godchildren. They grew up hearing the stories, seeing the photographs, even reading about it in the newspapers. They had their curiosity stoked early and often with trips abroad to places like Edinburgh, Judibana, St. Petersburg, Nazare, and Port of Spain. Their parents had fallen in together, went on a big adventure, and found their future. It wouldn't be a big surprise should their children pop up one day and make a big announcement. Enshallah, as Abbas would say, bring it on. The Merseyside Six would be fine; they were strong, smart, and forward thinking. He should know, he helped raise them.

Five time zones earlier and over 4,000 miles away, the Six were not concerned with the future, or the past, or even the new century that had just turned over. They were dancing in front of the stage with all their new friends to a 22-minute version of "Sand."

Phish entered the stage area from over the crowd on a 15-foot-long hotdog and bun just before midnight. They dismounted and wasted no time getting in a couple of songs before playing "Auld Lang Syne" after the countdown. After a few more tunes, they and their phans were on ABC with Peter Jennings during the unveiling of a new song, "Heavy Things." As it turned out, Big Cypress was the biggest New Years show on the planet.

The Seven had started the set at the sound booth again, only this time they had met a lot of the crew and were invited into the controls area itself. Robin was still there. The guys were showing off the gear, and giving her tips on some of the available equipment and set-ups for the Eclectibles.

The Six sat as long as they could, until the music called for them to help feed the beast, merging with the tribe and letting loose.

Phish soldiered on, following "Sand" up with "Slave," "Reba, " "Axilla, " "David Bowie, " and an "After Midnight" reprise, among others. The gang couldn't and didn't care to catalog every moment in their minds in real time; they just gave themselves up to it. The night passed in a swirl of light and sound, the participants savoring an experience unlike anything they might bear witness to again.

Dawn was nearing. "Piper" and "Free" gave em all a second wind as the band weaved snippets and teases into a tapestry of their catalog through the years. One of Robin's favorites, "Bug," was performed as light filtered through the eastern sky. And, as the sun broke the horizon, the opening fanfare, titled "Sunrise," from Strauss' "Also Sprach Zarathustra," greeted its arrival. A nice touch.

The set had lasted seven-and-a-half hours. Another nice touch saw the revelers back to their campsite, "Here Comes the Sun," The Beatles' version. Thanks guys!

Chapter 52
Tuesday, 11 January

In my Liverpool home
We speak with an accent exceedingly rare
Meet under a statue exceedingly bare
And if you want a cathedral, we've got one to spare
In my Liverpool home

It wasn't outwardly noticeable, but much of the clan had a bit of sparkle in their eyes, and extra spring in their step. Aleah had not been surprised; she'd seen it build in the time leading up to the new year. There had been uncertainty, even some angst, all brought on by the anticipation of what the first page of the new calendar would bring. She was happy; more than a few of her loved ones came to her for counsel, her calm demeanor a steady force to reassure their confidence. Now they all seemed back in the groove, speaking to her of the future excitedly rather than with trepidation.

This morning Aleah had decided to check on her charges in person. The day was sunny and she'd been indoors too much of late. She walked through Sefton Park and took the bus up Queen's Drive to

Allerton Road. From there it was only two-and-a-half blocks to Adam's Apple, one of a row of storefronts between Mapledale and Rosedale.

Abbas was wearing an apron and eating a plum.

"Hello Maman, this is a nice surprise!"

"Good morning, Abbas, love your style."

"Thank you, it saves on laundry. The staff calls me Pigpen."

"I can see. I think you have the shop's entire menu on the front of your smock. By the way, where's John and Sylvia?"

"They took advantage of the sunny day and went to the zoo in Chester."

"Splendid! They are learning to be pensioners."

"Old habits die hard."

"And where is my sweet daughter-in-law?"

"Out back, checking a delivery."

She put her hand on his arm, "How is it all working out so far, son?"

"It's good. Still a lot to get a handle on, but I like the routine. It's steady."

"Robin feels the same?"

"Very much so. She knew what to expect; the shop had been a part of her life all those years. Have you a shopping list?"

"No no, I'm just out and about, also taking advantage of the nice weather. I would like a plum though. And I'll say hello to Robin and be on my way."

She caught the bus on Smithdown and headed northwest towards the City Centre to the Edge Hill Animal Hospital. At the front desk Stacy said Dani was tied up with a client but sent her to the kennel area where she found Poppy.

"Look at you!"

"Aleah!"

They hugged, Poppy delightedly surprised at the visit and Aleah impressed with the new look.

"Poppy Carter, RVN. Registered Veterinary Nurse. I just saw Abbas. His new work cloak had only tomato and grape stains.

"Oh, I'm sure to acquire some even nastier stuff on this before long. How are you and Splotch getting on?"

"Wonderfully, now that I've accepted my place on her staff. And how about you and Gabriel, things are good?"

"I'm head over heels! Your grandson is so thoughtful and sweet. We really came together in Florida. I think it's because we were in a different place, experiencing new things."

"I agree. You had to escape the past to see the future."

Poppy had to get another cuddle. "You are so wise, always saying the right thing, put so simply." She had another immediate thought, but hesitated, then decided to go ahead. "I miss Hassan. I wish he were here to see Gabe and I together."

"He spoke of it, he and Neff both. They often sat around and predicted the future."

"Really, even matters of the heart?"

"Absolutely! And there's more to come."

Poppy was wild-eyed. "Oh, do tell!"

"Patience, my child, we mustn't rush Allah's plan."

"What a tease!"

"Nothing is certain. It is why we say Enshallah."

Stacy called a black cab for Aleah, which took her over and down to Duke Street, in the Ropewalks district of the City Centre. She hadn't seen Judith since just before Christmas so they had a catch-up while waiting for Lucas to finish with a phone call.

"Where's Benjamin?"

"Out on a photoshoot. Poor chap, he had to go up to Bootle for the opening of a beauty salon."

"And both boys are out, I suppose."

"Yes, Gabe's at the Phil and Jake is in Blackpool scouting a couple of players."

"So the agency has a solicitor now."

"Indeed, although Jake says lawyers, like doctors, never stop going to school."

"Especially where international law is concerned, I imagine."

"No doubt. Luke's excited. He said that's where things are headed, that all footballers will one day have agents and wages will soar with money from the broadcasters. Okay, he's off the line, hang on."

He came and chatted with the both of them, and he had some news.

"We finally got Darcy's new contract sorted. I didn't expect such a hassle."

"What was the problem?" Aleah asked.

"Money. Despite her being one of the youth symphony's youngest ever players, and despite the fact that they wanted her in the senior orchestra before now, they still presented us with a basic rookie deal."

"And?" Jude prodded.

"We weren't having it. Their claims of her being so young still, and therefore a tad immature, were baseless. They even suggested the 'bright lights' of the Royal Philharmonic may be a little much for her presently."

"That's daft!"

"And I told them so, along with the fact that less than a fortnight ago she was playing to 80 thousand under some very bright lights."

"What was the wind-up?"

"She got the same terms as her brother. Then we got him a raise."

"Well done Lucas," Jude complimented.

"In Iran we would say he talked the camel out of his hump."

It was nearly one when Aleah emerged out into the warming day, inviting enough to walk down Duke Street to the Anglican Cathedral and stroll the lower gardens on its east side. From there she took the bus back down to Sefton Park, stopping off in Waverly for some lunch.

The new owners hadn't changed the name of the chippy; the sign still read 'McTimons Fish and Chips.' They hadn't changed the recipes either, or the staff. No reason to jinx a good thing.

George and April were just about done with the lunch rush, so they sat and ate with Aleah, eager to be with such a kind and classy lady. They filled each other in on the latest news in general and specifically in each other's households. It was so heartening to Aleah to hear the happiness in April and George's voices. Both these souls had arrived in Liverpool with not a lot of hope or harmony in their lives before finding friends and building an existence to thrive upon. The final piece of the puzzle was finding each other. Their devotion to each other obvious and complete.

Aleah was so happy for them, April had her Georgie Boy and

George, well, he didn't care what month it was. To him it was always April.

CHAPTER 53
SATURDAY, 22 JANUARY

Poppies at the cenotaph
The cynics can't afford to laugh
I heard it on the telegraph
There's Uzis on a street corner

Lucas was going through the mail while munching on some plantain chips. Mundane stuff mostly, save a letter from Kosovo. It had an unfamiliar postmark; the stationery was unusual as well. The penmanship, however, was definitely Ermina's. She and Agnesa were in the capital, Pristina, in a refugee camp. Luke's mood darkened; the news got worse.

Keeping the peace in Kosovo after the war was nearly impossible; there was just too much ingrained hatred. The population was of mainly Serbian and Albanian descent, oil and water. The northern city of Mitrovica had become a forcefully divided municipality, similar to Berlin during the Cold War. Elsewhere sporadic incidents of violence broke out, like in Krushë e Madhe.

Ermina wrote that ten days ago a group of men, remnants of the Serbian Special Forces, rounded up the residents of a half dozen farms, including the Muratis, and put them on a bus to Pristina. Then they burned everything to the ground, livestock included. Ermina's two vizslas were shot.

Luke seethed; this was the kind of senseless cruelty that made him crazy. Innocent people, with no geo-political agenda, being set upon simply because of their heritage. Ermina and Agnesa, who'd already lost so much, now on the brink.

Daniela and Poppy were next door at the Ardavans. Luke took the letter and gave it to Abbas, the look on his face prompting his pal to sit down and start reading.

"What's up niño?" Dani asked, sensing the concern.

"Bad news from Kosovo."

Abbas finished reading the letter, dropped it on the table, and wordlessly walked into the kitchen.

Luke explained the situation; all four girls and he went to the table to suss it out.

"So is the war back on. Did it ever stop?" asked Darcy.

"All the principals came to an agreement, so officially there's no war," Luke said. "Some people just can't forgive and forget. And there's not much left of the country's law enforcement."

"What about NATO? They forced a cease fire."

"But they're only for military engagement, Poppy. They can't maintain any reasonable amount of local policing."

"So Lucas, how does it all end?" Robin posed.

"It doesn't, in my opinion. Not until the rest of the former Yugoslavia recognizes Kosovo as an independent state and Kosovo itself repairs its infrastructure."

Abbas came back and sat down with a glass of water. "That will take a very long time."

"Too long for Ermina," Dani remarked.

"What can we do, if anything?"

"Can we send her some money?"

"And a care package, like with clothes and personal stuff."

"Even with an address, would she get it?"

Lucas then came up with the obvious, although the girls would not say it out loud. "Someone has to take it there personally."

Silence. Poppy and Darcy thought it prudent to stay mum. Dani and Robin weren't going to say a word. They wanted to hear what these two were thinking. Abbas decided to dip his toe in the water.

"We would only have to fly in and out. They're in Pristina now."

"I wonder how far from the airport she is," Luke said.

"I imagine security would be good in the refugee camp," Abbas offered.

"We could be in and out in a couple of days," Luke added. "C'mon ladies, whaddya think?"

Dani had been fairly quiet so far, but she had been thinking. "We do need to help. It's horrible what's happened." She hesitated, and when she spoke again, it was with great resolve. "But a care package won't get it done. Ermina and Agnesa have nothing, and now they have nowhere to go. I'm doubtful they'll survive the winter, defeated and hopeless. I'm going to Kosovo Lucas. You get to Sir Philip, or Gene Pine, or anyone else you need to. I'm not coming home without that poor woman and her child!"

CHAPTER 54
TUESDAY, 25 JANUARY

To the hope and will you gave,
you were the brave.
And one day, when I hear your children sing,
freedom will ring.

Swissair flight #936 departed Flughafen Zürich just after eleven in the morning. It banked to the southeast after clearing the dense fog at ground level and reached cruising speed and altitude over the Alps.

It had been a busy three days, gathering as much information as possible and handling the logistics of the trip itself. Luke eased his seat back a bit and closed his eyes. He probably wouldn't sleep but needed to gather himself. Once the plane landed he would have to be sharp.

Dani sat beside him, nervous but resolute. She came for a reason with a clear objective. Not achieving it was out of the question, even though there was nothing to suggest that the quest would be successful.

Some groundwork was done. The first item of business was a call to Sir Philip. He queried a few of his contacts and told Lucas that given the situation in Kosovo in general, emigration to the U.K. shouldn't be a problem. Of course, this meant that all parties were subjected to the pace at which the bureaucracy operated, time that Luke and Dani didn't think the Murati's had. This they could get around if Ermina and Agnesa had valid passports. That way they could enter the country as tourists while the rest was being sorted.

They landed southwest of the city at Pristina International just before one. The weather was a little better than in Zürich—chilly and breezy under a partly cloudy sky. They cleared immigration and customs and found the taxi queue outside.

"Stadiumi Ramiz Sadiku, të lutem," Luke directed the driver. It was a short trip. The camp was on the south side of the city, adjacent to the University of Kosovo's vast medical campus, the Qendra Klinike.

The Ramiz Sadiku was a football stadium, the pitch dotted with communications equipment, medical and Red Cross stations, lots of security, and to Luke's eye, maybe 75 white tents.

They hung back, away from the gate, watching the come and go. Dani was anxious but stood by; she could almost feel her husband thinking, planning their next move.

Lucas sensed that something was not quite right. Assigned personnel were going about their business, the food tent was seeing steady traffic, and supplies were coming in sporadically through a smaller manned entrance off to his right.

But there was conflict here, and no small amount of unease. Something was simmering. Just inside, small groups of people were in serious but hushed conversation. These people were not in uniform and didn't appear to be acting in any official capacity. And there were watchers posted outside. They were subtle but they weren't pros, pretending to read the paper or haggling with a street vendor their ruse. What really concerned Luke was the posted security. They were lax, talking and smoking with each other, even at the gate. This entry point could be breached; Luke was about to prove it.

A small entourage approached, seven or eight people. They looked like the press, led by two uniformed officers. As they walked by, Luke turned to Dani.

"Look confidently straight ahead and stay next to me." With that he fell in right behind the group and together they were waved through the gate, peeling off once they were out of sight.

They maintained an officious air as they strode through the rows of tents, hoping to find the Muratis before being challenged. Most of the refugees were in their tents avoiding the chill. Dani was hesitant to start opening tent flaps but saw a group of children in an open area on the far side. As they approached, they saw a football being kicked about, a small swarm of boys and girls in pursuit. Luke waited for a chance to talk to them; it didn't take but a minute.

A young girl disengaged herself from the fray and stood still, staring their way. Luke smiled and walked towards her as Dani hoped beyond hope.

"Përshëndetje Agnesa, a ju kujtohet mua?" He wasn't sure if she recognized him or not or if she was just not believing it.

"Lucas," she finally said, walking the last few feet into his arms. Still, the kid's eyes seemed haunted.

"Mund të shkojme të takojme të nenen tende?" he asked, wanting to see her mother.

"Po, mund të mar," she said, and started to lead the way before calling out to one of her mates. "Jak, eja!"

A boy, smaller than Agnesa, broke from the pack and ran over, all pink cheeked and scruffy kneed.

"Përshëndetje Jak, unë jam Lucas. Kjo është Dani. Agnesa, Dani është gruaja ime." They were both quiet, taken by the presence and manner of this exotic-looking lady.

Ermina, seated on a folding chair, looked up when the children came in and started to remind them to close the flap. She began to rise as the two strangers entered, then froze, the look on her face indescribable. By the time she and Luke embraced, her and Dani were already crying.

Five minutes later Luke asked the big question, "Do you have passports?"

"Yes, we have them. My husband Arben was thinking we may have to leave Kosovo. Maybe we all go to Greece."

"Do you know anyone in Greece?"

"No."

Dani went to the cot next to where Ermina was sitting and took both her hands into her own.

"You know three people in England, and we all live in the same place where there is more than enough space for you and Agnesa. Ermina, come with us, and be a part of our family."

Tears were streaming down her face now, inside her emotions raged. "You are so kind, bless you."

Then she steeled herself and continued. "I have Jak now," looking at the tyke, who was wondering what was going on and looking pretty freaked out. "His family lived close to me. He had an older brother also."

She started to tell the story but, in the end, could only say they were all gone.

"This is not a problem," Dani said with a more cheerful tone. "We need another boy."

Ermina was incredulous.

"Does Jak have a passport?" Luke asked.

"Yes, his parents worked for the government. They also, I think, were looking at the future."

Lucas decided to scout around outside. They needed to git before his wife adopted the whole camp. "You guys get ready, but bring as little as possible. And be ready to move."

He went back to where the kids were playing; it was much quieter on this side of the stadium. There was a gate, apparently one used for turf maintenance equipment and the like, manned by only one guard. The guy looked bored, listening to a transistor radio.

"All right, we're on," he said to his newly expanded family. He explained the situation to Dani and Ermina as they walked toward this now alert guard. This guy was going to either accept a wad of cash or find himself under one of the stands in a bad way.

Luckily, he took the bribe and let himself be tied and gagged and hidden away. This gave Luke time to get away clean and the guard an excuse should there be a fallout later. The dude even insisted on Luke belting him a good one.

"Leave a mark!" the man said in Albanian. Luke liked that; glad the guy was not Serbian.

Their research beforehand led them on side streets to the Golden Hotel, where Ermina booked two rooms for the night. This kept management from asking Luke for his passport. Dani stayed with the children while Lucas and Ermina went shopping for a set of clothes, some personals, and some food for the evening.

The plan was to go to the airport in the morning and get the hell out of dodge. Tonight was all about bathing, eating, and sleeping.

The three Kosovans were pale, thin, and haggard. At least now their eyes had a spark, even if it was still deep within those thousand-yard stares.

CHAPTER 55
THURSDAY, 27 JANUARY

Everybody's at war these days,
let's have a mini surrender.
I need some sentimental hygiene.

Morning seemed to arrive a little early today, Dani thought as she put her housecoat and slippers on and started down the stairs.

"Morning mum."

"Hey Pops, thanks for putting some water on."

"Sure thing. You're not coming in today, are you?"

"I'm planning to, in the afternoon."

"Okay, but it's not necessary if you change your mind. We've no surgeries scheduled til Monday."

"Good, I didn't like leaving you alone. Thanks for stepping up."

"Not a prob, Ms. Fixer."

"No thank you. I'm not built for that kind of stuff."

"You guys lucked out I guess."

"Oh God Poppy, it's still freaking me out. We were less than an hour out of the camp when it was attacked. We may not have known at all if Ermina hadn't turned on the radio!"

"Ben said he was going to the *Echo* today for more details. Dad was pretty cool in the clutch, huh?"

"Yes, damn it, and thank heavens! He knew something was up, and spent a long time just in the shadows, looking and planning. Once he'd made up his mind, though, we were in and out of that stadium in less than an hour." She hesitated, realizing something she hadn't' before. "You know, except for some incidents around town, I've never seen your father in one of these situations. Hard to explain, but it's like a different person altogether. He's a very capable operator."

"Maybe he should be a private detective."

"Hush girl, my heart can't take it."

"Good morning."

"Ermina, good morning! How did you sleep?"

"Better. Thank you. The children, they don't sleep so good. Bad dreams."

"Poor souls."

"They need time," Dani said. "That starts today."

"It was hard for Agnesa to see the dogs," Ermina said. "Soon she will love them."

"Hopefully she and Jak will love all our clan. We got home too late last night; they'll all be coming by soon I'm sure."

And come by they did. Kevin and Cheryl with their morning cuppa were on the sofa when Agnesa led Jak down the stairs and peeked around the corner. Shy expressions and two shocks of black hair; for Cheryl it was love at first sight.

It was the same for Colleen, who had hot chocolate and shortbread with them while watching the telly.

Darcy stopped in on her way to the symphony. She and Viola entertained the youngsters with a song.

"That's Abbas' daughter," Dani told Ermina, who said Agnesa was taken with Abbas and his flute last year.

Abbas himself, sensing their new guests' diet had been lacking of late, brought a sack full of fruit home at noon. He teared up seeing how thin and pale they were, but it didn't dampen the reunion.

After lunch Dani took the three of them to the clinic. She busied herself catching up with the last couple of days' business while Poppy gave the tour. Ermina was wowed, something Dani was planning to tap into.

Rosie brought Elizabeth over from Calderstones mid-afternoon for a romp in the park. Lizzy was five, the same age as Jak, Agnesa was now six. Otis led the three of them around, chasing each other and exploring while Dani and Rose sat under the yew.

"So, the clan's got another crusader," Rosie noted.

"A one-off, that was."

"These two are adorable! It's just heart breaking what they've been through."

"They always say kids are resilient, I hope it's true."

"They'll come around Dani, they're still so young."

"Then so will Ermina. She's smart, and strong. I think once the children are okay she'll start to thrive."

"Cyrus suggested that I go through Lizzy's clothes for Agnesa. They look about the same size, maybe even Nathan's saved some of his old wardrobe."

"That's a great idea! Cheryl and Robin are getting some things for Ermina until we can organize a shopping trip."

"Oh, I want to come!"

"Of course!" Dani had a laugh. "You are your mother's daughter; she outfitted the whole Fab Five back in the day."

The evening brought a fresh new spate of callers to the Carter household. Lucas got home in time for a kickaround with Jak. The boy was football mad.

Robin took Ermina on a tour of her closet for a coat, scarf, and an old pair of wellies. They had a nice chat, Robin learning about Ermina's past life. It was good to talk about even the unpleasantness of what had occurred, part of the healing process.

The Pines and Colleen came over for dinner. Cyril promised to get there as soon as he could. Beer and roasted chestnuts served as appetizers. Poppy was showing Jak and Agnesa how to play Chutes and Ladders down on the floor while Otis was planning to snatch some of the game pieces. The rest were anxious to hear more details on what happened back in Pristina.

"What time did you say you left the stadium?" Ben asked.

"After three," Luke replied. "Probably quarter past."

"Well, the assault took place at three fifty. Four masked gunmen shot their way into the camp and detonated a small bomb at the NATO field office. At least thirteen dead, quite a few more injured. I'm sorry Ermina." Dani reached over and took her hand.

There wasn't much left to say. It was just more information, a sadness to realize, process, and let fade. Most everyone at the table had unspoken thoughts and feelings, but they weren't secrets. They were fully aware of both what did and did not happen. It was time to turn the page.

And change the subject. Thank goodness for Cyril.

"All right, everyone just relax. I'm home."

"Cy!" several of them called.

"Siwul Barcan!" the smallest of them shouted, then ran over just to stand before the man.

"It is you!" Ermina said, obviously amazed. "Your picture was on the wall in Jak's house. His father's most favorite football player!"

Cy picked young Jak up and hugged him tightly.

"Happens everywhere I go."

CHAPTER 56
WEDNESDAY, 2 FEBRUARY

Hope and Grace were breaking with tradition and taking a class together. This they tempered by sitting quite far apart in the small auditorium in Armstrong Hall. It was a class they were looking forward to, both for the topics it covered and because it was being taught by Sandi Wong.

Professor Wong, a petite woman of Asian descent, was educated at Rice and Yale and had a PhD in sociology. She was new at Colorado College, highly touted and sought after, her classes filling up quickly. Grace had met her last week; her easy smile and cheerful demeanor could not mask the obvious intelligence within.

The schools' block plan meant this was the second day of classes for the three-and-a half-week course. It wasn't a course the twins needed for their major in biology, but it was the type of subject that interested them greatly. Self and Society was its title, man, this could be taken in a lot of different directions.

There was no lecture today. The professor wanted to take the pulse of the class; see what kind of group she had.

"We're fortunate to have such a diverse student body here at C.C. This allows us to compare and celebrate the differences in our cultures. But how do we consider what we have in common? As a species we can differ in our appearance and behavior which can lead to judgement and classification by others. But again, as individual entities, we all begin our journey in the same boat." She looked around the room; wheels were turning. Now to set the hook.

"So, what changes, how is it we develop into what we become with respect to our place in society? Any ideas?"

"Regional influence," short, stocky, bearded white guy said.

"Culture," even shorter bespectacled white girl offered.

"Religion," this from a Latina girl with a Los Lobos hoodie.

"D.N.A., we're born only looking and acting similar; what's inside us shows itself with time," declared the probable science major with the punk haircut and leather jacket.

"The folly of man and the seven deadly sins. Our imperfections and overpopulation are combining to create an ever-worsening cause and effect reactionary society headed for extinction." Hello little mousey shy girl sitting in the back.

Sandi Wong thought it to be most entertaining.

The twins had lunch dates after class; there was a two-hour break before the afternoon session. Brothers Rolf and Heinz Muller, from Switzerland no less. They lived on campus, and had bicycles, so the four of them rode over to Mountain Mamas. It was a popular place, on Uintah, a little past Mesa. The market had some tables. They all browsed around and ended up with a bowl of soup each and a shared couple of sandwiches.

This was a first, for both sets of siblings. They were out with a pair of identical twins. Talk about a sociology experiment!

"Do you get stared at a lot?" Hope asked Rolf.

"Yes, it's typical. At least now we're not the only ones."

"And stupid questions," added Heinz. "We get those a lot."

Grace flashed a conspiratorial grin. "You know, we could really stir up some shit up around campus."

Rolf perked up, "I like your spirit."

"We do it at home," Heinz said. "Chaos and confusion are our specialties, but mind you, we only use our powers for good."

"And mischief," his brother added.

"What do you think of Dr. Wong?" Hope asked.

"I like her very much; she seems so smart. A real people person, as they say."

"That's her job, Rolf," Grace pointed out.

"Yes, but she knows what questions to ask."

"I get ya," Hope said. "It's like she knows how to push the right buttons, get people to engage without a bunch of boring lectures."

"I wonder what the afternoon will be like."

"I'm wondering about the whole month."

"What do you guys think about this morning?" Grace prodded. "I think we can agree the world could use some improving."

"For sure," Heinz said. "For me it's the way people change. We are born so innocent and pure, then the world changes us. In the end it depends how much."

"Basically, I agree," Hope started. "But also, I see it in terms of generation. Children look up to their parents, really prop them up as special. At some point they see that their folks are not perfect, just human, like everyone else. Some take it as an excuse to be less than they should, or could be. Then, as they age, they get bitter."

"But some people don't get a typical upbringing, sister. They have a whole different experience growing up where the world seems unfair."

"That's true," Rolf said. "Some people are the opposite, as well. They have, how do you call it, the silver spoon."

"And still they may be screwed up," Grace added. "What do you think Heinz, who or what makes people go wrong?"

"I cannot say. I am Swiss, we are neutral."

The afternoon session featured a debate, cultural or regional. Dr. Wong would introduce a subject, or item of pop culture, or even a pattern of behavior. Then the class would decide if it was cultural or regional in origin. It was a very spirited session.

The subject continued to be discussed at the dinner table that evening. Tim put it rather succinctly.

"Some people leave their mark on this world. Some just leave a stain."

CHAPTER 57
FRIDAY, 11 FEBRUARY

If I could through myself set your spirit free
I'd lead your heart away, see you break, break away
Into the light, and to the day

Daniela had been entertaining a wide range of emotions of late, pretty much ever since she boldly declared her intention to go to the Balkans on a rescue mission. It was her first experience going up country, as Luke would say—a real eye opener. Now the unease she felt was down to the sense of responsibility she held towards Ermina, Agnesa, and Jak. Thank goodness for the clan.

Cheryl's retirement was short lived; she'd become a part time combination student-teacher. She was learning Albanian while Agnesa and Jak were learning English. Lucas had taken an interest in the project; it was a great idea. Cheryl would give the kids a jump start in the subject, then, after a while, they would progress quickly due to their immersion in an English-speaking society. It would be interesting to see how long it would be until they would be ready for Bashir to take on at primary school.

Ermina's English was pretty good, but Dani didn't think it was quite good enough in one respect. In order for her to get her vet's license, she had to be more proficient in the technical and procedural language of the profession. Poppy had done the legwork, contacting the Royal College of Veterinary Surgeons to get the list of requirements necessary to certify Ermina to practice locally. Here they lucked out.

The government had a list of vet colleges abroad whose curricula they recognized. One of them was in Budapest, where Ermina learned her trade.

So, she had her passport, license, and was getting better in English. Besides paying the registration fee, she was supposed to have a reference stating she was in good standing with the veterinary establishment back home. Of course this was impossible at present. As a solicitor, Jacob might have to get involved. He could argue for an exception, citing her status as a refugee. Sir Philip had already secured visas for her and the children.

On a personal note, the three Kosovans were so thankful to be taken in by these kind strangers. Of course Agnesa and Jak couldn't fully grasp the situation. Things were better now, but there was a huge hole in their hearts with the loss of their loved ones and way of life. Ermina felt the same but understood the big picture. What an important day that was back in September when she met Luke and Abbas.

She was born Ermina Majlinda Shoshi, on the 29th of May 1963, in the northeastern Albanian village of Peshkopi. It was right in the middle of Prime Minister Enver Hoxha's reign of iron-fisted control of the country and its people. The Shoshis fled, emigrating to Prizren in Kosovo. It was here she met and married Arben Murati and moved to Krusha e Madhe. This was after her schooling had been completed, part of the reason she and Arben moved to this newly settled area southwest of the capital of Pristina. Arben worked the land and she set up her practice.

The Kuklis were neighbors, also new to the region, and the two couples became close, starting families and building a life. Dardan and Reina, and their sons, Luan and Jak. The Kuklis, gone now except for little Jak, who had witnessed much too much in his short life.

After two-and-a-half weeks the trio had come around some. More time in the sun and around the dinner table had improved their health and appearance. Laughter was rare but smiles were displayed more and more, along with eyes less hooded and more hopeful in their gaze.

There were less nightmares now; Ermina had a bedroom to herself. Poppy relocated to the downstairs study, Neff's old room, while Jak and Agnesa took over her bedroom. She was spending the odd night up at the Duke Street flat more often anyway.

Dani was glad to see a routine being established, important in terms of getting on with the adjustment of a new type of existence. Agnesa and Jak were tutored by Cheryl in the morning and spent the afternoons on outings. They would take turns going to the Duke Street office, the clinic, the pharmacy, or Adam's Apple. Kevin was often the chauffeur; he'd take them to the chippy for lunch then around the city to see the sights.

Ermina spent almost every day at the clinic. The girl had a way with animals. Pets were easier, for the most part, than farm animals. She was gentle and caring, and was learning the operational side of the equipment and the fine points of regulatory procedure.

Ben and Faith were fixing supper for the Greenbank Gang this evening—chicken and corn on the cob on the grill. The Ardavans were tossing a salad and Colly was baking cookies. Dani and Mina, yes, she had a nickname already, got home and bathed and listened while Jak and Aggy, yes, Aggy, she got hers too, spoke excitedly about their ride on the ferry.

Darcy and Poppy, who had classes in the afternoon, arrived with Jake and Gabe and a bouquet of flowers. After the obligatory kick around with Jak in the park, everyone filtered out into the Pine's back garden.

"That boy is destined for the number ten shirt" Jake declared. "He's already got an eye for the pass."

"Not so fast, Mister Agent Man. There are child labor laws to consider," Robin countered.

"Daniela, is that what I think it is?"

"Yes, Cy, would you like a tequeño?"

"Please!"

"This is a nice surprise. When did you find the time?" Abbas asked.

"Mina and I put them together last night. Luke was first home; he got them started."

Ben tended the grill while talking to Cheryl, beers at the ready. Lucas and Gabriel tended the fire pit; the temperature was dropping now that the sun had set. Aggy and Colly were sitting on the other side of the pit watching Jak, Amos, and Otis chase each other about.

Supper was great; food you could eat with your hands while outside was always a wonderful thing. Afterwards it was chairs around the fire and some music.

Ermina had always loved music even though she wasn't a musician herself. To her, Abbas, Robin, and their pair were magical in the way they performed together so effortlessly. Anything and everything they played, sometimes with vocal accompaniment. No one seemed too shy to sing; quite a few added their voices to the mix.

Darcy and Gabe wanted to play one they'd practiced recently, adapting the original's basic piano arrangement for strings. It was "Imagine," John Lennon's solo iconic call for peace. They began the familiar opening chord sequence. Robin and Abbas were going to alternate playing the verses instrumentally.

But just as Robin lifted her bow to begin, Ermina motioned for Agnesa to come sit on her lap. Then she began to hum softly, the melody sweet and low. It took a few lines but suddenly Aggy's voice was clearly heard, her eyes fixed into and beyond the flames

Mbine vetem qiell

Imagjinoni të gjithë njerëzit,

Duke jetuar për sot

It wasn't in English, but still there were smiles and a few tears. Such poignancy and so remarkable, a reminder from one so young.

For the first time in weeks, Daniela felt at ease. Luke noticed, almost immediately. He put his hand on her arm.

"Instant karma's got you girl."

CHAPTER 58
SATURDAY, 4 MARCH

And I used to fly like Peter Pan
All the children flew when I touched their hands

Football is life. A simplistic statement, bold in intent. Hard to argue with, really. A global obsession.

The numbers support the claim. Player salaries, T.V. ratings, ticket and merchandise sales all pointing to the sport's vast popularity.

These factors, however, are not what the enthusiast points to when he or she says football is life. It's the moments, those snapshots in time that become a part of both the psyche and the soul.

Jak Lirim Kukli was living proof of the sport's ability to maintain one's sense of self. The boy had been uprooted from every aspect of familiar life and witnessed far too much ugliness. At five years of age, he had no one to call mother or father. He was understandably timid and rather quiet, and it was anyone's guess who or what inhabited his dreams in the still of night.

Kids are resilient, they say, and Jak was coming around. Football was part of it; somehow he felt safe within the game. People didn't kill each other during a football match.

Jak was standing proud at the moment, and smiling broadly. He was emerging from the tunnel at Prenton Park dressed in a full home kit, walking towards center circle at Rover's captain David Kelly's side.

It was Cyril's idea. He, more than anyone, knew the boy was more at peace in the presence of a football than anywhere else. Ermina was nervous at first but there he was, almost beaming in front of the 10,000 in attendance. Confidently he shook the hand of the officiating crew and opposing players before running off the pitch. A steward escorted him up to the section where the gang was seated, waving at his well-wishers while almost strutting up the stairs.

He and Lucas were living large today, watching the match with a bevy of beauties. Poppy, Darcy, Mina and Aggy were along, Aggy in her own little kit.

It was Rovers versus Rovers today, scheduled kickoff at noon. Blackburn wasn't far away, north of Merseyside in Lancashire. Their side was further up the table than Tranmere; it would be a nice scalp to take.

The first half was cat and mouse, neither team creating much but committed in their endeavor. Tranmere got an early second half goal; Irish international, Alan Mahon, scored from the spot. Then he and Jason Koumas deputized on either side of Wilco Hellinga to lock down the midfield. Stoppage time saw both teams score, tired legs and a lapse in concentration the probable cause.

The 2-1 result greatly pleased the faithful, who remained to cheer their club. A new chant arose from the main stand. Luke wished his son was there:

Blow the whistle, he'll have a go,
On the ball, such a clever fellow,
Roger Wilco, Roger Wilco.
Under pressure, he's so clutch, man!
Wilco Hellinga, he's our Dutchman!
Roger Wilco, Roger Wilco.
Football is life.

A gathering was planned afterwards at the Duke Street rumpus room. It was becoming a tradition after weekend day games. Cy and

Shea showed up with Gareth Roberts, David Kelly, and Wilco, who was still feeling the love.

Jake and Gabe were already present, along with Dani, Geoff, and George. Abbas and Robin would be along after they closed their shop.

"Where's April, Georgie?"

"She should be here directly, Darcy. She's bringing dinner."

"Splendid! Just watching football makes me hungry."

"Hello Ermina, I'm Geoff. Pleased to meet you."

"Hello Geoff. You are in the band, correct?"

"Yes, George and I both. The rest you know, I think."

"The Ardavans, of course. And Dani and Faith."

"How about you?"

"No no," she blushed. "But I can listen very well."

Georgie was getting to know Aggy and Jak, showing the wide-eyed kids around his drum set.

"Percussion is the oldest form of communication, little ones."

Gabe and Jake were getting the players' account of the match; a big win was the general consensus.

"We had trouble creating chances in the final third, but Wilco and his mates stayed in control. It was always just a matter of time," David said.

"We're finally seeing the method in the gaffer's madness," Gareth said. "Your dad told me he was the one to hitch my horse to. Whatever that means."

"My dad was born in Kentucky. He's full of that kind of wisdom, if you will."

The Eclectibles wandered up on stage, one by one, beer in hand. George and Geoff started a groove, at first languid and rubbery. Gabe injected some funk and Darcy some melody. Soon they had it together —Ratdog's "Bury Me Standing." Poppy did the honors:

Once again the crossroads,
And there ain't no moon hanging in the trees.
Goddess lost my number, babe,
Leave me begging baby please.
Bury me standing, I've been too long on my knees.

It sounded really good. Dani took over for the album's next cut, "Lucky Enough," a bit more up-tempo and a bit more forward looking:

And we're going on faith here,
And all of that kind of stuff.
And even grace, if we're lucky enough.

The session lasted nearly an hour before April showed up. There was no lack of volunteers when she asked for the van to be unloaded.

"I can't be bothered," she said bluntly. "I simply must cop a cuddle from these two adorable little Muppets!"

Abbas and Robin came in as everyone was digging in. They grabbed a plate and sat with Lucas, catching up on the day's happenings.

Fresh drinks afterwards, and a trip to the back balcony for some enlightenment prior to another set of music. Poppy and Darcy ceded the stage to Obs and Robs so they and April could dance with the footballers. Mina, Aggy, and Jak, carefree for longer than they could recall, were still reticent to completely let go. They were mesmerized by the band though, and feeling a lightness of spirit.

After all, music is life.

CHAPTER 59
FRIDAY, 24 MARCH

Stand! There's a cross for you to bear,
things to go through if you're goin' anywhere.

"It sure doesn't feel like spring," Filly remarked, adjusting her scarf.

"Only the calendar is making the claim that the season has changed, luv," Rose said. "Mother Nature has yet to acquiesce." Nathan and Elizabeth didn't need to discuss the matter, they were already on the Carter's front stoop.

"Hey all, welcome!" Luke saw them all in and helped with their coats. "Honey, we've been invaded!" he shouted toward the stairs.

The Tweeners had come to Greenbank, all five of them. It was a social call. The Calderstones crew wanted to get better acquainted with the Kosovans. Dani was eager for Mina, Aggy, and Jak to spend some time with people their own age.

"Nate, pardner, comment ça va?"

"C'est bon, Lucas."

"Très bien! Hey, it's not dark yet, how bout you and Jak take Otis to the park for a bit?"

"Sure!"

"Help him bundle up, it's all in the mudroom. Oh, and take a football. But watch out, the kid's got game!"

"Even my cousin Caspar came!" Darcy squealed as she bussed his cheek.

He grinned. "Hey cuz, you know I love home cooking. It smells wonderful, by the way."

"Thank you!"

"You're the chef?"

"Me and Pops, we've got a pot of stew on. It's been simmering all afternoon, dad and mum are coming over."

Poppy came out of the kitchen drying her hands on a dish towel. "Well, well, all three of Cheryl's boys in one place. And such a turned-out lot. Some place fancy?"

"Casa Italia," Ian said. "We've a seven o'clock booking."

"Best lasagna in the city! Hi Lizzy!"

"Allo Poppy."

"Whatcha got?"

"Secret Sally, I have two. See?"

"Yes, very pretty!"

"One's for Aggy."

Agnesa, who was already curious, now perked up at the mention of her name.

Lizzy went over and sat next to her on the loveseat. "Here Aggy, her name is Sally."

"Tank you," then she leaned over and hugged Lizzy.

"Now that's precious," Seamus remarked.

"It was her idea," Cyrus added. "She bought it with her own money."

Dani and Ermina appeared from the hallway, Mina a touch sheepish. She looked good though, if probably a little self-conscious. This was going to be her first night out on the town, so to speak, in a very long time. She was looking forward to it, a necessary step she felt she needed to take.

Mina was of average height, with a solid frame and shapely body. Her dark brown hair was shoulder length and straight, parted on the side and held with a barrette. Her complexion was smooth, and she had hazel eyes and a rounded face with a welcoming smile that was more evident of late.

"Hello everyone."

Shea decided to address and dismiss the possibly awkward question of the evening right there and then. "Hello Mina, it looks like you'll be stuck with me as your dinner partner."

She appreciated the gesture and responded in kind. "Jak will be jealous, but I would be delighted."

The three couples piled in Ian's Morris and headed north. Casa Italia was up in the City Centre on Stanley Street. They parked nearby and walked, Ian pointing out the Eleanor Rigby statue across from the restaurant's entrance. Mina knew the song, beautiful but sad.

"Some things are the same everywhere," she remarked. "Lonely people."

"Paul McCartney said the inspiration came from an elderly lady that lived alone. He used to shop for her and sit and listen to her stories. Apparently, they became close; the relationship greatly influenced his writing."

"Did any of you ever meet any of the Beatles?"

"Yes, we did. It's quite a story, let's go inside first, get out of the chill."

Mina was thoroughly entertained during dinner, hearing of the clan's past. The Fab Five and their influence on all three brothers was clearly key to their story. Bashir and Penelope certainly were a big part as well—their children, Rose and Caspar, always best mates. She marveled at Cyrus and Rosie's first kiss at such a young age and how Filly, already a friend of the gangs, met Ian at an Eclectibles concert. And then there was that time in '74, when Paul and Linda McCartney crashed the New Year's party at Dovedale Towers.

"Lucas invited them outside to get stoned and told Paul he could try out for the band," Cyrus said chuckle. Mina was incredulous.

"He did perform," Ian added. "It was surreal."

The not so smooth past was remembered also. The revolution in Iran, Thatcher's reign of attrition, and Liridon Gashi.

"We're glad you came along, Mina," Shea said. "Our first Albanian experience was not good."

"It's very strange," she replied. "Gashi means butcher."

"Oh my word!" Rose exclaimed. "That's eerie!"

"Even my father got involved," Filly said. "The city has been saddened by its involvement in slavery in the past. Human trafficking he was just not having!"

"When will I get to meet Ben and Faith's children?"

"The end of May, I think," answered Rose. "Whenever their college term ends."

Supper was served. They all opted for lasagna so the waiter brough out a whole sheet pan full. Two large bowls of salad and lots of garlic bread made it a meal.

Afterwards they braved the cold and took a short walk up to the gardens outside St. George's Hall. Mina got the tour, courtesy of Filly, of statues of some of the historical figures on display.

The walk back was against the wind, the six of them coupled up, walking close together. Mina tightened her scarf and took Shea's arm, warm and comfortable.

The past few days had been important to her, days in which she'd gathered her thoughts and her resolve. No one knew, but tomorrow would mark one year since she'd lost her husband. Tomorrow would be the second saddest of her life. Tomorrow she would mourn. But the day after tomorrow would be different. She couldn't and wouldn't ever forget, but the day after tomorrow she would no longer look back. The bastards would not win.

CHAPTER 60
SUNDAY, 26 MARCH

Well I'm gone to Detox Mansion,
way down on Last Breath Farm.
I've been raking leaves with Liza,
me and Liz clean up the yard.

The twins needed some rehab. They were strung out and on edge. This was somewhat tongue-in-cheek, but they were in need of a break. The curriculum at Colorado College was challenging, the classrooms filled with bright young minds. It was possible that the academic powers that be across the nation foresaw this type of scenario, that late in the school year the students would falter, and lose focus. And so it was that God invented spring break.

Tradition called for an escape to warmer climes, rule number one. Also required was a sufficient supply of members of the opposite sex of similar age. Access to copious amounts of alcohol was a must, along with less cranial gray matter as a counterbalance. Add all the above, shake well, and what you've got is a headache for local law enforcement.

Grace and Hope were bucking the trend, at least in part. They did manage to land in the warm and sunny. Back in Tucson they were, Pima County, Arizona. They would pass on the keg tosses, beer pong, and wet t-shirt contests, opting for some R and R and a bit of sightseeing. And Mexican food, don't forget the Mexican food. A balanced diet is a burrito in each hand.

Ender and Anne Linares were their hosts, Anne had inherited the three-bedroom ranch style brick home from her father. It was in the old Terra Del Sol neighborhood on the city's east side on Avenida Planeta. Anne grew up here, and the Rawlings and Gorter families were still on the block, now a couple of generations removed.

"Cindy Rawlings and April Gorter were my chums. We chased each other around, played hopscotch on chalk-marked sidewalks, and pretended to be housewives with our doll houses. Such innocence."

The girls had been here a week and had established a languid routine. Up around seven for a cuppa and a walk around the hood with Buck, the Linares' old chocolate lab. The afternoon was spent helping Ender with some house projects or touring the area's points of interest. Supper in the evenings, after sunsets on the front porch with a cold one. Occasionally they would pry a story from the elders, tales of Daniela and Astrid's youth.

There was lots to do around Tucson; the topography itself was surprisingly diverse. The Santa Catalina and Rincon mountains lay to the north and east, feeding the Tanque Verde and Rincon creeks that ran towards the city. The central and northern city limits bordered the Tucson Mountain Park and Saguaro National Park, home of those giant cacti, sentinels of the Sonoran Desert.

South and west of Tucson was flatter in general, giving way to the desert landscape with the occasional mesa or arroyo. The Linares took the girls down there a few days ago to see two very interesting, but totally different sites.

The furthest away was the Titan Missile Museum, 25 miles south. A relic from the Cold War, it housed a now inert Titan II missile inside a 140-foot silo. Anne knew a lot about it; her next-door neighbor was the superintendent on the project when it was completed in '63. Awesome to look at, difficult to ponder.

At the opposite end of the karma scale was the Mission San Xavier del Bac. Make love, not war. The Spanish Catholic mission was erected starting in 1692, then rebuilt after the Apaches burned it down, the church's bell tolling again in 1797. It was a beautiful example of Moorish inspired Spanish Colonial architecture, still run by the Franciscans here by the Santa Cruz River.

One more outing was being considered in the few days they had left, but it required some considerable physical commitment. Mt. Lemmon, the highest point in the region at 9,159 feet, had a road to the top but they were planning to hike it. Maybe.

Chapter 61

Friday, 14 April

Sometimes you feel like you've lived too long,
days drip slowly on the page.
You catch yourself,
pacing the cage.

Lucas trudged up to the door at 62 Duke Street, paused, took a deep breath, and entered the foyer. He was not at it today. Judith noticed.

"How about a cup of tea Luke?"

"Yes please. Thanks Jude." He went to his office, took off his jacket, and sat behind the desk. Scruff had read the room and was treading lightly when Luke told him, "The world is gonna have to come to me today." And that it did.

"Mornin' Luke."

"Hey Ben, got a photoshoot someplace?" he asked, seeing his pal all loaded down.

"Yeah, up in Kirkby. I thought I'd check in, probably won't be back til after lunch."

"Cool. I'll be here all day, call if you need to."

"Alright, take it easy."

"Plan of the day."

An hour and a half later, and a second cup of tea, the intercom buzzed.

"Samuel Jackson to see you, Luke."

"Samuel L. Jackson?"

"Most definitely not."

His visitor overheard the conversation and smiled.

"Tell him it's Silky Sam." She did so.

"Send him in."

Wow, he was almost unrecognizable. A proper grooming and a nice set of clothes, flat cap included, which he doffed.

"Good morning, Mr. Carter!"

Luke looked around. "I don't see my father anywhere Sam. I'm Luke."

"Yes, of course, Luke. I just thought the occasion called for a bit of formality."

"Oh?"

"Yes, sir. I've come to see if the possibility of employment is still on the table."

"That's good to hear. Are you sure you're ready?"

"Absolutely. It's why I've waited a bit to come in. My time in Chester was well spent, an eye opener. I need to get off the streets Luke. Skint half the time, the bizzies on me arse. I'm too old for it now, and I have to admit, that business with the Albanian left me badly shaken.

He took a breath and continued. "I've been miserable feelin'; that girl's face haunting me. How is young Miss Grace?"

"She's fine Sam, really. Grace is in America, on a football scholarship at a prestigious college."

"That's brilliant, really good to hear. One day I hope to apologize to her personally."

"She'd like to meet you, I'm sure. It really wasn't your fault, you know. And you were a great help in finding the one responsible."

"I'm just glad he's off the table, and in a much-deserved manner."

"Apparently so."

"Scouse mums are not to be taken lightly," he said, with a conspiratorial grin. Lucas changed the subject.

"Well, I suppose we should talk turkey."

Sam looked confused.

"Sorry, an American expression. Let's discuss terms of employment."

"I appreciate it, more than you know. I would suggest, if I may, that I will start work whenever you like. Let me know when I've earned 200 quid. I owe you that and I'm paying it back."

Luke rose, offering his hand and a clap on the shoulder. "See you Monday morning."

As sharp as he was with his new look, Sam was no match for Luke's next visitor, Sir Philip Carter.

"So sorry old fellow, last minute and all that. Have you a minute?"

"Of course Philip, what's on your mind?"

"Everton Football Club."

"Understandable. Congratulations, by the way, you're club chairman again."

"Thank you, I think. If I'm honest just sitting on the board was sufficient to my liking. The F.A., however, have had enough of Peter Johnson's two faces and forced him to make a choice."

"Between Everton and Tranmere."

"Correct. He owned too much of both clubs, which creates a conflict of interest. So he sold his Everton shares."

"To whom?" To whom? What made him say that? Maybe because he was addressing a knight.

"Bill Kenwright, the theater impresario. My new boss. Bollocks!"

"Not a football man?"

"No idea, really. He seems a likeable chap, but the timing is terrible! All these questions he's had, starting in the middle of the season. The business of football is getting more complicated Lucas."

"How can I help?"

"I'm not sure you can, at least not now. I'll sort it, eventually. Tell you what, this summer will be important. Walter Smith, the manager, as you know, has had his way with the board thus far with respect to player movements. That will change, believe me. Then perhaps you and

I can get together and move some pieces around the chessboard, so to speak."

"Alright. In the meantime, I'll put Jacob on it. He's good at hanging round the lads. We can get a feel for the mood of the changing room."

"That's a splendid idea! He will be discreet, I trust?"

Luke just looked at him.

"Oh quite right, chip off the old block and all that. By the way, can I buy you lunch? I'm afraid you're looking a bit knackered today old chum."

"I could use some fresh air and a bite. Thanks cuz!"

The break had been refreshing, but he still planned to lay low this afternoon. Judith had other plans.

"Gabe's waiting for you, in your office. He looks anxious."

Luke entered to find the kid pacing the floor, head down in thought.

"Good afternoon, Master Gabriel."

"Oh, hi Luke. Sorry to ambush you like this. Are you busy, I can come back."

"No no, you're good. Have a seat. You're wearing the carpet out."

No sooner had his butt hit the chair when he was out with it.

"I want to marry your daughter."

"Right this minute?"

He took a deep breath. "No sir. I'm sorry, I need to settle myself down. I don't know when. I don't even know when I'm going to propose. But I do know that I'd like your and Dani's blessing. That's a good place to start."

"It is, soft lad. I appreciate it. Relax, let's have a chat. Are you sure, both my kids are kinda flakey."

"I'm very sure, and very much in love. I have been for a long time. We've talked about it. Not marriage, but being together. It was odd at first, growing up together then becoming lovers."

"Oh, you've slept together?"

The kid was silent, with big eyes. Then he smiled. "You got me. That was mean."

"Sorry, but the look on your face was priceless! Look, Gabriel, you're my second son, I love you. Poppy does too. Dani and I would be thrilled should you two decide to marry."

"Can we keep it between us for now? I've no clue when I'll ask her."

"Absolutely! Dani will find out when Poppy tells her. I personally hope to miss out on all the squealing."

Gabriel stood. "Thanks Luke. I just got out of rehearsals. I think I'll change and go for a run, get rid of this nervous energy."

Luke stood, and was going to offer his hand, Gabe beat him to it with a warm embrace.

Late in the afternoon Lucas was alone in the office and decided to call it a day. He freshened Scruff's water and food bowls and cleaned his litter, and was thinking about leaving the Vauxhall and running home before dinner. As it turned out he had one more visitor to contend with.

"Hello Lucas, still at it?"

"Just barely George, what's on?"

"Band practice, we're having a session this evening. That is, if all my mates survive til then."

"Yeah?"

"Uh-huh. They've been winding me up of late Luke, teasing me about my kit. It's too massive, it's too cumbersome to lug around to gigs. We were thinking about downsizing. Then they really stepped in it, and said those two words."

"Two words, what two words?"

"Drum machine! Those two words. It's like Ben and disco, don't go there! Sure, drum machines don't make mistakes. That's because drum-fucking-machines aren't human! Drum machines have no soul! Drum machines can't suddenly gain inspiration, take flight and soar with the Gods!"

"That's my Buddha Buddy! Tell ya what, I'm gonna run home, eat supper, and come back and watch you show em why they should never utter those two words in the same sentence again!"

"Bring your ear plugs brother."

CHAPTER 62
MONDAY, MAY 8

Come waste your time with me

Cyril found John Quayle out on his pitch, assessing what was needed off season to restore it before the next campaign.

"Permission to come aboard Cap'n."

John turned to the source and smiled. "Oy Gaffer, permission granted," he said warily, remembering their awkward first meeting.

"How's it looking?"

"It's held up well. The middle of the park needs some attention; the combination of winter and Wilco chopped it up a bit."

"The lad's a rager for sure."

"What brought you in today, Cyril?"

"I needed to clean up my office, plus I had a chat with the boss."

"Oh, what's her mood like now?"

"She seemed quite satisfied overall. Looks like we'll keep our jobs. By the way, are you hungry? I'd like to treat you to lunch."

"Much appreciated, Cy. Sure, I didn't really need to come in today. Habit, I suppose. Ready when you are."

Cyril drove to the Seven Stars, in the nearby village of Thornton Hough. Grilled chicken and chips with a pint of bitters was the fare, quite tasty. They spoke of family and football, and summer holidays, always important to those whose livelihood was tied to the sport.

Satisfactory was a fair appraisal of Tranmere's season, despite changes made in the chain of command. They'd improved their place in the league table and made a couple of good signings for the future. The highlight of the year had been two good runs in domestic cup competitions. They made the final of the League Cup, which brought a rare appearance at Wembley before a crowd of 74,000. They lost 2-1 to Leicester City, denying them their first major trophy in ten years.

Considering the competition, their F.A. Cup run was even more impressive. Rovers made it to the quarterfinals, knocking off two Premier League teams along the way. Good cup runs always provide a big boost to the club's coffers.

Cy was understandably light of heart on the drive back to Greenbank. The next month was basically his to do as he liked. His inward grin broadened slightly as he pulled to the curb, right behind Seamus McTimons' Austin. A quick glance round found Shea and Jak in the park with Otis.

Six weeks had passed since Ermina's night out with Shea and his brothers and their wives. It was hard to say, given all that had transpired, but she had seemed to turn a corner and gotten herself into a happy routine.

Dani and Poppy were well aware of the change in Mina's outlook. The three were constant companions. Kevin and Cheryl had noticed Mina's new sense of ease was reflected in Agnesa and Jak's more relaxed manner.

Cheryl was also cognizant of the fact that her middle son, Seamus, had been spending more time at Greenbank. This she kept to herself, at least for the time being. The personal dynamic was very complicated. She turned to Agnesa, who was listening to Elmo talk to Oscar.

"Aggy look, Cyril is outside."

She knew three of the five words spoken and could get the gist of the rest. She and Cheryl joined the boys outside under the yew.

Later on, they all started filtering in, home from their labors. The students, healers, players, merchants, and businessmen, all home in the warren down in Mossley Hill.

Spring had finally come to Merseyside, adding to the generally good energy that was building throughout the clan. Cheryl noticed more than a few who found reason to wander around outside for a spell before going back indoors. The football kick about ended up a four a side, and when Amos got home from the pharmacy with Faith and Colly, he and brother Otis had a frolic. She also noticed that when the veterinary crew arrived, Seamus broke from the scrum to come over and say hello, sharing an affectionate little cuddle with Mina.

"Me thinks Eros' quiver is an arrow light," she said to Kevin, sitting with Aggy reading a book. "I see one sticking in Shea's arse." Kevin mentioned Gladys Kravitz of the Bewitched show on the telly.

Meanwhile in the park, Cyril was huddled with Lucas, leaning against the yew, where so many important issues were discussed over the decades.

"Come na mon, let us go and feel de Atlantic pound us into blissful submission."

"Say again."

"Holidays, my brother. In Portugal."

"Ya know Cy, that very sentence was such a balm for my blistered psyche of late."

"Dere you go, gettin' all cosmic."

"Hey, ya think we could make it an all-guys vacation?"

CHAPTER 63
WEDNESDAY, 17 MAY

There is no childhood's end
You are my childhood friend
Lead me on

The holiday makers left for Portugal on Sunday, which was Mother's Day, ending any talk of a boys only vacation. Four of the five Greenbank couples went; the Ardavans staying home to 'mind the store.' A week was all the rest could manage, too much going on back in Liverpool.

The mass exodus from the rowhouse forced a reorganization of the week's logistical plan. Poppy and Mina both would go to the clinic every day. This was possible now; Ermina had been certified to practice locally. Caspar would be at Erins Pharmacy every day, dispensing meds and directing the rest of the staff. Faith's mum, Roisin, would come out of retirement for the week to help out as well.

Jacob and Gabriel were going to abandon the Duke Street flat for the week, joining Seamus on Greenbank to keep an eye on Agnesa, Jak,

Otis and Amos. Again, Cheryl taking note of Shea's increased presence. There was a pattern developing here.

The combined offices of Big Ben Photography and Carter Assets Management weren't completely quiet this week. Jake kept in touch with Judith while she and Samuel hired a crew for a thorough spring cleaning of the building.

Robin was home early today, busy in the kitchen. She was hosting supper for everyone. Darcy was home as well, she and Aggy helping out and providing companionship.

"Pasta."

"Yes Aggy, pasta. It's good."

"Very good."

"What were rehearsals like today, Darcy?"

"Shostakovich, fourth symphony."

"Oh, tricky. That was very nearly his Waterloo."

"Dmitri definitely had a bad boy streak. So, have you missed the Phil, mum?

"I miss the comradery and performing. But I'm glad to be away from the grind. And I like my new routine. I suppose I always enjoyed being around my parents and their customers at the store."

"I always liked hanging around there growing up. Gran knew everyone in the neighborhood."

"Aggy likes it. Eh Aggy, Adam's Apple?"

"I like it!"

Across the street Jak and his buddies were, you guessed it, playing football. He and Shea versus Gabe and Jake, hotly contested but in the end decided by the young number ten's deft passing. It was Jacob's plan to place the boy in Everton or Liverpool's academy as soon as they would accept him.

"The kid could nutmeg a virgin!" he claimed.

In addition to pasta, Robin roasted a turkey and steamed some veggies. Caspar came over, excited over the pharmacy's receipts so far this week, and happy that he'd seen the business run smoothly. In fact, all present were reporting no problems of note so far in the work week.

Drinks, music, and merriment with the kids and dogs was the plan afterwards. Most of the guys went out to organize chairs and prep the firepit. Gabe asked Darcy to grab Viola and go on out. He'd help mum and dad clean up.

"I'd like to run a couple of things by you two if I can."

"Sure Gabe, what's up?" asked Robin.

"I was planning to spend the night with Poppy in one of the Barcant's guest rooms."

"Really?" Abbas was confused; his son and Poppy's affair certainly wasn't a secret. They'd shown their class by being discreet over the past months, but everyone was together tonight. Couldn't they just wait?

Gabriel sensed his parents' surprise, even detecting a hint of disappointment. He pulled something out of his pocket to further explain his intention. "I was going to give her this."

"That's your grandmaman's engagement ring! Does that mean," Abbas hesitated.

"Of course it does Dopey!" Robin was already tearing up, and squeezing the rotini right out of her boy.

"That's wonderful news son," waiting to embrace him. "Your grandpa and Neff are having a chuckle. "

"I wish they were here," Gabe replied with a touch of melancholy. "Okay, let's maintain, I'm gonna surprise her later."

"I shall burst!" his mom complained.

The evening was warm as the sun's glow faded and the sky deepened from azure towards midnight blue. The conversation was light and cheerful, and the music followed suit. Folky stuff, and some sing-a-longs, with an occasional game of tag or hide and seek until Aggy and Jak tired and cuddled up with the rest around the fire. Poppy suggested a tune from a band whose albums were on the turntable a lot so far this year. She looked around at her gang and smiled, and thought about both the state of mind each was in generally and where their hearts were in this moment.

The pre-chorus is where she felt it, the words so simple in meaning yet spot on to what she wanted her loved ones to know:

So if I'm inside your head,
Don't believe what you might have read.
You'll see what I might have said,
To hear it.

Come waste your time with me.
Come waste your time with me.

Eventually they all decided to call it a night. Clean-up was a group effort, dousing the fire, stowing the chairs, and collecting the glassware.

"Gabe, would you mind taking the dogs for a short walk?" Robin asked, a twinkle in her eye.

"Sure Mum. Pops?"

"Yeah, I'll go, let me grab a jumper."

They did a lap around the park, stopping here and there when Amos and Otis had their snouts deep into it. A crescent moon had appeared in the southeastern sky, reflected in the dew already moistening the grass.

He proposed under the yew, her embrace and the look in her eyes unlike anything he could even hope for or imagine.

"Poppy Anne Ardavan, I rather like that. What do you think?"

"I don't know, all the blood's left my head."

Things got heated afterwards, and playful, and very personal. And, for the record, the lady eventually said yes.

Chapter 64
Friday, 26 May

Cradled in branches that stretched out their arms,
I must wait a while.
Bending my mind as I pick up the flowers in May.

There had been an underlying current of excitement throughout the rowhouse all month, Mina thought. Everyone had seemed to be looking forward to something, tacit but unspoken, but also seemingly unaware of its presence. It was a thing, though, palpable to her, and its identity, she felt, would be confirmed in just a few minutes.

Ben's Morris Traveler Estate wagon had just parked outside. He got out and went to the back to unload while Faith, Hope, and Grace emerged, smiling broadly.

Amos, who was at the front window after being alerted to the familiar sound of the Morris, started howling and bounded to the door. Mina let him and Otis out, the twins bearing the brunt of their glee. Amos in particular was joy unshackled, doing figure eights in the front yard.

And the twins themselves, Mina was sure they would be tall and fit, but she wasn't prepared for how lovely they both were.

"Agnesa, Jak, come look!"

The tykes ran to the window from the mudroom where they were putting on their shoes. Mina got a confused look from the pair, not sure what was happening.

"It's Hope and Grace, Ben and Faith's children."

"We go outside!" Aggy said.

"Okay!"

She followed them, amused at the way they scurried toward a couple they didn't even know. She guessed that if the dogs were so worked up about it there must be something special to these ladies.

"Oh my heavens!" Hope exclaimed. "That is the cutest little boy ever!" She kneeled down as he approached, dark eyes full of wonder.

"Hello, I'm Hope. Are you Jak?"

"Yes, Jak. Hello."

She opened her arms, and he showed no hesitation.

Agnesa was still a few yards away, staring back and forth. Grace stepped forward and knelt.

"Hello Agnesa, I'm Grace." Then she turned her head to the right, exposing the left side of her neck and face.

"Owee."

"Yes, owie. But it's okay now."

Hope came over and showed Aggy both sides of her face.

"Hi Aggy, I'm Hope."

That did it, they both got big hugs.

"It's possible that they have never seen twins," Mina said as she approached.

"It seems that they've taken it in stride," Hope said. "We get harder looks and inane questions from some adults. Ermina, it's so good to finally meet you." They embraced, then, with one arm still around Mina's shoulders, "And this is sister Grace. She's better looking, but I'm smarter."

Grace got her hug, feeling somehow not only Mina's strength but also some of her character and conviction. Despite the recent past, or maybe because of it, this woman was a force.

"Well, maybe now we'll get a proper game of football in the park." It was Seamus, with Cyril beside him, both grinning to beat the band. The girls loved em up pretty good.

Kevin and Cheryl got the same treatment, then there was a brief respite before the rest returned at day's end. The twins unpacked, showered, and sat around the front room talking with the folks. They had a successful nine months in the States, in the classroom, on the pitch, and at home with their second family.

Ben and Faith caught them up on the last few weeks. Tranmere's campaign, Silky Sam's new look and act, and the trip to Portugal. Then they sprung the big news—Gabriel and Poppy's impending nuptials. The twins were excited but not surprised.

"They had that look about them in December, both hopelessly smitten," Grace noted.

"Details?" Hope queried.

"None as yet," Faith said.

"Dani's got a hand in this; she tends to be secretive in such matters," Ben added.

Given the stir caused by the clan getting their wunderkinds back, a decision was made for supper—no one was cooking. Kevin, Cheryl, George and April were bringing fish and chips; the twins certainly weren't complaining.

The Pines were hosting, everybody wanting an audience with the Colorado collegians. The court jesters, Cyril and Jacob, were present, entertaining courtesans, commoners, and nobility alike. A troupe of minstrels also attended, entertaining all present with their tales and tunes. Wine and ale flowed, and the court celebrated the return of the princesses of the pitch.

The celebrated themselves were magnanimous with their well-wishers, bestowing their attention and charms with all who appeared before them.

"So tell me Kevin, it seems you're quite the body surfer now," Grace mentioned.

"Thanks to Lucas, it was the first time with he and Cy, before it was just meself in Trinidad, Cheryl undecided whether to laugh or call the lifeguard. Ya see, it was all about technique. I didn't have any. Just put your arms like you're about to dive into a pool, put your head between them, close your eyes, and push off," he took a breath. "All wrong it was. First, you size the wave up, take stock of the big bastard. Then you swim like hell, to stay a bit out in front. Then, you raise your head, eyes open, and hold your arms along your sides as you slide down the face, turning into the wave under the crest. You see, your arms not only broaden the surface of your torso, they also act like rudders, helping you navigate a longer ride. Let me tell you, eyes open, head up. That's the ticket!"

"Wow!"

"Yeah, and let me tell ya bout something rare and amazing, being in the green room."

"What's that?"

"The tube baby, cowabunga!"

"Tube eh, that's a Phish song."

"They surfers as well?"

Hope was huddled with Gabe and Darcy, ministering to their curiosity about the twins' adopted city.

"When we told Tim and Margaret about you and your folks, they took us to the Colorado Springs Symphony for a concert."

"I didn't know they had one," Gabe remarked.

"How was it?" Darcy asked.

"Surprisingly good! Not the Royal Liverpool or the Phil, but quality musicians in a really nice hall. The conductor's a hunk, that's for sure!"

As much as little Jak liked chips, he still offered some to Grace when she went over to sit with him.

"Shea says you play football."

"Yes, I play football, very much!"

"I play football Jak. Hope also plays football."

The kid stopped chewing and asked the question with his eyes.

"I think tomorrow we play football," she answered.

"Yes, tomorrow football!"

She gave him a high five.

Now Hope was giving the lowdown on Tucson to Colleen, who had lived in Arizona as a little girl. Together they decided the area had grown considerably. There was no Tucson Mountain Park when Colly was there, and the I.C.B.M. missile silo was very much active.

"It's called the Titan Missile Museum now," Hope said.

Lucas had just entered the twilight zone, that eerie, déjà vu inducing state of surrealism that now and again occupied his brain. He'd over-heard Hope and Colly.

"Did you say that Anne's family lived next door to the construction super on that project?"

"Yes, although she was an adult by then, grown up and in Venezuela with Ender and Dani and Astrid."

"And her father still lived in the same house?"

"Yes, where Anne and Ender are now."

"In Terra del Sol, on Avenida Planeta."

This was not a question. Hope couldn't answer anyway; she was speechless.

"What the hell Luke?" Colly asked, starting to get the heebie-jeebies.

"The super was my dad, Bus Carter. I was only 8 and 9, but I remember Richard Robbins."

"Ooo-whee-ooo!"

"Stop it Hope, I'm already weirded out!"

Up in the kitchen Shea was asking Grace to compare football in the States to the game here in the U.K.

"Chalk and cheese, Shea, there's nothing similar to the two. In America the women are better than the men. More people support them as well."

"Corr, that's unimaginable!"

"The men still get paid more, but that's not saying much."

Eventually all suitors bade the princesses a pleasant and restful sleep and departed, much cheered by the evenings' events and the good will of the court.

Later, under cover of night, the Merseyside Six were reunited under the yew. The hounds kept watch as they relived the past months and regaled the time spent apart. Then, under the spell of herbs from Merlin's pouch of potions and elixirs they spoke of the future, the seeds of which were now gathering life force within their very souls. A future together.

CHAPTER 65
FRIDAY, 2 JUNE

I can imagine the moment,
breaking out through the silence,
all the things that we both might say.

Over the years the clan had become fairly well known in the community, partially due to their sheer numbers. And, because of the various roles they played serving the community. Pharmacists, vets, teachers, grocers, all honorable professions, playing their part. Added value and quality of life was a part of their contribution as well, through the gang's musicians, artists, and sportsmen.

Those familiar with the clan remarked on how together they were, united in aim and purpose. It would be hard to argue the claim; it was basically one very big extended family, despite the differences in birthright and ethnicity.

How was it that such a large, diverse group enjoyed so much harmony, suffering only the occasional spat or disagreement. The clan's original elder, Neff Boler, summed it up some years ago, sitting under the yew with Sir Philip at one of the gang's annual garden parties.

"I believe this lot has managed to avoid the restrictive tenets of societal hierarchy, old chap. The children are taught to be kind, loving, and respectful. Then they're taught to be curious, to ask questions, even challenge their elders. Then they're encouraged to engage, anyone and everyone, and get involved. It's remarkable."

Simply put, the reason the clan got on so well together was because they got on so well one on one. The whole thing was built on individual relationships. One family didn't love the other; each member of one family loved all the members of the other. These relationships grew over time, one conversation at a time.

Mina walked through Sefton Park to the Stillwell house to have tea with Aleah. It was mid-morning, the late spring weather a boost to her outlook on yet another day of looking forward, the past occupying less and less of her thoughts.

"Good morning, Miss Ermina. You're looking on top of it today!"

"A brisk walk on a nice day Aleah. The city is starting to show me its colors."

They kissed cheeks and went to the back terrace and sat, a slight breeze causing the dappled light shining through the trees to dance on the flagstones in the garden.

"This is such a beautiful space, and very peaceful."

"I spend a lot of time out here, it's very meditative."

Mina sipped her tea, thinking of something she shared with her hostess. "Do you miss Iran still?"

"I miss the way it was when I was your age. In many respects it was the beginning of a long period of happiness. Hassan and I had our boys, our jobs, and Iran was modernizing. Our family was growing, and life was humming right along until problems between the church and state started to arise."

"I miss what Kosovo could have been. I went there still young, as an immigrant. But I went to school, started a family and a business. Then so quickly it went away. The immigrant became a refugee."

"Our pasts have much in common Mina, much of it sad. You have still some of that past in your head, and your heart." She paused and took Mina's hand. "You have suffered too much grief, more than anyone should have to bear. And you're a healer; seeing others suffer is a terrible burden. Don't feel guilty because you survived. Embrace life Mina, be joyous and show Aggy and Jak the way forward."

Ermina smiled, even though she was welling up. "That's so kind, and you are very wise."

"Well, you live long enough, you pick up a thing or two. Besides, I think you know these things already, you just need a reminder now and then."

"I suppose so. And I have been much happier lately. I still can't seem to bring myself to sing and dance. But I can tap my toes and hum!"

Aleah laughed right out loud.

There was another heart-to-heart happening as Ermina was walking back to Greenbank. It was up on Duke Street in the office reception area. Grace had been in the City Centre all morning and stopped by to see if her dad wanted to go to lunch.

"Oh, I'm sorry Grace, Ben's out until late this afternoon."

"My fault for not calling. How 'bout you, are you free?"

"Shackled to the desk, luv. Someone's got to mind the store."

The front door opened, and a man entered, purposeful of stride until he saw her.

"Miss Grace?"

"Sam?"

His confident manner fell away, replaced by a shrinking stature and submissive countenance, standing before the source of his greatest personal shame.

"I'm, I'm glad to see you're looking so well," was all he could manage.

"I'm doing very well Sam, and you look very sharp."

"Thank you," he replied meekly.

She and Jude were a bit embarrassed; they felt bad for the bloke.

"Have you got a minute?" she asked. "Let's go upstairs and have a fizzy and a chat."

"All right," he intoned as Jude gave her a wink.

They went out on the balcony with Cokes, the sun warm and comforting.

"I've wanted to apologize to you for so long, and now I feel awful for not doing so sooner."

"Well, then, do it and be done with it."

"I am sorry Miss Grace, and I feel a great deal of responsibility."

"I never thought you were to blame Sam. You've put yourself through too much."

"I could have followed those two down that side street instead of running off. Such a coward!"

"Bollocks! You were under threat yourself. Besides, you were never a part of what they were doing. You were Silky Sam, not popular with the bizzies, mind you, but not a physical threat to anyone. You just separated the stupid from all that unnecessary money they were carrying 'round and didn't know what to do with."

Finally, a smile.

"That's all done with now as well, thanks to Lucas," he said.

"We all end up giving thanks to Lucas. That part we keep to ourselves."

He nodded, knowing exactly what she meant.

"You played your part Sam. You came good in the end and it helped us all get past it. Now come on, let's have a cuddle."

It felt like salvation to him.

"We're mates now."

And with that he'd been set free.

Back down in Mossley Hill two long time mates were meeting at Dovedale Towers for a pint.

"Abbas, welcome!"

"Hi Emma, you okay?"

"Splendid, kind sir. And yerself?"

"Off work and thirsty. If you can fix that I shall call your splendid and raise you a most excellent."

"Done. By the way, Geoff's in the hall playing with his toys."

"He's become a sound nerd, but it's good for the band."

"If you insist, but tell him there's no free ale for soundchecks."

He found Geoff tangled in a mass of cables and cords, looking a tad bewildered.

"It's your wife's fault this! She's gotten in Luke's ear about her trip to Florida and how we need to get in the 21st century with our gear. Now Luke's tasked meself to put the Eclectibles at the 'technological forefront' of the local music scene!"

"Cool!"

"Well, it might be, if I can get it figured out. I need patience from those two, and less Paul Languedoc says this, and Chris Kuroda does that."

"Who are they?"

"Geezers with funny names, and employees of Phish, which is a ridiculous name for a band."

Abbas' giggle had turned to a chuckle. Geoff continued, softening a bit.

"Of course, I must admit I enjoy playing their music; it's clever and challenging. And I suppose that pair is probably the best one-two punch of sound and light in the business. Sorry for the outburst Obs, I'll get it sorted."

"Glad to be here for ya buddy. Listen, take your time, get it right, and enjoy the process. I'll keep the rest off your back."

"Much obliged mate."

"Hey, gotta take care of my home boy. I've known you longer than anyone in Liverpool save Bashir and Penny."

"And Luke 'Skywalker' Carter."

"Technically correct, I suppose, but that was a long time ago, in a galaxy far, far away."

Not far away, and very much in the present, Skywalker's daughter and Abbas' son were trying to get two different people off their collective back—their mothers. They were in the Ardavan's back garden making plans, or at least trying.

"We could ask for suggestions."

"No Gabe, this is our only chance at having any say in the matter."

"Yeah?"

"Absolutely. We're talking one Scouse mum and one combination Latina-Scouse mum. There's been cases in the wild where they've been known to eat their young."

"Pops!"

"No, seriously, if we show any hesitation they'll just take over."

"What can we do, after all, it's our wedding."

"Probably our best bet is to not aim too high. We decide on a few items that are important to us and make our stand."

"So, the big things are what you're talking about."

"Yes, exactly!"

"Okay, how about who, when, and where?"

"Translate."

"We dictate the guest list, the date, and the venue."

"Oh honey that's brilliant! Let them sort all the busy details like flowers, food, transportation, and the like."

"Uh oh!"

"What?"

"The honeymoon."

"Surely that decision is down to us."

"Yes, but what if we're wishy-washy, will they make suggestions, like Edinburg, or Paris?"

"Which is where they went. I see your point."

"We could elope."

"How many people are in the clan?"

"Probably close to forty."

"Which is how many people would disown us should we make that decision."

"A bridge too far, I suppose."

"That, my dear, is the bridge over troubled water."

CHAPTER 66
SATURDAY, 17 JUNE

Let's put our heads together,
and start a new country up.
Our father's father's father tried,
erased the parts he didn't like.

The Six met up a little before ten at the Edge Hill Youth and Community Center, not far from Dani's clinic. It was a nice facility, originally the Martindale House at 79 Durning Road, where it meets Royston Street.

Darcy arranged it, eager to introduce her mates to something she'd picked up from a colleague in the symphony. For a month now she'd been attending Tai Chi classes at the Kum Lau School of Tai Chi Chuan.

"We used to come here as kids," Gabe remarked.

"I remember," Hope said. "When the weather was harsh we'd have all sorts of games here."

"I remember being sent home once for fighting," Poppy reported. "I didn't start it but mum scolded me. Dad gave me a wink on the sly."

"So tell us Darcy, what are we in for this morning?" asked Jake, tightening the laces on his trainers. They were all in the entry area waiting to go into the sports hall.

"It's an exercise class of sorts. Tai Chi, in the old days, was a martial arts discipline. Over time it's been changed somewhat. Now there's been different styles to emerge, but it's slower, and more extended in its movements. The whole idea is to stimulate the energy centers to maintain fitness and overall physical and mental health."

"Let's do it!" Grace prodded.

There were probably thirty to thirty-five students present, milling around and talking quietly. At the top of the hour the group formed up into four lines, double arm distance apart and facing front. Darcy put her chums in the center of the middle two lines. They were a handful of classes behind the rest and would benefit from having more experienced classmates on all sides.

The instructor was Denise Halsall, a very pleasant lady, probably nearing middle age. She greeted the class and introduced a couple of advanced students that she placed at two opposite corners of the group.

Five of the Six were a little bewildered. What was about to happen?

"Begin."

Everyone began to move, slowly, rhythmically, and together. Thank goodness for the slowly part. Now they knew why the beginners were placed in the middle.

Performing a complete set of Tai Chi requires its adherents to execute 108 moves in order, matching the pace of the set leader. During the set, participants make a series of turns, constantly finding themselves facing a different direction. Having experienced classmates to follow, no matter which way you turn, keeps the group in sync.

This was a beginners' class; so far the first 40 moves had been covered. After the set Denise went back over some of the moves, performing them for the class for clarification. They practiced some more before taking a break.

Afterwards Denise and the two advanced students went over the next couple of sequences of new moves, followed by the class having a go. The hour-and-a half ended with a set from the beginning through the new sequences introduced today.

The Six mingled with the rest after class around the water fountain. Most were middle aged or more, happy to see some young blood in the mix.

"You'll find most of us wishing we'd started at an earlier age," said Sophie Davies, a pensioner whose short, squat figure belied the grace she displayed during the session.

"Already I can see some benefits of Tai Chi," Gabe said. "Balance and flexibility for sure."

"It'll flush your innards," one old geezer said.

"Say again?"

"He means it will free up your chi, your life force," Sophie explained.

Darcy suggested they stay to watch the advanced class for a while, to get a better feel for the art. They started with some warmup exercises, called jongs. These mostly dealt with hand and arm movements. Then the class did tor-yus and dan-yus, working their core muscles and reinforcing the basic lean and stretch motions used in so many of the moves.

Then, led by Master Lau himself, the class performed the entire 108 move set. Wow, when you do it correctly it looks like one long, fluid purpose of motion, syncopated and graceful. Darcy could see the hook had been set. Soon the Six would be all about strumming the pei pa, grasping the bird's tail, cloud hands, and fist under elbow. Thirteenth century practices, alive and well in the twenty-first century. Analog theory in the digital world.

None of them had any responsibilities for the rest of the day, perfect for hanging together, all together, increasingly rare as the years passed. They took a bus to the City Centre and walked to Duke Street, stopping off for a takeaway. Chinese was the obvious choice.

"Look at Darcy working those chopsticks! How 'bout you Jake, give it a try."

"No can do Gabe. I like this shirt."

"I noticed Grace and Hope, as usual, looking right at home in the physical world. They carried tiger to the mountain and parted the horse's mane like it was second nature."

"Aw, thanks Pops," Grace said. "I'm sold on Tai Chi. It's gotta be a nice go along with football. It's relaxing, and helps stretch out the kinks and knocks."

"It's possible, I think, that it's a boost for the mentality as well. Very centering," her sister added. "I can see myself at it for the foreseeable future."

"Speaking of the future, I've a question," Darcy said. "You guys are a year or four older than I, where do you see yourselves, say, five years from now?"

"Playing football professionally," Hope answered without hesitation.

"A doctor of veterinary medicine."

"First chair cello."

"Hang on. I asked where."

Silence.

"From that I guess I can assume it to be Liverpool, apart from the twins. If they do get signed to a contract, they'll be wherever that club is based."

"True that," Grace said. "Why Darcy, are you feeling the wanderlust?"

"I'm not sure. I would like to travel more, and emigrating to another country is something I've thought about."

"Me too," echoed Poppy. "It's easy, I suppose, to be tempted to relocate. We've heard the stories over the years, how the Fab Five came together and moved to England."

"I don't know sister. I've wondered whether or not mum and dad are expecting us to take over the clinic and the agency."

"Ya think so? I'm sure they'd like it, but I don't think there'd be too much of a row should we want to start something up on our own."

"Our parents, well, I can't see them expecting us to take over Adam's Apple," Gabe surmised. "But they'd miss us, as I'm sure all our folks would."

"And I would miss Liverpool terribly," Grace said. "But the idea is worth pondering. There's so much out in the world that I would like to be a part of."

"The Six, carving out their own little clan. It has its appeal," Jake said wistfully.

"It is exciting to think about, even if it's not evident that a decision is imminent."

"Careful Darce, you're about to put a knot in your tongue," her brother warned.

"It is exciting, at least to dream about," Poppy agreed. "Where would we go?"

"Morocco!"

"New Zealand!"

"Cool!"

"Wait now, let's be realistic," Gabe interjected. "We'll need a symphony, and football, a city big enough to give us a chance to succeed. What would you do Jake?"

"You know, I could probably still work for the agency. Just set up my own office, I'll be on the road a lot anyway."

"I think the States would be most sensible," Grace said. "Whether we play football or not, eventually we'll be falling back on our education to find a career. America would probably have the better opportunities."

"Florida's an easy choice," Hope suggested. "We've got Cye and Astrid to get us sorted, like Bashir and Penny did for the Five. Our grans will need some looking after as well."

"Tucson's a possibility," Poppy added. "With Anne and Ender."

"How about Burlington?" Gabe said, to the rest's confusion. "Cyril said Cat and Millie are thinking about it. Vermont's getting prepared to sanction same sex marriage."

"I'm thinking Utah," Jake offered.

"Utah?"

"Absolutely, the Mormons are in charge there. I could marry Hope and Grace."

"You wish!" came the reply, in stereo.

CHAPTER 67
FRIDAY, 23 JUNE

She led me by the hand to a room of dancing shadows,
And from the glowing tongues of candles
I heard her whisper in my ear,
J'entend ton coeur, j'entend ton coeur,
(I can hear your heart)

Seamus McTimons was thoroughly enjoying his summer holidays. This was an annual occurrence, begun in earnest thirty years ago when he began playing football for a living. Now, as a coach, his summers were even shorter, a trade-off, he supposed, for having to endure less physical toil. He had no complaints. He'd dreamed of a life in the game ever since he could remember, and certainly ever since he moved in next door to Cyril Barcant.

This summer had been different. He, and Cyril, as the top wage earners in the clan, in their playing days anyway, were normally off to warmer climes this time of year. Even time spent in Liverpool involved an almost tourist-like mindset, soaking up all the region had to offer. The difference was that Shea had fallen in love.

There could be no debate on the matter, Seamus McTimons was a seasoned purveyor of the opposite sex. His notoriety, personality, bank account, and roguish good looks afforded him the opportunity to have known more than his fair share of feminine companionship. All had shown him a wide range of charms and pleasure, but none had captured his heart. Then, from right under his nose and without warning, he'd been smitten.

The attraction had begun the moment he met her. Expecting a shrunken and defeated shell of a person, she was defiant and determined, fiercely protective of Aggy and Jak and her own sense of self. And, despite arriving in England pale and thin, she was very attractive, now looking more beautiful by the week to Shea's eye.

Mina was a gifted healer as well, with a strong will to partner with her compassionate nature. She'd also shown a more carefree side, laced with wit and wonder as time healed old wounds.

She and Shea had grown close, definitely considered to be a couple of sorts. But they weren't lovers. Hugs and kisses on the cheek were the extent of their physical contact. He knew he had to be patient; she'd let him know. Maybe it would never happen; she'd been through so much. He was betting on her, though. She had an inner strength that was rare, a life force within her that was tired of being held down.

She was treating him to supper this evening, right in his own house. His folks had taken Aggy and Jak to Calderstones for a cookout and evening in the garden. Summer on Merseyside is a wonderful thing.

She knocked on the door, arm laden and, it seemed, a little distracted. She looked so good, though, a naturally pretty lady.

"What all is in there?" he asked, taking the sack to the kitchen.

"Tave kosi."

"Oh, well, that explains it."

She laughed. "It means baked lamb with rice."

"I knew that."

She followed him, bussing his cheek and unpacking her ingredients. "It's all portioned out and ready for the oven. Probably it will take close to an hour to cook."

"Great, it already smells good. You want to walk the park while it cooks?"

"No," she said, and took both of his hands, looking hard into his eyes. "I want you to take me up to your bedroom." And with that she drew him to her, kissing his lips softly.

"Mina, are you sure? I can wait, you know. I don't want you to feel rushed because of me."

"You are a kind and gentle man Shea, and very patient. And I am more than ready."

They embraced, their kiss deep, gaining an urgency that swept them up, somehow ending upstairs. Shea was nervous; this was emotionally tricky. As it turned out he pretty much just had to hold on.

The meal, as good as it was, which was excellent, was almost an afterthought. They talked excitedly, about the future, the children, the clan, their work, the only subject not discussed was them as a couple. One step at a time.

They did take a nice long walk, enjoying the weather and greeting those from the neighborhood out doing the same.

They made love again that night, slowly, taking their time, afterwards just lying in each other's arms. Shea was hopelessly but happily lost in a place he'd never been before, right here in his own home.

Mina went to the Carters when the children returned, getting them ready for bed while hearing them talk about Nate and Lizzy. In her own bed later she wept, almost silently, strong conflicting emotions finally purged. There would be no more tears.

CHAPTER 68
SATURDAY, 1 JULY

Dancing days are here again,
as the summer evenings grow.

Tim, Margaret, and Jessica were leaning against the forward railing of the Royal Daffodil, reveling in the view of Liverpool's waterfront.

"The buildings are spectacular!" Margaret gushed. "I like the different styles; some look very modern."

"That's where we're going to land," Jessie said, pointing at Pier Head.

"That's right Jessie," Darcy confirmed. "Those three buildings behind it are called the Three Graces. And that long one to the right is the Museum of Liverpool."

"Look at those birds on that one!" she marveled.

"That's Bella and Bertie. They're called Liverbirds. They're mythical, which means there's really no such thing. A Liverbird is a symbol of Liverpool, half eagle and half cormorant, always with a clutch of seaweed in its beak."

"Cool!"

The Blacks had come to England for a visit to Merseyside, oohing and aahing ever since they got off the train at Lime Street Station. In the three days since, they'd been treated to the Greenbank Deluxe Introductory Scouse Sojourn. Today's tour guides were the Six and so far had consisted of an early outing with Amos and Otis, porridge, toast and tea, and a double-decker bus ride before the ferry trip across to the Wirral. There they'd seen Prenton Park, home of Tranmere Rovers, and the awesome Birkenhead Park, the model for New York City's Central Park.

Now they were strolling the waterfront's wide promenade, taking in the sights. The docks had come alive again since the '80s—museums, shops, restaurants, and other diversions to pass the time by the river Mersey.

Lunch was taken at the Pumphouse, on the Royal Albert Dock. It was a red brick relic of the past, repurposed into a large pub and restaurant with indoor and outdoor seating. They opted for the patio as most there did. It was a warm, sunny day.

"Chips, biscuits, and crisps. I'm glad Hope and Grace gave us the tutorial before we came," Tim said.

"Now you're ready for barms, pies, and butties," Gabe said.

"Huh?"

"More food options Tim," Poppy explained. "All good."

"I'm game."

The Coloradans were clearly enjoying their time abroad; they'd not traveled a lot before. They were enthusiastic, up for anything, already having seen the city from St. John's Beacon and checking out the funky shops on Bold Street. Last night was spent at the symphony. Tim and Margaret were guests of the Ardavans, seated in a choice loge side stage. The twins took Jessica over to Calderstones to meet Lizzy.

They continued south along the river, past the Echo Arena, and went inland at Queen's Wharf, turning back north to the Baltic Fleet pub.

"James!"

"Grace, Hope, my second favorite twins, yer looking sound!"

"It's good to see ya mate. How's Sarah?"

"Always more than I deserve, Hope. This is a made-up lot. Hello folks, I'm James Doohan. Welcome to the Baltic!"

"Tim Black, James," he said, shaking hands. "This is my wife Margaret and daughter Jessica."

"A pleasure Tim. It's a wise man that surrounds himself with pretty ladies."

"I like it here," Margaret said. "This is a crazy cool building, James. The shape is unique."

"Built to fit the space, Margaret. The old part of the city is one big, molded pile of brick and stone. Now, what can I get you nice people. You too, Jake."

They had a pint and sat with James, catching him up on all the moving parts that is the clan. He promised to bring Sarah to the Dovey tonight to hear the Eclectibles.

Once back home, the Ardavans and Carters went their way while the twins and Jessie went to the park with Jak, Aggy and the pups. Ben and Faith sat with Tim and Margaret in the front room, looking out the window and talking.

"What a fantastic city. Every day there's something wondrous and totally unexpected," Tim mused.

"Everyone's so friendly and curious, I wish I spoke the language better."

Faith laughed, "I can tell you've been down to the docks Margaret. It's thick, and the young are coming up with new slang words all the time."

"Jessie asked what a wanker was," Tim said.

"Jake told her it was a guy that liked to spend a lot of quality time alone," Margaret said between giggles.

"All our lads fancy themselves comedians," Faith said. "They grew up around Cyril and Ben."

"Both your girls are fond of comparing Tim and Ben, the corny dads."

The accused shared a conspiratorial grin.

"The whole arrangement has been better than we could've dreamt. Hope and Grace are two of the most well-adjusted and mature young people I've ever met."

"Oh Margaret, that's a wonderful thing to hear. So you're up for another year?"

"Absolutely! Don't take Jessie's big sisters away!"

"I feel safer with them around," Tim said. "Can we keep at least one?"

Ben laughed. "Sorry Tim, they're a matched set. We'll probably lose them next year anyway. They want to play professionally, which would probably be somewhere in the States."

"Yeah, the WUSA is popular, the world's first all-pro women's league in the world. They kick off next April, with eight clubs."

"I don't know much about soccer, I mean football, sorry," Margaret said. "But I know the twins were pretty dominant in their conference. Surely they'll get a tryout, at least."

"If they get signed that's when we'll know where they'll be living," Ben said. "Six of the eight teams are in the east and two on the west coast."

"We plan to come in the fall to see them play," Faith said. "Women don't play football as much in England. The level of competition is low."

"We'll try to bring Luke or Jake with us. I'm sure they'll want to represent them," Ben added.

"Your clan, as you call it, is amazing," Tim said. "I think you could break away and start your own country."

"It's always been very communal. When I came over with the other four it was out of necessity, just to survive. We became a family before starting families."

"Speaking of family, the Eclectibles are on at the Dovey tonight," Faith reminded.

"Oh boy! That I'm excited for. Poppy said you're the best pure singer in the band Faith."

"I don't know Margaret, Dani's quite the siren. Poppy herself is getting quite good now that she's embraced it. We should probably get cleaned up and ready. We can eat there before the gig."

"See Margaret, she said 'gig.' These are real musicians!"

As usual, the children led the entourage up Penny Lane to Dovedale Towers. Jak, Aggy, and Jessie, dressed for the disco, strutting their stuff.

Emma, Mae, and Colin, their hosts, greeting them warmly and got their food and drink orders sorted. The pre-gig atmosphere was lively and varied.

The Blacks met the rest of the band—Tim in the performance hall and Margaret at the bar.

"You're American, aren't you George?"

"Yes, ma'am, born and bred. New Jersey, by way of Florida."

"He and I are the backbone, Margaret," Geoff said. "Our foundational rhythm section sets the tone and allows the others to follow their muse."

"I saw and heard Darcy and Gabriel last night at the Philharmonic. They seemed to be excellent musicians."

"They are indeed. But just wait until you hear their parents. World class."

"Geoff and Abbas started the band, back in '68. Geoff's family owned the pub."

"Careful now, these two will lead you down the garden path. You must be Margaret. Hi, I'm April."

"Hi April. Don't worry, boys are the same the world over."

"Come on Geoff, the jig's up. Let's set up our gear."

They joined Paul and Abbas in the hall, chatting with Tim.

"You've got some beautiful guitars, Paul. I like how they're all blonde."

"Thank you, Tim. You a musician?"

He scoffed. "Couldn't carry a tune in a bucket."

Luke came in with the rest of the band and Margaret.

"Mister Manager!"

"Evening kids! What's on?"

"Abbas. The Persian Pied Piper has crafted a setlist to infuse the masses with mirth and merriment!"

"Cool. Everything looks good. Geoff?"

"All set."

"Okay, let's go to the green. Margaret, Tim, you should join us."

The ceremonial pre-set ritual was observed, adding a heightened conceptual anticipation towards the event itself. A fresh pint and some final audio adjustments as the audience filled the room signaled it was showtime.

"Good evening Mossley Hill!" Abbas said in greeting. "Let's do it!"

"We Can Be Together" was an apt opener, Paul Kantner's call to arms with the Jefferson Airplane set the mood for an intimate session and had all the band's singers warming up the pipes. Faith then belted out the Airplane's, "It's No Secret," matching Marty Balin's statement of intent.

The Wild Colonials were covered next, a fairly obscure group out of Los Angeles. They were female fronted and featured a violinist, good fodder for the Eclectibles. Dani did the honors, playing the protagonist's sympathetic friend:

Lying in my bed that night,
Heard you play Norwegian Wood,
And for you, I wish it could come true.

"This Misery" was followed by another Colonials' tune, "Childhood." The pace was slower, the lyrics contemplative. Faith sang, her voice deep and rich:

Back to childhood we must go,
To pay the price of what we sow.
Back to being innocent,
Left alone to conquer it.

Ian McTimons came on stage for a flute duel with Abbas, trading licks on the instrumental "Bouree," by Jethro Tull. He stayed for an extended "Low Spark of High Heeled Boys," Traffic's slow burner, Robin, Gabe, and Darcy's strings driving the improvisational sections with an inventive arrangement. The set ended with "Catch and Release," a band original and a crowd favorite, featuring a blistering solo by Robin. The normally lively crowd could only stand transfixed, her violin steadily building in complexity and intent. Tim and Margaret had never heard anything like it.

Good food and drink, music and dance, and an appreciative local clientele. The Blacks were getting their proper English pub on.

They cut loose for the second set. Even Jessica proved to be the twins match, almost. Late on, the band played a twelve-minute version of Phish's "First Tube," an instrumental that Abbas adapted to suit his string section as well as the core. George and Geoff were merciless in their groove, punchy and insistent, while Paul and the rest manipulated the time signatures into a patchwork quilt of hypnotic melody.

And, from the first note, Hope and Grace were at it. Like club dancers in steel cages, they combined their physicality with a rhythmic allure that was infectious. The floor was writhing with humanity, answering the ancient drum's call. Even Mina, til now only able to tap her toes and hum along, found her voice and her groove, much to everyone's joy.

Bacchus and Silenus, satyrs in the times of the Greeks and Romans, would've been proud of this modern bacchanalia.

CHAPTER 69
FRIDAY, 7 JULY

Clouds of love and laughter come without a care.
Clouds of dark and thereafter make the light seem rare.

The tour of all things Scouse continued, the tourists themselves regaled with all the local flavor and diversion. Gradually the Blacks were content to spend their time more simply, in the company of their hosts and their daily pursuits. An afternoon with Aleah, a morning at the Edge Hill Animal Hospital, a symphony rehearsal, or an Albanian lesson while learning how to juggle a football. All unique little experiences to add to their time in England.

"I'm developing a taste for pies," Margaret confessed, seemingly out of the blue.

"Oh, any particular kind?"

"No. Fisherman's, steak and kidney, shepherd's, all good."

"Funny, we don't make them at home much. Pub food, I suppose."

Cheryl and Margaret were with Jessie, Aggy, and Jak, walking up Penny Lane, still a very surreal thing to be doing in Margaret's mind.

They were headed to Erins for a few items before window shopping along Smithdown Road.

The pharmacy was not too busy. A half dozen or so people from the neighborhood were roaming the aisles.

"Hey all! This is a nice surprise."

"Hi Colly!"

"Hi Jak, how are you?"

"Fine."

"How about you, Aggy?"

"I'm fine."

"What's on girls?"

"A bit of shopping and a morning out."

Amos joined the conversation, alerted by familiar voices. He soaked up all the loving six small hands could provide. Faith waved from the control area; she was filling scripts. Caspar helped a bag laden pensioner to the door and came over to give Cheryl a hard time.

"I've lost my wing man Cheryl, though I can certainly understand why. Still, I have to blame someone."

"I've never seen him so, Caspar. This must be it."

"She's quite a woman, so resilient. Deserves any good fortune that comes her way."

"She's a strong one, I think," Margaret said. "She can make her own luck."

"Spot on Mogs," Colly said.

Margaret couldn't stifle an excited grin. "I've got my own nickname now. So cool!"

The shop bell rang, followed by four new customers in the front door.

"All hands to the pump," Cheryl said. "We'll leave you to it."

Outside she pointed to the roundabout at the intersection.

"There's your next Beatles sighting. The barbershop on the other side of the shelter in the roundabout."

"Of every head he's had the pleasure to have known," Margaret sang.

"Penny Lane!" Jessica added.

They circled the intersection, checking out the storefronts, then went into St. Barnabus' church, which began the trek back to Greenbank.

"Paul McCartney sang in the choir here."

"It's quite lovely."

"All brick and sandstone, with a slate roof."

"Maybe we could come on Sunday. It's the Anglican church, right?"

"Correct. And you're certainly welcome. Father Andrew is a dear man."

Dovedale Towers loomed large on the way home. It was past noon, and they were all hungry enough.

"What d'ya say Mogs, we could have a pie?"

Lunch was also being taken in the City Centre at the moment. The twins were treating the staff at Duke Street to sandwiches from Bill's. Tim was along, and all seven sat above the restaurant in Chavasse Park.

Tim had gone with Ben to the office in the morning and managed to make himself useful. He helped with a photo shoot, organizing and managing somehow nine children into suitable poses with a smile on each face. He'd also gone with Sam to collect a client from Lime Street Station for Luke and helped Judith by taking a pile of mail to the post office.

The day was nice, the park busy, great for people watching here on the edge of the shopping district.

"This is such an amazing city, but I would get lost in a heartbeat."

"We've no straight streets," Sam explained. "The Romans gave us roads, and we made them long and winding."

"Paul McCartney!"

"Full marks, mate, well done!"

"You haven't been to Strawberry Fields yet, have you?"

"Come on Luke, that's not a real place," he hesitated. "Is it?"

"Absolutely," Judith confirmed. "But it's nothing like you might expect. You should take it in though."

"We'll show you Tim," Hope offered. "It's a quick trip from Greenbank. Right now I'm taking in this BLT."

"The food is good, eh?"

"Very!" Ben agreed. "What about." He stopped. "Grace. Grace, what are you looking at?"

She was pale, and staring. He looked around, seeing nothing immediately untoward.

"Where Grace?" Lucas asked.

"Right up next to that building."

No one said anything because no one saw anything unusual.

"The Mancs," she said, her voice chilling.

Luke followed her eyes. There they were, the same two. "They're chatting up that girl."

Now Ben put it together. He immediately stood.

"Easy big guy, let's watch for a minute," Luke advised. He scanned the crowd. There didn't seem to be anyone else observing the little scene play out. "I think it's just those two."

Grace put her hand on Ben's arm, firmly. "Dad, look at me."

He did, slowly, hesitant to let them out of his sight.

"Dad let me do this, you'll go too far. They're nothing really!"

He looked hard at her eyes; it nearly broke his heart. "Take your sister."

"Aw now, Ben," Sam pleaded. "This should be down to me mate."

"We get it Sam," Luke said. "But it's okay, stay seated, but stay alert."

It was obvious the closer they got that these two were up to their old tricks, the filthy scum.

"Which one did you clatter before?"

"The one on the right."

"I got the other one."

"Now Hope, maybe we can just put a scare into them. I don't want things to get out of hand."

"You're right, I'm cool."

The guy on the left was facing away, towards the mark. The other one too, but on her other side, facing the twins. He looked over at them and smiled. Who wouldn't with those two approaching. No sign of recognition, however, just a bit of puzzlement in his gaze.

Still about ten yards away, Hope increased her pace and before the guy could turn, she grabbed his elbow in one hand, his shirt collar with the other, and bull rushed him face first into the side of the building.

So much for playing it cool. Grace confronted the other one, who looked confused but irate. "What the."

"Shut the hell up!" she spat, turning her face to the side. He went silent, his face blank with shock.

"You dare show your face here in" another unfinished sentence as the Manc turned and ran at a speed that his limited physique would suggest him not capable of.

"Look at that sucker go!" Hope exclaimed in wonder.

The other one had made it to his feet, one eye already swollen almost shut, nose misshapen, blood everywhere.

"Go find yer mate and disappear!" was all Grace could get out before he hastily exited the scene.

"Damn sister!"

"Sorry, I got lost in the moment."

They turned to look across the park for the rest, but found one very large man blocking their view.

"You bitches need a lesson," he said coldly, heavily accented. There was another behind him, bigger and rougher looking.

"Fuck you Gomer!"

He took a step forward as Ben, out of nowhere, stepped in front of the girls and was nearly in arm's reach of the guy, who merely stepped to the side and motioned for his associate to take his place.

The enforcer was only a couple of inches shorter than Ben, but probably weighed more and did not look fat. He did look experienced, a very hard man.

Ben raised his hands in submission and took a step back, which was the perfect position from which to spring forward and deliver a right cross to his adversary's cheek and jaw. He went down and remained motionless. A lot of feeling went into that punch.

Luke had alerted Ben to the pair arriving on-scene. As soon as his friend went to his daughters, he told Sam and Tim where to position themselves and asked Jude to start taking pictures of the two perps. He'd also warned Ben of the weapons they no doubt had. The bodyguard's boss was now advancing on Ben, knife drawn.

Sam, Tim, and Lucas closed in as the two engaged, in the end unnecessary. Ben allowed the guy one swing of the blade, slicing through his shirt and drawing blood, and then literally took the man apart. Judith had to lower the camera and look away.

Lucas had to think quickly. This was much too public. He took both guys' wallets and led his friends away from the park post haste.

They got back to Duke Street and called the clinic. Dani was in surgery, Poppy assisting, so Mina came over with a kit and cleaned Ben up, then stitched him up and dressed the wound.

"This family has to stay away from Albanians!" she said to lighten the mood. That's all she would ever say on the matter. Experience was the best teacher.

The Blacks were headed home tomorrow, so the gang gathered for a cookout at the Pines that evening. Tim, Mogs, and Jessie were gushing about the greatest vacation ever and thanking everyone for their hospitality.

"Please come back soon. You're all part of the clan now!" Robin said.

"Yeah, heck, we even put you to work!" Abbas added. "How did you get on today at the office, Tim?"

Tim shrugged, "Just a walk in the park."

Chapter 70

Monday, 10 July

And he keeps an eye out on this town,
the resignation Superman.
He'll keep himself amused, with the evening news.

Tom Carney sat at his desk, his expression a mixture of pique and amusement. Those cheeky bastards! He didn't know whether to commend them or arrest them.

Inspector Thomas John Carney was a part of Merseyside Police's Investigation and Intelligence Division. His office was in the St. Annes Street station near the Kingsway Tunnel entrance. His duties were varied; the division responded to threats to public safety from a number of sources, some organized and well-funded. Times seemed more complicated now, and Tom was nearing retirement, something he was looking forward to. Pride and dedication kept him vigilant though, his vast experience more than made up for any lack of energy.

A year ago, Inspector Carney was put in charge of a task force assigned to root out a human trafficking ring operating locally. Young women were being snatched off the street and smuggled onto ships bound for southeastern Europe, principally Albania.

A break in the case came with the escape of an intended victim, one Grace Pine, twenty years of age and apparently quite feisty. She was able to shed light on the kidnapper's methods and could identify the two-point men and the organization's local handler. Chief Constable Sir Norman Bettison assigned a three-man team to serve under Tom and together they walked the cobbles, questioned the citizenry, and monitored the CCTV in order to tighten the net and rein the crew in.

Their observations were providing some possible suspects. A lineup of photographs was being prepared for the witness. Then, one person of interest was found in a second-floor room in the Lord Nelson Hotel, the victim of a particularly grisly fate. Liridon Gashi, an Albanian national with a colorful past, once a mercenary in the Balkan wars known as the Butcher of Belgrade. He'd met his fate, quite ironic to Tom's thinking.

And so, nearly one year later, with other issues occupying his attention, young women began to go missing, again. The department kept it from the media; perhaps it was just a coincidence of isolated incidents. He and his team hit the streets, and eventually learned the opposite, it was happening again. Then, just three days ago, he had a front row seat for one of the most bizarre series of events, truly one for the books.

He was leaning against the railing at the top of the stairs on the edge of Chavasse Park, observing the two smooth talkers and their intended prey. Hoping the interaction would lead to an attempted snatch he waited; maybe more bad actors would make an appearance.

Instead, two more young girls strode with purpose up to the trio. They were twins for sure, and by the time he realized one of them was Grace Pine they'd terrorized the pair of lackeys into fleeing the scene.

He pushed off the railing, intending to dress the two down good and proper, when things started unwinding. Two very large and nasty looking characters confronted the twins, followed by the instant appearance of Benjamin Pine. Tom had interviewed Mr. Pine and his daughter after the incident last year and had been impressed. Grace was a strong and brave young lady, her father sharp and well-spoken, and obviously struggling to maintain patience and civility. Understandable, his world had nearly come apart.

The experience hadn't made them timid, or in any way diminished their ability to deal with a new threat. Pine was efficient and brutal in his taking down of the two men advancing on his daughters.

It was fairly clear-cut in his mind up to this point, what had occurred and why. Then it all got muddled up when four more persons of interest materialized from all points of the compass and converged to parlay with the Pines. That, combined with the packet received by his station the next evening, delivered anonymously, really stoked his curiosity.

It contained two wallets, a half dozen photos, and a typewritten note. Carney picked it up off his desk and read over it again:

To whom we hope it concerns:

Contained within is identification for the two men injured in Chavasse Park Friday afternoon. Also included is photographic evidence of their intent to inflict serious bodily harm to three local citizens. These men are involved in a kidnapping ring. Please take appropriate steps. Sincerely,

Mothers Against Human Traffickers

The tag line, that's what stuck in his craw. Multiple players, a link to the past, this was looking less and less like a random occurrence. He decided to re-introduce himself to Ben Pine.

Tom was glad to be in uniform today; he wanted to make a good impression. An associate dropped him off in front of Pine's listed place of business on Duke Street and he entered the office's foyer. There at the front desk stood two of the people that were in the park Friday. More food for thought.

Lucas wasn't surprised to see a member of Liverpool's finest at the front door. He was expecting them at Greenbank over the weekend.

"What's the plan Luke?"

"Tell him what he wants to hear Jude, we're cool."

"Good day Sir. Welcome to Carter Assets Management and Big Ben Photography. What may I do you for?"

"For starters, who do I have the pleasure of meeting on this splendid day?"

"I'm Lucas Carter, sir. This is Judith Baker." Luke shook the man's hand.

"Is Ben Pine in?"

"He is. Shall I see if he's available?"

"Yes please. In the interim perhaps we could have a chat."

"Of course," Luke responded. "Care for a cuppa?"

"No thanks. I'm Inspector Thomas Carney. Mr. Pine and I have met before. That awful business last year, I'm afraid. Unfortunately, a similar situation has arisen of late."

Luke sensed a bit of mischief on the inspector's part; he needed to get ahead of it. "Yes sir, we were made painfully aware of that just a few days ago."

Ben came out of his office, looking appropriately surprised. "Inspector, good morning! Glad you're here. Do you have some time? I'm afraid I've made a bit of a mess."

Sam walked through the front door. If he was taken aback, he didn't show it. "Hey all! Jude, have you been dating youngsters again?"

Well, this dynamic was getting out of control, Tom thought, another one from the park. "Is there someplace quiet we could talk, all of us?"

Jude asked Jacob to come down and watch the desk while the five of them went to Ben's office.

"I'm just coming out with it. Something has got me feeling very suspicious in that the line between hunter and prey seems to have blurred in this case. The fact that there were seven of you in the park and the manner in which events occurred would suggest some orchestration. Care to dispel that conclusion?"

"Absolutely!" Jude replied. "It was a total coincidence. Ben's daughters came by unannounced to take us to lunch. Grace is the only person in Liverpool that could recognize those two scally wankers, and she was in utter shock when they showed up."

"So, she was so afraid that she assaulted one of them."

"That was her sister," Ben said. "And that was preferred to my getting involved. Our whole family has had trouble getting closure from this nightmare."

"But you did get involved."

"Damn straight. My girls are brave, but those two would've taken them both from me."

"I suppose. By the way, how's your side?"

"What do you mean?"

"Your knife wound, is it looked after?"

Now Luke understood, and he was pissed. "You were there, weren't you?"

"A ringside seat."

"Then you saw how it went down. What little Ben and his girls are culpable for is nothing compared to what they prevented."

"Then why the cloak and dagger, Mr. Carter? Why didn't you just stay and sort it with the responding officers?"

"I can explain that Inspector. I'm Sam Jackson, an employee here. It's been twice by my count that Ben and his family have been terrorized by this outfit, which the authorities have still failed to bring under control. The Pine's names have managed to remain a secret the first time. Hopefully that will continue. Who do you think they'll send if they find out who's been mucking up the operation?"

"This little escapade was much more public than the first. You know how the fucking journos are. They'll splash this story all over the front page!" Tom said.

"Not if the police don't tell them," Ben put in. "I was one of those 'fucking journos' for twenty-five years. Alistair Machray will not publish my family's name in association with this."

"Good, that is a nice piece of luck. Now perhaps we can talk about the packet one of you no doubt dropped off at the station."

"Guilty as charged," Luke confessed.

"Why did you take their wallets?"

"In case they came around and left before help arrived. We'd at least know who they were."

"And the photographs? That was convenient."

"Ben was a photojournalist. He's never without his camera."

"The note was curious," Tom mentioned casually. "A bit cheeky. And where did you get that sign-off, Mother's Against Human Traffickers?"

"It was quoted last year in the paper, with that guy found in the hotel. Grace identified him as the one who slashed her. I composed the note, Inspector," Luke admitted. "I wanted to strengthen the possibility that some group out there was acting independently."

Fucking journos, Tom thought. He thanked them all for their time, left his card and departed.

Ben, Sam, and Jude were trying to parse out what exactly Tom Carney was thinking. Lucas felt that the man had already tipped his hand.

"He's not into us for what happened Friday, guys. He wants to know who was in that hotel room last year. He's worried about the vigilante thing catching on."

CHAPTER 71
TUESDAY, 11 JULY

Many is a word that only leaves you guessing
Guessing 'bout a thing you really ought to know

Jacob woke to the familiar sounds of the city coming alive around him. He remembered the hesitation he harbored when deciding to move to the flat on Duke Street with Gabe. Greenbank was leafy and peaceful, the only home he'd ever known. The transition to city life was a smooth one, however, and he was enjoying being more on his own here in the City Centre with his childhood chum.

Jake and Gabriel hadn't spoken yet about how this living arrangement might change after the wedding. He was going to propose the easiest and most obvious solution to the situation; he and his sister would just switch places. Poppy and Gabe would have their own place and he would live with his folks and his pal Otis. So far, all that was known about the wedding was the date. That was down to his mum and Robin, who were pulling all the strings for this affair.

He turned his attention to the day ahead, heading for the toilet and the wash basin. Taking stock of himself in the mirror, he noticed his hair was showing some extra length now; it hadn't been cut all year. Still good for the time being, he decided, although the stubble on his face would have to come off or shaped into a beard. He decided to shave, part of the plan to look a little sharper today than normal. The reason? Today was his twenty-fifth birthday.

After finishing up in the bathroom he dressed while eating some fruit, then saw to Scruff's needs before going downstairs.

A pot of water was started for tea and the front door unlocked, just in time for Jude's arrival.

"Good morning, Ms. Baker!"

"Morning Jacob. You're at it early."

"I went to bed early. I like it when I do that. The mornings are so nice now."

"It's habit for me. All those years at the *Echo*, I suppose."

"Here come the bosses. I'll get you a cuppa."

"Thanks Jake! Good morning gentlemen."

"Morning Judith. Nice look."

"Thank you, Ben. Nothing like a new summer smock to brighten one's day."

"Very nice Jude. The color sets off your eyes."

"Much appreciated, kind sir. Oh, by the way, I got a call late yesterday. Your tailor wants to move your appointment up a half hour."

"That's actually good news. Then I'll have time to do lunch before my afternoon meeting with Sir Philip."

"Oh?"

"Yeah, we've a few items to sort. A goalie I'm recommending from Wrexham, his family's nuptial invite for next month, and I want to give him a heads up on what happened Friday and yesterday."

"Good idea that. It's always nice to have an ally at the other end of the food chain."

"Why Moneypenny, I believe you're starting to embrace this foreign intrigue aspect of life."

"Think globally, act locally."

"Right on sister!"

"Okay, I've been entertained enough for one morning," Ben carped. "Off to work."

"Here Ben," Jake said, returning with a tray. "Have some tea."

"Thanks, birthday boy!"

Jake groaned, but it got him a warm cuddle from Judith.

"Oh Jacob, Jude said Ian called."

"McTimons?"

"No no, Hamilton-Doyle. We're needed at eleven, not half past."

"Cool, no problem."

"Alright, we've a plan. Now, to your stations lads. We've got to sign em and shoot em!"

Judith had it figured out—boys mature until they're about Jake's age, then they just stop.

Lucas and the birthday boy wheeled and dealed until ten thirty, then walked to Lord Street for their appointment. Made to Measure was the shop owned by Ian Hamilton-Doyle, a tailor who only had one employee, mainly to see to the odds and ends so he could concentrate on plying his trade. He was a talented craftsman, and a very nice man with a reputation for quality work.

"Like walking models you are lads," he complimented upon hearing the little bell over the door. He was of retirement age, peering almost hobbit-like over the top of his spectacles. A pension was not in the foreseeable future, though. He wouldn't know what to do with himself.

"I do like working with linen," he declared, almost apologetically. "A bugger to keep square but so worth the effort."

"This is the last fitting, I believe. Correct?"

"Yes Lucas, and they will be completed within a fortnight."

"Splendid Ian, you're the best!"

"There's enough to fret with a wedding looming. No need to worry about arriving not at your best."

"Careful now," Jake warned. "We don't want to outshine the groom."

"Not a chance, my dear boy. I'm outfitting Master Gabriel as well."

"Him you probably know by heart."

"Very nearly. I've been making or altering his formal wear for the Phil all along."

The Carters bought lunch from a street vendor and ate at Chavasse Park on the way back to the office. Luke relived last Friday's fun and games. He wanted his son to understand the mechanics of what happened, the reasons for and the implication of taking such actions. He knew Jacob was also one to get involved in these kinds of matters, and try to make a difference where needed. But his son did not have the same background as he. Luke credited his savvy as a product of his travels, because in the end, it was his knowledge of people and how to read and deal with them that allowed him to safely operate in tough situations.

"We're planning on you, counselor, to travel for the agency, far and wide. That's where you'll pick up your street smarts. Liverpool's been a good primer. Now you can get away from the clan some and become Jake Carter."

While walking back to the office Jacob brought up the subject of Grace's ordeal last year, and his dad's handling of it. Lucas responded by letting him in on some details that only Ben knew, knowing this was another good teaching opportunity.

"I got too personally involved Jake. Not about my feelings towards Grace, or that I didn't want this type of shit going down in my city. It was my impatience and the temptation I felt when I found that bastard. Going in that hotel room alone with him was a mistake."

The rest of the afternoon was business as usual, productive as well. Ben popped in Jake's office late on with a message.

"Don't know what you've got on for the evening, but Hope and Grace are hoping you'll come to Greenbank for happy hour first."

"Sure, it's hard to deny the twins."

"Boy howdy!"

"I've got to shower and change, then I'll be along."

Jake communed with Scruff while getting ready. The feline fury was more and more seeing the benefit of human companionship.

"I'd take you to Greenbank to live if I go, but we like our dogs with two eyes each."

He took the bus down to Mossley Hill, presentably clad and light of spirit. He wanted to check in with his mum, but no one was home, so he went next door to the Pines. Ben was just coming down the stairs, freshly attired and showered himself.

"The women folk are out back, let's join them."

"Yeah, I'm thirsty!"

He opened the back door and stood transfixed, somehow nearly all the clan was in Ben's garden.

"Surprise!"

CHAPTER 72
SATURDAY, 15 JULY

Dreams are lies, it's the dreaming that's real.

Darcy felt a bit put off. It had been a month since she petitioned her mates to ponder a big change in their lives, a decision to be taken together. They'd plenty of opportunity to respond, but so far she hadn't heard word one from any of them.

They were all at Tai Chi this morning, and she was happy that everyone was into this new discipline. It was funny in a way, a half dozen youngsters getting their 'boundless fist' on surrounded by other students older than their parents. In truth the group dynamic was welcomed. Being raised in the clan taught them all the value of the elder's wisdom and experience. Maybe that was it. She was the youngest of the Six, and therefore not heedworthy. Nah, that might be a bit unfair she thought. The Six were challenging but supportive.

Very well, they were to gather together later, another shot at redemption, perhaps with a nudge. She had time to further study her feelings on the matter and decided she might be jumping the gun a bit anyway. Perhaps the timing wasn't quite right.

In the meantime, some more research on the subject would be wise. She raided the fridge for lunch, a chunk of cheese and some grapes, and rang up Ian. He was home and available and said for her to come on over.

She found him in the garden with Nathan, conducting a bicycle maintenance lesson. The boy ranged far and wide on his trusty steed and was keen to keep it in top shape.

"Hi Darcy!"

"Hey Nate, I see you've put a rack on your bike."

"Yeah, I needed one. Dad said it's better on the back behind the saddle."

"Oh, why's that?"

"If you put one on the front, the weight of what's in it affects your balance."

"Oh, why's that?"

He hesitated, not really sure. She was curious, or maybe testing him. Ian smiled.

"I guess because on the front it's higher up, so the weight makes more difference." He thought some more, staring intently. "I think also because on the front, it's farther out and away from me."

"Makes sense. A back rack is almost right up under you, close to your body. Working on a bike is messy, eh?"

"Yeah, and hard to get off."

"I think we're done here anyway son. Why don't you get cleaned up. I'll stow the tools."

"Okay," he scooted off to the mud room.

"What a kid Ian, well done."

"Filly gets the credit."

"Not all luv. You're an inspiration, in a very major key."

He chuckled, a musician's joke.

"Where's Filly?"

"With Aleah, sorting decorations for the wedding."

"I wonder what they'll come up with."

"Useless to guess. It's always something unexpected and amazing every time those two put their heads together. But you've something on your mind Darcy, I'd rather talk about that."

She took a rag and wiped a smudge off his chin. "Well, I've been thinking a lot, and not getting anywhere, about leaving Liverpool."

He was stunned. He had no idea. "That's a big decision."

"One I'm unable to make. I guess I want company, but the others aren't showing much interest. It's a little more complicated for the rest, especially the twins. They're committed until next spring. Gabe, Jake, and Poppy all have plenty on their plate, so I understand that the whole idea's somewhat out of the blue."

"And you, are you conflicted personally?"

"I don't think I'll be satisfied until I've scratched this itch. Most of the clan has traveled extensively. I've been hearing about it all my life."

"Would you be willing to strike out on your own?"

"I suppose that you can speak to. What moved you to emigrate?"

"Basically the same reasons you have. My brothers and I were taken with the Fab Five, all from different parts of the globe. But I had a place to land, and Gene, Lou, and Astrid to live with."

"Which I could do, or even out in Tucson with Dani's folks. Grace and Hope have been there a couple of times. And I do wonder about going solo, a bit scary but a good challenge."

"A lot to think about Darcy. My advice is don't rush it, the thought process that is. Make sure it's what you want and makes sense. Once that's sorted, hell, you could leave the next day. You're capable enough to be successful, lass, I'd bet on ya."

"Thank you, Ian, it's great advice."

"Don't forget I ended up coming back. But there were no regrets; my time in the States was invaluable."

"You accomplished a lot Ian, and returned the prodigal son."

He laughed. "That could be debated. Still, it made no difference. I could've crawled home penniless and broken. You know that old saying, you can never go home?"

"Uh huh."

"Well, on Greenbank it's you can always come home."

And that's what she did. After bathing, she dressed nicely in a short summer dress and sandals, tying her wavy auburn hair back from her face. Three earrings and her ever present penguin pendant, plus a light buttoned jumper in case the evening cooled, completed the look.

Next door she found Jacob locked and loaded, sitting in the front room with her brother.

"Hey Darce, Poppy should be down tout de suite. Want some water?"

"No thanks. You boys look nice."

"Thank you, back at ya. Ever been to the Dandy before?

"Never even heard of it. Where's it at?"

"Cronton."

"Huh, I haven't been down in that area in ages."

"A client recommended it," Poppy said, appearing from the stairway. "They've got an extensive menu and beer list."

"Something for everyone," Gabe added.

"Where's Mina and the kids?"

"Two doors down," Jake said. "Watching Sesame Street with Kev."

"Aggy and Jak are soaking up the language like a sponge," Poppy said.

"Kevin and Cheryl are learning Albanian in the process."

"How bout you Jake, picking up any?"

"Very little, I'm trying to get better in German."

"Here come the twins," Gabe said, looking out the window. "Let's hit it."

The Dandy was the Dandelion Tavern, on the main road to Widnes in the village of Cronton, just to the southeast of Liverpool. Coming fairly early was a good move. It was a popular place.

Meg introduced herself and saw to their drinks order while the menu was perused. A variety of dishes were ordered, including a halloumi wrap.

"What's halloumi Darce?"

"A type of cheese, my brother. An ancient food but now starting to get more attention."

"Interesting."

"We'll see, probably a lot depends on how it's prepared. Denise Halsall, our tai chi instructor, turned me on to it."

"That reminds me," Poppy started. "I didn't get a chance after class this morning. Gabe and I have talked some about the future."

"Really?" Hope asked. "You mean after the wedding and honeymoon?"

"Yep. We'd be willing to relocate. Not at the drop of a hat, mind you. Mum and the Phil deserve fair warning."

"Me too. Dad and I discussed a lot of stuff on my birthday. We spent the whole day together. He said it may be a shrewd move for the agency to have two offices. Better access to the talent. So, I can live nearly anywhere and keep my job."

"Hope and I can join you after we graduate. We'll not be the ones to break up the Six."

"Nice of you to say. But as the resident scout and assayer of athletic endeavor, I predict high draft picks for the both of you."

"Then let that decide our destination," offered Gabe. "Surely all eight cities have symphonies."

"And lots of vet practices. Or I could start my own."

Darcy had sat quietly as soon as the subject had been breached, curious as to her mate's thoughts. A warm flush had filled her body as they spoke. They hadn't dismissed her plea after all. Now she felt emboldened.

"I've a plan," she began, confident now and clear of thought. "The Women's United Soccer Association's inaugural season kicks on next April. Franchises have been awarded in D.C., Atlanta, Boston, Carolina, New York, Philly, San Diego, and San Jose. Jacob, you're to go to the States this fall and establish a relationship with all these clubs and assure at least one of them that trading up to get two picks in a row would get them an all-star pairing at center back. Then deliver letters of introduction for Gabriel and me to that club's city symphony, along with some recorded performances and a set of headshots. Don't forget the head-shots—my brother is quite handsome, and I am to die for. Poppy, follow your mum's path. It was brilliant. Work for an older, established vet and you can move him on and take over. And find us a big house, big enough for Jake's office and some kids and dogs. I'd like a nice garden and a place to jam with our new band, 'The Immigrants.' Any questions?"

Silence, and slack-jawed, wide-eyed stares.

"Oh, and a hot tub. A big one, with lots of jets."

Chapter 73
Tuesday, 25 July

And we're going on faith here,
and all that kind of stuff.
And even grace, if we're lucky enough.

It was an exciting and busy week at Greenbank. For one, Aggy and Jak were getting their own rooms. Mina was changing hers, as was Seamus. Even Kevin and Cheryl were playing musical bedrooms. Otis was much amused, camped out on the Pine's front stoop watching the goings on next door.

A rare and seismic development was responsible for the moves, made after much talk and deliberation, and in the end fairly straightforward and simply concluded.

Kevin and Cheryl were moving to Calderstones to live with the Tweeners. The idea had been on the table for some time—an offer from Ian and Cyrus' families to spend their retirement around their grandchildren. Seamus was aware of the possibility and brought the subject up again last week, subsequently discussed by all three McTimons households. The timing was sound and the whole plan made good sense. "The children need some structure now, added stability so they can move on from the past and get on with their lives," he'd reasoned.

Of course, Shea himself had as big an adjustment to make as any in this scenario; his life would change the most with the new arrangement. And that was fine by him, hopelessly smitten and ready for a 'made to order' family. He was mature enough to accept the responsibility and more devoted to Mina by the day. The name on the post box would still read McTimons, but with a new cast of characters.

So, a couple in their thirties were moving in with their young children, replacing the couple who moved in over thirty years ago, also in their thirties with young children. Must be a generational thing.

"Puttin' me out to pasture, they are," Kevin groaned, feigning injustice.

"Not havin' it," Cyril replied. "You'll be waited on hand and foot."

They were out under the yew, reminiscing while watching Shea, Grace, and Hope load the chip shop's van with Kev and Cheryl's personals.

"I remember pulling the lorry to the curb, back in the fall of '69. A gamble it was, putting the chippy up for a mortgage on a big, beautiful home for Cheryl and the boys. Scary stuff, but we managed it. Now this, an end and a beginning, just turning the page."

"You sound wistful, old chum. Any regrets?"

"None. I'm happier than ever."

"And deservedly so. You and Cheryl can put it on cruise control now. Your lives have changed a lot the past year Kev. Enjoy de transition."

"That's the plan. Some of these changes are a little surreal. It looks like I've doubled my allotment of grandkids."

Cyril smiled. "Yes sir, and dis one is special. Shea and Mina, a real love story. Has to be to affect this kind of commitment from the playboy."

"Ermina is special Cy, character and soul."

"Indeed. Check it out."

She emerged from the Carters, Aggy and Jak in tow, loaded down and headed two doors north, picking Otis up on the way. She looked over and waved.

"They look nearly done, Cy. Should we go and offer assistance?"

"You sure? I've only seen clothing and personals being moved about."

"That's all that's going. The furniture stays. We may get a new bed soon, but otherwise both places are suitably furnished."

"Makes sense, and makes it easier, a good thing."

"You've enough on your mind anyway. How's the preseason going?"

"Good. The lads have come back looking nearly fit."

"They know you'll make them suffer. The more they look after themselves during the summer the better."

"They've run a lot the past ten days. I gave them today off."

"So you can torture them tomorrow. What's the trick, how do you get them to work so hard?"

"I train with them, Seamus too. They stay focused and push on. Can't let the old man show them up."

Inside the house the flurry of activity had started to die down. Nearly everything in the house that was supposed to be there was there, just not necessarily in the right place. Mina, Aggy, and the twins were gleefully discussing the possible arrangement of all thing's girlie upstairs in the bedrooms. Seamus and Jak were having a fizzy and a biscuit at the dining table, resting from their labors. Shea was more nervous around the kids than he was Ermina now, opposite to his feelings just several months ago. She'd explained to them carefully about their new lives, how she felt and what the future held. The young were always being informed on matters they had no control over, and sometimes didn't fully understand. Trust was so important. Children needed to feel safe and loved, and to believe in what they were being told. Kids were resilient, but they had to have something, and more importantly, someone to hold onto during such confusing times. Shea was replacing Jak and Aggy's fathers and hoped that one day they would call him their father. That was one hell of a long road. In the meantime he was going to be someone they could trust and count on.

Cyril and Kevin paused out front before coming in.

"Do you think they'll have a child together?"

"I dunno Cy, I suppose it's possible."

"Likely, I'd say, given the reproductive influence Greenbank has on its residents."

"There ya go again, there's 'something in the water.' Isn't that what you claim?"

"It's on my list. I'm not so concerned in this case though."

"Yeah, how so?" Kev was really curious now; Cy had some wild theories.

"Well, we're introducing some more foreign blood into the gene pool, which is a good ting. I was starting to get confused as to who was related to who. We have to be careful; we could have problems a couple of generations down de line."

"Still not following ya mate."

"Let me put it dis way. A wise old Trinidadian once said, 'trees planted too close together bear bad fruit.'"

CHAPTER 74
THURSDAY, 3 AUGUST

Nothing I see can be taken from me

"Good morning," she said softly.

"Good morning. Happy Anniversary."

"Yeah it is, a bit lost in all the hubbub."

"Not as long as I'm lying here holding you."

She snuggled up closer and kissed him sweetly. "Let's stay right here a little longer."

"A lot longer," he replied, pulling her on top of him.

Downstairs Poppy had just returned with Otis and was boiling some water for tea.

"There you are!"

"Morning Gran!" She hugged Anne, then Ender, who was shuffling along behind. "Y Abuelo, dormiste bien?"

"Si si, siempre mi cara."

"How do you both feel?"

"Great! I needed a couple of days to shed my jet lag."

"Me too," Anne said. "I want to get out and about today. It's been a long time since we've come to Liverpool."

"Let's get a good breakfast in ya, I'll whip up some eggs."

Similar scenes were unfolding all along the rowhouse where family was in for the big event. The crew from St. Pete were in town. Cye and Astrid were next door at the Ardavans and Eugene and Louise on the other side at the Pines.

The Trinis were camped at Cyril and Colleen's. Michael and Allison were taking tea with Cy in the garden while Colly was next door introducing Catherine and Millicent to Mina.

The pair were much impressed, as well as horrified, upon hearing Ermina Murati's story, and anxious to meet her. Their embrace was almost embarrassing to Mina, such was the sincere emotion it carried. Amusingly the greeting and introduction was so effusive that their island lilt was beyond Mina' grasp.

"It is beautiful to listen to, but I cannot understand a lot of what you say."

That brought more hugs, and a considerably slower and a more distinct choice of words.

Seamus was delightfully entertained, and always happy to see these two. He remembered meeting Millie for the first time when she and Cat came for a visit and stayed with the McTimons. That caused a sensation amongst the brothers, their father as well.

"I'm so glad you ladies could make the trip over."

"Any excuse to come to Liverpool. All my favorite people are here. This is a pretty massive occasion Seamus."

"That it is, the kids are all grown up now."

"Not all!" Millie exclaimed, looking at the hallway.

Jak and Aggy had been curious about the goings on downstairs and came to investigate.

"Agnesa, come and meet Catty, she is Cyril's sister."

Jak beat her to the hug. Anything or anyone connected to Cyril Barcant had to be special. Long, tall Millie was a nice bonus too.

"She's beautiful Mina," Catherine cooed. "And Jak is adorable!"

"Their English is improving by the day," Shea said. "We have to be careful what we say now."

"I know what you say," Aggy chided.

"I play football!"

"Yes, I know," Millie said. "Can we play later?"

"You betcha!"

"Hey, that's Carter talk!" Cat said.

"The Carterian influence on Greenbank is as strong as ever," Colly informed. "It's been an eventful year."

"So we hear. How's Ben?"

"He's fine Cat. We're hoping all that business is done now."

"Grace, Lucas, and now Ben," Shea said. "The clan needs to stop going to Albanians for their elective surgery." Mina poked him in the ribs.

Next door Ben himself was forced to succumb to his mother's request and bare his wound, now mostly healed.

"Oh Ben," was all she could say.

"Ermina did a good job son," his father began, not sure how to proceed. "I suppose you have mixed emotions."

"Since the beginning. When Grace was attacked, and that's been over a year now, I was teetering, rage and despair. I was ready to burn the city to the ground to find the man responsible. Lucas sorted it, and I was only able to sit and wait, and seethe. Then you think it's over, and when it isn't, it's like a nightmare."

"I'm proud of the way you handled it."

"Thanks Dad, I wish I had your experience, and your cool."

"Don't kid yourself. My time in the field was spent avoiding drastic measures. This was personal Ben. They forced your hand."

"What a rush. I'll have to admit it was cathartic, but I nearly killed them."

"It was their intent to kill you son. And the young girls they target, their fate is worse than death. What's the latest?"

"The two finally were healthy enough to travel. Two tickets to Tirana, courtesy of the British government, one way."

"Any backlash?"

"One very curious and mildly suspicious inspector paid us a visit. I think his interest was personal. Nothing since. I suspect we have someone looking after us."

"Oh?"

"Yeah. Sir Philip Carter."

"Of course. Part of the clan."

"That and Lucas. Sir Philip respects Luke a great deal."

"That seems unlikely, in theory," Gene thought.

"It started out that way, I'm sure, changing over time."

"A conservative is a liberal that's been mugged."

"A liberal is a conservative that's been arrested."

Louise left the boys to it; a debate was taking shape. She found Faith and her granddaughters in the kitchen, dicing fruit and working the toaster.

"Morning Gran."

"Good morning, Hope. You ladies are looking fresh today."

"It's the countdown to consummation Lou. We have to be at it."

"Mother!"

Louise was laughing. "Nonsense Grace, that was hilarious, although I doubt the intended have been chaste all this time."

"That's for sure. Jake's been driven from the love nest up on Duke Street more than once. How about some coffee, Gran?"

"Yes please, I need to clear the cobwebs. By the way, when are you two headed back to school?"

"The end of next week," Hope announced. "We've football training for a couple of weeks before classes start."

"Senior year, how exciting!"

"And a little intimidating," Grace said. "We're going to try to be able to graduate, with enough credits anyway, after second term before Easter. Then take some elective afterwards."

"Why the rush?"

"The new pro league starts in April. We're hoping to get drafted."

"I see, if you're selected you can slot right in and finish college in the off season. Good idea."

"It was Darcy's idea. She's seen the future."

"Has she now?"

"Oh yeah, the Six, together, pioneers of the new millennium."

"You two are a blast! Makes me wish I was your age again."

"Nope, we love our Gran just like she is."

"And I'm anxious to see your other grandmother again, and those charming Mason brothers!"

Two doors down Gene and Lou's neighbors were in Robin's kitchen figuring out breakfast over tea.

"Porridge and toast," was Cye's vote. Astrid agreed whole heartedly.

"It's probably not popular here in the summer," Astrid reasoned, "but it's in the 60s here. That's chilly for us. St. Pete will top 90 today."

"Then porridge it is," Robin decided.

"Cye, come into the front room and meet Alpina," Abbas urged excitedly. Robin rolled her eyes.

"How's Cye's new business Astrid?"

"Gangbusters Robin. He turned an old paint and body shop into a day care center that sold for three quarters of a million dollars. Then it started to snowball. Gene's been using his contacts to get prospective clients and grease the skids at City Hall."

"Shades of Hassan and Neff."

"With the same name on the firm's masthead."

"How about you and the aquarium?"

"Loving it! The atmosphere, the people, and we're doing some very important work."

"It's got to be a challenge, when you think about the environment, particularly the seas. Uh oh, there they go!"

"What are they doing?"

"Just wait, you'll know in an instant."

Abbas, proud as a peacock, in the attic with his brother, his baby assembled and ready. He opened the dormer, placed her bell end on the sill, and let'er rip.

Let the games begin!

CHAPTER 75
THURSDAY, 3 AUGUST

I knew her when summer was her crown,
and autumn sad how brown her eyes.
I knew her when winter was her cloak,
and spring her voice she spoke to me.

Scruff hopped up onto Gabriel's bed, chose a spot next to his hip and curled up, beginning to purr. Gabe was already awake, laying quietly while trying to anticipate the day's events. He had a minor role in the proceedings, basically to just show up and say I do. A lot of planning and effort had taken place, paving the way for a day of celebration with all his family and friends present. He was glad his plan of the day was relatively straightforward and easy to fulfill because all he could think of was Poppy Anne Carter.

He couldn't imagine life without her. He was two and a half when she was born. The Six grew up together in the communal spirit of the clan, the definition of a shared life experience. The strangest part of the whole situation was that they'd become lovers. He was more nervous the day he declared his intentions towards her than he'd ever been in his life.

Her reaction made it the happiest day of his life. In an instant he was made to feel accepted and loved, and desired.

That was Poppy, the epitome of '60s ethos in a modern young woman. Outwardly she was the classic 'it' girl—stylish, pretty, lively, and open. Inwardly she was strong of character, with her father's sharp intellect and her mother's grace and shrewd judgement. And she was a healer, with great heart and compassion. Gabriel felt himself to be a very lucky fellow.

"Hey man, you gonna sleep all day?"

"Mornin' Jacob."

"He's alive!"

"What's up?"

"I have care and custody of the condemned today, and I take my responsibilities seriously."

"Oh brother. Scruff, kill!"

"Come on now, don't waste your last day of bachelorhood."

"I'm still getting over my last night of bachelorhood."

"Yeah, that was epic!"

Gabe got up and headed for the bathroom. "So what's the plan?"

"Breakfast at Tabac. Rita will want to hear about your impending nuptials."

"She's been pinching my cheeks since I was a toddler."

"She'll cop more than that today, I suspect. Anyway, afterwards we can come back here and hang for a while, then go for a long run."

"Good idea, I need a workout."

"Ditto. Then we can eat lunch and get you ready for the big event."

"Thanks for being my best man, and best mate."

"We've always been mates; if youd've chosen someone else for today I'd kick your ass!"

"Dream on!"

"Oh hey! I've seen the bride in her dress. Man oh man!"

The bride to be had been up for a while already. No choice really, the whole rowhouse was full of people. She stayed in her room initially, playing out the day in her mind. Everything was in place and ready to go, and the anticipation, building all along, was peaking. Poppy was thankful to have so many loved ones about to pass the time and occupy her thoughts.

Tradition called for her to stay in the background until the ceremony. Attendees were supposed to be shielded from seeing the bride until the appointed hour. Her plan was to spend the morning with her Gran Anne in the City Centre, and be calmed by her peaceful demeanor and sage advice. A run in Sefton Park afterwards, followed by a meal midday and she'd be ready to bathe and let Robin, Darcy, and her mum get her ready for the wedding.

Poppy hoped Gabe hadn't become the victim of tradition and overdid the bachelor party thingy. She hadn't seen him for days. Who knows what he'd been up to, especially with her brother as his guide. Gabriel was smart, and always had a good feel for the situation, but he was quiet by nature, and could be led astray from time to time.

She loved him so much, their almost sibling relationship evolving over the course of their lives. She knew before he, how it would end up. Girls are quicker than boys in that respect, also the reason that she nudged the process along. This was not by design, just another manifestation of the feminine psyche, sometimes occurring unknowingly. Pheromones, the love drug, an integral part of the feminine mystique.

Gabriel's seduction of Poppy was unplanned if not unintended, and deeply rooted in the past. As soon as she started to notice that boys weren't all gross and icky she realized that Gabriel Ardavan had the look. Her adolescence and his Celtic Persian visage combined to create a strong reaction in her, one she still couldn't clearly define. The day he walked her along the waterfront and said how much he cared for her was a shock, even though it was what she longed to hear. That was the best day ever, until today.

The ceremony was to be held under the yew. That's where Gabe proposed, and where they both wanted to be to make their vows. It would be a first; past weddings were held at various other sites. Now the yew would once again shelter the clan at yet another big occasion.

By noon the massive old tree had been transformed by a power trio of artistic intent. Aleah's creative vision, Filly's coordinated logistical plan, and Nate's skilled application had resulted in a living display of form and beauty. The stage was set.

The celebratory atmosphere that pervaded Greenbank all week was kicked up another notch. People scurrying to and fro, getting themselves ready, borrowing hair thingys and ironing their Sunday best for a Saturday. Shined shoes, ties knotted and reknotted, and cowlicks tamed. The invitations listed the dress code as 'summer serious.'

"Let them interpret that any way they like," Robin said.

A lorry pulled up across the street and disgorged a couple dozen chairs and an arbor. The latter sparked a debate between Ben and Cye, Ben claiming it was big enough to be called a pergola. Whatever the correct term it certainly was fancy, more than suitable for their needs.

Prayers, offerings, and even a pagan ritual was performed in order to ensure good atmospheric cooperation for the day. Outdoor affairs on Merseyside were always odds against. Mother Nature had smiled on the two young lovers today; the weather was glorious.

An hour before the appointed time people started to gather, at the rowhouse and in and around the park. They came from the neighborhood, the suburbs, the city, the region, and points around the globe such as Port of Spain, St. Petersburg, Tucson, and Schindellegi. Yes, even Schindellegi. Luca and Laura caught a flight from Zürich and arrived Thursday night. They were busy back home in Switzerland but couldn't resist the opportunity to see Jake and Gabe again and meet the clan. They stayed at the Ardavans, adding another nationality to the mix, cultures colliding in a most familial manner.

The Doohans and Waters came together, along with their daughters and their families. All the various workmates attended, Jude and Sam, along with representation from the pharmacy, clinic, the *Echo,* and Tranmere Rovers. Some friends from the Phil were providing pre-ceremony music and, of course, the Eclectibles all came dressed to the nines.

The groom showed up with the best man, greeted their parents, and escorted them to their seats. They sat and talked while the twins, who were in charge of security, as always, also served as the cutest ushers ever. They seated those who opted to sit while the rest of the guests filled the semicircle, around the chairs under the east side of the yew's canopy facing the lake.

The power trio's handiwork was front and center now, lots of oohs and aahs were heard amongst the assembled. Multi-colored streamers were interlaced throughout the lower branches, creating a latticework of wood, crepe, and needles, alive in the breeze. Ribbons hung from the branches to within three feet of the ground. They were white, with a red bow at the bottom and different types of flowers pinned along their length. They were everywhere.

Aleah and her team added a personal touch to the event. Each guest received their own small corsage or boutonniere to mark the occasion and have as a keepsake.

Four o'clock came. Grace gave Jake the high sign, and he and Gabe took their places. Across the street the procession was taking shape. The guests suspended their conversations and gathered closer as the chamber group changed their tune.

Elizabeth Rose followed behind Agnesa and Jak as they spread flower petals, leading the wedding party into the park. Adorable!

Next came Nathan, walking between Amos and Otis, the ring-bearers.

Dani and Robin didn't want the processional spotlight on them, so they stayed seated. They both beamed as Abbas escorted the maid of honor to the arbor. Darcy was giggly with excitement, and one beautiful young lady.

The main attraction did not disappoint. Poppy pretty much burst from the house out onto the front walk, forcing Luke to scramble to catch up. She took his arm and leaned in, sharing a personal aside that they both laughed at. She was breathtaking—the local 'It' girl turned cosmopolitan cover model. Everyone was transfixed, gazing at the lovely lady walking their way, swept up by her energy and grace.

Lucas escorted her to the arbor, kissed her cheek and winked at Gabriel. "Good luck."

The intended smiled at each other and turned towards the man who would sanctify this union, Eugene Pine. Gene was honored, and thrilled to be asked to perform the ceremony. The Six were very dear to the Pines. He lent a heightened sense of class and dignity to the occasion; the former statesman and diplomat could really work a room.

"Oh my, this is a splendid looking bunch, I must say. Welcome everyone, thank you so much for coming. We're here, of course, to witness and to celebrate Gabriel and Poppy's wedding, much antici-pated and looked forward to by us all.

"Despite their youth you certainly couldn't accuse them of rushing into anything. Apparently they've been acquainted for some time. Indeed, it was their shared life experience, growing up around the very people gathered here today, that informed the values and tenets that guided their paths forward.

"Today those paths will converge, and the remainder of their journey will be taken together, for better or worse, as they say. I can tell you right now, you're facing long odds if you bet against them.

"Their love is obvious, their commitment is complete, and their will is strong, so let us now perform the traditions of ceremony and present Poppy and Gabriel to the world as one."

Now he addressed the happy couple personally, his voice softer now, one of experience.

"When you two became engaged, you've since had to make plans, and promises, all along the way. Decisions, agreements, choices all common to the process of getting married. Privately you've dreamed, dreamed and schemed about how your life together will unfold, playing out among the loved ones around you.

"This you've done as friends, and as lovers. Now, after the utterance of just a few simple words, you will realize these plans and hopes, and dreams, as husband and wife."

"Nathan, may we have the rings, please?" Nate led Otis and Amos to Poppy and Gabe, where they each retrieved each other's wedding band from the dog's collars. Gene nodded at Gabe.

"Poppy, I have loved you all my life, the rest of which will be spent proving it. And suddenly I feel like luckier than I deserve to be. We'll figure it out together, and we'll be happier than we can right now even imagine." He slipped the ring on her finger and gave her hand a squeeze.

"Gabriel, the only reason you've loved me longer is because you're older. And when you told me you didn't want to be my chum anymore, I thought I'd die. You should have led with the part about us being lovers. And I shouldn't be dressing you down at our wedding, but that's you and me Gabe, a proper couple, we look after each other. I want to take your name and bear our children. I love you Gabriel, then, now, and forever." She jammed the ring on his finger and snuck a quick kiss on his cheek.

Lucas leaned to Daniela's ear. "That's your daughter."

Gene was delighted. He continued.

"I'd like to read from a poem by Bee Rawlinson."

Love me when I'm old and shocking

Peel off my elastic stockings

Swing me from the chandeliers

Let's be randy bad old dears

Take me to your special places

Watching all the puzzled faces

You in shorts and socks and sandals

Me with warts and huge love handles

Hold me safe throughout the night

When my hair has turned to white

Believe me when I say it's true

I've waited all my life for you

"Gabriel, do you offer yourself fully to Poppy, to marry and forever stay true to her?"

"I do."

"Poppy, do you accept Gabriel's commitment, and promise to remain true to him always?"

"I do."

"Well, then, I'm convinced." He addressed all those present, "I'll forego the part where I petition those assembled as to any hesitancy or protestations towards this union, if only to spare you the pain of dealing with my granddaughters.

"And so, by the powers invested in me by all those assembled, I pronounce you, Gabriel and Poppy, husband and wife. Carry on!"

And so they did.

They took their time parting the sea of well-wishers, doling out affection and gratitude. A post ceremony procession formed, exited the park and walked one block down Streatham, accessing Croyndon and onto Penny Lane.

Lizzie, Aggy, and Jak led the way, dispensing flower petals from a seemingly inexhaustible supply. The newlyweds followed, along with the rest of the eighty or so attendees, forming the largest entourage of Greenbankers ever headed up the lane.

Dovedale Towers had closed to the public at two in the afternoon in order to prep for the reception. Emma, Mae, and Colin were all set, excited themselves for the coming festivities.

Most of the tables were against the walls, a couple by the hearth for gifts, the opposite wall lined with them for food. Finger food for the most part, fare to graze on whilst in the throes of celebration.

The reception line formed, the bride and groom, their parents, and Gene. Louise commanded the guest book, managing a chat with everyone that signed it.

The bar was the epicenter of activity early on. Beer, wine, and champagne filled the glasses, flutes, and mugs, everyone toasting their loved ones.

"Congratulations Gabe, you've got yerself a real live wire!"

"Amen Sam, a new adventure every day."

"Hey Nate, what's in the mug?"

"Root beer Cy, it's not stout. Yet."

"Patience lad, your time will come."

"It's okay, some people shouldn't drink."

"Too true, my wise, young friend. Come on, let's get a tequeño."

"Hey Callum, how's life in the Midlands?"

"Purring along nicely at the moment Abbas, knock wood. Simon and I are busy at work."

"Good, glad to hear it. Did you bring your instruments?"

"Indeed we did," he said, a question in his voice.

"Great, we'll need all the notes we can find. Let's go into the hall and see how things are progressing."

Paul Pilnick sat at the bar, looking every bit the rockstar in an embroidered western shirt with a bolo and a lilac sport jacket, surrounded by the fairer sex.

"I'll bet Led Zeppelin's your favorite classic rock band," Filly guessed.

"Nearly luv, I've slotted them in at number three. I'm writing a book you know."

"No, I didn't," Jude replied. "Is it about music?"

"It is. The title's to be *The Pil's Encyclopedia of Rock Music*. I've taken a cue from Ben's 'Missives on Merseyside' in that each page is about a different band, in order of importance. So with Led Zep being third you have your first page, your second page, then your Jimmy Page."

Equal parts groans and laughter ensued.

The McTimons brothers were at the buffet, clearly enjoying the variety. Cheryl and Sir Philip's wife Harriet were nearby, sipping some chardonnay.

"Your sons are a handsome lot Cheryl, and all three so good at completely different jobs."

"They were lucky Harriet, discovering their passions at a young age."

"And all three have families. Seamus certainly has made up for a slow start."

"We're seeing more of them at Calderstones of late as well. Aggy and Jak are thriving now, Filly and Rosie are big influences."

"That's cause Scouse mums are the best!" Luke said, hugging them both from behind. Harriet bussed him on the cheek.

"What a wonderful reception Lucas, I'm sure it's set you back a farthing or two."

"Not really. The wedding venue was free, and I don't have to pay the band."

"What?" Geoff protested, joining the conversation. "What kind of manager are you? We're joining the musician's union!"

"Free food and drink amigo. That and the company of all these lovely ladies."

"Hmm, maybe you have a point. Party on!"

Mass mingling was taking place, in groups and one on one, boundless in subject and verbal inflection. Cat and Millie sequestered with the Mason brothers, something about an investment in the travel industry. Faith, Colleen, April, and George were huddled in a corner, also in talks about a business venture. Kevin was with Michael and Allison, describing his recent mastery of the art of body surfing. Meanwhile Robin, Dani, and Poppy sat and were happy to watch the guests enjoy themselves.

The Eclectibles were tuned up and plugged in, and enthused, Geoff had upgraded the set up and the boards with a lot of current innovations. Nearly everything was wireless now, and the lights and other special effects were pretty much a self-contained, turnkey system.

Tradition called for a father daughter first dance.

The band obliged with "In My Life." No bass or drums, just two acoustic guitars and strings, and Faith. It was the kind of song that made one pause and reflect. People tended to stop and listen when Faith sang anyway.

Abbas figured things would get very unscripted later on, so he plotted a course for the first set list.

War's "Low Rider" kicked off the proceedings, the first in a string of up-tempo numbers, including "Bad Karma" and "Trouble Waiting to Happen," by Warren Zevon and the Wild Colonials' "Charm." Dani's come-hither crooning took a dark turn as she took on the protagonist in "Charm, " luring in then chastising the song's villain with her sexy snarl:

Lying awake in the dead of the night,
Seeing my life and it's not looking bright.
I'm freezing to death in the warmth of your arms,
I'm wasting my charms.

The dance floor was buzzing. Of course the twins didn't need an invitation; they grabbed the groom and his best man and got with it from note one. The Tweeners got their groove on. Young Nathan even coaxed Darcy off the stage for a dance, causing Ian to raise an eyebrow. He was glad to see his son start to bloom socially. The kid had a lot to offer.

The first set break cued a trip to the bar, the buffet, and in some cases the green out back. May and June Doohan brought Poppy a beer, anxious to catch up with some of the Six in general. They'd watched them grow up from afar during the years.

"Well, if it isn't the original Merseyside twins!"

"Oh Poppy, the band is fantastic!" June exclaimed.

"Thanks so much. Always a work in progress."

"And progressing quite nicely. By the way, when do you leave for your honeymoon?" May asked.

"Not until tomorrow. We're spending tonight up at the flat. Hey, I'm not missing this party!"

Luca and Laura were also more than impressed at hearing the Eclectibles. They'd succumbed to the music's pull and danced. They found the newlyweds near the stage sharing a plate.

"It is amazing Gabe, the Ardavans can play anything, I am sure!"

"I don't know Luca, you can never master your instrument, you just learn how to coax more from it."

"You sound like an artist Gabriel. And Poppy, your voice is special, very evocative!"

"Thank you, Laura. Gabe has spoken a lot about your art. We've talked about coming to Switzerland someday so I can see it. Your sailboat too Luca. I've seen pictures. That is a work of art!"

"Okay you two," George said, walking into the room. "We're about to start back up. You wanna sit this one out?"

"No sir. As a matter of fact, Poppy and I want to start it off, just the two of us."

"Alright kids, have at it!"

Five minutes later the hall had filled back up. Gabe sat, bow at the ready. Poppy stepped to the mic.

"We're baaack. I hope you don't mind; Gabe and I are gonna play a little song for ya. Bear with us, it's slow and sappy, but heartfelt. And thank you everyone for coming. It's made our day the best. Stick around, we're gonna have an epic throwdown!"

She turned to Gabe, "Play it sweet maestro."

He began, his arrangement of the acoustic guitar driven ballad instantly haunting, drawing the listener in. He extended the intro, weaving the notes methodically into the melody. Poppy leaned in, closed her eyes, and sang. She'd found her confidence in Florida, before eighty thousand people. These eighty were hearing the results:

With you standing here, I can tell the world
What it means to love.
To go on from here, I can't use words
That don't say enough.
People shouldn't cry at a wedding.
Three songs by the Crash Test Dummies followed, breaking the

trance created by the Airplane's "Today." The Canadian indie rockers were a blast, clever lyrics and hook heavy instrumentation their forte. The dance floor became the scene again, second verse same as the first.

More traditions were followed, albeit with a Greenbank twist. Wedding cupcakes were served, a whole slew of em. The best man offered up a toast to the betrothed in which he thanked his buddy for getting his sister out of the house and openly pondered the possibility of finally getting the love and attention he deserved from his parents. And when the happy couple did leave, they were not pelted with rice. Instead, they departed under a hail of flower petals. Were there any plants with blooms left on them in the whole of England?

Regardless, the celebration raged on with music and dance, food and drink, wit and wonder, and a dash of naughty.

Soon it would all be a memory, but for now Dani, Faith, Colleen, and Robin sat on a sofa in the performance hall as Abbas' thrilling and dynamic arrangement of David Bowie's "Heroes" was being performed. The whole band, except for the singers and Robin, were really laying it down. And at the mics? Luke, Ben, Cy, and Abbas, none of whom had ever sang a lick in their lives, not only singing but strutting around the stage, a mix of Bowie, Jagger, Daltry, and Cocker.

"Have I drunk too much?" Colly asked.

"No dear, you're fine."

"Then give me some more. I want no recollection of this in the morning."

"It is the morning luv."

CHAPTER 76
MONDAY, 21 AUGUST

These are the seasons of emotion,
And like the winds they rise and fall.

Robin didn't go into work, rare for a Monday morning. Instead, she was being fawned over by her kids. It was her forty-eighth birthday. The occasion kinda snuck up on her with all the hubbub of the last few weeks.

Darcy and Gabriel had the day off as well, after a couple of weekend symphony concerts. The Philharmonic's calendar was getting busy with fall coming, coinciding with much of the clan's increased labors that came with the change of season. Ian, of course, was at the symphony, challenged by the upcoming programs. Bashir and Cyrus were teaching again, and Cyril and Seamus were steering Rovers into the new season. The twins were back in Colorado Springs and even Erins Pharmacy and the Edge Hill Animal Hospital were busy, a byproduct of all the hustle and bustle around the city.

"Great omelet Gabe. You spending time more in the kitchen?"

"Come on sister, you know I can cook."

"That lasagna you prepared a while back was very good."

"Thanks mum. I suppose I will be cooking more in the future. My schedule isn't as rigid as Poppy's."

"Well, you're up close to the Phil on Duke Street, and able to spend more time there. How are the both of you liking your first home together?"

"Oh it's boss! Easy to look after and close to work as you say. We're fixing it up some. A lot of the wedding gifts were things for the house."

"Did you find a spot for Laura's quilt?" Darcy asked.

"Very first thing, front and center in the sitting room."

"You were right Gabe, it's useless to try to describe her work—so unique!"

"Scruff likes it, maybe too much. I can picture coming home and find him using it as a climbing wall."

"Aw, the happy couple are nesting."

"Stow it sister."

The happy couple's other half was catching a bit of flak as well.

"Hello stranger, I don't believe we've met."

"Gotta get used to it. Your baby's married and moved away."

Dani, Mina, and Poppy were in the clinic's break room, grabbing a bite to eat. Mondays can be tricky at the vet's; shit happens on weekends. Today was fairly calm, gladly, giving Dani and Mina a chance to catch up with their young colleague.

"We've got a few minutes. Tell us about the honeymoon," Dani suggested.

"Orgasmic!"

"How about we start with the away from the hotel room part."

"It was all wonderful. Amsterdam's for everyone, so much to do and see. We did some touristy stuff, the Rijksmuseum, a boat trip along the canals, renting bicycles. We saw Ajax play a friendly with Feyenoord. Oh, and the Concertgebouw, wow! We went to a concert there; the Dutch Royal Symphony are the resident players. It's the first hall I've been to that can match the Phil."

"It's actually known as one of the top three, along with Boston Symphony Hall and the Musikverein in Vienna."

"How did you know that mum?"

"A few of my favorite people are classical musicians," she quipped.

"I have been to the symphony two times, but it was some years ago."

"Really Mina, in Pristina?"

"No, in Budapest when I was in school. It was the Hungarian State Opera House. Very nice!"

"But you haven't been to the Phil yet, right?"

"No, not here in Liverpool."

"We shall have to fix that," Poppy promised. "I don't think Seamus is much for the classical scene. We'll go if he doesn't want to take you."

"Brother Ian is quite the flutist," Dani said.

"I think our favorite part of the honeymoon was just hanging out with the locals," Poppy continued. "Sleep in, have some tea, walk around the neighborhood. Find a place for lunch, window shop, in the evening a stop at the hash café and some live music. Wilco turned us on to a great little jazz club. We went there a few times."

Molly, one of the vet techs, stuck her head around the corner. "Ladies, we've got a couple of patients just arrived. A dogfight. Looks like both lost."

"Blood and guts on a Monday, I knew it was too quiet."

Jacob had blood and guts on his mind. He was too late to save Scruff's prey, and glad of it. Rats were a problem in Liverpool, and definitely not limited to the docks. Scruff was an efficient mouser; Jake would gladly dispose of as many as the little dude could produce.

He was used to his new routine now, living again at Greenbank. He had to get up earlier on days in the office, but he was spending less time feeding himself. There were plenty of willing cooks at the rowhouse.

Carter Assets Management had paused to take a breath. The busiest time of year was football's summer transfer window, and the agency had been active in the market. The wedding, and all the house guests associated with it, were poorly timed, but they managed it, and now could recharge and address clients in other fields.

Jake's mind was on the Six, specifically Hope and Grace. Darcy's mandate of shit or get off the pot had stirred him to action. He wasn't going to be on the wrong end of one of her tirades.

He'd been researching the eight clubs in the newly formed WUSA, keying on their coaching staff and scouting network. Only one manager was a Brit, Ian Sawyers, from Sunderland. He was a midfielder that played at Rotherham in a very short and unremarkable career on the pitch. Scouting personnel were harder to track down. This whole movement was strictly grassroots at the moment. He would need to plan a trip to the States. His dad was interested in the talent in the Americas anyway. It might turn out to be a very productive undertaking.

The fall and winter were going to be big for the Six, possibly a preamble to their lives for a long time. Why did that sound familiar?

The Six seemed to be following the same path, but in a different order. One major step remained. Were they going to take their act on the road?

CHAPTER 77
SUNDAY, 28 JANUARY 2001

Fear is the lock, and laughter the key to your heart.

Dani looked out the bedroom window, trying to locate Lucas. Mossley Hill was fog bound and cold, the day brightening incrementally. Finally she spotted him, materializing out of the mist, walking from the lake towards the house. Ben was with him. They were talking while Amos and Otis worked the brush along the shore.

Pausing under the yew they continued their conversation, waiting for the dogs to catch up.

"Thanks Ben, I really appreciate the advice."

"Any time pardner. We all need an emotional reset now and then. Don't carry that crap around Luke. We gotta share the load, all of us."

"You're right." He put his arm around Ben's shoulder as they started towards the rowhouse. "I think all that business is behind us now anyway."

They split up, headed for the warmth of the fire and a mug of something sweet and creamy.

"Well, that only took a year and a half," Ben said to himself, stripping down in the mudroom. He fed Amos while rehashing Luke's confession. The clan's alpha dog had a strict set of ethics and operated under self-imposed tenets that were quite clear in his own mind. The guy's moral compass was always pointing true north.

Ben knew that his buddy was well aware of the real world, and that sometimes exceptions had to be made. Something fundamental was changed that night when Grace was attacked, something that touched everyone that knew her. Loved ones could only imagine how it affected he, Faith, and Hope, but no one could predict that the incident would turn something loose inside Lucas Carter that even he had trouble recognizing or controlling.

"It was like I stopped processing information like I always did," he had said. "I was sharply focused, but on one thing only. Then, in the end, when I found the bastard, it was so out of character. I went feral Ben, coldly doing something I didn't think I was capable of."

Ben hoped he'd settled things for Luke. This was unchartered territory. Analyzing it all now, he realized the matter was handled quickly and privately, and with no repercussions. Surely Luke realized this. He just needed to unburden himself.

Sometimes the world gets ugly, and sometimes you have to get your hands dirty. The latest chapter was handled by himself, and he was glad Luke witnessed it. Now the whole affair was probably over and they could all forget whatever part they were forced to play.

A saying came to mind. It was a phrase used in the newspaper business as somewhat of a credo. 'Comfort the afflicted and afflict the comfortable.' That could be the clan motto.

Next door Lucas was considerably more at ease than he'd been all week. He was surprised at the funk he was in; the subconscious is a fickle and mysterious thing. Ben straightened him out, reminding him of the time it would take to put the matter to rest. Funny, had Ben come to him with the same concerns he would've given similar counsel. Reinforcement from the ones you love and trust, your emotional get out of jail card.

Lucas had other issues to ponder anyway. A week ago, Sir Philip asked him for a copy of his CV, or Curriculum Vitae, which is Latin for the French word resume. It's the same in English, just pronounced differently. It didn't make any difference how you pronounced it; Luke didn't have one. This wasn't technically correct. Everybody had life experience, he just had never formalized his onto paper. It wouldn't be overly impressive anyway, bachelor's degree, twenty plus years teaching school, less than five running his own business. He could list hobbies, music, football, meddling in foreign affairs, and the odd vigilante gig. Definitely a one-page document.

Philip wanted to nominate him for Everton's Board of Directors, a total surprise. Luke was honored. The seat carried power and prestige, and he felt lucky to be thought of so highly. His problem was how to politely decline. This position was too front and center for a guy who preferred to stay behind the scenes. Also, he felt it to be a conflict of interest of sorts to be an agent with such close ties to one club. Carter Assets Management was on the ups anyway, a growing entity in a growing industry.

He was reminded of Brian Epstein, the agent, manager, and talent scout that guided the careers of so many musicians in Liverpool during the '60s. He saw a hotbed of musical creativity and turned the world onto it, something Luke intended to do a generation later in not only sport, but the arts as well.

He would give Philip a few days before contacting him, time to recover from the Blues' performance yesterday. Everton hosted a fourth round F.A. Cup tie at Goodison Park. Nearly all the clan attended. The match was one of heightened interest on Merseyside. The reason why it was a big to-do was because the opponents were Tranmere Rovers.

Cyril was the talk of the town today. He and Shea revisited their old club, warmly welcomed by the Toffee faithful, and proceeded to thrash their hosts three-nil. Steve Yates and Jason Koumas scored the goals, but it was Andy Parkinson who ran riot through the home side. They simply had no answer for him.

Cy was still abed, snuggled up to Colleen, the house quiet and dark. They were up late last night, feted by everyone from the Everton ball boys to his own club director. It was the biggest scalp taken by Rovers since he'd become manager.

Big wins are a plus. The team survives to the next round and banks a nice supply of funds, and the players gain a new level of confidence. It's wise to keep emotions on an even keel; fortunes and results can change quickly. The lads would go again, training and matches, trying to maintain momentum.

Cyril felt at ease, and at peace, both this morning and in general. The reason was not football but rather the woman lying beside him, breathing softly. Colly was a treasure, one that takes a long time to discover all she has to offer. She could be quiet, content to go along with and be entertained by the rest, but also possessing a lively wit, and that mischievous spark in her eyes that he so adored.

She'd shown her independent side of late, a complete surprise of an idea that Cy thought brilliant. She went to Faith and April with a plan to buy Dovedale Towers, and she went prepared. The stars had aligned to present the opportunity. She'd learned the owners were open to an offer, and, coincidently, Caspar had lobbied her privately on taking a more active role at the pharmacy. This coincided with April's declaration of how much she and George like owning Kev's chippy, but wished it was bigger and offered a more varied menu.

In carefully orchestrated moves behind the scenes, she'd lobbied the principals to gauge interest. Faith was up for it. The three of them worked at the Dovey, the place where they all met their husbands. Good times they were, although sometimes a struggle. Caspar would manage Erins, and Faith and Colly would still put in shifts and share ownership with him. George and April put the chip shop up for sale and papers were being drawn up to sell the pub to the gang. Dovedale Towers was soon to have the best house band ever!

The Eclectibles themselves had caused a stir recently, Abbas was at the dining table with a mug of cocoa looking at the pictures. They played the Empire Theatre on New Year's Eve. The Empire was on Lime Street near the train station and was the largest two-tier theater in Great Britain, seating over 2,300.

Lucas put on a master class in promoting the gig, complete with party favors and Aleah's stage design, and Abbas came up with his most interesting set list to date. The band played one song released in every year, in order, from 1966 through to 1999. Thirty-four songs, the show lasting from nine til one in the New Year. A prominent London music journo dubbed them 'the best pub band in the world,' at odds to understand why the Eclectibles never went for the big time. That issue had been hashed out years ago, Abbas thought. Still, it was easy to see why others may be curious about the band's apparent lack of ambition. They just didn't get the lure of clan life on Greenbank.

The clan's most recent initiates got it. Mina, Aggy, and Jak still had scars from the past, but were safe and happy on Greenbank. A nice little family unit had evolved in Shea's childhood home, and he felt like the luckiest one under that roof.

He was over at the Carters, asking if Dani could watch the kids for a while.

"Mina wants to go to the cathedral this morning," he said. Dani detected something in his manner. He seemed a little distracted. "I'll bring them over as we're leaving."

"No need, I'll come over there. We can cozy up in front of the telly."

Twenty minutes later she scurried to their front door in a housecoat and slippers, Aggy showing her in.

"It's cold Dani!"

"It sure is. I'm going to the fire!"

Aggy hugged Dani standing before the hearth. She loved this little girl.

"Bundle up Mina, it's Baltic out there."

"For sure. We should be back in a couple of hours. Thanks for coming over."

"My pleasure. The boys are boring this morning. Where's Jak?"

"Up in his room," Shea said, appearing from the stairwell. "Thanks again Dani."

"You're very welcome. Be careful."

Jak had his door closed, something he did often. Who knew when, if ever, the last time was that he had his own place to go, and be. He kept his room tidy, everything in its place. He had stuff of his own now, things he could hold onto. His own football, some cool toys, and lots of warm clothes. He was offered Cyril's prized possession, Cruyff's Dutch National Team shirt for the '74 World Cup, which he passed on. The Barcant number six and McTimons number eleven were his preferred items of football idolatry.

Dani tapped lightly on the door.

"Come in. Dani!" He ran to her from the window and hugged her fiercely.

"Good morning, Jak!"

"I'm glad to see you."

"Me too honey, are you hungry?"

"We ate porridge!"

"Oh good, how about some hot cocoa?"

"Cocoa? Yes, cocoa! Please!"

"Come downstairs when you're ready."

"I'm ready."

Man, this little dude was precious. Children are resilient, she realized, but she also knew there could be some dark stuff still inside their hearts and minds. She had hoped they would not completely forget the past, and that the older they got the better they would understand it.

For the moment Dani was in the past herself, reliving times spent with her little boy and girl with cocoa and shortbread by the fire. Otis had come over with her, now luxuriating in Aggy's attention.

Occasionally she eyed the window, awaiting Shea and Mina's return. Shea had added to the mystery of his demeanor this morning as he was leaving, winking at her and whispering something about the news of the day. He was no doubt still on cloud nine over yesterday's result. Probably he had more to add.

They were gone longer than she had expected. Perhaps they walked the gardens after the service. When they got out of the car they went into the park and stood under the yew. Then Shea took Mina's hand, and spoke to her, his look sincere.

Dani squealed as Mina embraced Shea, then kissed him passionately. She must've said yes.

EPILOGUE

They had been rechristened the Catalan Crew, the 2.0 version of the Merseyside Six of Mossley Hill. The sons and daughters of the Fab Five had let the pilgrim blood of their elders guide them to foreign shores in the new millennium, a time of opportunity in a world of expanding technology and shrinking human connection.

Now established in their fields of endeavor, the businessman and the healer, and the athletes and the musicians heeded the call of Catalonia, the land of Dali and Messi. Here they would ply their trade at the Teatro del Liceu, the Veterinaria Calabria, and the Camp Nou. Barcelona, home of sensuous scents and soaring spires. A city by the sea, the passion of its people reflected in their immense regional pride.

They would speak like natives, and live in a villa in the foothills, and integrate themselves into their community while learning how to add to its value. There would be a little bit of Liverpool in Iberia, with a Catalunyan countenance and a Scouse soul.

May all that is, bless you one and bless you all,
Under gun on our planet, spinning like a cannonball.
Sonny Landreth

Quoted Lyric Index